HOME
BODY

HOME BODY

GERRY BOYLE

BERKLEY PRIME CRIME, NEW YORK

A Berkley Prime Crime Book
Published by The Berkley Publishing Group,
a division of Penguin Group (USA) Inc.,
375 Hudson Street, New York, New York 10014.

HOME BODY

This book is an original publication of The Berkley Publishing Group.

Visit our website at www.penguin.com

First edition: June 2004

Library of Congress Cataloging-in-Publication Data

Boyle, Gerry, 1956-
Home body / Gerry Boyle.—1st ed.
p. cm.
ISBN 0-425-19611-9
1. McMorrow, Jack (Fictitious character)—Fiction. 2. Journalists—
Fiction. 3. Maine—Fiction. I. Title.
PS3552. O925H66 2004
813'.54—dc22
2003063931

PRINTED IN THE UNITED STATES OF AMERICA

10   9   8   7   6   5   4   3   2   1

For Emily, Carolyn, and Charlie.
I count my blessings.

CHAPTER 1

A Monday morning and I was waiting for Roxanne at Portland District Court. She had a hearing about a little girl who was being molested by her uncle, who had done time for doing the same thing to his daughter, but I didn't know that because it was all confidential. I stood in the corridor with the defendants: drunken drivers and bar fighters, check bouncers and methadone junkies. We were slouched against the wall, eyeing the cops and lawyers and listening to their cheery, grating banter. The guy next to me, tall and gaunt and wolfish, looked at the people in suits and shiny shoes and dismissed them with an obscenity. Along the wall, there was silent agreement. And then a deputy pushed the courtroom doors open from inside and a knot of people emerged.

A puffy-eyed woman and her emaciated husband. Their lawyer, a pale, doughy guy who looked about fifteen. A counselor or something, a woman toting folders for each of her young and tormented clients. And then Roxanne, pulling on her trench coat, looking for me. I peeled myself off the wall and took her arm.

At the foyer, we paused. Roxanne held my arm for balance as she switched her pumps for running shoes. She stuck the shoes in her briefcase, and zipped it up.

"What would I do without you?" Roxanne said.

"Topple," I said, and we went out into the cold and down the stone stairs.

It was snowing, a dry flurry that swirled like dustballs on the brick sidewalks. We walked arm in arm, past the federal courthouse, across Market Street, behind the *Portland Press Herald* building, across Exchange up the courtyard at Monument Way. The courtyard had benches and round concrete planters that looked like giant ashtrays. It was lunch hour and people from the downtown offices were hurrying in all directions, heads down, intent on their errands. Executive-types in cashmere coats pretended to be on important business, solemn and serious as assassins.

We went to our usual place, the Victory Deli, and took our usual table in the front window by the neon Rolling Rock sign. Roxanne hung her briefcase and pocketbook on the back of the chair, then her trench coat, too. She brushed at her hair, which was frosted with snow, and she eased herself down. I sat, too. Roxanne sighed.

"Did you win?" I said, folding my hand over hers on the table.

"Oh, I guess so. If you ever do. I don't know. We got what we asked for. The mother is in total denial, which was hard. I don't know. I just don't feel so good."

I looked at her. Her skin usually was milky white, but today it was tinged with blue-gray. There were shadows under her eyes.

"You're beautiful when you're tired," I said, smiling.

She smiled too, but wanly.

"I know. I look awful."

"No, you don't."

"I just think maybe I'm getting some kind of bug."

I frowned and said, "Maybe you should go to the doctor."

"Jack, just because I'm pregnant doesn't mean I have to run to the doctor every time I get a sniffle."

"Sure it does. Now you need to eat. How 'bout chicken soup?"

"Jack, I'm not an invalid. I'll have spicy Asian noodles. You want to split an order—"

Roxanne looked toward the window. I paused. She listened, and then I heard it, too. Slapping. Pounding. Muffled footsteps, growing louder, coming closer. I turned to the window just as a figure flashed by. Then another and another and another.

Kids.

"Oh, god," Roxanne said, and she was up, her chair sliding on the floor. People looked as she slipped between the tables and eased her way through the take-out crowd at the door.

"Hey, lady," somebody said. "Watch it."

I started to move through, too, and a little guy in a suit tried to block my way. I moved him like he was a potted plant.

But by the time I got out the door, Roxanne was gone. I hesitated, then turned left, the direction the kids had run. The next building was a parking garage and I ran to the entrance and stood by the ticket machine and listened. A car pulled up and I crossed in front of it and heard the horn blow behind me. The sound echoed as I trotted from the garage, past a line of cars parked in the alley outside. The alley ran along the back side of buildings on Monument Square, and I ran along it. I slowed to listen. Stopped. I heard voices. Shouts.

Roxanne.

CHAPTER 2

"Stop it," she was yelling.

I could see her as I rounded the corner. She was pulling a guy by the shoulders from behind. It was a kid but he was her size, or a little bigger, wearing a black baseball cap on backward. As I ran toward them, he reached behind him and gave Roxanne a shove. She held on to his sweatshirt and they both staggered. I hit him at a full run, took him by the neck and shoulders and flung him over a curb and into a parked truck. He banged against the metal, and I turned back as Roxanne, in her suit and sneakers, bounded up a flight of steps and disappeared.

I was behind her as she shoved another kid aside. There were four of them standing and one was on his knees in a corner filled with trash. He had his arms over his head and two of them were kicking him in the back, another was kicking at his face, which was streaked with blood. As I came up the stairs, they shoved the boy onto his side and he put his arms out behind him and a girl kicked him in the mouth and he screamed. She was whooping and grinning as I took her by her shoulders, spun her around and threw her off the stairs.

"Hey, you—" she said, but then another one was on the kid on the ground, crouching as he punched him in the back of the neck, kneed him in the back of the head. The kid on the ground was making a sobbing animal shriek, and I booted the bigger boy off, taking the wind out of him, then kept shoving him back until he hit the graffiti-covered wall. He had black feral eyes, a scrubby moustache, and brown-stained teeth. He came off the wall like a weasel, arms and feet flying.

I stumbled in the trash and fell back for just a moment, and he was on me, snorting and spitting and grunting. I didn't want to hit him, but he was clawing at me, scratching my hands and arms, then kicking for my groin. I took him by the arms, whirled him around until he came off the ground, then heaved him off the steps. He flew ten feet in the air and landed hard, and clutched at his leg and didn't get back up. The first kid, the one with the hat, stood beside him and screamed at me but didn't come closer.

Roxanne was beside the boy on the ground, saying, "Stop it, stop it," to one of the girls, trying to wrap the girl in her arms, but the girl was kicking at the boy and at Roxanne's shins, stepping on Roxanne's feet. I grabbed the girl from behind, and she turned and tried to bite me, her teeth white against black lipstick, her green-and-red hair pressed against my face.

"You asshole," she said, and I dragged her away from Roxanne, and shoved her down the stairs. As she stumbled back, the weasely kid came bounding toward me, up the steps, and then leapt into the air so fast I couldn't even get my arms up. His sneaker caught me in the mouth, and I felt a white-hot flash of pain, and then he was jumping up again, like something on a video game, kicking and punching at my face in this flurry of limbs. I staggered, grabbed an arm, and yanked him toward me, then spun him toward the cinderblock wall. When he hit it, still facing me, I took him by the throat and slapped him in the face, hard, over and over, until he started to go limp. I stopped and let go.

A siren whooped and the kids scattered, two going down the alley past the parked truck toward Free Street and the two others going the other way, around the corner toward Exchange. For a moment, it was just the three of us, me and Roxanne breathing heavily over the boy on the ground. My mouth was bleeding and one of my front teeth was kicked in. I could feel it with my tongue, slanted inward like a broken slat on a fence. Roxanne's hair was in her face, and her suit jacket was torn at the shoulder. There were long scratches on her neck. Four of them, parallel like jet entrails in the sky.

"You okay?" I said.

"I don't know," Roxanne said. "I guess so."

"You can't do this."

"They were killing him," she said.

She leaned down to where the boy now was sitting up. He leaned forward and coughed blood on to the litter of leaves and fast-food trash, flattened cans and broken bottles, all dusted with snow.

"You all right, Rocky?" Roxanne asked gently.

He sniffed and didn't answer. His glasses were bent, but still on his face. His nose was bleeding. There were scuff marks on his cheekbones and on his temple on one side. He was breathing in quick shallow breaths, but he got himself to his feet. Blood ran from his mouth down his chin. He wiped his face with the sleeve of his red plaid wool jacket, then took his glasses off and examined them. He was slight, bookish. His wrists were thin and hairless.

"I think you need an ambulance, buddy," I said. "You got kicked pretty hard, and you don't know if something inside is—"

He bolted as soon as he was out of arm's reach, and scurried around the corner of the building. I started to follow, but he was already crossing Exchange Street, slipping through traffic. I didn't want to leave Roxanne alone so I loped back up the alley, just as the police cruiser slid to a stop, blue strobes flashing in the grill.

Two cops got out, a blond guy and a dark haired woman. They were both carrying flashlights, and the guy called out to me and started to run.

"Hold it right there."

I did, and then he saw Roxanne walking slowly toward us.

"Roxanne?" the woman cop said. "You okay?"

"You don't move," the guy told me, pointing the flashlight. "You get on the ground, now."

"It's okay, Jimmy," Roxanne said. "He's with me. This is Jack."

"You want to sit in the car, Roxanne?" the woman cop said. "You know you shouldn't be doing this, not in your condition."

"I'm fine. It was Jack they got into it with."

"Who?" Jimmy said.

"Kids from the square. The one who hangs out with Crystal with the green hair. A couple of guys I've seen, but I don't know them. Another girl. I think her name is Hillary or Helena or something. They had that new kid, the little kid, Rocky. They were beating the hell out of him."

"You know you really should be more careful," the woman cop said.

"Thanks, Mom," Roxanne said. "Jack, this is Delena."

She nodded at me sternly, like it was somehow my fault.

"They all split?" Jimmy said.

"In different directions," I said.

"The Rocky kid, too?" Delena said.

"Went toward Exchange, but I don't know if he went up or down," I said. "He's got glasses. Red plaid jacket. Face pretty beat up."

"Weapons?" Jimmy said.

I shook my head.

"Just fists and feet, that I saw. One of the little bastards kicked me right in the mouth. Came at me like some sort of ninja warrior."

"They start that crap, I just use this," Jimmy said.

He popped a can of Cap-Stun off his belt. Held it up and popped back in.

"Takes the ninja right out of 'em."

I felt my tooth with my tongue, spat blood on the pavement.

"You need Medcu?"

"Nah," I said. "You okay, Roxanne?"

"Yes, for god's sake."

"Hey, this is a very crucial time," Delena said. "What are you, five months?"

It seemed odd, talking about pregnancy in the back alley. It seemed odd that this cop was talking about my baby. Roxanne said she and the baby were fine.

"It's Rocky who might need to be looked at. They were kicking him in the face and the back. Kidneys maybe?"

"Little darlings," the woman cop said.

"You sure you don't need to be checked out, Rox?" Jimmy said.

"Ahhh," Roxanne said, shaking her head. "No, Jimmy. I just need to go home and take a hot bath."

We stood in the alley in the cold. Jimmy held out his hand in a Dickensian fingerless black leather glove. I shook it.

"You're the newspaper guy?" he said.

I said I was.

"You should write about these kids," Delena said. "Out here loose and all the laws keep them here. Like stray dogs. Little kids, got no chance of making a life at all. Fourteen or fifteen and they're done."

She looked to Roxanne.

"Unless somebody like her gets hold of 'em before it's too late."

Jimmy looked over at me, peering at my mouth.

"They might be able to save that tooth," he said. "If they can't, hold on to your wallet."

He opened his mouth and touched a finger to his tooth, top, right front.

"Post," he said. "High school hockey. Cost, like, four grand."

He closed his mouth.

"We round up these tykes, you want to file an assault complaint?" I shook my head, touched my tooth with my tongue.

"Screw it."

"The kid getting beat, his name's Rocky? Got a surname?"

Roxanne thought for a moment, then shook her head.

"No. He's not one of mine. I just heard about him. Landed in town from somewhere up north. Stayed at the Port House, with the rest of them, at least he was, but he just kind of stands out. Sort of wimpy and studious looking."

"What's the name, a joke on the little Poindexter?" Jimmy said. "What's he doing on the street?"

"I don't know," Roxanne said. "I was trying to figure that out."

"Looks like he'd get eaten up," I said. "Little skinny guy with glasses. Arms like sticks. Kicking him like that, they could kill him."

"They get on the street, they change," Jimmy said, looking up from his notebook. "What was that movie about the kids on the island? It was on cable the other night."

"*Lord of the Flies?*" I said.

"Right," he said. "These kids. Leave 'em alone, they turn into little goddamn animals."

CHAPTER 3

We talked on Market Street. I stood by the door as Roxanne sat in the driver's seat, the Explorer idling, the snow falling, Roxanne running her fingers over the rips in her tights, the scratches on her thighs.

"So what's the deal with this Rocky kid?" I said.

"I don't really know."

"Name's a misnomer."

"Yeah," Roxanne said. "He's anything but, from what I can tell. I don't know why he's here, really. He doesn't fit. He doesn't have that hard shell."

"Not yet. How long has he been down here?"

"I don't know. I noticed him a couple of weeks ago. These kids, even if they're soft underneath, they swagger."

"Their defense," I said.

"From years of being treated like dirt. Rocky was sort of wary, but he didn't have it. The cockiness."

"The bravado."

"No. He looked like he needed a hug," Roxanne said.

"Where was this?"

"At Port House. The shelter. I was looking for somebody else. But he just looked so vulnerable with these other kids. I said, 'Who's that?'"

"What'd they say?"

A seafood truck passed on the cobblestone street, compressor motor roaring, bound for the docks. I waited to hear Roxanne's answer.

"They said the kids called him Boonie, because he was from the country somewhere."

"You think anybody is looking for him?"

"That was the odd part. Usually, you get a kid like him, you've got parents calling every shelter in the state, putting up posters all over town. Nobody had asked for Rocky at all."

"So he doesn't have anybody?"

"Or nobody who cares," Roxanne said.

"Boonie," I said. "I wonder where in the boonies."

Roxanne gave me her warning look.

"Jack, don't head off on some wild goose chase. He's a DHS problem, not yours."

I pictured his skinny arms, folded over his head as he curled up like an armadillo and the blows rained down. Roxanne said she had to go, had to get cleaned up and get back to the office. I said I had to go, too, didn't want to be late. I said I loved her and kissed her on the cheek. She said she loved me too, and put the truck in gear. Then she turned to me one more time.

"Jack," she said. "Don't."

I didn't answer.

CHAPTER 4

It was quarter to one and my shift started at the *Clarion* at three. Three to eleven, Monday through Thursday. Two o'clock on Fridays and every other Saturday. A hundred and fifty dollars per shift and health insurance for twenty-five bucks a week. That was key. You needed health insurance to have a baby.

Ours was four months away, good Lord willing, as my father used to say. One day Roxanne had said she'd have to go back to work after the baby was born because we couldn't go without health insurance and my freelancing didn't provide any. I said I'd go get us insurance and then she could stay home as long as she wanted, take care of one child instead of fifty. Try to raise our child well rather than trying to fix the problems of children gone so far astray.

She said I was a dinosaur. I think she meant it in a nice way.

So that was the impetus, and off I went. I hurried back to Congress Street and picked up the truck. Headed down the hill toward the highway. I glanced down at the CDs, looking for something to pass the two-hour ride. I sorted through music, glancing up at the traffic, back to the radio—

Over at the kid in red plaid.

He was standing in the doorway of a seedy corner store. I saw the jacket, the glasses, and then I'd passed the corner and traffic was moving me along down the hill toward the next light. I stayed in the right lane, turned on the red light, drove a block, and turned up the hill again. A block up, I took a right onto a street of tenements that faced the backside of downtown, circled until the store was in sight, pulled over and parked.

There was no sign of Rocky.

I shut the truck off, got out, and started walking on the sidewalk toward the corner. The doorway was visible now, but only part of it. The windows of the place were spray-painted white from the inside and I couldn't see through to the alcove where the kid had been. I hesitated, then kept going. In front of the store, I stopped. Listened. Turned the corner.

He was gone.

I stepped back and looked down the block. No Rocky. I looked back the way I had come. I looked the other way, and then opened the door of the store. A bell jingled and I went in.

The counter was on the left. It was low and made of metal, dented like it had been drummed by a hammer. On the counter was a jar of eggs in a yellow solution, like something from high school biology. Behind the counter, someone coughed.

I stepped forward and turned. Behind a cash register was an old smoke-colored woman. She looked at me and coughed again, as if to clear her throat to speak. Then she stopped and didn't say anything. I looked closer and saw that her chair had wheels. On one of the armrests was a revolver hanging in a holster. On the wall behind her head were racks of cigarettes and cardboard displays of condoms.

"Hi," I said.

"Yup," she said.

"I'm looking for a kid."

She looked at me.

"Glasses. Red plaid jacket. Kind of skinny."

"Ain't seen him."

"He was just standing in the doorway."

"Can't see the doorway."

"I thought he might have come in," I said.

"Might've. It's a free country."

She looked at me and rubbed her nose.

"I'll look around," I said.

I started to turn.

"You a cop?" she said, behind me.

I turned back.

"No," I said.

"You his dad?"

"No."

"Then what you want the boy for?"

"I know him. I need to talk to him."

I looked at her but she didn't say anything. I glanced around the store one more time, then turned to the door and opened it. The bell jingled like I was leaving Santa's workshop. I stepped out onto the sidewalk. And the door jingled closed. I stood there for a moment, then walked to the corner of the building and turned. Stepping over trash and glass, I eased along the brick wall of the store and then paused again. Listened.

I heard a scuff. A sniff. I turned the corner.

"Rocky," I said.

He took a step back, but there was nowhere to go. Behind him was chain-link fence topped with barbed wire. He ran toward it and leapt, scrabbling up until his feet were at eye level. There was a clanging sound as he tried to climb higher, but then he grunted and slid down and turned and faced me, wide-eyed as a cornered animal, arms wrapped around his belly.

"Relax," I said, walking slowly toward him. "Nothing to be afraid of."

Rocky looked behind him, his eyes searching for a way out. I stopped five feet from him, hands in my jacket pockets.

"I don't want to scare you. I was driving by, that's all. I saw you in the doorway. You know, you still should go to the hospital or something."

"I'm fine," he said.

His voice was a child's, the sound of an eight-year-old coming from a fourteen-year-old's body.

"You're not okay. Even I can tell that. You could have broken ribs, or I don't know what. I'm not a doctor. I'm just a friend of Ms. Masterson's. You know her, right?"

His eyes searched me. His arms still were wrapped around his midsection. Snow flaked on his glasses, and he reached up with one finger and wiped the lenses, first one, then the other.

"The state lady," Rocky said.

"Right. She was trying to help you, too."

"I don't need any help."

I shook my head.

"They would have stomped you into jelly, Rocky. Why were they doing that to you? You know those kids?"

He looked at me. Nodded.

"What'd you do to them?"

"Nothin'."

"Then why would they do that?"

He shrugged.

"They just decided to beat you up, for no reason? What'd you do? Wear the wrong color hankie?"

Rocky stared at me, then looked down at the trash-strewn ground. He kicked at a flattened can with his sneaker. The sneakers were Nike Air Jordans, one red lace, one white. The can was Colt 45.

"They said I was annoying," he said quietly.

"Harsh punishment for rubbing somebody the wrong way."

He shrugged again.

"I can take it," he said.

"Why would you want to?"

Another shrug. I shifted on my feet, blinked snow from my eyes.

"Where you from, Rocky?"

He didn't answer.

"You from around here?"

Rocky scowled. Then gave his head a little shake.

"You from far away?"

The shoulders came up, dropped back down. They were narrow shoulders, like the jacket was draped on a metal hanger.

"I just mean, if you live nearby, I could give you a ride home. I don't know why you're kicking around on the street, but you don't seem cut out for it."

"I'm fine," he blurted, then clenched his teeth. He was angry.

"I didn't mean to insult you," I said.

"What do you care, anyway?"

"I don't know. I just thought you might be more hurt than you realized. And Ms. Masterson, she was worried. When she's worried about something, it rubs off on me."

He looked at me, squinting as if to search for some seed of truth, or a hint of a lie.

"If you want a ride, I'll give you one. If you want to go to the hospital, get checked out, I'll give you a lift over there. But I've got to go. I'm late for work. I've got to drive all the way to Bangor."

His eyes seemed to brighten behind the smeared lenses.

"I used to go to Bangor."

He started to say something else, then caught himself and stopped.

"I work in Bangor. I live in a place called Prosperity. It's between there and here. Closer to there."

"Why you work way up there?"

"I don't know. It's where the job is."

"What do you do for a job?"

"I work for a newspaper."

"You mean, like a reporter—"

"More like an editor. I do reporting for other papers. At this one I fix up other people's stories."

"The spelling and stuff?"

"Yeah."

"Well, if you write about me, my name's not Rocky."

I smiled.

"My name's not Jack. Nice to meet you, not Rocky."

"It isn't," he said, the anger rising to the surface like a hungry fish.

"Okay, okay," I said.

"It's David," Rocky said.

I smiled.

"Okay, Dave. Good to officially meet you."

I turned and started to walk away. As I glanced back, I saw him take a couple of steps and clutch his abdomen again. I kept walking and he followed, five feet behind me. I turned the corner of the building and continued past the abandoned cars, toward the street. At the sidewalk, I turned back. He still was there, holding his belly and looking up the block, away from me.

"My truck's up here," I said.

I started off down the sidewalk. I sensed that he'd turned the other way, and then I heard the jingle of the bell on the door of the store. So he'd gone back in there. That was okay, I thought. The store lady seemed to be looking out for him. And then I heard the jingle again.

At the truck, I looked back. He was walking along the sidewalk toward me. I opened the truck door, took out my big L.L. Bean duffel, and heaved it into the truck's bed. I got in and popped the passenger door open from the inside. I moved CDs and the phone off of the passenger seat. He got in and reached over and closed the door, still clutching his belly with one arm.

I turned the key, put the truck in gear and drove.

"I told Lannie I was okay," he said.

"Who's that?"

"The lady in the store. She lets me eat there sometimes."

I glanced over at him. He seemed to be relaxing, the hard coating melting off. The more it melted, the younger he seemed.

"That's nice of her," I said. "What do you eat?"

"Cheez-Its and Doritos. Sometimes doughnuts. She gives me the doughnuts at the end of the day."

"All the basic food groups, huh?"

"Yeah. She has a gun, you know."

"I know. I saw it."

"You went in?"

"Yeah. I was looking for you."

"She didn't rat me out, did she?"

"No. Didn't say a word."

He smiled.

"Then how'd you know I was out back there?"

"I felt the draft. The cold air when you opened the back door."

I could see him processing that.

"I should've closed it quicker, huh?"

"Maybe," I said. "Where to?"

We stopped at the stop sign at Congress Street.

He hesitated. Wrapped his arms around himself, and pulled his legs up.

"You hurt in the front or the back?" I said.

"Kind of all over," Rocky said.

"Down low on your back?"

"What's down there?" he asked.

"Kidneys, spleen. I don't know. All your innards. Hospital?"

"Will they call the cops?"

"I don't know," I lied.

"Cops will bring me home."

"But what's worse? Going home or having your spleen rupture or something."

He considered it, his mouth set in a frown, forehead furrowed. It appeared to be a toss-up.

CHAPTER 5

I drove for a couple of blocks, waiting for Rocky to reveal some hint of why he had left home, what had turned his life down this dead end. The city was gray and cold, everything cast in the color of dirty cement. The heat had turned the truck cab into a sauna but Rocky still was hunched in a near-fetal position, his hands between his thighs, his cheeks still white and cold.

"They can't make me go anywhere," he muttered, then turned toward the window. "It's the law."

"Who?" I said.

"The cops. The state ladies. They can say what they want and I'm, like, 'Kiss my butt.' "

"You say that, huh?"

"Well, I think it."

"Where do they want you to go? Home?"

"I'm not going home. I don't have one."

"That's too bad," I said. I braked to let a woman cross the street. She was heavy, legs like gnarled stumps. She shuffled along in unlaced basketball shoes.

"Lots of people don't have a home. Like that lady there, I'll bet. When I lived in New York City there were homeless people all over the place. Living in cardboard boxes, under bridges. You know, highway overpass bridges? They get in there out of the rain and—"

"I'm going to New York," Rocky said.

"Really. How you getting there?"

"Hitch a ride. With a truck driver."

"Is that right? What are you going to do in New York?"

We were alongside the park, where paths wound through the arching black trees. A couple of people were walking dogs. A skinny guy in a red stretchy outfit was shuffling through the snow on skis. An unshaven guy in mismatched boots held up a scrap of cardboard that said, "Please help." I had a vision of Rocky in Central Park, helpless as a pet-store rabbit.

"I'll get a job in a big museum or something," Rocky blurted.

"Oh, yeah? My father worked in a museum in New York.

He studied bugs. You mean that kind of museum?"

"No, I mean the kind filled with old stuff. I like things that are old."

"Your house, the one you don't have, is that filled with old stuff?"

"No. It's new and boring. But I don't go there."

He glowered, and I didn't say anything. Then he said, "This the way to the hospital?"

"Yup."

"I don't think I want to go there."

"Why not? They'll check you out."

"They want permission to look at you. Your parents or something."

"You tried to get looked at here before?"

He hesitated. We were grinding up the hill toward the hospital.

"They wouldn't help you?" I asked.

"I left. They were wanting to know who I was with and stuff, and I said, 'Nobody,' and they said, 'Well, we'll have to call so-and-so.' Some social worker. I'm like, 'No thank you.' And I'm gone."

I glanced at him, smiled at his tiny bit of bravado. We came out of St. John and into the circle in front of Maine Medical Center. Three cars in front of us an old woman was being hoisted from a wheelchair into the passenger side of a taxi.

"You'd think she'd have somebody to come and get her," I said.

"Maybe everybody she knows is dead," Rocky said solemnly.

I glanced at him. He'd said it with empathy and I wondered if he was an orphan, bolted from some foster home. Brand new.

"So what was wrong with you?"

"When?"

"When you came here and changed your mind."

"Ah, nothing. I had this, like, cut on my foot. It was getting all infected and stuff. It had pus coming out of it."

"Yuck," I said. "So what did you do? After you left, I mean."

"I got this stuff at the drugstore and I put it on it and it went away. It got better. I didn't need these doctors and nurses. Your body, it has all these lymph nodes and stuff."

"Is that right?" I said.

"Yeah. It's how you heal. White blood cells. They march right in and kill the infection germs."

"You learn that in school?"

"Yeah."

"Who was your teacher?"

"Mr. Leonard."

He caught himself, like divulging even that much made him jumpy. I could see him looking for the door handle. The woman finally was loaded into the taxi, and the driver wrestled the wheelchair into the trunk. He got in the taxi and pulled away, and we moved up a place in the line.

"I could just get out here," Rocky said.

"No, I've got time. Wait just a minute and I'll drop you right at the door."

"No, that's okay."

"No, really. I don't mind."

I could see him tensing in the seat.

"I'll get out here."

"Hang on," I said.

He was fumbling for the door handle.

"Rocky, buddy. You could have internal bleeding. You could hemorrhage or something. You really shouldn't—"

I started to put my hand on his shoulder, but he opened the door, slid out, and started down the driveway, bent at the middle like he was carrying an invisible load on his back. There were cars behind me and I couldn't back up. I watched in the mirror as Rocky disappeared around the corner of the hospital building, running away like a wounded deer, heading for deeper cover.

CHAPTER 6

We were the doddering daily of Bangor, junior to the *Bangor Daily News.* Circulation was modest, ad lineage was slipping, but the *Clarion* was family-owned and run with an odd lack of concern for the bottom line. The family, the Danforths, had made big bucks in land speculation, timber and shipping, originally, and, oddly enough, the newspaper. The younger Danforth clan had degenerated or evolved, depending on your point of view, into a scattered band of trust-fund hippies from Blue Hill, Maine to Marin County, California. They were sculptors and painters and musicians. One of the granddaughters made violins and a grandson made necklaces from deer antlers. Their grandmother, our fearless leader, made only occasional editorial dictates to the *Clarion* from her Victorian mansion overlooking downtown Bangor.

The staff plodded along with impunity.

Her name was Tippy Danforth and in the three months

I'd been on the staff I'd gotten to know her pretty well. Her cause was primarily cats, but any other stray animals would do. She was known to stake out trash cans in restaurant parking lots, baiting her Havahart traps with salmon and swordfish. Cats and kittens trapped by Tippy Danforth were handed off to other animal lovers in her network, like hostages taken by jungle insurgents.

Robust and mannish, Tippy came to the newsroom every week with the latest installment of her column, "All God's Creatures." The column usually retold an animal story sent in by one of Tippy's many compatriots, but it sometimes was more hard-hitting. Once she told how animals were used in horrible experiments so companies could produce important products, like mascara. Each column ended with a plea that a featured cat be adopted. Tippy warned that potential adoptive parents would be subject to a background check.

When I walked into the newsroom that day Tippy Danforth was standing by my desk, waiting for her personal editor.

She nodded, but kept talking.

"Just because it's winter, don't think they can't have fleas," she was telling one of the news assistants, a young woman named Marna who also pampered her cat. "They breed year round. Ditto for ear mites."

They looked at me.

"Sorry I'm late," I said.

"What happened to your mouth?" Tippy said.

They both stared.

"Oh, that. A little bump."

"Don't tell us. You walked into a door," Marna said.

She was young and sharp, a single mother and part-time student from the boonies, scraping out a life. Tippy, in her L.L. Bean boots and smudged parka, gave my swollen mouth a last look and went right on to more important matters.

"There's the column," she said, pointing to the pages on the keyboard of my terminal. "It's rather a disturbing one, but I think it needs to be said. These Satanist people."

I took off my jacket and hung it on the hook by my cubicle. "Satanists?" I said mildly.

"Stealing cats for sacrifices," Tippy said, waving toward the column. "It's all in there. I heard about it from a friend of mine on the coast. Sickening. Well, I'm off."

And she was, striding through the still-quiet newsroom like the Queen off to the hunt. Sound the horn. Load the Havahart.

Marna shook her head.

"I'm glad I just work here," she said.

"Likewise," I said.

And oddly enough, I was.

The *Clarion* wasn't the *New York Times.* Its world was smaller and its news judgment sometimes provincial. But it covered greater Bangor with diligence and affection, and most of the time was a serious newspaper. When it wasn't, I said so. Sometimes they listened. As Tippy said, I'd improved her pet column a hundred percent, and the animals thanked me.

I smiled and shook my head.

"What?" Marna said, behind me. "Didn't they do cats in the *New York Times?*"

"Only on Broadway," I said.

"I'd die to be in New York," she said, looking dreamily at her computer screen.

"Some people do," I said.

"When I was a kid, about fourteen, me and my best friend, Alicia, were going to run away to New York and become writers," Marna said.

"I did a series once on kids who did that," I said. "Ran away to New York."

"Did they become writers?"

"One actually did. Wrote for magazines. The rest became store clerks. One was a waitress. There were drug addicts and a prostitute and one of them got killed," I said.

"Leave me my dreams, McMorrow," Marna said, and she started punching her keyboard. I ran my tongue over my swollen lip and thought of Rocky, hunched in his red plaid jacket, hurrying away on skinny legs into the snow, visions of skyscrapers dancing in his troubled little head.

CHAPTER 7

It wasn't a bad night on the desk. No major crisis. No breaking news to keep me late. I began with obits, those little prose nuggets that attempted to sum up an entire life in a hundred words.

On that day's death list there was a woman who'd worked in a woolen mill for forty-two years. A man who had cut wood and raised eleven children. A man who kept a garden, supported his family, and didn't raise his voice. "His word was his bond," the obituary said.

I thought of the obituaries in the *Times,* where simple goodness, the most fundamental of virtues, didn't often make the list of illustrious lifetime achievements.

I smiled.

"Good one?" Marna said.

"Very," I said.

Reporters and editors swept into the room, released from the afternoon news meeting. A couple of the reporters waved. The city editor, Ronald Randall, rounded the corner, grimly serious as always, like he'd just gotten off the phone with the president—and the president was not happy.

"Mister McMorrow," he said as he strode by, headed for the photo department.

"Mister Randall," I said.

He said he had two stories for me to rewrite. One was rough, he said, and the other was ten inches too long. "So fix 'em," Randall said loudly, knowing he was within earshot of both reporters. "Save the originals so maybe somebody will learn something." One reporter was young and earnest, a woman on the way up. The other was older and tired, a gray-haired guy on the way down. Randall wasn't making either ride any easier.

Pathetic little tyrant, I thought. Is this how you get your jollies?

I tapped at the keys. Opened directories and closed them. The health insurance, Jack, I told myself. Hold your tongue.

There was a time when I would have told him to kiss off, but this was the new me. Four nights a week and home. Write the freelance stories in between. Don't take it so much to heart. Insurance for the baby.

I took a long, deep breath, stretched in my chair. Randall went to his desk and got on the phone.

"Can you spell, 'Pompous ass?' " Marna murmured behind me. "Of course you can't. You're a moron and I'm god's gift to journalism."

"Five o'clock," I said quietly. "He'll be gone."

And he was, home by five fifteen, recounting the day's victories to his cross-bearing wife. They didn't have children, thank goodness, but word was that when Randall came to work at the *Clarion* and met Tippy Danforth, he went right out and bought a cat.

He knew whose milk to lap.

But the fearless leader did leave the rest of us to our business. I edited the stories. One was about a zealous town constable who was making himself unpopular in his little town up north. The story was a little rough but not bad. The other was about a robbery at a branch bank out by the mall. It wasn't clear whether the guy really had a gun; he was definitely wearing a ski mask. The story needed trimming, but not a hatchet job. I made a point to tell the reporters I thought they were good stories. They said, "Thanks," but warily, still not sure if I was friend or foe.

With the exception of Marna, that was true of most of the newsroom. I was an outsider, one with an intimidating big-time past. And they didn't know the half of it.

So I was left to myself. I drank tea, read stories, and at seven fifteen, I called Roxanne in South Portland. She answered, sounded worn out. She said she might be coming down with something.

"Get to bed," I said.

"I've got reports to finish."

"They can wait," I said. "They're only matters of life and death."

I could feel her smile.

"Thanks, Jack," she said.

"Anytime."

"How are you?" Roxanne asked.

"Okay. Still feeling a little isolated in the newsroom. Peer acceptance is coming slowly."

"I meant your tooth."

"Oh," I said. "It's fine."

"Does it still move?"

"Only if I want it to. I do it at recess to gross kids out."

"Did you make an appointment yet?"

"No. I've been tied up."

"Will you do it in the morning?"

"Sure."

"Sure you'll do it, or sure you won't?"

"Sure, I'll try to remember to do it," I said.

"The great equivocator," Roxanne said.

"We don't use words like that here at the *Clarion*. Randall says the average subscriber reads at a fourth-grade level."

"Only if you give them fourth-grade writing."

"We try to be vigilant but sometimes some seventh-grade words get by," I said. "But hey, speaking of seventh grade, guess who I ran into on the way out of Portland."

I told her about Rocky, the store, the hospital.

"You drove him in your truck?" Roxanne said.

"Yeah. It was cold. He's hurt."

"You should be careful of that. Especially if you're alone with them."

"He's harmless."

"No, I mean be careful for you. These kids will say a lot of things that aren't necessarily true."

"Oh," I said. "I get it."

"Yeah," Roxanne said.

"You know, it's almost like he's not really running away. It's more like he's hiding."

"Maybe from an abusive adult," Roxanne said.

"But he didn't seem like a kid who's been abused for years and years. Don't they develop a pretty hard shell?"

"Or they're obsequious, like an abused dog," she said. "Always cowering and fawning, looking for approval."

"I don't know," I said. "He just didn't seem to fit any of

that. He just seemed like sort of a quiet little guy. And you know, I think he liked me. Liked talking to me."

"Maybe he needs a father figure."

"I wonder what was wrong with the old one," I said.

"Could be any number of things," Roxanne said. "There are countless ways that relationships come apart."

"Not ours," I said.

"No, not ours."

"And not our kid."

"I hope not," Roxanne said.

"What if this Rocky kid hemorrhages or something? What if he has a broken rib sticking in his lung?"

"It's out of your hands, Jack. You tried to help."

"Maybe I didn't try hard enough."

"Don't be so hard on yourself. He's a big boy."

"No, he isn't. He's a little skinny runt."

"Who knows how to take care of himself, probably more than we think," Roxanne said. "He'll find his way."

"But to what? Some flophouse? Some place full of drunks or junkies? A few years from now I could be here editing his obit. Drug overdose or AIDS or he gets killed and dumped in a ditch."

"I don't know, Jack," she said. "Most of these kids are survivors. They'll surprise you. They really will."

CHAPTER 8

The route home was down the interstate for ten miles, then off the highway to the east until that road intersected with a road that went south, over hills, along ridge crests. I drove through the woods, passing occasional hamlets, silent in the still-falling snow. They were inexplicable settlements, remnants of places that had sprung up around farms and churches. There had once been small wood-framed mills propped beside streams that ran down steep, rocky pitches. Now the old buildings—the big barns, the farmhouses where craggy maples stood sentry—were falling down, pitched to their knees. As I drove through, just before midnight, everything was dark and still.

I pictured Rocky in places like these. In the country where did you hide? The woods? He'd freeze. Abandoned houses? He'd starve. Soup kitchens and shelters? There weren't any. Knock on doors? They'd call the sheriff or worse—grab him by the shoulder, toss him into the pickup and drive him home.

"What do you mean you're running away? Get in that goddamn truck before you freeze, for god's sake."

I pictured it as I swung off Route 9 and headed east to Prosperity. The back roads hadn't been traveled at all and the snow covered the pavement like white moss. The black woods rose steeply to my left and the road twisted and dropped and then climbed again, following the path some homesteader had trod some two hundred years before.

It was another ten miles to home, through Knox and Freedom, and then another back road. I turned off onto a dirt road through the woods, and off that road to the track through the trees. There were four houses on the little track, which crested a ridge just past my place, a half-mile in.

The road was rutted by a late December thaw. The dooryards of the houses—the college girls, the widow Mrs. Soule, Clair, and me—served as laybys where you waited for oncoming cars to pass, like in Ireland. But that didn't happen much. A strange car on the road was an event. The driver usually was lost, or trying to be.

Which was why the footprints struck me as strange.

They led along the edge of the road in front of the truck, plodding up the rise. The snow had partially filled them but still they showed plainly in the headlights.

The college girls? They were in Montana on a winter survival training course. They'd asked me to watch their house.

Mrs. Soule wouldn't be out. Clair wouldn't be likely to walk this end of the road, and if he did, his tracks wouldn't look like these. These tracks meandered, wove a gentle slalom in the snow. I followed them like a hound.

The tracks continued along the edge of the road, then veered into the woods and back onto the roadway. I stopped the truck and got out and looked. The person had stepped into the trees, urinated and continued on. So it was a male, and it looked like he'd put something down on the ground as he relieved himself. I climbed back in the truck and followed.

The tracks scuffed in the snow. At one point they stopped, as though the person had paused to listen or look, and then they continued until they came to the college girls' oversized cabin. I felt myself tense. The girls were active in the school's gay-rights organization, and we looked out for them. Drunken guys had driven by a couple of times, stopped once, but Clair had gone out and enlightened them. He always took his rifle; they didn't tend to come back.

So was this one of them?

At the girls' house, the tracks turned in. I stopped. The tracks stopped ten feet from the house, meandered a bit toward the car parked in the driveway, then veered back toward the road.

I drove on.

The tracks were straight now, on the right side of the road, close to the trees, and when he approached my house, on the same side of the road, the prints drew closer together. He had slowed, walked nearly past the house, then turned in.

And hadn't come out.

CHAPTER 9

I eased the truck into the yard and stopped. The headlights illuminated the front of the house, the tracks to the side door dark shadows in the snow. No lights showed from inside. I waited a minute. I looked toward the shed, to the left. Nothing showed. I waited some more, looked for some movement in the darkened windows.

Nothing moved.

My rifle was inside, in the kitchen closet. The shells were

in the drawer beside the sink, behind the towels. There were no other weapons in the house, except for the arsenal of knives in the block on the counter. Was the person in there? Had he gone out the back? Was this a burglary, somebody looking for a house that looked empty? Was he looking for cash? Beer? The DVD? If he was gone, he'd be easy to track. If he was still there, I didn't want to wrestle.

I reached for my cell phone between the truck seats, dialed the operator. When he answered, I asked for the number of the Waldo County Sheriff's Department. The operator asked me if this was an emergency.

"I don't think so," I said.

He told me to wait for my number. I did and then I dialed. Waited. The truck motor ticked. The dispatcher answered. I identified myself. I said I lived on the old dump road in Prosperity. I said there was somebody in my house. I told her about the tracks. She asked me if anyone else should be in the house. Roxanne was in Portland. The tracks were too small to be Clair's. I said no. She asked if there were guns in the house and I said yes, but only one. She said she'd send a deputy but it could take a half hour. She said I shouldn't try to enter the dwelling myself.

I sat. A minute went by, then another. One more and I eased out of the truck, shutting off the motor but leaving the headlights on, trained on the house. Then I backed away from the truck and walked up the road.

At the edge of the woods, I walked toward the back of the house, shuffling through the new snow and trying not to break through the frozen crust underneath. When I could see behind the house, I fell to a crouch.

I watched. Back on my feet, I circled the clearing behind the house, looking down for tracks. I walked the perimeter of the yard. Nothing. I stopped again and watched. The house was still, the snow falling in the darkness. I could see the faint green glow of the light on the microwave. Nothing else. I eased closer. Closer. Stood beside the house, alongside a window. Moved slowly over and peered in.

Shapes of furniture showed in the dark. Nothing moved.

I walked slowly to the front of the house, by the road. The truck lights blazed on the door. I walked to the truck and shut them off, then walked carefully to the side door. The tracks were to my right. They stopped at the door, shuffled in place. And then he must have opened the door, which hadn't been locked. Why lock a door when the cops are a half-hour away? I reached out and pressed down on the latch.

It moved. I gave the door a tap and it swung open. I tapped it again and it swung wider. I listened. Thought I heard something. A snort or a grunt. I stepped in. Stopped and listened, but didn't hear it again. Then, in the dark, I eased my way to the closet, and opened that door. It creaked. I waited. Nothing. I reached in past the jackets, past the broom and the mop, and took out the rifle by the barrel. I eased it into my arms, put my finger on the trigger guard, then with my left hand reached for the light switch.

And there he was.

"What are you doing?" I said.

Rocky awakened with a jerk, eyes wide and white. He started to get up from the couch but saw the rifle and froze.

"What the hell?" I said. "How'd you get all the way up here?"

He was on the edge of the couch, a paper grocery bag beside him.

"Hitched," Rocky said.

"Why? How'd you find me?"

"I, um, I didn't really mean to. I just did."

He looked disoriented, jarred from a deep sleep.

"What do you mean, you 'just did'?"

"I just sorta did. I mean, I was gonna go to New York."

"Wrong turn," I said. "Didn't they teach you north and south?"

"The guy was on the ramp. How was I supposed to know? Then he says he's going to Unity. He's in this big truck, it, like, has these ladders to get in, and he just keeps on driving. It was really warm. I fell asleep."

"Why'd you leave Portland?"

"I couldn't go to the shelter. This kid told me they were gonna, like, hurt me bad during the night. I had to get out of there. I mean—"

"So how'd you find me?"

"I asked the lady. The lady at the restaurant."

"What restaurant?"

"I don't know. The one the guy with the truck stopped at. It was right near here, sort of. I saw the sign, it said Prosperity. She told me where you lived."

"And you walked?"

"Yup."

"That's four miles. You're lucky you found it in the dark."

I stepped to the closet and put the rifle back.

"She made me a map."

"A map? That's nice, but you know what? There's a Waldo County deputy on the way, coming out here because I thought you were a burglar."

"Shit," Rocky said, coming off the couch like an animal bolting for an open cage door. He was by me, with his hand on the door, when he remembered his grocery bag. He turned back.

"You can run, but that's the best way in the world to get

picked up. Wandering the roads around here in the middle of the night."

"They won't get me," he said, going by me again.

"If they do, they can hold you this time. You'll be a suspect in a burglary."

"The door was open."

"Doesn't matter."

At the door, he paused.

"I'll go in the woods."

I looked at his thin, wool jacket. His sneakers.

"You'll freeze," I said.

"I'll be okay," Rocky said.

"No, you won't. Let me tell you. I've got nine toes because of the cold."

He looked at me skeptically.

"I'm not kidding. I'll call the cops," I said. "I'll tell 'em it's okay."

His hand dropped from the latch.

He stood there while I went to the phone and dialed, pausing to recall the number. The same dispatcher answered. I told her who I was, that it was okay. The intruder was a neighbor. She asked if everything was ten-four. I said it was and apologized for the inconvenience.

I hung up. Rocky stood by the door holding his bag.

"Sit down," I said. "You hungry?"

"Nah."

He stood.

"Yeah, sure. I've got to close my truck door."

I did, and when I came back in, I took off my boots and jacket, and told Rocky to do the same.

"At least take your jacket off. And you can get the stove going while I look for something to feed to a kid who isn't hungry. How 'bout some lettuce?"

He looked doubtful.

"Just kidding. The paper and kindling are beside the woodbox. You heat with wood at home?"

"Yeah," Rocky said, then catching himself again. "I mean, I don't . . ."

"I know. You don't have a home. You were born in a pumpkin patch. How 'bout tuna fish sandwiches? It's a house special. The bread's frozen but I can toast it."

He didn't say no, and he even started the fire. He knew just how much newspaper and kindling to use, selected the logs, and set them just right. He'd grown up in a wood-burning home. That was a clue that narrowed the possibilities to three-quarters of the homes in Maine.

I opened two cans of tuna, got out mustard and mayonnaise and celery and onion. He squatted by the stove and watched the flames through the glass panels in the door. Then he noticed me watching him and started to get up and winced.

"Still hurts?"

"Not as much. A lot better than before."

I chopped the celery.

"Good," I said. "Onion?"

"Sure."

"A lot of people don't like onions, but they're really good for you. I read that some place. Purple onions are supposed to be really good for your heart. I don't know. Maybe they made the whole thing up. They're in the onion business, so they invent this theory about—"

"No, it's true," Rocky said. "My mom, she—"

He stopped.

"She what?" I said.

I peeled the skin off the onion, and waited. Rocky stood there, his lips compressed, then turned toward the fire.

"If you want to say something, go ahead. I'm not a cop.

I'm just an innocent bystander. Or something like that."

Rocky opened his mouth, then closed it. He held his hands up to the fire to warm them. His fingers were long and slender, like his wrists. I watched him for a moment, then continued to mash the onion and celery, mustard and mayonnaise, into the tuna. I wondered if he got a hard time in school, looking so young. I considered whether that might be what he was running from. I decided it wasn't.

I toasted the bread, deli rye Roxanne had brought from Portland. As the toast popped, I made the sandwiches, quitting after four. The sandwiches went on a plate, and I put two glasses on the table, and turned to the refrigerator.

There was Sea Dog brown ale, mine, Diet Pepsi, Roxanne's. I took out both, poured a glass of each. Rocky shyly pulled up a stool. I sat across from him and raised my glass. He held his Pepsi awkwardly. We both turned when the headlights darted through the trees.

And then the spotlight.

"It's the deputy," I said.

"Oh, my god," Rocky said, lunging from the table.

The stool clattered to the floor.

CHAPTER 10

The cruiser pulled up outside, the spots on the end of its light bar strafing the windows of the house. Rocky was pressed against the door, his mouth open, face pale, eyes unblinking. He looked to the sliding door at the rear of the house, but he didn't move.

"Please don't let them take me," Rocky said. "Please don't."

"I'll go talk to him," I said.

I came out of the house into the dooryard. The cruiser was parked across the end of the driveway, blocking my truck in. The door opened and the deputy emerged slowly, disappearing behind the glare of the lights.

"Sir, did you report a break?" a woman's voice called.

"Yes, I did," I said, walking toward the car. "But I was mistaken. It wasn't anything. I told the dispatcher—"

"Stop right there, sir."

"But I told the dispatcher it wasn't—"

"Do you have any identification on you, sir?"

I stopped. Stood in the lights, with the snow in my eyes, and patted for my wallet. It was in my back pocket. I started to pull it out.

"Could you hold it right there, sir?" the voice called.

I did.

"Hey, listen. I just—"

"Just turn so I can see your back, sir, if you don't mind. That's good. Now take it out. Slow."

I heard her murmur something, then the radio coughed and I heard my name. The deputy came around the front of the car and I finally saw her. Dark wavy hair. Fair skin, pale in the lights. Heavy-set, but that might have been the flak vest under her uniform. A wide, high-cheeked face. A resolute, unflappable set to her mouth.

She kept her right hand low, near her gun.

"What's your name, sir?" she said, approaching me.

I told her.

"You live here?"

"That's right."

"You reported a break in progress?"

"Not exactly. I just saw footprints going in. I just got home from work. In Bangor. But it turned out to be somebody I know. I just didn't know he was coming by. So I'm really sorry you had to come all this way."

"Not a problem, sir," she said.

She looked at me neutrally, her gaze flickering past me toward the house.

"You have your driver's license?" the deputy said.

I said I did. She kept eye contact, still wary.

"So you saw footprints? Your friend walked here?"

"Yeah. Down the road."

"Are these the prints?"

The deputy flicked the flashlight beam over the ground. I pointed to Rocky's prints in the snow.

"That's some of them. I guess I walked on them a little. Once I knew it was him."

"What's your friend's name?" she asked.

I looked at her. She stared back. The motor in the cruiser huffed patiently, like a panting dog. She was in no rush.

"Rocky."

"Rocky what?"

I hesitated. She caught it.

"I don't know," I said.

"You don't know your friend's name?"

"No," I said. "We just met. Just recently. He's not really a friend. More of an acquaintance."

"Since when?"

"Since this morning."

"And this new acquaintance dropped by at almost one in the morning? You must have really hit it off."

I shrugged.

"Is he still here?"

"Yeah."

"Why don't you have this person come outside, sir. Is there anybody else in the home?"

"No," I said.

She looked toward the house. The radio blared from the cruiser, then was silent. Her hand dropped to her gun again.

"Tell this Rocky to come outside," the deputy said. It wasn't a request.

"Hey, Rocky," I called. "Come out here."

We waited. I was half-turned to the house. I could see the lights in the kitchen, the glasses on the table. And then the figure bolting across the room.

"Hold it! Police!" the deputy shouted. "Hold it right there."

I saw Rocky fumble with the sliding door at the rear of the house, then disappear from view. The deputy saw him, too, and started to trot toward the house, still shouting, "Hold it. Police." Then she turned back to the cruiser, trotted around and leaned in for the mike.

"I've got one in the woods, one in hand," the deputy was

saying. "I'm not sure what the situation is here. Is there a canine close?"

The radio crackled. She came back to me, her expression hard and determined, a flashlight in hand. I was standing there in my sweater, starting to shiver. She said she wanted my ID. I handed her my license. She looked at it, then put it in her pocket. She motioned for me to go toward the house. I walked to the doors, following Rocky's footprints. She followed. When I turned I could see the gun hand low, the light held like a club.

Inside in the light, she looked the place over, the way cops do, then did the same with me. I saw her note the scuff mark on my mouth, but she didn't say anything. I walked to the woodbox and got another log and she told me to put it down. I did.

"So why'd he run?" the deputy said.

"I don't know. He has this thing about being taken into custody."

"Who is he?"

"His name's Rocky. That's all I know."

"Where's he from?"

I hesitated, fully realizing for the first time what this was going to sound like.

"I don't know. I met him in Portland."

Her eyes showed the faintest flicker of disgust.

CHAPTER 11

Her name was Divan, like the couch. I was sitting at the table in the kitchen. She was standing at the counter. She'd told me to keep my hands in sight.

"Met him in Portland? When?"

"This morning."

"I thought you said you worked in Bangor. And he walked here. From up the road. Why don't you cut the crap now, Mr. McMorrow, and tell me what this is about."

"I said up the road, not from up the road," I said. "And he's a kid."

This time her eyes showed more than a flicker. Her mouth hardened in distaste.

"A kid? How old a kid?"

"I don't know. Thirteen. Fourteen. A runaway."

Her eyes narrowed, pronounced me a pervert.

"You brought him here?"

"No," I said. "He hitchhiked. I didn't invite him. Listen, it's not what you're thinking."

"Never mind what I'm thinking."

"I didn't pick the kid up. I was with my friend. My girl-friend."

I paused. Was this going to get Roxanne in some sort of trouble for fraternizing with the clients? The deputy waited. I looked down. Melting snow from her boots had puddled on the pine floor. She dug in her pocket for a pad and pen and I could see the line of her flak vest. When she was ready I told the story, from the deli to the alley to the *Clarion* to home. She asked me to spell Roxanne's name and I did.

"So you invited the kid to come and stay with you?"

"No," I said. "I didn't invite him anywhere. Like I said, I just tried to get him to go to a hospital to get checked out."

"But he got all the way up here somehow. And he looked like he could run pretty good. He couldn't be hurt too bad."

I shrugged. "I saw him taking a pretty good beating."

Divan scribbled on her pad. The puddle at her boots was widening.

"Why would he think he could stay here?"

"I don't know."

"You didn't tell him he could sleep here?"

"Hell, no."

"But you didn't kick him out."

"In the snow? A kid? Would you?"

"Then why'd he run?"

"I don't know," I said.

"What happened to your mouth?"

"A kid kicked me in Portland. Another kid. One of the ones who was beating on Rocky."

Her eyes swept the room, stopping at the table. The sandwiches. The ale.

"You give him alcohol?"

"No," I said slowly. "Pepsi."

"That's not Pepsi in that glass."

"That's for me, not him."

"So you were gonna have a few beers and then both of you were going to go to bed?"

"What's that supposed to mean?"

"Take it how you want," the deputy said.

"I hadn't thought about going to bed. I hadn't figured out what I was going to do with him."

"Had you called your friend? From DHS?"

"Not yet."

"Why not?"

"I was making the kid something to eat. He was hungry."

"Nice of you," Divan said. "You have this Roxanne Masterson's number in Portland?"

I recited it. She wrote it down and I motioned to the phone. She picked it up and I went to the sliding window, watched the snow falling in the window light, filling the tracks that Rocky had left as he'd run in his sneakers into the dark, cold woods. In an hour, all evidence of him would be gone. The rock would be sunk and I'd be left with the ripples.

I stood there, back to the deputy as she talked to Roxanne. It lasted ten minutes and then she hung up and I turned around. Her expression had softened but only slightly. When you loathe someone, it's hard to shift gears.

"Some people prey on runaways," Divan said. "And they're not always the people you think they'd be."

"Hardly ever."

"You'd be surprised at what we see," she said.

"No, I wouldn't," I said.

She looked at me like I'd sassed her.

"I was a reporter in New York City for years," I said.

"Oh," Divan said. "So you've seen what I'm talking about, Mr. McMorrow."

"Times ten," I said.

She looked at me curiously.

"If we don't find him, I want you to call me if he turns up," Divan said.

"Tonight?"

"Any night. I want to talk to this kid. I want to know what he's running from."

"That," I said, "makes two of us."

CHAPTER 12

At two thirty-three by the clock on the microwave, Rocky came out of the darkness. I was sitting in the big chair in the living room with a mug of tea. The lights were off. The phone was beside me from when I'd called Roxanne. She'd said she was sorry she got me involved in this whole mess. She said to call her when Rocky showed up, and she was sure he would, but not until the coast was clear. Cold woods, a warm house, cops gone.

And sure enough, I watched as he emerged from the trees and picked his way down his own path, still carrying his grocery bag, placing his sneakers in each faint footprint like a deer. At the edge of the deck, he paused and peered up, then walked up the steps and over to the door. It slid open and he stepped in.

"You could have called," I said. "I was worried sick."

Rocky jumped.

"Close the door," I said. "You frozen?"

He slid the door shut.

"I'm okay," he said.

In the darkness, I could see him trembling.

"Good. That cop'll be glad to hear it."

I could see him stiffen. I got up from the chair and poured a little more tea from the pot on the counter.

"Don't worry. She left. What's with this shyness when it comes to police officers? What's with you?"

He stood there.

"Nothin'."

"That's why you're running around in the snow at two in the morning? Jimmy Cagney gave up easier."

He didn't say anything, probably because he'd never heard of Cagney. I didn't bother to explain. I did get up and turn on the lamp on the counter. Rocky's head was crusted with snow. The end of his nose was white. His glasses were fogged, which made him look almost blind. His hands, clenched together as though in some sort of supplication, were blue. The bag was under his arm.

"Stand by the stove. Can you feel your toes? Take off your sneakers and move your toes around. I'll get you a towel so you can dry your hair. How 'bout hot chocolate?"

Rocky didn't say no, which I took for a yes. I went to the bathroom and got a towel and came back and tossed it to him, then put a mug of milk in the microwave to warm. When it beeped, I took it out and dumped in some chocolate syrup, one of Roxanne's few vices other than me. I stirred the steaming, brown milk and handed it to him. He took the mug without dropping his bag. He'd unlaced his sneakers but hadn't taken them off.

Maybe there were holes in his socks.

I leaned against the counter and sipped my tea. Rocky faced the woodstove and blew on the hot chocolate for a couple of minutes, then drank it in gulps. When he was done, he held the mug for warmth, hands wrapped around it like a priest holds a chalice. I went to the refrigerator and took out the bag of sandwiches. I handed it to him, and he opened it and fished one out with his slender fingers. He ate it in four bites, swallowing it in chunks, like a dog would.

"Could you eat a little faster? I'd like to get some sleep," I said.

He looked at me.

"Just kidding," I said.

Rocky took another sandwich out and took a bite, then another. I watched him, and suddenly felt very tired and annoyed. This was my house. I hadn't invited him and here he was, just standing there, shoving food in his mouth. Where did he think he was? Burger King?

"So what's the deal?"

He looked at me.

"What are you running away from? Get a D in algebra or something?"

He eyed me and kept chewing, like a cat that didn't want to give up a kill.

"You get beat up at home?"

Rocky chewed, poked his glasses back up his nose, which was turning from white to pink. I could smell the odor of warming, wet wool.

"Where is home?" I tried.

He looked away, my little amnesiac.

"You have parents? Mother and father. Want to call your mom and dad?"

"My mom's sick," Rocky said quickly, almost reflexively, as though it were a well-worn explanation.

"Oh," I said. "Sorry to hear that. Well, maybe she'd like to hear from you then. Is she in the hospital?"

"No," he said.

"Oh. Then you want to call your dad? He can tell your mom you're okay."

"No."

He chewed. I stood there for a moment, and he did, too, looking away from me, looking far away. So it's the father, I thought.

"Okay. That's fine. But I've got to get—"

"Thank you for your help, sir," Rocky said suddenly. "I hope I'm not too much trouble."

It startled me, this outburst of courtesy. Somewhere along the way, he'd learned some manners.

"No, it's no trouble. And I won't toss you out in the snow tonight, but you can't just park here. I'm sure there's some-place you can go—group home or something. Ms. Masterson will know. But you can't be staying here because she's here, living here, a lot of the time and I'm sure there's some rule or something that says you can't just move in with the state lady. You know what I mean?"

"Yeah," Rocky said, swallowing a last chunk of bread and tuna. "I'll go."

He bent down to lace his sneakers.

"Oh, come on. I didn't mean that. You don't have to go this minute, for god's sake. Take your shoes off. Or don't, I don't care. I'll get you a dry shirt, if you want. You can sleep on the couch."

I went up to the loft and got a pair of sweatpants and a T-shirt, and came down and tossed them on the couch.

"Bathroom's in there," I said, nodding to the door under the stairs. "You got your toothbrush in that bag?"

It still was under his arm, clutched protectively. He didn't answer.

"If you don't, and you don't want your teeth to fall out

when you're twenty-two, there's a couple of new tooth-brushes in the cupboard under the sink. Help yourself. And there are towels in the closet in there. You can take a shower if you want. I don't know, get yourself squared away for an-other few days on the street. Whatever. I've got to be up by seven, so I guess you'll have to be up, too."

"You going to Bangor?" Rocky asked.

"Not until the afternoon. You want to go to Bangor? You know people there?"

He shrugged. "I've been there before."

"Well, I don't know. We'll see in the morning. I've got to work on my truck, and I want to finish it before I go to work, so I don't know."

I turned to the loft stairs.

"So good night or whatever."

"Good night," Rocky said.

It sounded strange here, these words that belonged at his home, not mine. I started for the stairs, then turned back and went to the counter for the phone. I took it off the charger and brought it with me. He was standing in the same place. I walked over and closed the damper on the wood-stove.

"How's your insides?" I said.

"Okay," Rocky said. "Better."

"Good," I said. "There's some . . ."

I was going to tell him where the ibuprofen was, but thought better of it. What if he took the whole bottle? His parents would sue me. I wondered if I should take the me-dicinal stuff upstairs with me. No, I thought. I'd have to clean out the whole house. Knives. Toilet bowl cleaner.

If somebody was bent on self-destruction, there really was no stopping them. And Rocky didn't seem like he wanted to hurt himself. He just seemed like a kid who, for some reason, didn't want to go home. For some reason . . .

I went up the stairs, started to undo my trousers, then reconsidered. Kid in the house, me in my shorts? Uh-uh. I unlaced my boots and yanked them off. Then I put the phone on the bedside table and stretched out on the bed in my clothes.

I didn't call Roxanne.

She couldn't be up all night, arranging for someplace for this kid to go. She couldn't overdo it, get exhausted. She had a baby to think about. We had a baby to think about. I'd call her in the morning, let her know somebody had to do something with Rocky.

I couldn't baby-sit him. I was supposed to be at Clair's, up the road, at seven thirty. I supposed the kid could come along. Clair wouldn't mind, but then Mary, Clair's wife, would want to take Rocky into the big kitchen, fill him full of pancakes or something. She'd have him half-adopted by lunchtime and he would have wormed his way even deeper into my life, and what did I do to invite that, other than yank those little creeps off of him, and that was more for Roxanne than for him . . . .

The phone rang, but in my dream it was on a ship, on a metal wall, and the ship was pitching and I kept sliding away and the phone was just out of reach, and I had to call Roxanne because I didn't want her to try to swim to the ship, and the phone was ringing and it was her, calling from the water, holding our baby, calling for help.

Half-conscious, I picked up the phone.

CHAPTER 13

"Yeah."

"Mr. McMorrow," the voice said from the darkness. "This is Deputy Divan. How are you, sir?"

How was I? Who the hell knew?

"Fine," I croaked. I looked at the luminescent glow of my watch. It was twenty minutes before six. The deputy's day was winding down.

"Did the boy ever come back?" she asked.

Did he come back? My mind struggled to put everything in place. Yeah, he'd come back, but should I tell the police? Should I have called them when he walked in? I considered it. The truth, my father had always said. Always tell the truth.

"Yeah," I said. "He's asleep on the couch."

"You didn't call?"

"I gave him some food and I fell asleep. I'm going to call the DHS and ask what they want to do. I can't have him here."

"No," Divan said. "You can't."

In her tone was the faint ring of innuendo. In the background, I heard the gruff voices and buzzing phones of a police station. I heard Rocky stir.

"I made some inquiries," Divan said. "There's a boy named

Arthur Doe who's been missing from the town of Woodfield since December nineteenth."

"Arthur Doe? Sounds like a dead body," I said.

"No, that's his real name. Actually, there are quite a few Does in Waldo County."

"And one on my couch?"

"I called the father. If it's him, he'll come and get him. He said the boy's still gone."

"What's he look like?"

I heard papers shuffle.

"Five-five, hundred and five. Brown and blue. Build is thin. D.O.B., one-eighteen, ninety-one. Glasses. Last seen wearing red plaid wool jacket, jeans, black-and-white sneakers. High tops. Nike Air Jordan. Left sneaker has red laces. Right one doesn't. Doesn't say what color it is."

I pictured Rocky's shoes, snow melting onto the floor.

"White," I said.

She kept going.

"This came from the school. He showed up at school one morning, got off the bus, went in the front door and out the back."

"What about the parents?"

"They didn't report it. The school finally did, I guess. Father said he figured the boy would come home when he was ready. Said it's been an ongoing problem."

"Nice," I said. "No wonder he took off."

I vowed to never be a father like that.

"I don't know," Divan said. "Might be one of those tough-love things. Sometimes kids need to decide to come home on their own."

"He's not even fourteen yet and he was on the streets in Portland getting the crap kicked out of him. That's pretty tough love."

"So you think it's him, Mr. McMorrow?"

"Yes."

"Why?"

"The sneakers. The laces."

"Okay, I'm gonna call the dad back. I told him I thought we'd located Arthur but I'd confirm it and get back to him. I'll give him directions and he'll take him off your hands."

"If the kid'll go," I said. "You know none of this addresses why the kid ran in the first place."

"That's not up to law enforcement, unless there's something obvious or he alleges something," Divan said. "I'll write up a report for DHS. They'll take it from there."

"Okay, Pontius," I muttered.

"Pardon me?"

"Nothing."

She wanted to know where I could be reached later. I gave her the number at the *Clarion* and my cell phone. Divan took the numbers and hung up. I pressed the button on the phone and rested it on my chest.

The house was quiet but I could hear the first morning doves coming to life. Through the skylight, I could see the sky turning from blue black to dull gray. The snow on the skylight glass had slipped off, which meant it had warmed up overnight. That's good, I thought. The kid won't be quite so cold, but then I remembered that he'd probably be home, in his house, probably in his room. I wondered what sort of scene that would be. Shouting and screaming? Taking away his privileges? No more Play Station? No more Internet? What did you do to a kid these days? Would the father hit Rocky, once he had him home? The kid seemed able to take a beating. Maybe he'd had practice.

I took a deep breath and readied myself to go down and break the news. Or should I wait or not tell him at all? Let the dad just knock on the door. If Rocky ran, I wasn't going to stop him. Hey, I'd let the father chase him through the woods. It was his son. It wasn't my fault he was screwed up.

"Oh, brother," I said.

I heaved myself off the bed and staggered. I felt like I hadn't slept at all, and I lurched stiffly down the stairs. I looked at the couch. The kitchen. Turned toward the bathroom. The door was open, the light still on. The bathroom was empty.

Rocky was gone.

"Son of a bitch," I said.

I went to the door to the deck and looked out. In the dim light, I could barely make out the remnant of the tracks Rocky had made the night before, going out to the woods and coming back. I reached for the light switch and turned on the floodlight. Next to the old tracks, gauzy with new snow, was another set of prints that crossed back and forth over the old. The fresh tracks went one way, leading into the trees.

"Oh, man," I said.

The father was on his way and I'd lost the kid. Well, he could follow the tracks himself. Stake out the roads. What was I supposed to do? Tie the kid down? No, they frowned on that down at DHS. Hell, if the cops couldn't hold him, what chance did I have?

I shook my head and walked to the side door and opened it and looked out to the road. Snow was slipping from the branches in sticky clumps, like color washed from a painting. The sky was pale to the east, and I could see that snow still covered the truck. Rocky's tracks from the road to the house still were visible, and my tracks to the door. But nothing else. He hadn't come back this way.

Standing there for a moment, I wondered if I should go look for him. I could loop around to Route 137 and see if he was hitchhiking or just walking. Would he hide in the woods? Would he risk being followed? Did he think his father would trail him? How badly could the guy want him if he hadn't even reported him missing?

"Goddamn it," I said.

I turned back into the house to get my boots and my jacket. If Rocky had taken off after hearing me on the phone, he couldn't have gone too far. And traffic at this hour would be almost nonexistent. A hitchhiker at six in the morning in the middle of nowhere? Then again, it would probably work to his advantage.

I went up the stairs to the loft and sat on my bed as I put on my boots, then came back downstairs and grabbed my parka off the hook by the door. Maybe I could find the kid and turn him over to his dad and go back to bed. No, Clair would be out in the barn, getting a fire going in the stove. Maybe I could take a nap, after lunch. Even an hour would help, I thought. I opened the door. Felt for my keys. Heard a truck coming up the road.

It was a green Dodge pickup, a big four-wheel drive diesel, dressy and new, and it slid to a halt in the snow in front of the house. I stepped out. The driver did, too. He was a very big guy, tall and rangy with a flattop haircut. He was wearing a tan field jacket, tan leather gloves, and a determined expression. On the door of the truck were the words, RUSTY CLEMENT, LOGGING CONTRACTOR. They were painted in gold.

Stepfather.

He closed the door. I walked toward him, and he toward me.

"You the guy got my boy?" he said.

His voice was disdainful, as though he'd like to toss me aside.

"I don't know. I said slowly, as he stopped in front of me. "There was a kid named Rocky here. But he's gone. Just left."

"What the hell you mean, he just left?" the guy said. "Where'd he go?"

"I don't know. Into the woods. But probably just a few minutes ago."

"Then go get him. Go get my boy."

He stood over me, which meant he was six-three, anyway. I told myself to stay calm. The guy was worried about his son. If I were in his place, I'd say things like that, too.

"So move," the guy snarled.

I exhaled slowly.

"I know you're upset. I would be—"

"You bring him out here, or I'll tear this shack apart with my goddamn bare hands. I'm gonna count to ten. Now move your friggin' ass."

His teeth were clenched. His fists, too. My hands were in the pockets of my jacket, but ready to come out if the need arose.

"I can't bring him out," I said slowly. "He's not in there."

"I don't care. Get him. What the hell you doing with my kid, anyway? I hear you laid a finger on him, I'll kill you."

I took a step toward him.

"Listen, I saved your kid from getting stomped to death in Portland. I didn't ask him to come here. He just showed up because he was cold. I fed him. I gave him a couch to sleep on. I could've—"

"That kid's got psychological problems. He's not right. Mister, you touched him and I'll have you put away. What the hell is your name? I want to know your name."

He paused. I looked right at him, a foot from his face. I told him my name.

"And if you want to know where he went, I'll show you

the path. Otherwise, get in your goddamn pimp truck and get off my property or I'll call the cops."

I turned and walked back toward the house, then around the side of the shed. Behind me, I could hear his boots crunching in the snow. I crossed the yard in the back of the house and stopped. Pointed to the ground.

"There you go. I'd say he has about a ten-minute start. Maybe less."

He looked at the tracks, then toward the woods.

"Where's that lead?"

His tone was less threatening, more authoritative. A man who was used to pushing people around.

"Depends," I said. "If he follows the path that's there, he could pop out at the main road. A half mile or so. He could listen for the trucks. He might do that. He got a ride up here from Portland with a trucker."

"He told you that?"

"Yeah."

"What else did he say?"

I looked at him. It was an odd question.

"Not much."

"What's he been doing for food? You said he went all the way to Portland?"

The tone was more reasonable now. Maybe he was just one of those people with incendiary tempers. Screaming one minute, calm the next. I'd known a few editors like that.

"Stayed at a shelter for kids," I said. "Hung around with some street kids."

"He's all right?"

"More or less."

"What's that mean?"

"He's a little beat up. Got kicked pretty good yesterday."

The guy didn't react to that. I waited. It was lighter and

a band of chickadees arrived at the feeder, six feet away, cheeping and whistling. The guy didn't react to that either.

"Don't suppose the little shit said why he won't come home," the guy muttered.

The little shit. I vowed to never say that about my son.

"No," I said. "I didn't get into that with him. He didn't say much at all, really."

"Never does."

I looked at him.

"He said his mother is sick," I said.

"Why'd he tell you that?" Clement said. His voice was sharp, newly angry.

"How the hell should I know?"

"Yeah, well, she's got leukemia."

"Sorry," I said.

Leukemia? What an odd thing to confide, but it was an odd conversation all around. I stood there in the snow and didn't say anything. The birds came and went. Clement turned toward me suddenly, and thrust out his gloved hand. I looked down. He was holding a business card. I took it. It read, RUSTY CLEMENT, LOGGING CONTRACTOR, just like the truck door. There was a sketch of a truck in the background. A string of telephone numbers.

"I'm gonna drive up to the road, see if I can cut him off. If he shows up here again, call me."

A chickadee fluttered by his head, blithely cheery. Rusty Clement turned and started back around the house, then stopped and turned and jabbed at me with a forefinger.

"If you touched him, you're in deep shit," he said.

"Likewise," I said. "I'm sure."

CHAPTER 14

Clair was using a torch to cut the rusty bolts that held the bed of my truck to its frame. The torch hissed, then the bolt clinked onto the concrete floor. Clair rolled out on the mechanic's creeper, and turned the torch off. The flame glowed blue, then went out with a pop.

"Guilt," Clair said, laying the torch on the floor. "Guy's feeling guilty 'cause he didn't chase the kid down in the first place. Now he needs a bigger villain than himself. So he picked you. Chester the Molester."

"I hope the kid doesn't tell him some tale," I said.

"I'll vouch for you. A changed man since you found Jesus in state prison."

"Thanks."

"Don't mention it."

It was nine thirty and we'd been at it for two hours. With Duke Ellington playing in the background, I'd told Clair about Rocky and Rusty and Deputy Divan, and he hadn't said much as he'd moved from the bench to the truck and back. Now he flipped off his welder's mask. His hair was close-cropped and silver. His hands were big and muscular.

"Isn't it amazing how bad people can screw things up?" he said, shaking his head. "Even something that should be easy. Like a kid."

Clair got to his feet, and turned to the truck bed and started to lift.

"Wait," I said. "Your shoulder."

"It's fine. I did rehab."

"Yeah, for three weeks."

"What do I look like? A hypochondriac?" Clair said.

"It was a gunshot wound. That's not hypochondria."

"Just get over on the other side and lift."

I did, on three. The bed made a crunching, ripping as it pulled away from the truck and shards of rust shook loose. Clair eased the gas-tank filler nozzle through the gas-cap hole and we lowered the bed to the floor.

"There," I said. "Now we turn it into a Woodie."

"Should build them this way in the first place. This oak'll still be solid when the rest of the truck is squished the size of a hay bale."

We turned to the stacks of oak and hemlock.

"Rusty Clement had a nice truck," I said. "Thirty thousand easy."

"Shoulda spent that money on his son," Clair said. "What I hear, he steals a lot of that money. Gives a lot of hardworking, honest loggers a bad name."

"His reputation precedes him?"

"Hard to keep secrets around here."

He took one of the hemlock shims and placed it on the chassis.

"Strange combo," I said. "Kid looks like he'd be in the chess club or something. And the dad is this big, aggressive macho type. It's like the son got switched at birth. Must be a stepfather."

"A lot of it's genetics, anyway," Clair said. "You been reading about that? They've identified genes for just about everything now. Violence. Ambition. This kid's genes probably skipped a generation. Instead of daddy's, the boy gets Great Aunt Mabel's. Old ramrod there is macho man and his kid wants to do needlepoint."

"Nothing wrong with that."

"Nope," Clair said.

"But he isn't doing any needlepoint where he is now," I said.

"No, that's true."

"You'd think a kid like that, I don't know, kind of soft, would just want to stay home."

"Something must've happened," Clair said, fitting a stringer over the wooden shim.

"You think you suddenly run away because you've been ignored by your father for fourteen years?"

"It builds. One hurt on top of another. And then one day, the whole thing collapses. Guy's probably oblivious to the hurt he causes. Had some kids in the Marine Corps. You felt like you had to undo eighteen years of damage. Start from scratch. For some of 'em it was too late. They'd given up on themselves."

"I don't think it's too late for this Rocky kid. He seemed nice. Just troubled. Worried."

"Worried about what?" Clair asked.

"I don't know. He said his mother was sick, but I don't know if running away had anything to do with that. Why would you run away if your mother was sick? Seems like she'd need you."

"Unless she was dying and maybe you didn't want to watch."

I remembered my own parents' passing. Part of me had wanted to run, and I had been twenty-three, not thirteen.

"Maybe that's it," I said.

Clair shrugged, then bent to fit another U-bolt in place.

"What'd Roxanne say?" he said, his back to me. "She's the expert at putting all these Humpty Dumpty families back together."

"Didn't know him. And I missed her this morning. Besides, it's all confidential."

"Be nice to at least know the kid's home and okay," Clair said.

I pictured Clement's wrath.

"Home and okay may not be the same thing," I said.

We worked until noon, and with the exception of the taillights, the truck bed was done, the beams bolted down, the planks screwed in place, the rusty metal bumper replaced by a varnished oak four-by-four. Clair was unwinding electrical wire from a reel when Mary came into the barn through the side door. I was putting wood in the stove.

"Warmer out here than it is in the house," Mary said. "I made soup, if you're interested. Jack, what happened to your mouth?"

"A long story," I said.

"Aren't they all," Mary said. "You know you are the most accident-prone man I know."

"Thank you," I said.

"It was an accident?"

"Well . . ."

Mary shook her head. "Roxanne's a saint," she said.

"Now that's the truth," Clair said.

Mary left the barn, the door closing behind her. Clair smiled to himself, and then bent to attach the wire to the snipped wire-ends on the frame. I used the driver to screw the taillights to the top of the wooden bumper. Clair connected the wires with plastic wire nuts, and taped them with black electrical tape. Then he went to the cab and turned the key on and tried the brakes and blinkers. I checked the lights as I screwed the license plate to the oak beam.

"Okay," I said.

"Just like we knew what we were doing," Clair said.

The blinkers blinked. The brake lights glowed. The Duke played on, and in the truck, the phone rang.

Clair moved to the bench and turned the music down. I leaned into the cab and picked up the phone.

"Hey," I said, expecting Roxanne.

"Mr. McMorrow," a voice said.

"Yeah."

"This is Deputy Divan. We spoke this morning."

Her voice was distant and fuzzy.

"Right," I said.

"I just wanted to let you know that we think we've located Arthur Doe."

"Oh, really," I said.

"Well, sort of. We had a report of a boy that may have been struck by a motor vehicle, on Route 202 in Dixmont. We think—"

"Oh, my god. How is he? I mean, was he—"

"We don't know, at this time. A witness said the truck stopped. A pickup truck. A boy—I guess he was walking north on the side of the road, maybe hitchhiking—was picked up and put in the truck, but he hasn't shown up at any hospitals. He fit the description, I think."

"Red plaid jacket?" I said.

"And black sweatpants," Divan said.

I remembered.

"Oh, yeah. Those are mine."

"He was wearing your clothes, Mr. McMorrow?"

"Well, no," I said, still leaning into the truck. "Not my

clothes. Just the sweatpants. His jeans were soaked from the snow last night. You know, when he was out in the woods? I gave him something to sleep in."

"Right," she said.

"Something dry."

"I understand," Divan said, but I didn't think she did.

"He was frozen."

"Right."

"They were black sweatpants. Cotton. Regular sweatpants. And he had on that jacket, and maybe a flannel shirt. Plaid flannel shirt."

"I don't know about that," she said. "Now, Mr. McMorrow . . ."

I waited.

"Tell me. That Toyota at your house. Is that the vehicle you drive every day?"

CHAPTER 15

"What is this?" I said, rubbing pink hand cleaner between my fingers. "Does she really think I tried to run the kid over? Saved him in Portland to kill him in Prosperity? That doesn't make any sense."

Clair shrugged.

"It does, if you start with a couple nasty givens. That you lured him to your house for the purpose of exploiting him in some way. Then he takes off. You get scared because, I don't know, maybe he says he's gonna tell people what you did to him, and you can't let that out. Or maybe he wanted money. Tried to extort money from you. Threatened to make up some story about you molesting him. You can't let that happen, so when he runs, you wait for him up on the road."

"But I was the one who called the cops in the first place."

"Because you thought he was a burglar. You didn't call to say he was back."

"It was two in the morning."

"Cops don't care what time it is," Clair said.

"I do. I had to sleep. I work till eleven o'clock at night, and drive an hour home. I can't stay up all day and night jibber-jabbering about this nonsense."

"It's not nonsense, Jack," Clair said.

"No," I said. "It's not nonsense at all."

I passed on the lunch, and Clair said he understood and would give Mary my regrets. He also said he'd take a ride around that afternoon and see what he could see, ask around about a kid in a red jacket. I told him I'd give him a call later, and he slid the barn door open and I backed the truck out.

It was snowing again, granular flakes that fell like smoke-stack grit. I turned the truck in Clair's barnyard and pulled out onto the road, and even as I drove the short distance to my house, I found myself scanning the woods for Rocky and his red plaid jacket. Hit by a truck? Maybe they did try to bring him to a hospital. Where? Belfast, ten miles to the east on Penobscot Bay, was closest. The cops would have checked there. Bangor and Waterville, too. The rural health center in Albion. The clinic in Unity.

Goddamn it, I'd do it myself but I had to be at the *Clarion*.

I had an hour to change and eat, try Roxanne again. Should I call the father? Divan would have done that, wouldn't she? Maybe I should just back off, let the thing play out without me.

I parked and went in, saw the answering-machine light flashing on the counter. Four messages: Roxanne, saying she'd try me later; Divan, saying she'd try me at the other number; Marna, saying a lady named Joelle or something like that had called me at the newsroom; a lady named Joelle Duguay, saying she was from the Department of Human Services in Bangor, and she'd try to reach me at the office.

I could run, but I couldn't hide.

I went up the stairs slowly, my knees creaking, untied my boots and fished in the bureau for clean khakis, and in the closet for an ironed shirt. The only shirt was white Oxford cloth, which seemed dressy for the *Clarion* newsroom, or at least for me. The officious, obsequious ones dressed up, like Randall in his silly suits and power ties. I covered the shirt with a drab blue sweater.

Dressed, I came back downstairs. There was a streak of black grease on my left wrist, and I went to the bathroom to scrub it off. The door was half closed. I pushed it open, hit the light and there they were, askew on the floor.

Two black legs.

It was Rocky's jeans. I paused, startled, then picked them up. I held them for a moment, then reached for the shower curtain and yanked it open. He wasn't there. The jeans were Lee brand, beltless, with a 30-inch waist and 28-inch length. They still were damp around the ankles. Damp and cold.

I walked back to the living room; the pillow was on the couch, the blankets tossed off on the floor. I picked them up and shook them. Nothing fell out. I got down on my knees and looked under the couch. There was nothing there but dust. I got back up and lifted the cushions. Cracker crumbs. A Ballantine Ale cap. One of Roxanne's socks, lost during one romp or another. For a moment, I pictured her, sockless and in other states of abandon, but then those images faded away.

I was left with the jeans.

They were dirty, smelled like boy. In one of the front pockets was seventy-five cents and a book of matches from a Portland restaurant. The other front pocket was empty, with a hole. The back pockets were empty, too. I turned the jeans again, reached inside the legs, then into the pockets again, one by one.

And then I fingered the watch pocket, the little one in front, on the right. I felt a piece of paper and fished it out. It was white, folded until it was the size of a sugar cube, and hardened, as though it had gone through a washing machine. I picked at the corners and bent them back, and it slowly unfolded.

It was a piece of paper, half of a page, white and lined and starting to tear at the folds. On it, someone had written:

April 7 1987. Kitty Kitty Kitty. How can you live?

The words were written in the schooled hand of a child. And then there were doodles. Squiggles and slashes, and cubes piled one on the other, like a city skyline.

I turned the paper over. The other side was part of what looked like a test or a homework assignment. *In this novel, Johnny Tremain shows his character because even though his hand was burned . . .*

That was all, at least on this half of the page. Someone—Rocky?—had grabbed this piece of paper and scribbled the note on the back and saved it. He was carrying it in a safe, relatively well-hidden place. Rocky considered it important for some reason.

April 7, 1987 . . . Kitty . . . How can you live?

In 1987, Rocky wasn't born. Did the parents have a cat? What happened April 7? How can he live? Who, the cat? Kitty, Kitty, Kitty. Like someone calling a cat. A cat ran away? But why would Rocky care about that?

I turned the paper over, then back again. I read it over and over. *Kitty. April 7, 1987. How can you live?* It was strange, but probably made perfect sense to Rocky. Maybe it was a song. Maybe he'd written it himself.

Kitty kitty, kitty, how can you live?

But the date? Somebody's birthday? Who knows, I thought. Rusty Clement had said his son had psychological problems. Maybe this was an indication of something like that. I'd had a running conversation with a man in New York who'd seen my byline on a story about a murder on East Seventieth Street. A madame had been shot in some sort of turf fight. The story was on page 24, and he was twenty-four. His mother was seventy.

"So you can see how it all fits," he'd say.

And this Rocky story probably all fit, too, but I didn't see how. Was he nuts? Behind the store, in the truck on the way to the hospital, Rocky had seemed perfectly sane. A little troubled maybe.

April 7, 1987 . . .

I folded the paper to its original size and shape, and put it in my wallet, then went to the kitchen. There was tuna salad left from Rocky's midnight snack, so I spread some on stoned-wheat crackers and ate them with a glass of orange juice as I stood by the window. The chickadees and nuthatches and finches had gone, but a lone female cardinal was huddled reluctantly in the old honeysuckle, like some troubled person who'd stayed after mass to see the priest. The cardinal came forward warily, hopping from branch to branch, then onto the step of the deck and then up onto the deck itself, where it ate hurriedly, head rocking up and down. I thought of Rocky, the kid who came in from the cold and ate sandwich after sandwich with that same jerking movement.

The cardinal was worried about being eaten. What was worrying Arthur "Rocky" Doe?

I finished the tuna and put the dishes in the sink, then put a travel mug of water in the microwave, spooned China Black Tea into the mesh strainer and dropped it into the mug. One mug would get me to Bangor, or at least close. At my "work station" in the newsroom, I had another canister of tea, another strainer. The coffee guzzlers at the *Clarion* eyed me suspiciously when I poured my zapped hot water through the strainer, as though I were performing some mysterious religious rite. After the news meeting, we could all chant.

When the tea had steeped, I jammed the cover on the mug, grabbed my keys and leather jacket, the one I wore in the big city, and went out to the truck. The sleet rained down and the sky was gray, the road slashed by a single track. I followed it down to the main dirt road, and as I turned, a buck deer loped across the road in front of me. It was odd that a deer would be moving at this time of day, unless something had frightened it. Somewhere back in that range of woods, Rocky had passed, and then his father, on his trail, tracking his son like a hound.

As I drove out to the main two-lane road that wended its way northeast, I thought of Rocky and his dad: the hunter and the hunted. There was something odd about the father, a lack of despair or worry. No, he seemed worried, but not in the way I would have expected. Was he worried that his son was cold and hungry? Or was he more angry at the inconvenience of having to be worried? Rusty Clement was a very hard guy, it seemed, and yet the son seemed so soft.

"Mom must be a real cream puff," I said aloud. But was her name Kitty?

I pondered it as I drove, following the ridge line to the northeast. The road split farms, big dairy operations where yellow loaders were poised in front of the gaping brown manure pits, torn open like strip mines, ballasted with tires and black plastic. And then there was the bustling little town of Unity, and that left behind, there were fields and woods and houses with peeling paint like flayed skin, and sagging stairs, and satellite dishes mounted on posts, aimed skyward as if to receive communications from another planet, orders beamed to outposts on the frontier.

The road climbed and the land fell away steeply to the west, and the houses were scattered and solitary. Trailers sat next to rotting homesteads, vans on blocks served as storage sheds, cars and trucks sat in dooryards in states of both decay and disrepair.

It was tough, living on these ridges, and it took a certain optimism. I'll get that car running one of these days. I'll get a hundred dollars ahead. I'll win the Megabucks. It was a fine line that separated hope and despair. My son will straighten out.

The sleet turned to snow and the tire tracks in the road turned to narrow black lines. And then a sign said Dixmont, and I slowed and eyed the shoulder of the road, looking for something to show where Rocky had been hit. I eased along, one eye on the rear-view mirror, but nothing showed on the roadside. Then I was at the crossroads, with a store and a scattering of houses, and then back in the woods and it seemed there should be footprints or something, but the snow apparently had covered any sign of the accident.

No evidence that it had happened at all, and for a moment, I pictured Rocky faking his own mishap from some shopping-center pay phone.

That would get them worried, wouldn't it? Run over and spirited away. How do you like that one, dad?

I sped up after the Dixmont town line, into Newburgh, where I'd turn northwest toward the interstate. Or I could turn east, toward the town of Woodfield, seven miles away. I looked at my watch.

CHAPTER 16

Woodfield was a neat little town with an odd prosperity, gleaned from a couple of small electronics plants and a home-grown construction company that had mushroomed into a big player in New England. On the edge of town I passed a subdivision, "Woodfield Meadows," that looked like a ranch-house version of a Civil War encampment. It flanked a strip mall with a video arcade and a styling salon. Then there were some older houses, overlooked in the town's makeover, and in the downtown were a pretty old church, a couple of brick banks, and a restaurant. Cars and trucks were parked around the restaurant like animals around a watering hole.

I figured I'd find a phone booth and look up Rusty's address, then take a spin by his house and his business. If a guy threatened to kill you, it was wise to know where he was coming from.

I parked and got out of the truck and walked up the sidewalk toward the restaurant, past an insurance office, a gift shop, a bookstore. Everything had an air of, if not affluence, then comfort. I looked in the windows, at the secretaries, the ceramic chickadees. I was passing the bestsellers when I heard a familiar sound, a roar and a clatter.

A diesel.

I turned and saw a mini-van backing out of its space in front of the restaurant. Behind it, Rusty's truck waited, its blinker on. Rusty was at the wheel.

He waved to the blond woman driving the van. She smiled and waved back. Rusty wrestled the big green pickup in and climbed out, like a cowboy easing down from his horse. He left the truck running.

Rusty went into the restaurant, the Downtown Diner. I eased my way along until I could see inside the restaurant. I passed once, squinting in. There was a lunch counter on the left, tables on the right. Behind the tables was a deli counter. The lunch counter was full, the tables a third occupied, a couple of people at the deli. I hesitated for a moment, then walked back, pushed quickly through the door, and sat at a table by the window. I looked out.

He was behind me, at the lunch counter.

"Hey, Mandy honey," Rusty was saying. "There's a man down here needs your services."

"Oh, he does, does he?" a woman's voice said.

"Better watch what you say, Rust," a guy called from one of the tables. "She's feeling feisty, today."

"Hey, I like 'em feisty," Rusty said.

"Oh, yeah," the woman said. "What else would you like?"

"I'll tell you later. When we're alone, and Harold isn't listening in. Harold'll get all jealous. Isn't that right, Harold?"

"Jealous of you? That'll be the goddamn day."

"Whoa, I think I rubbed Harold the wrong way. Speaking of rubbing, Mandy, I got this stiff muscle."

"That's not what she said," Harold said.

Everybody guffawed at the counter. Harold cackled. I turned slightly and looked.

Rusty was hunched over the counter, his big boots perched on the foot railing. Mandy, blond and pretty in a weathered sort of way, poured coffee in Rusty's mug. He said something and she said, "In your dreams" and started in my direction. She was fortyish and sturdy. Her jeans were tight and there was a confident swing in her walk. I turned toward the window and put my right arm up in front of my face as she approached.

"How are you doing today?" she said, putting the mug down and starting to pour.

"Good," I said quietly.

"You did want coffee?"

"Sure."

"Need a menu? We have homemade vegetable-barley soup, and meatloaf with gravy and mashed potatoes."

"No, thanks. Coffee's fine."

I gave her a quick glance and a smile. She smiled back, and seemed to give me an extra look. I was a stranger.

"Just sing out if you change your mind," Mandy said, and she headed back to the counter.

"What do I have to do to get service here?" Rusty bellowed. "Can't you hear my stomach grumbling?"

"Not when you're flapping your gums," Mandy said.

I glanced as she circled the end of the counter. Rusty's

gaze followed her rear end, his radar locked in. I sipped the coffee and listened as he joked with Harold, then ordered lasagna and garlic bread. Harold pulled a hounds-tooth sportscoat on over his shirt and tie, made his way to the counter. He punched Rusty on the shoulder as he passed.

"Thought I felt a mosquito," Rusty said. "Oh, no, it's just Harold giving me his best shot."

Everybody laughed. This was dinner theater and Rusty was on stage. Finally the lasagna came. Mandy put it on the counter in front of him, then leaned confidentially. I strained to listen.

"Flossie isn't feeding you?" Mandy flirted.

"I haven't been home," he said. "Been chasing the goddamn kid around half the state."

"He still hasn't come home?"

"Hell, no, why would he? Must think I got nothin' better to do than drive around the puckerbrush huntin' him."

"Where the hell does he go?"

"Where doesn't he? This morning he turns up with some guy in Prosperity. Guy says he met him in Portland. I said, 'Mister. Let me tell you something. You touched my boy, I'll be back here to kill you myself.'"

"Who was he?"

"I don't know. Some goddamn flatlander."

"These people are sick," Mandy said. "So you didn't bring Rocky home right there and then?"

Rocky, I thought. Not David.

"Kid took off in the woods. I'm out there in the goddamn snow, like I'm tracking deer. I mean, I got jobs going. I can't be chasing the kid all day."

"'Course not," Mandy said.

"Now I got messages to call the cops in Belfast or something. I call back, the cop ain't there. I mean, I gotta be the other side of goddamn Skowhegan in an hour. Explain to some wingnut from New Jersey that I can't cut every third tree."

"Thinks you cut wood with tweezers."

"You said it."

"Well, maybe the cops picked him up."

"Who?"

"Rocky."

"If they did, I hope they talk some sense into him. He was a pain in the ass before he took off."

"It's that age. When Eric was fourteen, fifteen, he was a miserable little punk. They grow out of it."

A bell rang and Mandy turned to a shelf with a window to the kitchen, brought a plate to a table and came back to Rusty. She put both elbows on the counter and leaned close.

"So this must be always on Flossie's mind. Paying any attention to you?"

I could see Rusty's jaw muscles flex as he chewed. Mandy waited. He shoveled another load into his mouth and she waited some more.

"She's too easy on the kid. Always has been. I know she's been sick and all, but I think that's half the problem. He hits the real world and he's dead meat. I figure in two years I could have him on a crew. Christ, I started working when I was fifteen, shoveling shit for Old Man Haskins. I'd pay him good money, put him with some good boys. But he wouldn't last an hour. Hell, wouldn't last fifteen minutes."

Mandy shook her head.

"Now I get home, it's all I hear about. Call here, call there. Hey, he wants to see what it's like out there, let him." Rusty chewed some more. " 'Talk to him,' she says. Friggin' A, my old man would've tanned my ass. He said, 'Jump,' you said, 'How high?' Now there was one tough old bastard. Said ten words to you a day, but, boy, you listened."

He tore at the bread. I sipped my coffee and looked out the window. At the next table, two white-haired men were talking about ice fishing. Beyond them, three stolid women were slurping their soup.

"You all set?" Mandy asked me suddenly from the counter.

Rusty started to turn my way. I nodded and put my hand alongside my face.

"Hey," he said. "That's the guy."

CHAPTER 17

I turned, saw him facing me, still on his stool, fork in his hand. I tried to appear surprised.

"Hey," I said. "How you doing? I thought I'd heard that voice before."

"What the hell you doing here?"

"What are you doing here?" I said.

"I live here. What are you doing here? I thought you worked in Bangor."

I sipped my coffee and smiled. Mandy smiled back, unsure how to place me.

"That's right. For a newspaper. I had to stop and talk to somebody on the way up there."

"Pretty weird. I'm in here every day. I never seen you in here before."

"Never been here before. Nice place."

Mandy smiled again.

"Friend of yours, Rust?" she said.

"No," he said. "This is the guy I was telling you about. The guy with my kid."

"Ucck," she said.

"Nice to meet you, too," I said.

"So what the hell?" Rusty said, gesturing toward me with his chin.

"What the hell what?"

"What the hell you doing?"

I looked in my cup.

"Drinking coffee," I said. "How's the lasagna?"

The fishermen had stopped talking. The three soup-slurping ladies were watching, eyes glittering at this unexpected diversion. Entertainment was sparse since they'd banned bear baiting.

"Don't make no difference," Rusty said. "What're you doing? Following me?"

I snorted.

"No. Just a pleasant coincidence."

"Don't give me your coincidence shit."

"Trust me. I spent more than enough time with you this morning for one day."

"Hey, asshole, you remember what I said," Rusty said, his voice lower, meant to be menacing.

"Which pearl of wisdom was that?"

"Jeez," Mandy said. "Who does this guy think—"

"I'm warning you. You laid a finger on my kid, you'll regret it. And I want to know if he came back. I didn't see a goddamn sign of him out in those woods."

"You didn't hear?"

"Hear what?"

"The deputy called me this morning. They think he was hit by a car."

"Oh, my god," Mandy gasped.

"You son of a bitch," Rusty said, coming off his stool.

"Whatever," I said. "Don't you want to know how he is?"

He didn't answer, just moved toward me, all big boots and red-faced glower.

"They said whoever hit him put him in their truck and kept going. So maybe he's okay."

Rusty stood over me and pointed a big finger in my face.

"You better goddamn hope so, 'cause if he isn't, I'm gonna take you apart piece by piece. He wouldn't've been up there, if it wasn't for you."

"He wouldn't have been there if he'd been happy at home," I said.

"I could make you eat that, you piece of shit," Rusty said.

He shoved my shoulder and his palm was hard as lumber. I raised my cup and took a sip. Then I shoved my chair back and stood and squared around and faced him.

"You know, all this may make you feel better but it doesn't have anything to do with your son."

"Stepson," Mandy murmured.

"You stay away from him," Rusty said, his eyes narrowed, teeth clenched, cheeks flushed. In the corner of his mouth, there was a spot of red sauce from the lasagna. "Last warning."

"No problem. Personally, I wish I'd never heard of the kid."

"You better watch your mouth. Or I'll be asking you to step outside."

"Ask away."

"So where the hell is he?"

"I don't know. Call the deputy. I hope he's okay."

"You better do more than hope," Rusty said.

"I'd better go to work. And you better ask yourself why it is when Rocky heard you were coming to get him, he took off like a rocket. Why is he so afraid to come home?"

"None of your goddamn business," Rusty said.

"Rocky made it my business, when he showed up half-frozen to death."

"You shoulda called."

"I called the cops and he took off. They called you and he took off again. And now who knows where he is."

"That's what they probably wanted, Rust," the waitress said. "To tell you about this accident."

I took two dollar bills from my pocket and tossed them on the table.

"If it were me and my son were missing, I'd return a call from the police," I said.

"Hey, I'll be talking to them. And I'll be telling them about you."

"Why don't you get out of here," Mandy said.

"Gladly."

"Before I toss you out," Rusty said, but there was just the faintest hint of hesitation in his voice and I wondered why. My bulging biceps? An allergy to cops?

"Go," Mandy said. "We don't serve perverts."

I glanced around the place, the cold staring faces. I smiled.

"Now that," I said, "I find very hard to believe."

CHAPTER 18

I drove up the block and turned into a convenience store lot. There was a phone on the wall of the store and a rain-swollen phone book hanging on a cable. I pulled up and hopped out, leaving the motor running. There were a dozen Clement listings, but only one in Woodfield, on Orchard Field Terrace. I dropped the book and went inside and asked the expressionless guy behind the counter where that was. He pointed back the way I had come.

"Left at the light, two miles up, on the right."

At the light, I took the left, and then sped up, all the while thinking how strange the encounter in the restaurant had been.

The guy hears that his son, or stepson, has been hit by a truck, and he lashes out at me. His reaction was all anger, no concern. His reaction to his son running away was annoyance, not worry. And yet he'd driven right over when he'd heard Rocky was in Prosperity. It was as though he wanted Rocky back, but for all the wrong reasons. There was no love there, certainly none that you could see. Was it all for his wife? And what kind of marriage was this? I wondered what poor ailing Flossie would have thought of their little banter over the counter. I wondered what Rusty did when he really had a chance to step out.

And then there it was, Orchard Field Terrace, denoted by a short fieldstone wall with a white wooden sign set into the stones. I turned in.

It was a wide street with new houses set on treeless lots. The lots were big and the houses were, too, set away from the road and each other. The intent probably had been for the homes to appear stately, but in the snow and the cold, they looked temporary and out of place, like they were going to be dismantled and loaded on trucks.

I drove slowly, peering at the names on the roadside mailboxes. Other names, some with no name at all. And then, on the side of the mailbox. *Rusty Clement, Logging.*

I looked up at the house. It was white, a raised ranch with a two-story addition coming off the back. There was a two-story garage on the far side of the house. Next to the garage was a snowmobile trailer with one machine sitting on it, wrapped in a black cover. The cover said, SKIDOO. Parked next to the trailer was a black rack truck with a plow attached.

I drove past and then pulled into a driveway and turned around. As I approached the house again, I slowed almost to a stop—as the side door swung open and a woman crept out.

She was wearing a long, quilted black coat that came nearly to the ground, and she moved monk-like down the driveway toward me and the mailbox. I stopped the truck but looked down at the passenger seat, as though checking an address, and the woman came closer.

I looked up. She did, too.

She was small, with blond hair pulled back tightly and a round, snub-nosed face that once might have been cute. It was a look that was sometimes called perky, but this woman had set her mouth in a baleful, permanent sort of frown that grew taut as she approached. I smiled and nodded, and she gave me a barely perceptible nod, and pulled the little door down on the mailbox and slid a sheaf of envelopes out. Standing there at the edge of the street, she quickly flipped through them.

Then, even under the shroud of a coat, I could see her body sag. Her thin-lipped scowl opened into an anguished gasp. "Oh, my god," she mouthed.

What had she been looking for? Was it news of Rocky?

I quickly rolled the truck window down.

"Mrs. Clement?" I called.

She looked over at me, startled.

"I'm Jack McMorrow. I can tell you about your son."

CHAPTER 19

"You're the man?" Flossie Clement said.

"Yeah," I said. "I'm the one where Rocky stayed last night."

"My husband, he—"

"I wouldn't hurt him. I know what your husband thinks, and that's one reason I'm not going to talk to you long. I don't have that much to tell you anyway."

We were standing beside my idling truck, in the street. She was looking up at me. Her eyes were big and dark like her son's; her expression was like his, wounded and mistrustful.

"Where is he now?" Flossie Clement said, her tone more desperate than demanding.

"I don't know where he is. I know where he's been."

"Why didn't you bring him home?"

"I didn't know where home was, Mrs. Clement. And Rocky wouldn't tell me. He wouldn't tell me anything."

"Well, what are you doing here?"

"The police told me where Rocky lived. Early this morning, before they called your husband. Or you."

"No, Rusty is handling it. I didn't talk to them. He told them to call him on his car phone, and he'd go get Rocky. He . . . well, I've been sick and . . . So is he okay?"

"He was all right. Not great."

She nearly gasped.

"What do you mean, not great?"

I told her about the fight in Portland, that Rocky might be hurt. I told her about Rocky standing out in the cold. I started to tell her about the accident, but stopped. I asked her if she or her husband had talked to the Waldo County Sheriff's Office yet.

"I don't know. I haven't. Maybe Rusty has. Why? Why should we talk to them?"

I hesitated, looked down at my feet and at hers. I was wearing tan work boots. She was wearing white sneakers, with pink designs on the sides and pink laces. I thought of Rocky. One lace red, one lace white.

"I don't know. I don't think I should be the one to tell you," I said.

Her face went white as the snow on the street, and a shiver seemed to go through her.

"Tell me what?"

This wasn't what I had planned. This kid had turned into a vortex and I could feel myself being sucked in. I looked at Flossie Clement, shaking with fright and cold.

"What is it? What is it?"

I took a deep breath.

"They said this morning that somebody fitting Rocky's description was struck by a truck—"

"Oh, my god," she wailed.

"But he might be fine. He went in the truck. Maybe he's okay."

"Oh god, oh god," she cried. I stood there helplessly.

"I'm sorry," I said. "I didn't want to upset you. You should talk to your husband and—"

"He's up north. He's got jobs going. They've got to get all the wood out before mud season so he's straight out for—"

"I just saw him in town. At that restaurant. I think he said he was going to a job but he hadn't left yet."

She looked bewildered.

"Oh. Well, then I'll try him in the truck. Oh god, he's got to be okay. Please god. I'm going to go call."

She started to turn away.

"Mrs. Clement. Your husband, he thinks, well, I don't know why, but he thinks I molested your son or something. But I didn't. I wouldn't. I just tried to help him. My girlfriend works for DHS and she knew him and I just happened to be there. He seems like a nice kid and—"

"He is," she said. "He's the nicest boy you'd ever find."

"Well, I won't keep you. But if I see him again, if he comes back to my house or whatever, what should I tell him?"

She turned toward me. She was crying, alternately wiping her cheeks and pressing her hand over her mouth.

"Tell him I love him and I want him to come home. I just don't understand why he won't come home. I don't understand why he left."

"It's not something he's done, I don't know, even for a day or two?"

"No. Never. Never ever. He liked it here. He liked it. He was always home. Always in his room. Just hanging out, reading or doing his models. Model planes and things. Just liked to be indoors. And I know it was kind of frustrating for his stepdad, but he's a good kid. He really is."

"Why was it frustrating?"

"Rusty played football," she said, as though that explained it.

"I don't understand," I said.

"I mean, he tried, marrying somebody with a baby already. We went out in high school and then he graduated and we didn't see each other and then I had Rocky and then he came back and we got back together, but he didn't know much about kids. And Rusty works a lot, I mean, half the time I don't know where he is, and before car phones it was, like, who knows where he is?"

She looked away and seemed to be reliving something, and then she gave a little shake and gathered the coat around her and looked at me again.

"So you've got to understand. He didn't see much of Rocky when Rocky was real small. But when he got older he bought him his own four-wheeler, his own snow machine, and Rocky used it, like, twice, and then it sat. Rocky said it was too loud."

"Not his thing?"

"Nope. But what can you do?"

"Nothing."

I looked at her, helpless and small, a well-intentioned handwringer with a small-town bully for a husband.

"Okay," I said. "Now this isn't my business, but I feel like I have to ask. If I'm going to talk to him. Do you really know why he left? Can I tell him whatever it is, it's okay now?"

"I don't know what it is," she said. "I don't know. He just left. He just left this house and didn't come back. He and Rusty, they don't get along great, but there was nothing that happened."

"Nothing at all?"

"No. I mean, they bicker. Rocky he was—"

She hesitated, wrapped her arms around herself, shuffled her feet on the frozen pavement.

"I'll let you go."

"No, it's okay. See he was playing with—this sounds funny, but it isn't—he was playing with Legos. He's always liked Legos. Building whole cities, with little streets and everything—oh, my god—he's been hit by a car? I'll call the hospitals and see. Where would they go? Bangor?"

"Probably," I said, but Flossie didn't seem to hear. She seemed distracted, her mind wandering. I wondered if she was medicated.

"Oh, god, and anyway, the Legos, I was telling you about the Legos. They were all over the place and Rusty, he, well, Rusty just doesn't like that sort of thing and he says Rocky is too big to be playing with blocks and once he threw them all away, but Rocky went and he just dug them all out of the trash, and oh, god, but Rusty doesn't mean anything. He says Rocky has to get ready for the real world and I baby him, but if he likes to do these things, build stuff with Legos, I say let him be, you know? But he's never left. Oh, god. I mean, if there wasn't any ambulance or anything, he's probably okay, right?"

"I'm sure," I said, though I had no reason to be.

"Well, tell Rocky, come home to us, baby. We're right here. Everything's okay. Everything's fine."

Flossie Clement closed her eyes and shuddered, and her

face flushed. She looked suddenly unwell and unsteady, wavering on her feet, clutching the mail to her chest.

"You all right?" I said.

"I gotta sit down. You can . . . you can come in if you want. I'll make coffee and you can tell me. You can tell me more about Rocky."

I considered what Rusty would think if he came home to find me parked on his couch, chatting up his wife.

"Thanks, but I've got to go to work."

"Oh. Okay. What do you do?"

"I'm a copyeditor at a newspaper."

She looked at me and brightened.

"So you could put a write-up in the newspaper, saying for Rocky to come home, or to call."

I thought of Tippy Danforth. She had stray cats. I had a stray boy.

Flossie took another step to the house. I hesitated, then said to her half-turned back, "Mrs. Clement, do you know somebody or something named Kitty?"

She froze in the cold. Turned back to me, her pale hands clenched.

"Kitty?" she said.

"Yeah, like a cat. Rocky had a piece of paper stuck in his pocket, all folded up, so it was about this big."

I held my thumb and forefinger out, an inch apart.

"It had a date, in 1987. And it said, 'Kitty kitty kitty. How can you live?' Does that mean something?"

Flossie looked at me and her mouth opened. She gasped softly and then she made a guttural sound, something between a sigh and a cry of pain. She turned away and, in the long black coat, walked up the driveway and into the side door of the house. The door clicked shut. The street was quiet. I got back in the truck, knowing that what I'd suspected was true.

When Rocky had run, he'd taken a family secret with him.

CHAPTER 20

The microfilm machine was in the news library, a cramped, windowless room lined with gun-metal gray file cabinets and yellowing stacks of newspapers. I'd skipped out after the news meeting, turned on the lights and the microfilm viewer, which whirred reluctantly to life. The microfilm reels were in a cabinet at the end of the room, and I fingered the drawers until I found 1980 to 1989. April 1987 was in the back of the drawer. I pulled it, wiped the dust from the box, and took out the film reel. Pushing the door almost closed—reporters were a nosy breed, even at the *Clarion*—I threaded the film into the machine and onto the reel, and turned the knob. First there was a blurry white light, then newspaper pages whirred across the screen like one of those time-passage devices in old movies. I stopped but I was on April 13. I reversed the film and it ground to a halt on April 5. I eased the film forward, and bits of history strolled past.

On Tuesday, April 7, the day in question, AIDS was reported to be the hot topic in Los Angeles, not because it was a terrible disease, but because it was a terrible disease that could kill heterosexuals, too. In Washington, John Hinckley, locked up for six years after he shot Ronald Reagan, was saying he, Hinckley, wanted to live with a woman who had killed her sleeping daughter. In Central Maine, the *Clarion* editorial decried the Soviet bugging of the U.S. Embassy in Moscow. The rest of the state was recovering from its worst floods in a century.

There was another flood story with a photo of "weary victims." The Soviets said an unmanned space "module" had failed to link with the orbiting Mir laboratory. Six West German skiers died in an Austrian avalanche. In London, the prime minister's cat, Wilberforce, had retired.

Could that be the "kitty, kitty, kitty" in Rocky's note?

I pored over the pages on the humming machine. Catholics training for marriage. Scientists cloning mammals. Admissions to the hospital in Bangor. A ferry capsized in Belgium, with 134 people feared dead. The Pope kissed a sick woman in Chile. Five members of a family in the town of Pittsfield escaped a fire. In the photo they were wearing pajamas and parkas, standing in mud and snow.

There was no mention of their cat.

But if the date was April 7 then maybe whatever it was, it had been reported April 8.

I heard stirrings in the newsroom, but whirred into Wednesday nonetheless. Attorney General Ed Meese denied blocking an investigation of gun-running to the Nicaraguan Contras. The Bangor Planning Board pledged to tighten up subdivision requirements. In Augusta, a woman was sentenced to twenty years in prison for selling her child for sex for thirty dollars.

A police dog was used to capture a burglar in Hampden. The Celtics were on a roll. The burned-out family was looking for donations. Reagan said there were no easy answers to the problem of acid rain. In the Maine town of Newport, a woman was killed in a hit-and-run.

I paused.

It was on page 2. A woman had been found dead on something called the Horseback Road. Police said she was between twenty and twenty-five, wearing jeans and a white parka with "aqua" trim. She'd been found by a nurse on his way to work. The nurse had almost hit her again, in the early morning darkness, but had picked up the white parka in his lights and swerved his truck in time. A state police detective named David Turgeon said it wasn't known whether the woman had been killed when she was struck or had died afterward of shock and exposure. The woman's name was being withheld pending notification of next of kin. There was no photo.

I hit the print button; the machine spat out the page.

Spinning through the rest of Wednesday, I started in on Thursday, looking for the follow-up. There were more Soviet-spying hostage stories, a big story about flood victims getting low-interest loans for new mobile homes.

From the newsroom, I heard somebody say, "Anybody seen McMorrow?"

I bent to the screen, letting the pages pass in a slow procession. And there it was.

It was at the top of the local section front, two columns on the right. Her name was Katia Poulin. The story was written by a staff reporter named Bonnie Cue, no longer with us. It said Poulin was twenty-three, a waitress who'd been living in the town of Scanesett, southeast of Newport. Police now said they believed Poulin had died of hypothermia in the thirty-degree cold after being struck and left unconscious in the road. Turgeon, him again, said police didn't know what Poulin was doing on that road, twenty miles from her apartment. The investigation was continuing. He asked anyone who had seen anything suspicious to call the state police. In other words, at that point the cops had squat.

Katia? Kitty? Or did Rocky's note refer to something that had nothing to do with the newspaper? A cat? A kitten? What had it said?

Kitty Kitty Kitty. How can you live?

From the newsroom, I heard voices, my name again.

I hit the print button again and locked the door. Rewrites could wait.

Turning the knob, I moved ahead quickly, scanning the passing headlines. On April 9, a Thursday, a story on the front of the second section said there were no new leads. That story added the detail that Poulin was a waitress in a lounge that featured Jell-O wrestling and hot-oil shows. It didn't say that she was a participant.

I printed that page, too.

On April 13, a Monday, Turgeon was reported appealing to the public again. The story ended there, where a better reporter with better editors would have gleaned something from other sources. What was the direction of the investigation? Who was Katia Poulin? What had her life been like? Was she a hooker? A kid trying to work her way through college? Where were her parents? Why hadn't they been interviewed?

The *Clarion* should have done a full-blown profile on the short life of Katia Poulin, but instead had just regurgitated the police press releases. And then the newspaper had stopped doing even that.

Two weeks after the death, the *Clarion* printed the last story I could find for that month. It was three paragraphs, with Turgeon saying there was nothing new to report, that the investigation was continuing. That was it.

Had there been another follow? An anniversary story? I looked at my watch. It was three twenty-five. I turned and listened for my name, but they'd stopped calling. Turning back to the machine, I rewound April 1987, pulling it off the spindle and returning it to the box, then returned the box to the drawer. I closed it, moved up one drawer, and pulled out April 1988. Anniversaries were artificial news hooks but papers used them all the time. *How long has it been since the Jones murder? Let's do a follow-up.*

Had the *Clarion* been that vigilant?

The film slipped through the spools and the images whirred across the screen. The fourth of April. The fifth. I slowed the machine and scanned the headlines. Reaganomics. Car accidents. A cocaine bust in Bangor. Four Portland men convicted of molesting children.

No hit-and-run story that day. No hit-and-run story on the sixth or the seventh. I backed up to the sixth, and went through page by page.

Nothing.

Until page 16. A one-by-two ad, near the bottom.

"In Memoriam. Katia Poulin." A photograph, fuzzy, black-and-white, with Katia looking over her shoulder toward the camera. Lots of blond hair, feathered with bangs, the way they wore it back then. Three lines of copy:

> *Katia Poulin, May 19, 1963–April 7, 1987. Killed by hit-and-run driver. Gone but never forgotten. From one loving friend to another. I miss you. Love, Sandra.*

Katia? Kitty? There was alliteration, if nothing else. Maybe nothing else. I hit the print button again, and waited for the page to slip out. Did they keep a record of who bought these ads? If they did, did they keep it this long? I knew they were careful keeping records of death notices. Death notices and obituaries. Obituaries.

Damn. Why hadn't I checked that before?

I wound April 1988 back on the reel, and crammed April 1987 back into the machine. I found April 8, and slowed until I found the obit page. A woodsman, 93. A teacher, 41. A salesman, 69. A homemaker, 96. A waitress, 23.

There was no Katia Poulin obit on April 8. Nothing on the ninth or tenth. Maybe they hadn't bothered, whoever "they" had been. Maybe she wasn't from the Bangor area. Maybe she was from out of state, and the obit would appear there. Maybe she was . . .

> . . . *born in Newport Beach, California, the daughter of Raymond Poulin and Jessie Bertone. She attended school in California and at the time of her untimely death was pursuing a career in modeling and in the restaurant industry. She enjoyed dancing and the company of her friends. She was a good person and brought joy to everyone she met.*
>
> *She was predeceased by her mother and father. She is survived by several cousins of California and a friend, Sandra Baker of Scanesett. Services will be private and held at the convenience of the family.*

"But did they call her Kitty?" I asked aloud.

I printed that page, too, and then rewound the film and put it back in the drawer. As I gathered up the papers, Marna knocked on the door and I wheeled the chair back and opened it. I folded the clips and stuck them in my back pocket.

"Jack, I don't mean to—"

"I know. Tell our fearless leader I'm coming."

"No, it's not him," Marna said, her eyes wide. "It's that lady who called. Joelle Duguay? From DHS?"

"She called again?" I asked.

"No," Marna said. "She's here. She came right in. I looked up and she was asking Randall if you're here."

"Oh, great."

"She said she was from child protective. She needed to talk to you because of some investigation. Child abuse or something?"

"Oh, for god's sake."

"And Jack."

"What? What's the matter?"

"Tippy was there, too."

CHAPTER 21

Joelle Duguay was waiting in the lounge at the far end of the newsroom. As I walked through, the reporters looked up from their terminals, then turned away. Randall was on the phone but he started to motion to me. Tippy Danforth, wrapped in her big coat, was talking to one of the reporters but paused when she saw me.

I kept walking.

Duguay was parked on the plaid couch next to the fake rubber tree. There were newspapers and magazines on the table, but she wasn't reading them. She was staring straight ahead, a small but blockish woman in her twenties. Glasses. Hair tied back with tendrils spilling down onto her forehead. Corduroy slacks and suede shoes. A dark blue parka and a briefcase on her lap. Incongruous turquoise earrings.

I strode up to her and held out my hand. She reached out and gripped it hard and stood. I felt like I was lifting her out of a ditch. She smiled but kept her lips firmly closed, like she was hiding a missing tooth.

"Joelle Duguay. Department of Human Services. I'm so sorry to bother you in your workplace, but I felt it was really imperative that I talk to you today."

I started to say it was okay, but she kept talking.

"First of all, what I'm going to tell you is confidential, Mr. McMorrow. Anything you tell me, of course, will be kept in the confidential case files of the department. Now, if we could just go someplace—"

"I've got to work. I'll try to be helpful but this isn't the best time."

"Rocky Doe isn't having the best time, either."

She gave me her pursed-lip smile again. If it was meant to be soothing and to put me at ease, it wasn't working. Her gaze was as firm as her handshake. Only her long, turquoise earrings wavered as she stared.

"Out in the hall," I said. "For Rocky's privacy, not mine."

I led the way to the end of the corridor past the elevator. I leaned against a dusty file cabinet. Duguay stood erect, hands folded in front of her, briefcase at her knees.

"I'm trying to determine whether Rocky is at risk," she said.

"I'd say he is. Or was. Have you talked to him?" I asked.

"No, sir, but I've talked to the deputy at the Waldo County Sheriff's Department. Deputy—"

"Divan."

"Exactly. She's very concerned about this boy's well-being."

"She should be."

"And I talked to the boy's father."

She hesitated.

Here we go, I thought.

"The father was concerned about his son—"

"Stepson."

"Right. He was concerned about his son's association with you."

I could feel myself bristle. Easy, I thought. She has to ask these questions.

"His association with me kept him from being beaten unconscious."

"No, I think the father—"

"Stepfather."

"Right. Whatever. I think he was more concerned with the boy sleeping at your house."

"Why?"

"He thought it improper for his son to be alone with a strange man."

"He thought it improper?"

"He said he was worried about you messing with the kid."

"Messing in what way?"

"A sexual way, Mr. McMorrow."

"Well, you can tell him he's got nothing to worry about. I was just trying to keep 'the kid' from freezing to death."

The smile. She understood. She just had to ask the questions, just as Roxanne did.

"That's fine, Mr. McMorrow, but it doesn't address the question," she said.

"I haven't heard a question yet."

"You know I'm legally required to investigate all allegations—"

"Of course. But let's back up a minute. Allegations by whom? Rusty? This isn't an allegation or anything, but it's my impression that this guy couldn't care less about Rocky."

"That's not really the question. The question—and please don't be defensive—the question is why you invited the boy to your home."

"I didn't. He just showed up. Hitched a ride up to Prosperity and asked around until somebody gave him directions to my house. I didn't invite him. I didn't want him. But once he was there—it was snowing and cold and I live way out in the country—I couldn't just toss him out. He's got sneakers on, you know? Hadn't eaten in who knows how long. I mean, what would you do?"

"I'd call the proper authorities."

"It was one in the morning. I didn't want authorities. I just wanted to go to sleep. So I made him a sandwich and gave him a blanket. Told him he could sleep on the couch. What's wrong with that?"

"Nothing, Mr. McMorrow. Maine is full of Good Samaritans. But we do have to be aware that some adults have other motives when it comes to children."

"Not this adult. I have a very longtime partner. We're having a baby. I mean, I'm not some sicko."

She looked at me. Didn't smile. Didn't immediately agree that I was a good guy. Behind me I heard someone pass, then the men's room door slam.

"Mr. McMorrow," Duguay said. "I understand that this is difficult. No one likes to be accused of something like this."

"Something like what?"

"Improper contact."

"Is that what the stepdad said?"

"He was concerned."

"He had no reason to be. If I were him, I'd be more concerned with finding my boy. And maybe you should be asking why he took off in the first place. Once you make sure he's not in an E.R. someplace."

"I would be, Mr. McMorrow, but I've been informed that he was dropped off right here in Bangor. The citizen called and reported it. The boy wasn't struck. He was almost struck, and then given a ride here."

My turn to pause. She gave me the thin smile again.

"Well, that's good news. So he's okay?"

"That's all I know. You seemed to have such an interest in the boy, I thought I'd talk to you."

"Such an interest? I let him sleep on my couch."

"And he fled into the woods. Can you tell me what precipitated this event?"

"Precipitated this event?" I said. "Didn't they tell you that you don't have to talk that way. You just have to write that way in your reports."

"Okay. Why'd he bolt?"

"Much better. Because the cops came. He's afraid of cops because he knows they'll send him home and he doesn't want to go there. The second time it was because his stepdad showed up."

"Why won't he go home?"

"I don't know."

"He didn't confide in you?"

"Confide in me? Hell, no. He barely speaks."

"He must have said something," she said.

I looked at her, this persistent little terrier of a woman. She looked soft, but inside was the hard heart of a zealot.

I'd have to ask Roxanne if she knew her, what her rep was.

"No, he didn't say anything. He's never even told me his real name. But I didn't press him. I just gave him a sandwich."

"And he ate and ran."

"Basically, yeah. You know, you should be asking his parents these questions. You might have better luck."

"But you're the only one who was with the boy before he ran."

"He's been running for weeks."

"And he's in a vulnerable state. I'd like to talk to him."

"Go right ahead."

"I don't know where he is, sir."

"That makes two of us."

"If he contacts you, will you call me?"

"I don't know. I guess so," I said.

"Why do you hesitate, Mr. McMorrow?"

"I'm not hesitating. I said I thought I would. Or maybe I'll tell him to call you, but I can't guarantee he will. The kid seems to know his rights under the law. He says he's fourteen and you can't hold him."

"Is that what he told you?"

The smile again. Feet planted close together in the flat, suede shoes. The shoes were scuffed at the toes, worn at the seams. The earrings swung like a hypnotist's baubles. Behind me the men's room door opened and slammed shut again. I could feel someone walking down the hall behind me. Joelle Duguay kept her eyes locked on mine. The urge to tell her who I was welled up inside me. Tell her about who Roxanne was. Did she know who she was talking to? I was one of the good guys.

I swallowed it.

"He told me he didn't have to go home if he didn't want

to. The cops couldn't make him, and DHS couldn't make him. I wouldn't call him savvy, but he knew that much."

She nodded.

"Well, that's sort of true. But we can remove him from a situation where he is in danger."

"Then take him off the streets."

"Or if he's in danger of becoming a victim of a crime."

"He could get mugged out there. He's just a little guy."

"There are other forms of violence. A lot of things can happen to a little guy."

"And where do they usually happen?" I said. "In the home. And who is usually the perpetrator? In the vast majority of cases, it's a family member. Ms. Duguay, you're looking for answers in the wrong place, with all due respect. Go after the family. There's something very wrong there."

Again, the implacable smile.

"Right now we're talking about how the boy is making it on the street. And there are only a couple of ways for a kid to get money on the street," she said. "One's theft. The other is performing services for adults."

"Shoveling snow? Running errands?" I said.

Duguay shook her head. The earrings swung like wagging fingers.

"The guy who picked up Rocky on the road said he offered to buy him a meal. Rocky reached in his pocket and took out at least three twenty-dollar bills. Said he was set."

"I didn't give him any money. If it was mine, he stole it."

This time she gave me a little shrug. Shoulders up. Shoulders down.

"I had cash at home. In the kitchen. I'll check to see if it's gone."

"And if it is?"

"I'll call the cops and report it. Or should I call you?"

"Both, Mr. McMorrow."

She held her hand out, extended her card like it was an ace from her sleeve. I took it the card but didn't read it. Then she shook my hand. It was a long, hard squeeze, tight as handcuffs.

CHAPTER 22

The newsroom was as silent as a courtroom. I ran the long gauntlet between the reporters, none of whom looked up. Dropping into my seat, I gave the keyboard a slap. Marna began to type furiously, eyes fixed on a pile of news releases. I aimlessly scrolled through the directories, pounding the keys.

Without turning around, Randall said, "Jack. The scam story by Miss Child. I gave it a once-over, and I think it needs some tightening. Trim off the fat. She's got to learn she isn't getting paid by the inch. And Souza's got a marijuana bust. Make sure he doesn't convict the guy in print, will you? We don't want the story to look like it was written by the district attorney. And the only other page-one candidate is a feature on that teen-shelter place, whatever the hell it is. It's by a freelancer. Don't let the counselor types go on and on. Let 'em justify their jobs someplace else."

"Gotcha," I said.

The teen shelter, I thought. My first stop.

I opened the story and started in, deleting unneeded words and phrases, fixing style stuff. The place was called Penobscot House. The director said it was a safe haven for runaways who might otherwise be victimized on the streets.

"There are predators out there," the guy said.

"So I've heard," I said aloud.

Randall turned around and looked at me, then got up from his chair. He walked over to me, and leaned down. The typing subsided. Ears pricked around the room like dogs had awakened.

"McMorrow," Randall said. "Everything all right?"

I could smell his aftershave. See the little beads of sweat on his upper lip.

"It's fine," I said.

"What'd that woman want?"

"Oh, nothing. She's looking for a kid I saw in Portland. Some runaway."

"Came a long way, didn't she?"

"The kid's supposed to be here now. Maybe at this shelter."

"Yeah, well, tell her next time to chase the kid on her own time, not ours. We have a paper to put out. Early deadline. Snow, heavy at times, beginning after midnight."

I nodded. Randall paused, then jerked his head toward the hall. He walked out of the newsroom. I heaved myself out of the chair and followed. He was waiting by the water cooler, arms crossed on his chest, feet apart, shoulders back.

"Give it to me straight, Jack. Something funny going on?"

I hesitated. Cleared my throat.

"Depends on what you call funny."

Randall looked away, then gathered himself up.

"Child protective. They do child abuse. Kids getting

beat up and . . . well, molested. Jack, she asked me if there'd been any teenage boys in the newsroom."

"How is that internship program?"

"Jack, she meant—"

"I know what she meant. She's looking for a runaway. I helped him out and he left and now they want to find him."

"That's it?"

"That's it."

"Because all I need is the *Bangor Daily* getting hold of some dirt. You know what that would do, don't you? Advertisers would run like we had the plague. Doesn't have to be true. Just the accusation."

"It's nothing like that," I said. "It's a runaway kid from Woodfield."

" 'Cause I never asked why you left the *New York Times.* I figured it was your business and—"

"I said it was nothing."

"You're sure?"

"Yeah. I helped a kid out. He went on his way. End of story."

It was what Randall wanted to hear, but even as I said it I knew the last part was a lie.

We walked back into the newsroom, where the heads were bowed as if in prayer. I went to my desk and sat down. Randall went to his desk, where the phone immediately rang. I heard him say, "Yes. Sure," and hang up.

"Jack," he said, without turning around. "Tippy wants to see you. Her office."

Her office was on the fourth floor, on the southeast corner, with windows all around. Tippy held meetings of the Bangor Area Animal Rescue Society there. Very rarely had I heard of her inviting members of the *Clarion* staff to her aerie.

I took the stairs. The foyer was dark and the door was

closed. I held my hand up to it, hesitated, then knocked. Twice. Tippy told me to come in and I did. I closed the door behind me.

She was sitting sidesaddle on the front of her desk, reading something, her L.L. Bean boot swinging absently in the air. The room was cold and Tippy had her big parka on. Behind her hung an oil painting of a fat white cat on a red velvet pillow. It looked like it was being served for dinner.

"I'd tell you to have a seat but there's no need for either of us to get settled," she said. She still was peering at the paper, a newsletter by the looks of it. As I got closer, I could see there was a drawing of a puppy on the back page. Tippy tossed it on the desk.

"Vivisection," she said. "It never ceases to amaze how cruel humans can be."

The phone rang. Tippy said, "Oh, bother," and swung off of the desk and walked around to pick it up. I moved to the window and looked out over the city: red-brick rows of the old downtown, with gray-black rooftops. The Penobscot River, an open channel running black as oil between rafts of snow-covered ice. Beyond the river, the city of Brewer, highways and mini-malls, and then the distant hills to the east, still bristling with trees, flanked by low clouds.

Behind me, Tippy said, "Well, we'll talk, dear," and then hung up. I turned back to her. She turned to me, direct, as usual.

"Jack, I'm not going to waste too much of your time. I know we have a paper to put out. But I'm going to tell you what I cannot tolerate. Cruelty to helpless things. The most helpless things are animals. Pets who look to us for food and affection. The second most helpless thing is a child."

I nodded, barely. She fixed me with her blunt gaze: reddened nose, salt-and-pepper hair, and the blind self-assurance that came with money.

"As you know, you've worked with my column, part of my role here is to protect the helpless pets among us. I've always loved animals. That was just born to me, part of my wonderful heritage."

If you don't say so yourself, I thought.

"I never married, so I never had children," Tippy went on. "But if I had married and had a family, I suppose I could have taken up children as my cause. After all, it really is cruelty that I oppose, cruelty of all sorts."

She gave me a searching look, then turned away, took a couple of steps and stopped. Her parka smelled of animals.

"There was a woman downstairs from the state. She was looking for you. Did you see her?"

"Yes, I did."

"Randall said she said she needed to talk to you because of some sort of investigation."

Covering his butt, the little weasel.

"That's right," I said. "She did."

"Well, I'm not going to pry into your business, but I read the paper, I know the things that go on. Is this something—"

"Tippy, it's nothing. I helped a kid and they're looking for him. He's a runaway and she thought—"

"Because any association with something like this would be very damaging to the *Clarion*. As you know—"

"Tippy," I broke in. "It's nothing, like I just told Randall. You're getting all bothered for no reason. I fed this kid, like you'd feed a stray cat."

She looked at me like it all suddenly made sense. It was very pretty to think so.

CHAPTER 23

The newsroom was spooling up to full speed, the spattering sound of fingers on keyboards, the bark of impatient voices. I took a deep breath and opened the editing queue. The marijuana bust. It seemed almost wholesome.

I started in, picking at typos and misspellings as I gave it a first read.

A husband and wife were arrested at their apartment on outer State Street. Police found four pounds of processed pot, a few hits of LSD. They also came away with an assortment of weapons: a shotgun, three rifles, and two handguns, including a loaded nine-millimeter the cops said was under the woman's pillow. The couple went to jail. Their six-year-old son was remanded to the temporary custody of the Department of Human Services until relatives or other suitable placement could be arranged. The kid was crying as he was led from the house.

They were armed drug dealers to us, but to him they were Mom and Dad.

But even that hadn't kept Joelle off my back. Had she handled that kid? Maybe they only unleashed her on grown-ups.

I culled the cop jargon from the story, then made sure the incriminating statements were attributed to police. Souza wasn't a bad reporter, but he tended to get caught up in the semi-hysteria that surrounded an event like this. It was my job to keep that emotion from making it into print, and I was pretty good at it.

For a child molester, I was a hell of an editor.

The teen-shelter story needed less editing, only because there was less to work with. The freelancer had talked to the guy who ran the place, just a couple of blocks up the hill from the *Clarion* building. Predictably, the guy said his facility addressed an urgent, growing need in the community. He waxed on, and then the freelancer described the inside of the place, right down to the starched white curtains and gleaming Formica counters. And then the story ended.

"There aren't any teenagers in this story about the place for teenagers," I said aloud.

Randall, getting up from his desk, overheard me.

"Yeah, I guess there weren't any there when she went for the interview. They leave during the day."

"People to see? Burglaries to commit?" I said.

"Probably. Ought to put the little bastards to work or something."

"Juvenile chain gangs. Now there's an idea. You want to run this as is?"

"Yeah, dump it. It's been hanging around for a week. I've got it pegged as a bottom dweller. It's thin but it's done and I'm sick of her calling me, asking me when it's gonna be in."

We were nothing but for our high standards.

Randall went down to the conference room to meet with the sports editors. I plugged away until my stomach growled loud enough for Marna to hear. She asked if I wanted to order something. I said no, I was going out. Crossing the newsroom, I told gray-haired Souza and earnest Miss Child that I'd liked their stories. They said thanks but looked at me skeptically.

It was going around.

I started for the door, and then turned back, stopping at Souza's cubicle.

"Question for you," I said.

He looked up, surprised.

"Yessir."

"This teen shelter place. It doesn't open until six o'clock. Where do you think the kids hang out during the day? You see them around town?"

His eyebrows raised ever so slightly, but then he seemed flattered to have been asked.

He said he could find out. He picked up the phone and dialed.

"Hey, Billy. John Souza. You been busy? . . . Yeah. . . . Didn't let that lady get her hand under her pillow, did you? . . . Just a T-shirt? No, she wasn't bad looking, either. Yeah, right. All look better around closing time. . . . Hey, listen, you know these street punks who go to this new shelter place? Yeah. Kids. Your future job security. You know where they're likely to go during the day? Uh-huh. Right. . . . Uh-huh. . . . gotcha. . . . Owe you one, partner."

Souza hung up.

"In the morning, some of them go to the mall. They take the bus out there, make trouble. Later on, before the shelter opens, they might go to the Cave. It's that sleazy arcade next to the bus station. But he said some of them go down by the river, under the bridge. They drink, sniff paint. Cops run 'em out every once in a while. A few days go by, they're back. Like chasing raccoons outta your garbage."

"Thanks," I said.

Souza paused, then the competitive reporter in him kicked in. He added with poorly feigned nonchalance, "What's your interest, McMorrow? Thinking of doing a story?"

"No," I said. "Just curious. I know a kid who might be one of those raccoons."

"Crafty little bastards," Souza said. "Hang onto your wallet."

"Not this one. Crafty is the one thing he isn't."

"Or he just has you really fooled, McMorrow. The sneakiest sneak is the one who doesn't seem sneaky at all."

His phone rang. He turned away. His words hung in the air, so I snagged them and took them with me.

CHAPTER 24

I left the Clarion building and trudged down the hill past City Hall and around the corner. The sidewalk was slippery with sand and the air was cold but heavy. To the east the sky was dense, dark gray, and it felt like it was going to snow. I turned up the collar of my jacket and walked.

This was Main Street, set in the shadow of the handful of six-story high-rises. Where there once had been family-owned department stores, a movie theater, shops, and restaurants, there were storefront churches, a second-floor dance studio, an Indian restaurant. A shoe store, surviving against all odds. And the arcade, serving the street kids who, like alchemists, could somehow turn their idle hours into a little gold.

It was a block up, across the street. Outside was a knot of

girls, standing in the cold, heating themselves with cigarettes. I slipped around them, shoved the door open and
walked in.

Lights flashed. Lasers hummed. The building shuddered
with pounding, pulsing music, punctuated by electronic
grunts and raining blows. My ninja friend's training ground.

This was the cantina in *Star Wars* and kids were the
aliens. They clumped around the machines, peering into the
glowing screens. One kid saw me and elbowed the kid next
to him.

Was I a cop? A social worker with a bad attitude? Somebody's father, ready to yank his kid out of the place by the
scruff of the neck? An old guy looking to buy drugs or com-
panionship?

I made a quick circle of the room but didn't see Rocky. I
considered asking but didn't think any of these kids would
answer, even if they could hear me in the din. The guy dol-
ing out change behind the counter was a possibility but
when he saw me looking at him, he scowled and busied
himself behind the glass cases of cheap baubles.

He didn't know who I was but he knew I was trouble.

So I moved to the back, stood behind a kid playing "Battle in the Bronx." Bare-chested thugs hit each other with
clubs against the backdrop of the Manhattan skyline.

"Die," the kid muttered.

I shook my head and left, and as I came out of the door,
the girls looked up.

"Hi, daddy," one of them said. "Looking for somebody?"

The rest turned toward me and giggled.

There were five of them, all fourteen or fifteen, made up
like exotic birds. Peering at me from behind black eyeliner,
they put cigarettes to their red-lipped mouths and blew
smoke into the cold air.

"How you doing?" I said.

"Freezin' our asses off," one girl said. "You got a car with heat?"

"Tammy," another girl protested.

"I'm friggin' freezing," Tammy said. "I don't care."

I moved closer. She looked at me defiantly. She was pretty, in a big-boned sort of way, with large brown eyes and a ring in her eyebrow. Her denim jacket was open and her shirt was short so her pale white midriff was bared to the cold.

"I don't have a car, but I'll buy you a cup of coffee," I said.

One of the girls said, "Nice line."

"No, it's nothing like that," I said. "I'm from the newspaper."

There was a moment's pause and then they started gabbling like geese.

"Hey, you want to interview me? . . . I'll give you my life story. . . . Is this really gonna be in the newspaper? . . . Where's your camera? . . . I was in the newspaper. This douche bag, like, spells my name wrong."

Tammy, the alpha female, sucked her cigarette until they subsided.

"What's the story about?" she said. "How us kids got no place to live?"

I hesitated.

"Not exactly. It's more that I want to find a specific kid."

"What kid's that?" Tammy said.

"His name's Rocky."

They looked at each other, then back at me, suddenly stone-faced.

"What do you want to talk to him for?" Tammy said.

She waited for an answer.

"I met him. He's a street kid from Portland but I think he's in Bangor now."

"Does he mean Twiggy?" one of the girls, a short squat white-blonde, said.

"He hates it when you call him that," another girl, also blonde, said. "I remember he got, like, so pissed."

She grinned at the thought.

"Is this guy gonna buy us hot chocolate?" a girl toward the rear said.

"Gotta show him your boobs first," the white-blonde said.

"She ain't got any," another girl said.

"Then you do it. You'll do anything."

Tammy looked at them and shook her head in dismay. They quieted.

"You guys act like you're two years old," she said, and turned to me.

"What do you want to find him for?"

"I need to talk to him."

"Yeah, well, no shit. I didn't think you were gonna sing him a song."

The gallery tittered. I smiled. Tammy looked at me, eyes narrowing as she assessed me. I tried not to stare at her eyebrow ring but couldn't help it.

"Didn't that hurt?"

She shrugged, pushed her hands in her jeans pockets so the jeans pulled down and more belly showed. I didn't know if it was deliberate.

"Pain don't bother me. I just tune it out. Just go floating away in my head."

"But you can't float away from cold?"

"Sometimes. But right now I can't even feel my feet."

"How 'bout the coffee?"

"I hate coffee."

"Okay. How 'bout hot chocolate?"

"Sure."

The group giggled.

"Everybody else?"

"I'm going back in," the white-blonde said.

"He said we were kicked out for the night."

"Oh, he always says that. He said that, I'm like, 'Right.' "

They turned and followed the white-blonde girl into the arcade. Tammy looked at me, then started walking down the sidewalk. I fell in beside her, and we both looked down at her black sneakers as we walked. Neither of us spoke. At the end of the block Tammy stopped in front of the Indian restaurant. I peered in doubtfully.

"They have hot chocolate?"

"Yeah. I been here before, like, lots of times."

"They don't mind if you don't have dinner?"

"Nah, they're goddamn Egyptians or something but they're all right."

She opened the door and a bell jangled. We went in and the place was empty. I went to a table in the front window. These days, if I had cocoa with a kid, I did it in public.

We sat. Off the street, Tammy seemed younger, more vulnerable. She sat straight in her chair and then grabbed a paper napkin off of the table. Looking out the window, she began to shred the napkin into confetti.

"So you do know Rocky?" I asked.

"I don't know. Sort of. I might've ran into him."

"Here? In Bangor?"

"No. Portland. We was at Hope House together. He came from the friggin' boonies with this other kid."

"How long ago was that?"

"Oh, gee. I don't know. Like, three weeks. Before Christmas. I don't keep track."

"I saw him down there. These kids were beating the heck out of him."

Tammy shrugged.

"Yeah, well. That's the way it is. I mean, when I first was on my own, I got it. I mean, nobody knew me. It was like, 'Let's go kick her ass.' I mean, I didn't even know how to fight. I was, like, twelve."

I thought of the Portland cop. *Lord of the Flies.*

"You ever do that to anybody?"

"Sure. It's punch or be punched, you know what I'm saying?"

I looked at her hands. They were dirty, with dark blue fingernails, and illegible words scrawled on the palms with pen.

A waiter came, an older man.

"Hi, there, honey," he said to Tammy, but gave me a hard look. I ignored it and ordered a hot chocolate and black tea and picked up the menu.

"You sure? Not hungry?"

Tammy shook her head. The waiter left, leaving us glasses of water. Tammy took a sip.

"So I heard Rocky was back in Bangor today. You seen him?"

"Today? No."

"If he was in town, you think you would?"

"Don't know. Sometimes Rocky hangs out with us. Sometimes he's, like, by himself."

"Maybe he's afraid of getting beat up."

"Yeah, well, maybe in Portland, but here it's, like, more mellower and shit."

The guy came back. He smiled at Tammy as he put her mug of hot chocolate in front of her, and then a bowl of marshmallows beside the mug, and then a big cookie on her saucer. He winked at her paternally, then dropped my tea in front of me with a bang, and strode off.

"So you haven't seen him?"

"Nope. Didn't know he was here. Why do you want to find him?"

I sipped my tea. It was lukewarm. Tammy's hot chocolate was steaming.

"He came to my house last night."

Her eyebrow ring twitched.

"He was freezing. Got dropped off by a trucker in the middle of nowhere and it was either my house or the woods. I live way out in the country."

Tammy sipped, peering into her mug like she was reading tea leaves. Then she put her mug down, reached into a pocket and pulled out an elastic thing and gathered her hair back. I couldn't tell if she was listening. I took a chance and told her about Rocky's tracks and calling the cops, and his stepfather coming to get him.

I paused. She didn't say anything, then blurted, "Oh, he hates his stepdad. He'd rather be like dead than living with that guy."

"Why?"

"Why do you want to find him?"

"Well, it's mostly because he took off when the stepfather came. Ran into the woods."

"Go Twiggy," Tammy said.

"And I felt bad, because I didn't call the guy, the stepdad, I mean. The cops did. But I think Rocky probably thinks I set him up or something. But I didn't know the guy was coming to get him."

Tammy took a marshmallow and popped it into her mouth. Then a handful.

"He likes his mom," she said, swallowing.

"Yeah?"

"He says she's great. But she's, like, sick or something."

"What's wrong with her?"

"I don't know. He didn't say exactly. He just said he missed her and stuff. I mean, saying that kind of stuff? That's what gets you beat on."

"Saying you miss your mother?"

"Shit, yeah. I mean, he could tell me that, but, like, one time these other guys heard. They busted his glasses and stuck his sneakers in the toilet."

"That's pretty low," I said.

"Yeah, well, you gotta know when to keep your mouth shut."

"Rocky learn that yet?"

"He's learning. He's okay. He's wicked smart. A wicked good artist."

I sipped my tea, looked out at the street.

"Is that right?"

"Oh, yeah. He draws these mazes and stuff. If you couldn't find Twig in Portland, you know where he was?"

"Where?"

"In the art museum place. He goes in there and sits and draws and stuff. They don't even kick him out."

"No kidding."

Tammy finished off the marshmallows and started on the cookie, not taking bites, but picking it apart with her fingers and popping morsels into her mouth. I waited.

"You know what he said? He said his stepdad used to make fun of him when he was littler. Call him a little pussy and stuff in front of, like, all these other guys. Old guys. His friends. Doesn't that totally suck?"

I agreed that it did.

"I mean, he's his stepdad but that's like your dad, and the

guy's busting his kid's nuts in front of these people and laughing at him. Rocky said they all laughed at him."

"That's sick," I said.

"Yeah, that really bugged the shit out of me. I mean, if the guy's mad or something, and he loses it and whacks the kid. But busting him like that?"

She held out her middle finger to the spirit of Rusty Clement.

"I hope that man has something really bad happen to him. Don't you think something really bad should happen to him for doing that?"

I smiled gently.

"Sure, if you believe in justice and all that."

"Well, why not? Don't you?"

I smiled again. Underneath the toughness and makeup, there still was naivete.

"Sure," I said. "You've got to believe in something."

"Uh-huh," she said, and popped a piece of cookie in her mouth.

"Listen, Tammy, where else would Rocky go?"

"I don't know. Sometimes he just runs the road with us. Goes to the mall. We go in the stores, do some shopping. Five-finger shopping."

She grinned.

"If we get bored, we can always go pick on the rent-a-cops. We make fun of them. Those guys hate us."

Tammy drank her hot chocolate and came up with a brown moustache on her red lips. She licked it off languidly, her tongue writhing like an eel, her big brown eyes suddenly fixed on mine. I looked away. She dropped the Lolita act and wiped her mouth with the back of her hand.

"Just kidding," Tammy said. "I hate guys. My mother's boyfriend, he pretended to be my daddy and that was fine and then he stopped pretending. Get me drunk, I'll tell you the whole fucking pathetic story. Anyway, I said, 'I'm outta here, you piece a shit.' And I ain't a lesbian, so what does that leave? Maybe I'll be a nun. I'd be a wicked good nun."

She sipped again. I smiled.

"So where would he go?" Tammy said. "I don't know. District Court. Sometimes I go there, 'cause it's warm and really quiet and you can sit on the benches in the lobby and sleep. But the cops know me now, so they kick me out. These old farts, they put 'em there 'cause they're too old to catch criminals. I'm like, 'Hello? Is anything going on inside that bald head of yours, you senile old bastard?' But Rocky, he looks straight so they don't bug him."

I sipped my tea.

"So anyplace else?"

"Oh, Dunkin' Donuts. McDonald's. Places like that. Sometimes people get up and just leave the stuff on the tables, and we, like, sit down and start eating. I don't eat the sandwiches, though, 'cause people's teeth have been on them, but I eat the french fries. Or if there's Chicken McNuggets that haven't been touched. They're separate, you know what I'm saying?"

I nodded.

"Rocky does that?"

"Sure. I showed him. I said, 'This ain't gonna kill ya. Get used to it.' "

She ate more cookie. From underneath the table, I could feel her leg drumming nervously. She looked out the window, then back at me.

"You know I can get pot easier than I can get cigarettes. Getting to be a pain in the butt."

The pun was lost on her. The leg drummed some more.

The table shook like a table on a train. Cars passed slowly and Tammy watched them, then suddenly turned back to me.

"I stuck up for him, 'cause he's not like these scabs. These guys who are just these, like, total jerks but they think they're just so cool. This one time we were at the mall in Portland and these guys were goofing on Rocky and I'm going, 'Leave him alone, you assholes. Just 'cause he's got a brain, you fuckin' huffers. Go suck paint.' I ain't afraid. I'll kick their asses and they know it."

"So they left him alone?"

"Yeah. They pushed him around a little but they didn't, like, beat on him."

"Nice of you, Tammy."

"Yeah. He owed me that day. Big time."

She popped the last pieces of cookie into her mouth.

"Hey, I gotta go. Thanks for the drink."

"Thank you," I said.

I got up, fished in my pocket and dropped a five-dollar bill on the table. Tammy already was headed for the door. I followed her out on to the sidewalk, where we hesitated and watched the traffic, the exhaust rising like fog in the cold. I was going left, back up the hill to the newspaper. Tammy was going right.

"Nice talking to you," I said.

"Yeah, right," Tammy said, her facade back in place. Body pierced. Face painted. Little girl street warrior.

"No, really. Listen, if you see Rocky, tell him—"

Tell him what? Tell him his stepfather had the wrong idea? Tell him to call home, his mother was worried? Tell him I needed him to get this DHS lady off my back? Tell him I wanted to know who Kitty was?

"Tell him he dropped something at my house," I said. "A note. Tell him it was folded up really small."

Tammy was walking backward, away from me.

"What was it a note about?" she said.

"I don't know," I said.

"Whatever," Tammy said, and with a shrug hurried off into the night, her band of bare belly pale in the streetlight.

I slipped back into the newsroom, settling in at my terminal. The reporters looked down. Randall picked up the phone. Across the room, the other copy editors bent to their tasks with renewed concentration, as though the stories were written in a code that they were on the verge of breaking. The guys in sports never paid much attention to anybody else, anyway. Marna was away from her desk.

I sat down and poked the keys. There were stories in the editing directory: A snowmobile accident that left a guy paralyzed from the waist down. A dinner and dance to raise money for a five-year-old girl with terminal cancer. *With horizontal pic of kid and mom.*

Starting at the top, I worked my way down, culling words like stones from a harrowed field. After fifteen minutes, I closed the snowmobile story and sent it on its way. The dinner dance was next, and I scrolled through it. Miss Child's work and really pretty good. *"When Molly Seguin asks when she'll be able to go back to kindergarten, her mother says, 'Soon.' And then she turns and whispers to a visitor, 'I still believe in miracles.'"*

Very nice. I considered breaking the silence by complimenting her, but when I looked over, Miss Child was looking toward the door to the corridor. Then Souza turned and looked, too. Randall hung up the phone and said, "Christ, what now?"

A partition blocked my view, but I saw Miss Child get up from her seat and start toward the door. Then she reappeared, looking over at me.

"There's someone here to see Jack McMorrow," Child said, and then there was Tammy.

She stood there, with her dyed hair and garish makeup, and looked down at Randall like he was a stiff in the front row at a strip show. She took a long drag on a cigarette and glanced around.

"Shit," she said, smoke billowing from her mouth. "This is just like on TV. WKRP."

"I'm sorry, but you can't smoke in here," Randall said.

"Oh," Tammy said. "Okay."

She put the cigarette to her mouth, took another deep drag and blew a mushroom cloud of smoke toward the ceiling. When she leaned back to exhale, Tammy's bare belly stared Randall in the face. He stared back as she stubbed the butt out on her hand.

One of the copyeditors said, "Jesus." Randall turned to me with a cold stare.

"Friend of yours?" he said.

CHAPTER 25

I scrambled out of my chair and hurried toward her.

"Hey, newspaperman," Tammy said, as Randall listened. "I found him for you. I think he'll talk to you, too."

"Oh, good," I said, as the reporters stared. "Hey, these guys are trying to work so let's go down here."

"Yeah, well, he hasn't eaten much in, like, all day and I thought if you could give him five bucks he could get, like, a burger and some fries maybe, 'cause . . ."

I took her by the arm and eased her away. At the end of the room, I let go.

"Tammy, I've got to work another three hours or so. Where could I find him at, let's say, eleven?"

She put her hands in the pockets of her jeans and shrugged.

"I don't know. He said he ain't going to Penobscot House."

"Well, then where would he go?"

"I don't know."

"Where are you staying?"

"These kids I know, they know this guy's got this apartment. I'll probably go there, maybe."

"Would Rocky go there?"

She frowned skeptically.

"Nah, these guys, they'd trash him."

"So where can I meet you?"

"Me or Rocky?"

"Rocky."

"I don't know. I could tell him to come here."

"I don't think so. They're kind of edgy about people just coming in."

"How come?"

"It's hard to explain."

Tammy's eyes darted around the room.

"They're all watching us, you know," she said, grinning. "I think they think I'm gonna steal something. Got any doughnuts or anything?"

I moved her into the corridor, by the elevator, then dug in my pocket and brought out some bills. I peeled off a ten and gave it to her. She slipped the bill into her jeans.

"Can you and Rocky get some dinner?"

"Sure."

"And then I'll meet you guys?"

The elevator started to hum. It was on the first floor, headed up. I started to maneuver Tammy toward the door. She kept talking.

"I don't know. I might be partying."

"Rocky, then. Did you tell him about the note?"

"Yeah. He said, 'Does he have it?' I said, 'What do I look like? A mind reader? I don't know.' I'm like, 'Ask him.'"

I did have it. I could feel the little square in my pocket. And I'd give it to him. I'd give him the note, and he could talk to Ms. Duguay and tell her to leave me alone.

"Tell him I have it and I'd like to talk to him."

The elevator's hum was louder. Then it stopped.

"Okay," Tammy said. I opened the door to the stairwell.

"So you'll eat? Where you going?"

"I'll bum a ride to Burger King. Hey, I think I'll take the elevator down. I like elevators. We used to just ride the one at the bank until they kicked us out."

"No, why don't you—"

She moved past me to the elevator door. I was standing beside her when the humming stopped and the door slid open.

"Oh, my god," Tammy squealed. She darted into the elevator and dropped to her knees.

"Mr. McMorrow," Tippy Danforth said.

"Hi, there," I said.

"He's so cute," Tammy said.

She was kneeling on the floor of the elevator, where Danforth had set down a Havahart trap. Inside the trap was an enormous white cat. The cat yowled. Tammy cooed. The elevator door started to close, but I reached out and blocked it and it rolled open. Tippy, with the trap, stepped out, Tammy followed, crouching beside her.

"Hey, pretty kitty," Tammy said.

"Miss Danforth," I said. "This is Tammy. Tammy, this is Miss Danforth."

Tippy looked down at the expanse of Tammy's bare back.

"Hello," she said, neutrally.

"Hi," Tammy said. "This cat is so beautiful I can't believe it."

Tippy almost smiled.

"Yes, she is. She'd been living on Hammond Street. I think she was dumped off by somebody. And she just recently had kittens, but I couldn't find them, poor dears. She has rather a nasty gash on her hind leg and she was quite cold. Her whole system is weakened, so I didn't think she should be left in the car. She needs plenty of TLC, that one. You like cats?"

"Oh, I love 'em."

"Do you have cats at home?" Tippy asked.

"No. I had this cat when I was, like, really little, but my brother killed it. My mom's like, 'Get over it. It's just a cat. We'll get you another one.' I'm like, 'Yeah, right. So Dickie can kill that one, too?' Frig that."

Tippy blanched. The white cat meowed.

"And where are you from?" Tippy asked her.

"Oh, here and there. I used to live in, like, Rockland area, but I don't anymore."

"Tammy's staying in Bangor now," I said.

She still was on her knees. Tippy looked at me.

"Tammy knows the boy I was talking to you about. Rocky. She located him for me."

"Oh. Where is he?"

Tammy looked at me.

"You can say it. Miss Danforth isn't going to bother him. She's a good person."

"Well," Tammy said. "He's down by the river. He met up with this kid he ran away —I mean, left with."

"And what are they doing down there?" Tippy asked.

There was no judgment in her voice, just curiosity. Tammy poked her finger in the cage and the cat licked it.

"Oh, I think she likes me. I'd take her home, except—"

"Except you don't have one, do you?" Tippy said.

There was an awkward pause. I didn't fill it. Tammy didn't answer, but after a moment, her shoulder blades lifted in her trademark shrug.

"Hi, kitty. Hi, honey," she said, in the high-pitched voice that people use when they talk to animals.

"You're a stray, too," Tippy said, matter-of-factly.

"Yeah, so put me to sleep," Tammy said softly, almost to herself. "Hi, little kitty. Hi, little mama kitty. Where's your babies, huh? Where's those little babies?"

I looked at Tippy, in her big jacket and boots, her nose pink from the cold. She stared down at Tammy, her vertebrae showing like the bones of a snake, her green-and-red hair like something growing on a tropical reef. Tammy was singing softly to the cat.

"Lost your kittens, you poor little Mittens . . ."

"Do you have a job?" Tippy said. "Stand up, now, so I can talk to you."

I waited. Would Tammy spit in her face? Tell her where to go? Tell her she'd stand when she was good and ready?

She gave the cat a last finger pat and straightened, her fingers stuck defiantly in her belt loops.

"Do you have a job, young lady?" Tippy asked again.

"Yeah, right. Do you?"

"Miss Danforth owns the newspaper," I said.

"No shit. The whole thing?"

Tammy moved one hand from her belt loop and brushed at her hair, her eyebrow ring.

"But I also try to find homes for wayward animals."

"What's wayward?"

"Lost," I said.

"You like animals?" Tippy said.

"Well, yeah," Tammy said, her voice warbling on the last syllable to indicate it was a stupid question.

"Do you mind changing litter pans?"

"Well, I ain't going out of my way to find cat poop, if that's what you're saying. But I can do it. Hey, you wouldn't believe the gross shit you see, living on the street."

"You want a job helping with the animals?" Tippy asked flatly.

"Hey, I don't need no charity, no fake people. They tell you they want to save you and then, after two days, it's like, 'Okay, that was fun. Let's play some other do-gooder game now.' I been down that road."

"Miss Danforth isn't fake, Tammy," I said. "Anything but."

"I'm not talking about charity," Tippy said. "I'm talking about work. Twenty-five dollars a day and a place to sleep and eat, if you want it."

"I don't know, Tippy," I said. "You don't know what you're—"

"Where's this?"

"West Broadway," Tippy said. "The animals are in the carriage house, mostly."

"Can I smoke?"

"Outside," Tippy said.

"So what am I supposed to do? Like, pick up poop all day?"

"No, not all day. I do it now myself. It takes a good three hours to clean and water and feed all the animals. And they need human company to be resocialized, so you need to talk to them, pat them, if they'll let you."

The cat yowled. Tammy looked down at it and made a kissing sound with her garish lips.

Then, still looking at the cat, "This isn't, like, some dyke thing, is it? 'Cause I'm sorry, but I'm not like that."

"It's a job," Tippy said. "You do the work, I pay you money. That's all."

"Do I have to stay? All the time?"

"Not if you don't want to."

"Well," Tammy said. "Like when? Tomorrow?"

"You can help me with them tonight."

"I've gotta get my stuff."

"Where is it?"

Tammy said it was at an apartment behind City Hall.

"But I don't like it, I'm gone."

"And vice versa," Tippy said. "You can start by carrying that cage for me. I've got to get some things upstairs."

"When do I get paid?"

"When the job's done."

"Tonight?"

"If the job's done."

"Where do I sleep? Like on some busted couch in this garage or something?"

"No, there are rooms," Tippy said.

Rooms galore, I thought.

"Well, okay," Tammy said.

I looked at Tippy.

"You sure?"

"The quality of mercy and all that, Mr. McMorrow."

"Is that why you called me upstairs?"

She smiled, eyes only.

"I may owe you an apology," Tippy said. "Tammy, you carry her."

Tammy picked up the cage and the cat started a bleating mew of panic.

"It's okay, honey," Tammy said.

Tippy hit the button and the door hissed open.

"We have to go up and then down," she told Tammy. They stepped into the elevator.

"Hey, but where's Rocky?" I said.

The door started to close and I blocked it and it opened.

"Hobo Hotel," Tammy said. "You know where that is?"

"No. Never heard of it."

"Down at the bridges."

The door started to close again, and, again, I blocked it.

"Right by the river?"

"Yeah," Tammy said. "Yeah, like you fall off you land in the water. They're partying."

"Rocky?"

"I don't know. That's where Crow Man said they were going."

The door again. I held it and waited and it opened.

"Who's Crow Man?"

"Just this guy."

"You weren't going?"

"Frig that," Tammy said, as Tippy shook her head in dismay behind her. "I ain't gonna cook my brains. It's a guy thing, you know what I'm saying?"

"But Rocky? Would he—"

"Maybe he'd just, like, hang on the fringes. But not too close I hope 'cause it's a long way down. This kid fell last summer. He busted his legs and got all cut 'cause there's metal and junk under the water."

"Yeah, well," I began, then paused.

I wanted to tell Tammy not to screw this up. I wanted to tell Tippy to watch herself. But instead I just looked at them: Tippy in her parka, Tammy in her Technicolor hair, and the cat crouched in the cage.

"So how many cats you got?" Tammy was asking as the door rolled shut.

"At the moment, twenty-two," Tippy said.

"That's a lot of poop," Tammy said, and then the door was shut and the elevator was on its way. Like a lot of things I'd started, this was out of my hands.

CHAPTER 26

The streets of the old downtown were white, like snow-covered frozen canals, and I rolled the truck quietly down the hill to Washington Street, and turned left toward the river and the Penobscot Bridge, and the railroad bridge just beyond it. It was a little before midnight and the downtown was quiet. The Penobscot Bridge was lighted, but dimly in the falling snow. The railroad bridge was marked by a couple of faint red beacons. All else was blackness.

I rolled the truck to the side of Washington Street and stopped, then pulled into the parking lot of an office building. Lights showed through the snow from across the river, which was otherwise lost to the darkness. I peered out for a moment, then fished a flashlight from the glovebox and swung out of the truck.

The parking lot ended in a retaining wall, followed by a five-foot drop to the rubble and railroad tracks below. I flicked the light down over the wall and saw trash and shopping carts and a refrigerator and unidentifiable pieces of metal, piled up like buffalo driven over a cliff.

I stopped. Listened.

The snow seemed to rustle as it fell, like falling bits of paper. From the direction of the river, I heard glass break. I tried to fix the direction but only heard the snow and a distant car horn. Taking another look down, I turned the light off, climbed to the top of the wall and, turning around, eased myself down.

I dropped the last couple of feet onto the refrigerator, then half jumped, half stumbled, off the refrigerator, off a tangle of metal and onto the ground.

Froze. Listened.

Heard the murmur of the snow.

Picking myself up, I clicked the flashlight. It worked and I clicked it off and started toward the river. The tracks were black lines, four sets of them, and I stepped from rail to rail, silently.

But did I want to surprise anyone? Or did I want to announce my presence? I didn't want to spook them; I just wanted to talk to Rocky.

The railroad bridge was upriver, to my left. The highway bridge was to my right. In the darkness, I could make out boxcars, a crane on a truck, some sort of tugboat heeled over on the bank. I listened again, then walked toward the abutment under the railroad bridge. The light played on the snow, and there were beer cartons, a vodka bottle, and footprints, but they were filled in with fresh snow.

I turned back and walked slowly along the rails, peering at the black shape of the highway bridge. A car passed overhead, and the joints in the bridge rattled and clanged. I played the light over the riverbank, through the fringe of scrubby birches and alders. Tammy had said they might fall in the river, but where would they be? On the ice? Behind the abutments? I walked slowly, making no sound in the snow.

And then I heard voices.

I looked up and saw a flare of orange light, a flicker of flame.

They were on top of the first abutment in the river, in the space between the granite and the metal beams of the bridge. I listened. Heard a soft whoop, laughter. I walked closer, heard someone talking. The light of the flame dimmed, then flared again. I stood on the riverbank and looked out.

There were tracks that led down the bank to a rusty metal pipe, about a foot in diameter. They'd crossed the pipe, six feet above the ice. I peered into the dark, then gave a quick stab with the light.

On the side of the abutment were iron rungs, implanted in the granite. The kids had crossed the pipe and climbed the rungs, twenty feet up to the top of the graffiti-spattered abutment. Their den was hidden from view, sheltered from the snow. Hobo Hotel, with its scenic view of the mighty Penobscot River, was a four-season resort.

I stood for a moment. The light of their fire flickered again. I called.

"Hey, Rocky."

My voice was driven back by the snow. I called again, louder.

"Hey, Rocky. It's Jack."

The firelight dimmed. I heard voices from atop the granite. I played the light on the the top of the abutment.

"Hey, Rocky. It's Jack McMorrow. I need to—"

Faces appeared at the edge of the stone shelf, like owls peering from a nest. First two, then two more. Baseball hats. Knit caps. One guy older than the rest. Then a fifth face, pale in the flashlight. Rocky.

"Hey, Rocky," I called. "Tammy told me where to find you. We need to talk for a minute."

They squinted at the flashlight, and I started to shine it away, but then noticed something seemed odd about them. I left the light on them and looked closer.

There was silver above their lips, like metallic milk mustaches. I played the light down the row, which looked like a casting call for Tin Woodsmen. All of them had it, except the older guy, who looked like he was in his twenties and had a real mustache. The kids in the knit caps had the spray-paint version. Rocky, too.

Rocky had been huffing.

"It's your pepé," the older guy said.

"It's a cop. Don't shoot me," another kid cackled.

"Faster than a speeding bullet," another kid, one in a knit hat, said. And then he gave this strange, sing-song laugh.

Rocky stared at me and said nothing.

"Rocky, you okay?" I said.

He smiled weakly.

"You his daddy?" The older guy said. "Come to read you a bedtime story, Twig."

"What's he been doing?" I said.

"Getting the old chrome mustache," the older guy said. "These kids are little paint junkies."

"Is he all right?" I said.

"He's fine. You a cop or what, 'cause if you ain't, how 'bout running down the store and getting me a goddamn bottle? I'll pay you."

"You don't got no friggin' money left," the kid squatting next to him said.

"This dude's got cash. I can tell. Oh, yeah, the man can tell who's got dinero. He's looking for Twig. What do you think he's gonna pay Twig for?"

He grinned, and it was a lecherous drunken leer.

"Twig. Earn us some cash, you little whore. I have another drink, I might do you myself, you little girl."

The others grinned with their painted mouths. Rocky stood suddenly, then staggered, whirling his arms to get his balance.

"Look out," I shouted, scrambling down the bank.

"He's gonna fly," the older guy called out.

Nobody moved to help him, but Rocky regained his balance himself and dropped to his knees, the vacant grin still on his face.

"Hey, Twig, do another bag," the older guy said. "You ain't high enough to fly."

"Leave him alone," I said.

"Hey, I'll leave him alone. I'll go and have another drink and then we'll sell Twig to the highest bidder. First case of Bud takes him. Make that two cases. And some wood. We need some wood up here. This is Maine. Goddamn place is full of trees and we got no wood? What the hell? I mean, what the hell?"

The last of it was a bellow that echoed metallically under the bridge. "Crow Man," one of the kids said. "You're baked."

The older guy staggered out of sight, and one by one, the kids followed. Rocky went last.

I stood looking up at the edge of the abutment for a moment. Waited. Looked down again and started across.

CHAPTER 27

I took one step, started to slip, and backed off. The pipe was bare at the very top, but icy if you wavered from that two-inch line. Below, the ice was white, then pale gray, then, closer to the abutment, greenish and soft, with the current showing through it.

Fall there and you might not come back up, at least not where you went through. And Rocky was supposed to negotiate this with a head full of paint fumes?

I held my arms out for balance, and then, like a tight-rope walker, made a feint, with the flashlight beam stabbing in front of me. Paused. Plunged.

One, two, three, four steps. A slip. A crouch. Back on the pipe, and onto the abutment, scrabbling up on my knees, the flashlight in my hand. It went out. I shook it and tried the switch. It came back on. Above me, someone shouted an obscenity.

The rungs were iron, the color of dark chocolate, cold even through my gloves. I looked up once, then clicked the light off and started to climb. Ten careful steps, then my head poked over the edge. I reached out and felt broken glass, a crushed can. Beyond a concrete pillar there were shadowy figures in the light of a fire. The sweet smell of paint hung in the air.

I hoisted myself over the edge and got up off my elbows and knees. They were talking and I heard the rattle of a paint can being shaken.

"You don't shake it, you idiot," a voice said.

"I can if I want," someone else said.

I approached slowly and stepped around the pillar.

One kid was crouched by a pile of burning trash, stirring it with a stick. Another kid, one with a baseball hat, was spraying paint into a plastic bag filled with what looked like wadded paper or rags. He dropped the can onto the concrete and jammed the bag over his mouth.

God, I thought. Was this Bangor or Brazil?

The kid inhaled. I put the light on him and he turned toward it and stared, hat on backward, the bag still on his face, more befuddled than surprised.

"Off to Planet Metallica, dude," the older guy said, his voice coming from the darkness to my left.

I put the light on him. He was leaning against the concrete wall, and he gave me a half-toothed grin. Peter Pan and his very Lost Boys.

"Thought you was going to get me a drink," he said.

"Yeah, right. Where's Rocky?"

"No, you said you'd get me a drink," the older guy slurred. "A man oughta keep his word, unless he's a goddamn lying son of a whore."

I ignored him, swept the light over the kids next to the fire, then beyond it. There he was, leaning on the other side, his mouth half open, his head lolling.

"Rocky, let's go," I said.

He gave me an absent smile.

"Where's my drink?" came the voice behind me.

I stepped over one kid, crouched in a litter of bags and paint cans and paper towels, then kicked a can. It skittered,

ringing on the granite. I went to Rocky and lifted him to
his feet. With one arm around his shoulders I started to lead
him across the stone platform.

Glass broke. I put the light on the older guy, saw the
broken bottle in his hand. His hand was bare. The bottle
was clear. Miller Genuine Draft. He held it in front of him
like a knife and moved unsteadily toward me, the grin fixed
on his face.

"I don't think I like you," he said.

"I'm all broken up," I said.

I stopped, Rocky beside me.

"Cut him, Crow Man," one of the crouching kids said,
but none of them moved.

"You got money," Crow Man said. "Gimme your money."

"Get lost," I said, "you worthless piece of human garbage."

The grin vanished. I swallowed. Still, no one else moved.
I got between Rocky and Crow Man and started to ease my
way toward the opening and the ladder, shuffling in half
steps.

"I'm talking to you," the drunk said.

I didn't answer.

"Hey, I'm talking to you," he said again. "Gimme all
your money and I'll let you go."

I moved a step. He half staggered to his right, to cut me
off. The bottle wavered in the air in front of him. He was
five feet away, then closer.

A feint with the bottle. I stopped. Kept the light in his
face. He grinned again, two spaces for every brown tooth. I
thought of my tooth. Maybe I would see a dentist.

"Never flossed, did you," I said.

"I'm gonna cut your balls off," he said.

To my right and behind me, someone stirred. It was time
to get moving.

"Another time," I said. "I'm leaving and he is, too. We'll leave and you can get back to the party."

"With what? I ain't got no money."

I shrugged.

"Not my problem."

"I'm gonna make it your problem, dude. Gonna make it a problem like you never seen. I don't like you."

"You said that."

"I'm gonna say it again. I don't—"

It was half lunge, half stagger, but the bottle was in my face. I grabbed his arm and forced it down, and then the bottle was in my gut against the leather of my jacket. I could smell his foul alcoholic breath, his bristly face brushing mine, his hand on my shoulder, the bottle hand jerking, trying to get loose.

It did, but I grabbed his wrist again, the bottle sticking up between us.

"Get him," Crow Man called, but the kids just watched, like it was a movie with subtitles in a language they didn't understand.

"Rocky, go," I said.

He moved between the posts and out of sight, while we staggered like sumo wrestlers. I kept my eyes on the bottle, the jagged points of glass, and both hands clamped on his wrist, the flashlight caught in the grip. Our feet ground in the trash, and a can got underfoot and I stepped on it and almost tripped, but hung on to the wrist and swung him around and pushed, while he had momentum, toward the edge of the abutment. One step, another step, close now, close to shoving him right off and down onto the ice, and he'd be dead, the stinking piece of crap, he'd be—

I eased off. I couldn't kill him, but he could kill me, and he pushed back toward me, straining to get his wrist loose, scratching at my face with his other hand. And then we were tripping over the kids, and they were saying, "Hey," and shoving back. He stepped on one and the kid said, "Ow," and Crow Man staggered and I took one hand off of his wrist, slammed him in the face with the flashlight. That jolted him and I dropped the light and got him by both arms and drove him back until he caught a foot on the kid by the fire, and fell flat on his back.

The bottle smashed. The fire sparked and crackled. For a moment, I thought of just leaving him, but then remembered the ladder. I'd have to get Rocky down and across the pipe. I needed time.

I kicked Crow Man while he was on the ground, once in the thigh, once in the gut, the third time in the groin. He said, "Oooh" when I hit the groin, and he writhed in the smoking ashes.

"Awesome," one of the kids said.

I leapt over that kid, and trotted in a crouch through the opening. Rocky was standing near the ladder, too close to the edge, and I took his shoulders and moved him back. Then I turned and eased my way over the lip and found the top rung with the toe of my boot. I stretched out until I caught his ankle, and pulled him toward me. He came passively, and I turned him, then told him to kneel. I had to tell him twice.

"Okay," he said, and he did it.

"Where is he?" I heard Crow Man shout.

"Come on," I said. "Now toward me."

Rocky shuffled back on his knees, but slowly.

"Hurry up," I said.

"I'm gonna friggin' kill him," Crow Man screamed.

I took Rocky's right ankle and drew it over the edge, and then eased my way down, stabbing for the rung in the dark.

With one hand on the top rung, I took his foot with the other and pulled him to the first rung. When that foot was planted, I took the other and pulled it down, too.

Rocky started to fall back.

"No," I said, wrapping my free arm around his ankles. He swayed like a tree.

"Back," I said.

I forced him against the granite with my shoulder.

"You let him go, you pussies," Crow Man was shouting. "I oughta kill all of you. If he's gone, you're dead."

With Rocky's legs pinned to the wall, I began the slow descent. Pressing against him, I let go of one rung and grabbed for another. With each grab there was a moment when we both wavered. We wavered again, my shoulder pinned to the back of Rocky's legs, as his feet scuffed the stone, searched for the ladder.

Scuffed. Probed. Swayed above me in the dark, as my face pressed against his thin buttocks.

Three steps down. How many did that leave? And then the pipe. I'd have to carry him.

I grabbed for a rung. Searched with my boot for another. Rocky's foot slipped, and he was half-sitting on my shoulder.

"Hold on, will you?" I snarled.

"Assholes," came the shout from above.

Something hit me in the shoulder. I heard Rocky cry out, then something hit me in the head. A piece of ice. Then another. Then a can that missed and clanged on the granite below me.

"You mother, you're dead meat," Crow Man bellowed.

I pressed my face against Rocky, as more stuff rained down. That was fine. As long as he was throwing things, he wasn't following. But then the rain stopped.

"Son of a bitch," I heard, but more muffled, and I glanced

up to see him sliding over the edge. One rung, then another. I grabbed for the rungs. Told Rocky to hurry, but he still wavered in place.

Like Jack fleeing down the beanstalk, I held tight to my goose and continued down. And then Crow Man reached Rocky and kicked for his head. I dropped a rung and he missed, and said, "Shit," and almost fell.

I pressed for another rung and scuffed the concrete. Crow Man kicked again and connected, and Rocky cried out. "Ooohh," and I was on the abutment. Should I stop and put this guy over the edge? Would he pull me in the river with him?

No. I swung Rocky off the last rung and over my shoulder, pausing at the edge to shift him higher on my shoulder. Behind me, I heard Crow Man's feet hit the concrete.

Off the ledge, on to the pipe. One step. Two. My legs straining under the weight, pressing to stay on center. Three steps. Four. Five, then six. My leg slipped and my knee slammed the metal, and the pain jolted right up to my hip, and I pitched forward and Rocky tumbled off my shoulder.

Onto the snow.

I rolled off the pipe, and dropped a foot to the riverbank, scrambling to my hands and knees. Looking back, I saw Crow Man leap from the abutment to the pipe, take two steps and stumble and fall. He grunted and hugged the pipe, lying on it, his legs pumping to get himself back up. I got to my feet, rushing forward, and took Rocky by the red plaid jacket and hauled him, still on his knees, up the bank. The snow and ice smashed beneath us, and branches snapped. One lashed my face, and then we were in the open, across the railroad tracks, and Rocky was loping along as I dragged him.

At the retaining wall, I looked back and saw Crow Man cresting the bank, persistent for a drunk. I clambered up the pile of junk, pulling Rocky up after me. His foot fell in, and he said, "I think my shoe's caught," but I took him by the armpits and yanked him out. At the top of the heap, he reached up for the lip of the wall, then hesitated. I stood on a shopping cart, and took him by the arm and the buttock and heaved him up, then pushed him over. He rolled. I vaulted up. Crow Man was starting up the pile, but he fell and there was a clang and he cursed and I knew that in the tangle of metal, he'd met his match

CHAPTER 28

"*You need to* choose your friends more carefully," I said.

"Don't have any," Rocky said.

His voice was slurred. He was slouched against the door of the truck, his skinny legs pressed together. I drove up Exchange Street, away from the river, to the safety of downtown traffic and people who wouldn't kill for a bottle of vodka. At State Street, we turned right, following a single pair of tire tracks in the fresh snow. Rocky's mouth gleamed in the light.

"Have you done that before?" I said.

He shook his head.

"You shouldn't do it again. It can kill you. Even if it doesn't, it kills big chunks of brain cells. I interviewed a kid once who had reduced his IQ by twenty points. And he didn't have a lot to begin with."

Rocky looked out the window. Pushed his glasses up on his nose. I stopped for the light at Broadway. The wipers made angel wings in the snow.

"I only did it once. Some kids kept doing it. I feel a little better now."

"Why did you?"

He shrugged.

"Because you don't get along with your stepfather? That's pretty stupid."

He smiled at the glass.

"It doesn't matter."

"What doesn't matter?"

"It."

"What's it?"

"It's it. It's everything."

"Everything doesn't matter?"

Rocky gave a short, high-pitched chuckle, and smiled. The paint on his mouth made him look like a clown.

"You may think this is funny, but to me it's getting to be a royal pain, you know that? You know I have a DHS worker asking what my interest is in you?"

"Interest," Rocky said. He seemed to be considering the word.

"Right," I said. "Interest. As in unhealthy interest. Like Crow Man back there was talking about."

He didn't say anything.

"So you know what would be a good idea? For you to talk to this DHS lady and tell her exactly what I did. Saved you from getting your butt kicked in Portland. Let you stay for part of the night at my house, after you showed up uninvited. That's it."

"Thanks," Rocky said. "It was cold. That truck almost ran me right over. I said, 'This is not good. This is not good.'"

"But they didn't hit you?"

"It was like, 'Look out!'"

He made a sound like tires screeching.

"And then they gave you a ride?"

"Country western."

"What?"

"Country western. All the way. Country western."

The light turned, and I turned left onto West Broadway. It was after midnight and most of the big houses were dark. One was lighted, a big old mansard-roofed place.

"Palatial," Rocky said, his head turning as we passed.

"Yeah, this is where the rich people used to live. There's a few of them left. You like old houses?"

"Mmmm."

"You like your house?"

Rocky sagged, then frowned. He took his glasses off and peered at them, then put them back on.

"Why don't you go home?"

His frown deepened. He took the glasses off again. Above the silver mouth was a red spot where the nosepiece rested.

"Can't," he said softly, as much to himself as to me. "Never, ever. Never, ever."

"Why not? You know your mother's very worried about you?"

He turned to me for the first time since he'd gotten in the car.

"I saw her," I said. "I told her I'd seen you. I didn't know you hadn't been hit by that truck. That's what the police thought. They thought it hit you and the people picked you up and drove away with you and tossed you in the woods or something."

"No," Rocky said.

"That's what your mother thinks, Rocky. Don't you think you should at least call her? Let her know you're okay?"

He turned away.

"Can't."

"Why not?"

"Just can't."

"You afraid of your stepfather? What, does the guy beat you up or something?"

Rocky didn't answer for a moment, but I could feel something coming, so I waited.

"He doesn't even like me," he said.

He said it as though it were worse than a beating. I looked at him, a skinny little kid in Rusty's long shadow.

"Your mom's good to you, isn't she?"

"My mom's awesome."

"So why don't you go home? Your mother's frantic. She misses you, Rocky. She's worried about you."

He was turned to the window. I downshifted and slowed the truck, and turned to look toward him.

"So what is it?" I asked.

He still was turned away, but I could see his jaws working, then his hand wiping his face. It came away wet. Rocky was crying.

"Well?"

He shook his head resolutely.

"And what's this kitty stuff?"

Rocky jerked around and leaned toward me. Silver mouth. Reddened eyes. Glasses fogged.

"Don't talk about that," he snapped.

"About what?"

"I can't talk about that. Never, ever."

"Then why did you write it down?"

"I didn't."

"I saw the paper. You left it in your pants. In my bath-room."

"I didn't," Rocky insisted.

I dug in my pocket and took out the folded piece of pa-per. Rocky's hand shot out and he grabbed the paper. I thought he might eat it but he stuffed it in his pocket.

"Who or what is kitty? Is it Katia?"

"I never heard of any kitty."

"You know that's not true. Why can't you talk about it?"

"Because she—"

He stopped.

"Because she what?"

Rocky paused, as though confused.

"I didn't. I can't."

"What? What is it?"

His eyes were still vague, but the words came through clenched teeth.

"Because she's my mom."

"Who is? This kitty? What do you mean?"

But he wouldn't say anything else, so we turned into the drive of Tippy's big old manse, stopped by the side of the house—headlights on, motor running, staring straight ahead. A dog barked and then others took up the chorus. There were lights on in one of the gable-ended dormers in the ell and in the second floor of the main house. We waited.

"What's this place?" Rocky said finally.

"I know the lady who lives here. Tammy's here, I think. You know Tammy?"

He nodded.

"You like her?"

Another nod.

"Would you rather stay here than the shelter?"

"I'm not going to that shelter. Crow Man'll tell those guys to kill me."

"Then it's decided, if she'll take you. Her name is Miss Danforth. She takes care of stray animals and Tammy's here to help with them. At least that's the plan for tonight. You like animals?"

"They're okay."

"Act like they're more than okay," I said. "This'll be a safe place for you tonight. Tomorrow you can talk to the DHS person and then we'll be even."

Rocky didn't answer. Lights came on over the back door. It opened and Tippy emerged. She was wearing boots and her parka over a bathrobe and bare white legs. I got out of the truck, but left the door open and the motor running. Rocky squinted in the glare of the dome light.

"Sorry to bother you," I said.

"What's the matter?" Tippy said.

She peered into the truck.

"Who's he?"

"He's a friend of Tammy's," I said. "Rocky, this is Miss Danforth. Miss Danforth, this is Rocky. Rocky is the one that the state person was asking about today."

"Hello there," Tippy said.

"Hi," Rocky said.

Tippy leaned past the open truck door and stared at his silver mouth.

"What's this? Some sort of theater thing?"

I looked at Rocky. He scowled and looked away.

"It's paint," I said.

"They're painting their faces now?"

I paused, not sure how to explain.

"Sort of," I said. "They spray paint in a bag and inhale the fumes."

Tippy looked incredulous.

"Why?"

"Because there's nothing on TV."

"What?"

"I don't know, they do it to escape. They're too young to buy beer."

"That's barbaric," Tippy said.

"In some circles," I said. "Rocky just tried it once, just enough to get it on him. I think he's okay now."

"But he needs a place to stay?"

"He doesn't want to—"

"Isn't he able to speak?" Tippy interrupted. The paint thing had thrown her off but now she was taking charge.

"You all right, son?" she said, leaning into the truck cab. Her robe hiked up and I could see the broken blood vessels behind her knees.

Rocky replied but spoke so softly that I couldn't hear him over the dogs, who had settled into a rhythmic baying, like hounds trailing a fugitive. Tippy asked him if he'd like something to eat, and he said, "No, thank you." She asked him if he wanted something to drink, and he said, "Yeah. I mean, yes. Please."

"Well, come in then."

She eased backward out of the truck and turned to me. There was snow in her hair. The truck exhaust rose in a cloud around her, but she didn't appear to notice.

"He can't go to some sort of shelter, Mr. McMorrow?"

"I'm afraid he might be beaten up. We just had a bit of a run-in with some other kids and an older guy. They'll be looking for him."

"What about his home?"

"He won't go there. I'm not sure why."

Tippy watched as Rocky swung out and came around to the front of the truck. He stood there, ten feet away, looking toward the carriage house, where the dogs had picked up the pace.

"I thought you did mostly cats," I said.

"I don't turn anything away," she said. "I have a goat right now—don't tell the neighbors."

"And two kids?" I said.

"He can stay tonight, but this can't get out of hand."

"It won't. I'll call you in the morning. I couldn't just turn him loose. It's cold and it's snowing and he doesn't even have gloves or—"

Tippy held up her hand to stop me.

"You're preaching to the choir, Mr. McMorrow. But tell me, with this paint thing, is he dangerous?"

"No," I said. "He's a nice kid, I think. But if you're worried, I can take him someplace else. With all this DHS stuff, I didn't think it would be right to bring him home with me."

"Probably not."

"And you already had Tammy, and I think she sort of looks out for him. How's she worked out?"

"Fine. Swears like a sailor but good with the animals. She's in the shower now. Been in there for a half hour, but that's okay."

"He's okay, too. Not as tough as her. He's just sort of—"

"Lost," Tippy said, and that was enough for her.

"Let's go in," she called to Rocky. "I don't suppose you have any luggage."

He hesitantly started for the door. She turned back to me.

"I'll call in the morning," I said. "I'm off tomorrow. I'll come back up if I have to."

"Before nine. I've got a busy day, Mr. McMorrow."

I turned to the truck, then back to Tippy.

"You know, you can ask him. About this DHS thing. Whether I ever—"

But she was moving away, another stray to be tended, another lost creature with a mysterious and unknown past.

I hadn't been fed, or watered, for that matter, but I didn't stop. I drove through the city's dark streets to the highway and then slowly south, in the one lane that had been traveled. Just south of Bangor, I fell in behind a tractor trailer and the rest of the highway portion of the trip was spent in the swirling, white maelstrom of the truck's backwash.

My hands clenched the steering wheel, and my mind wheeled through the day's events. Rusty and Flossie. Crow Man and Tippy. Rocky and Tammy. Kitty and Katia? What was it that Rocky wouldn't speak of? If he loved his mother, if he was close to her, why wouldn't he want to see her? What was keeping him away? What, as I'd tried to quiz him, had kept his mouth clamped shut?

Don't talk about that. Never, ever.

Talking about "that" was worse than a beating. Worse than being cold and hungry. Worse than paint fumes burning your virgin lungs. Worse than Crow Man, his dirty mind and foul breath. Worse than sleeping in a strange woman's house.

The snow swirled. My mind played it all, again and again.

In Hampden, I tried calling home, but the line was busy. That was good because it meant Roxanne was there, talking to someone. God, I'd barely thought of her all night, but then again, I'd been busy, hadn't I?

I called every five or ten minutes, down the interstate,

across to the meandering ridge-top route that took me over the hills to home. The phone was busy? What if something had happened to her? What if something was wrong with the baby? What kind of father didn't think of his wife?

In Dixmont, I pulled to the side of the road and set the front hubs of the truck to better track through the ruts in the snow. Before getting underway again, I called again. Still busy. I was forty minutes from home. It was twelve-forty in the morning. I considered calling Clair, but he'd be sound asleep, resting up for his five A.M. reveille. Maybe Roxanne was just chatting. Maybe she'd called one of her friends out West. Her old skiing crew loved to gab, and it was before eleven in Jackson Hole or Park City. Maybe I was getting jumpy for nothing.

The truck caught in a rut, and pulled to the right and jolted me back. I said, "Jeez," and pulled it back into the two-track lane, and continued on, peering into the meteor storm of snow. If I could have willed myself home, beamed myself home, I would have. Something was wrong.

On the outskirts of the little town of Unity, the ruts gave way to plowed road and the yellow blips of a plow truck's strobe lights showed in the distance. I sped up and overtook the truck as it reached the town center. The strobe lights reflected off the snow like fireworks, and the truck lumbered along like a dazzling Mardi Gras float, down the deserted main street, sparks cascading as the plow blade scraped the pavement.

Oh, the strange things you see.

And I followed the truck south, out of town, where the fields and farmhouses were lost to the snow. The flakes were bigger now, and slower. They flew at the windshield like bugs, piling up beyond the reach of the wipers. The plow had slowed moving up a long grade, and I eased my way into the other lane and gave the accelerator a testing tap. The snow was two or three inches deep, and the truck wove from side to side as the tires grabbed. The plow truck roared, lights flashing, and I fell back into my lane and cursed. At the crest of the hill, I slid the truck out again and blasted by the plow into the white-flecked darkness.

Roxanne.

Coming into the farm town of Albion, I almost went off the road, the truck starting to go sideways, then grabbing again on the shoulder on the opposite side. I yanked it back onto the roadway, then grimly started off again, sliding around the corner onto the road to the little hamlet of Freedom, beyond which was my hamlet, Prosperity. The fat snowflakes were giving way to sleet, and I drove grimly and gingerly, forty, forty-five, then eased off as the rear end of the truck started to break loose.

There were no other cars, no headlights but mine, no lights at all. The road twisted like a chute between walls of spruce. I was riveted to the few square feet illuminated by the lights, to the road flowing toward me like a rushing river. Miles passed, and I was deeper into the Waldo County hollows when I had an odd premonition. Roxanne was sick. It was something very grave. It was about the baby. She would put her hand on mine to calm me as she gave me the news.

And then there was my turn, the road sign flashing past, and I braked and the truck skidded, coming to a shuddering halt fifty yards up the road.

I backed it up. Turned off. Down the paved road, then off onto the snowbanked path through the woods, where a single set of tire tracks led the way. Past the big oaks, past the college girls' house, and scrabbling deeper into the woods, and then home.

The lights were on. Roxanne's car was in the dooryard. Her footprints led from the car to the house. I parked and got out, heard the gritty sleet pelting the truck hood as I hurried in.

Opened the unlocked door that I'd told Roxanne to lock. Closed the door behind me, and turned the key. The bolt slid across.

I listened.

The house was silent. The woodstove ticked. The refrigerator hummed. The lights were on by the big chairs, but Roxanne wasn't there. There was a light on in the loft, too, but I didn't call to her.

My jacket still on, boots still snowy, I crossed to the stairs and quietly started up.

Her jeans were on the chair, her underpants and socks on the floor. I stepped toward the bed, and at first I couldn't see her at all, then I saw a swatch of dark hair. She was on top of the bed, covered by the down comforter. There were magazines strewn on the bed beside her, one near her head. Travel magazines. One was open to a story about "Classic Castile." I slid the magazine away from her, and leaned down close to her to hear the always-reassuring sound of her breathing.

Peering at her, I hovered there. Her breathing faltered and caught. Was she sick? I reached down and put my hand gently on her forehead.

Her eyes opened and she turned.

"You okay?" I said.

Roxanne smiled.

"I think so," she murmured.

Again, not the right answer.

"What's the matter?" I said.

She didn't answer, and in that moment, my mind raced. My panic must have shown, because Roxanne smiled sleepily and slipped an arm from beneath the comforter and took my hand in hers. She squeezed, then held on tightly. Without letting go, she shifted and turned toward me.

It was coming true. She had the same soft smile, but her eyes were filling with tears.

Oh, no.

Roxanne squeezed my hand tighter, reached out and touched my cheek. A tear slipped from her eye, and left a silver trail on her skin. All these silvery faces.

"What?" I said.

"Jack," Roxanne said. "We'll be good parents, won't we?"

I sat on the edge of the bed and we talked. Roxanne said she'd been on the phone, a page from work but the issue had been resolved. We talked about how most parents start out with good intentions but still things get screwed up. And then their kids ended up in her hands. I said our child would already have her so she or he would be all set.

"But those kids in the alley. They all had parents who thought everything was all set. That little guy, Rocky, I'll bet his parents always thought they were doing the right thing for him."

"Maybe," I said. "Maybe not."

"What do you mean?"

I leaned on one elbow beside her and told her the story, as much of it as I knew. When I was finished, Roxanne said, "I wonder if Rocky saw this guy abusing his mother?"

"Then why would he leave her alone?"

"Maybe they fight about him, how to treat him, discipline issues. So Rocky takes off to keep them from having these disagreements."

"That could be, but who's Kitty? And this date from a long time ago."

"I don't know," Roxanne said.

"I don't know, either."

"But you're going to try to find out."

"The kid needs some help," I said.

"Be careful, Jack," Roxanne said. "You have another kid to worry about."

"When it rains it pours," I said.

"Tell me about it," she said, and she sighed and gave my hand a good-night squeeze.

CHAPTER 29

The house was quiet. I stirred the coals and put wood in the stove, then went to the refrigerator and peered in. There was Ballantine ale and Murphy's stout. I took out a Ballantine and opened it. Turning out the light, I stood by the stove and lifted the bottle into the air.

"Here's to you, my son, my daughter," I said. "May the roads rise to meet you and the wind be always at your back."

I drank some of the stout and went to the big window and looked out at the woods. The sleet had mixed with rain, and the snow was flopping off the branches like something treed and shot. I watched it absently, and sipped the ale, and then the questions began to come at me, like snow in my headlights.

What kind of father resented his son? A Rusty Clement

kind of father. And that kind of father produced a Rocky kind of kid, wandering the streets like a spooked dog.

"Never," I said aloud. "Never, ever."

But things were going to change in this life I'd carved out for myself, carved out like a cave in these dark woods. Another witness to my life, another person looking to me for answers. Funny, I was much better at questions. Maybe my kid would be a questioner, too.

Daddy, why don't you have a regular job? Daddy, how come we have two houses, one in the woods and one in the city? Daddy, what happened to your little toe? Daddy, how'd you get that big scar on your face? Daddy, is your tooth going to fall out? Daddy, who's that big kid sleeping on our couch? Daddy, why do we have a rifle? Daddy, there's somebody on the phone who says you're dead meat. What does that mean?

The stakes suddenly had been raised.

I stood there for two ales, my mind whirling. Diapers and poop. Little swings and seats with wheels and plastic things kids chew on. Peek-a-boo and lullabies, and baseball and walks. A stroller and people leaning over it saying, "My, how she's grown." Three of us in the car instead of two. A car seat. A bigger truck. A van?

I prayed it would go well.

Well, Clair and Mary did it with their two girls, all grown now with kids of their own. People did it all the time. Even Rusty and Flossie Clement did it, after a fashion. And Rocky hadn't turned out bad at all, really. A little confused. A little frightened. And that had been only lately. Maybe he'd come out of it.

I wondered how Rocky was doing at Tippy's house, her home for wayward mammals of all kinds. He'd be with Tammy, but she was a different type: hardened and emotionally calloused, hurt so deeply for so long that she didn't feel anymore. For all her exuberance, she was a cold, calculating kid. Why had she gone with Tippy? She could smell a warm bed and meal a mile away.

Rocky wasn't like that. He didn't have that feral survival instinct, and I still wondered what had driven him out. Rusty didn't even like him, Rocky had said. He'd said it like it hurt, but could it hurt enough to drive him into the streets? To leave his mom behind, all alone with Mister Macho?

I finished the last swallow of ale and put the bottle on the counter. In the morning, Roxanne would be up early, and I wanted to be up with her so we could talk some more. Or I could just look at her and wonder. Boy? Girl? Her eyes or mine?

I put two big chunks of maple in the stove and closed the damper. The stovepipe ticked and the firelight faded to an orange glow. The rain and sleet made a hissing sound on the roof. I climbed the stairs and the hiss was louder, but when I stood still and listened closely I could hear Roxanne's soft breathing. I slid under the sheets, moved over to be closer to her. In her sleep, she nestled into me. I put my arm around her and didn't let go.

Clair was building something, hammering timbers into a frame. I was telling him I wasn't sure it was a good idea, building it so far from the house, because it was a baby and if it cried at night, you'd have to put on your jacket and boots to go get it.

"They have to be isolated because of disease," he said, and he kept pounding away with a big framing hammer. Bam, bam, bam.

I slowly opened my eyes. Light filled the room and the sky was blue through the skylight. The hammering continued.

"What's that?" Roxanne said.

I tried to focus.

"Somebody's at the door, Jack," she said.

"They're knocking it down," I rasped.

I rolled out of the bed and found my jeans on the floor and, hopping on one foot, pulled them on. Roxanne pulled the comforter around her and I looked at the clock. It was five after eight. I started down the stairs.

"Hold on, for god's sake," I called.

I twisted the bolt. Fumbled with the latch. If this was some goddamned religious nut, I was going to . . .

I yanked the door open. Squinted into the glare.

"What the hell do you—"

"Mr. McMorrow."

It was Divan, the deputy. Standing beside her was a guy wearing a tie and brown sportscoat. The tie was blue with little red pistols all over it. Divan's cruiser was in the yard. The guy's car was behind it. It was blue and unmarked, cop written all over it.

"What's the matter?" I said.

"Mr. McMorrow, this is Detective Cobb of the Maine State Police."

"What's the matter?"

"Could we come in, sir?" the detective said.

"Sure. But what is it? What's the problem?"

I backed away from the doorway and they followed me. Barefoot, I moved toward the front of the room and paused.

"What is it? Is it Rocky?"

"Do you mind if we sit down and talk, sir?" Cobb said.

"No," I said. "Of course not."

I showed them to the dining table. The detective was my size but chunky. A round face and a bald spot like an underdone pancake stuck to the back of his head. He glanced out the big window.

"Pretty woods," he said. "Lotta deer?"

"Some," I said. "You hunt?"

"No," he said. "I see enough, you know what I mean?"

I didn't offer a reply and he didn't seem to expect one. He looked around more and unzipped his parka. I said I'd be right back and went to the bathroom behind the stairs and washed my face and brushed my teeth. As I opened the door, I heard the stairs creak above me. Divan and the detective were looking up. Roxanne was coming down.

"Hello," I heard her say.

"Hi, there," the detective said. "Sorry to bother you, but we just needed to have a word with your husband."

"Oh," Roxanne said. "Is everything okay?"

They didn't answer. She came down the stairs and introduced herself. The detective nodded, then awkwardly shook Roxanne's hand.

"Would you like coffee?" she said.

"Sure," the detective said.

Roxanne turned back toward the kitchen and met me. She was wearing jeans and one of my flannel shirts. She took both of my hands in hers and squeezed them.

"I'll be right out," she said. "Or do you need me to leave?"

"No," I said. "Stay."

Roxanne went into the bathroom and closed the door. I went to the table.

"Sit down, officers," I said.

They did. The detective put a small black tape recorder on the table in front of him. His hair was thin and fuzzy but his forearms were taut and muscular, the arms of a guy who did something other than ride around in a car and ask questions.

"Mr. McMorrow, Deputy Divan here told me about her last call here. The one where the boy was here but then he ran away? Is that right?"

"Yeah. Rocky. But is he okay?"

"We were going to ask you that. When did you last see him?"

I hesitated. Swallowed.

"Last night," I said.

"Where, sir?"

"In Bangor. I left him with a friend. Well, she's not really a friend, she's sort of an acquaintance. She owns the paper I work for. The *Clarion*."

"Who's this?"

I told him.

"And you left the boy with her?"

"Yeah. He didn't have any place to stay. And he was—"

Roxanne came out of the bathroom and walked past me to the kitchen side of the room. Her hair was pulled back. She opened a cupboard and took out mugs.

"He was what?" the detective asked.

He did the talking. Divan watched me closely. A red light showed on the tape recorder like the eye of a snake.

"He'd been sniffing paint."

"How do you know that, Mr. McMorrow?"

I told him what I'd seen, down by the river.

"So he's huffing and then he goes with you voluntarily?"

"Yeah."

"Just said, 'Okay, pops, let's go?'"

"No, he didn't say much. It was kind of a scene. One of them tried to stop us."

"But he wasn't successful," Cobb said.

"No," I said.

He paused. I didn't elaborate.

"So Rocky left with you voluntarily?"

"Yeah. I'd say he was glad to get out of there. He was in over his head. This wasn't a bunch of Cub Scouts. All juveniles except this one older guy they call Crow Man. A real dirtbag. If you want to go after him for endangering or something, I'd be glad to—"

"We can talk about that, Mr. McMorrow. Now, the kid went with you to this lady's house. Then what?"

"Then I drove home."

"Here."

"Right. Home. Where I live."

"Oh. Well, Officer Divan here said she thought you lived in Portland some of the time."

I looked at her. She didn't speak, didn't let me off the hook.

"Sometimes. Roxanne has a condo there. South Portland, on the harbor."

"So you came here and just went to sleep."

I felt a tingle of irritation but fought it off.

"I talked to Roxanne, had a beer, and went to sleep."

Roxanne walked over and put the mugs down in front of them.

"We talked about Rocky, about our baby," she said.

They both glanced at her belly, then away. Divan said, "When are you due?"

Roxanne told her April or early May.

"How exciting," Divan said, but she didn't sound excited herself. I supposed she meant it would be exciting for us. Cobb took a sip of coffee and said, "That's good, Ms. Masterson," about the coffee or the baby, I didn't know which.

"So what is this about?" I said. "Is Rocky dead?"

"Getting to it," he said. "So that day when the kid was here. Can you tell me about that. You got up early. The kid was here, right?"

"Right. But he was gone when I got up."

"And then what?"

"And then the stepfather showed up."

"Looking for the kid?"

"Right."

"But he's G.O.A.?"

"Gone on arrival?"

"Right," Cobb said.

"Yeah. He bolted out the door and into the woods."

"So the dad must have been a little unhappy, huh?"

I stared at Cobb.

"He was angry. He said if I'd touched his son, he'd kill me. Stuff like that. I figured he was just emotional."

"And what made him think something like that might have taken place?"

Cobb smiled. Roxanne looked at him coldly.

"I guess he didn't believe that I'd help the kid for the sake of helping him," I said. "That anyone would do that just to help out."

"So if you bothered with the kid, it had to be because you were a pedophile," Cobb said.

"You got it."

"So you had words?"

I shook my head.

"He had words. I didn't want to listen to it so I left."

"And you went?"

"Down the road."

"To where?"

"To work on my truck. At a friend's house. In his barn. It's got heat. Then I came back here and got ready for work."

"That's in Bangor."

"Right."

"Drove right up there?"

It was Divan all of a sudden. I could see Cobb watching my reaction.

"No," I said.

I told myself to remain calm.

"I stopped in Woodfield on the way. Where Rocky lives."

"Why did you go there, Mr. McMorrow?" Divan asked.

"Just curious."

"About what?"

"About Rocky. Where he lived. Why he wouldn't go back there."

"So what'd you do?" Cobb said.

"I stopped for coffee. Right in the little downtown. This little lunch-counter place. But you know that."

"What do you mean, we know?"

"You've talked to Rusty Clement, and he fed you some line of crap and now you're coming here to check it out. Why is it you can't even talk to a kid these days without people thinking you're a pervert? I don't know what that guy's problem is. I know he can't stand the kid. You should ask him why his stepson won't go home."

"Did Rocky tell you?" Divan said.

"No. Not really. But I'll tell you, he left this piece of paper in his pocket, all worn like he carried it everywhere. Something about Kitty. I mentioned it to the mother—I drove by the house and she was outside and we talked for a few minutes—and she went white as a ghost. You should ask her about that."

Divan looked at Cobb. He looked at me.

"We'd love to, Mr. McMorrow," Cobb said. "But she's dead."

CHAPTER 30

"How'd she die?" I asked, still stunned, still picturing the fragile woman in the big black coat, collapsed before my eyes by some sort of grief.

The cops said they couldn't say how she died. The autopsy hadn't been completed.

"When?" I asked.

They said they didn't know that, either.

"Who found her?" I asked.

"The husband," Cobb said. "He said he was out of town on a logging job and she called, all upset."

I waited. Roxanne listened intently, too. Under the table, she reached over and took my hand.

Cobb brushed at his hair, working on the thinning spot.

"He said she was distraught about the kid," he said. "He said you stopped to talk to his wife about her son, and whatever it was you said, it must have made the wife, Flossie Clement, despondent."

"So you think she killed herself?" Roxanne asked.

"That's what the initial investigation seems to indicate."

"But I barely said anything. She said she was worried about Rocky, and I told her how he was. She was worried. But not hysterical or anything. I told her what you—" I looked to Divan "—told me about Rocky being hit by the truck. Which turned out not to be true. He told me they almost hit him, but missed, and then they gave him a ride to Bangor."

"And that upset her?" Cobb said.

"Yeah, but not to the point of killing herself. We talked after that. This was just standing there in the street. I was going to stop and knock and she came out to get the mail. So we talked right there in front of the house."

"About what?" Divan asked.

I took a deep breath, tried to remember it all. Flossie had just rambled, and I did, too. I told them about the Legos and the four-wheeler, but that was a year ago. The kid reading all the time, the stepdad saying he was too soft for the real world.

"She kind of just went on, how she didn't understand it, there hadn't been one thing to make him run. And then I told her about Kitty. And that seemed to shock her."

"This is this note?" Cobb said.

I told him what it said, word for word.

"And you told Mrs. Clement?"

"Yeah. I thought maybe she'd know what it meant."

"What'd she say?"

"Nothing. Just turned white. Said, 'Oh, my gosh,' or something like that, and walked into the house."

"That's it?"

"That's it. I went to work."

There was a lull. They looked at each other and the red eye on the recorder looked at me. Roxanne sipped her coffee. Cobb looked up at her and brushed hair over his bald spot.

"So where's this note?" Cobb said.

I told him I'd given it back to Rocky. I told him what I'd found checking out papers around that date: the woman named Katia, killed in the hit-and-run.

"Katia?" Cobb said.

"Right. Katia, Kitty. Maybe it was a nickname."

They looked at me, unimpressed.

"And that's all you said to Mrs. Clement?" Cobb said.

"Yeah. She walked away. Up until then, she seemed glad to hear about Rocky. I could at least tell her he was all right."

"Unless he'd been run over by a dump truck, right? That wasn't such good news, was it?" Cobb said.

He smiled.

"You think this is funny?" I said.

Roxanne squeezed my hand to shut me up. Cobb's face hardened. Divan's, too.

"No, sir," he said. "This is what I think. I think I've got a guy—you—who's got a history of attracting trouble like flies attract—whatever. I've got a thirty-three-year-old woman who's dead. I got a guy—you—who keeps turning up with her fourteen-year-old son."

"He keeps turning up with me."

"Uh-huh. I got DHS involved with this juvenile who's on the streets. Now I've got a note that's supposed to be some sort of clue, about some kitty, but maybe it's some other name that sounds like kitty or starts with K or something. This information shocked the deceased shortly before her death. And the note is gone."

"No, it isn't. It's with Rocky. I'll bet he still has it. Just ask him."

"We'd like to do that, too," Divan said.

She took a notebook out of her breast pocket and flipped the pages.

"At zero thirty-three hours today, a Theresa Danforth, 161 Broadway, called the Bangor Police Department to report a theft. A boy she identified as Rocky had stolen sixty-three dollars and a pizza from her home and fled."

"The little bugger."

"You know where he might be now?" Cobb said.

I started to shake my head.

"He isn't here, is he, Mr. McMorrow?" Divan asked.

"No, he's not here," Roxanne snapped.

Divan gave her a cool stare. No more baby talk.

Cobb looked at her curiously.

"Now, you work with—"

"Department of Human Services," Roxanne said. "Child Protective."

"Right. I've seen your name. In reports. Our paths have crossed, at least on paper."

"Homicide cases?" Roxanne said.

"Sometimes," he said. "Sometimes just C.I.D."

"So does it look like a suicide?" I said. "Gun in her hand or something? I really need to know."

"There's been no ruling on cause of death," Cobb said. "Until there is, I can't comment on that at all. She's dead. It doesn't appear to have been natural causes."

He pursed his lips, and looked up at me and said, "So maybe Rocky had a cat?"

"I don't know."

"But you discussed it with him?"

"He said he couldn't talk about it."

"Why not?"

"He wouldn't say. Just said, 'Because she's my mother.'"

"Who's his mother?" Divan said.

"I don't know," I said. "I figured his mother was his mother."

"Okay," Cobb said slowly. "So where can we find this kid, do you think?"

"I don't know. He could be in Bangor. When I first saw him, it was in Portland, Monument Square. He doesn't like shelters. In Bangor, he was afraid the huffer kids were going to come after him because of what happened to this older guy, Crow Man."

"What happened to him?" Cobb said.

I looked at Divan and Roxanne.

"I had to kick him a couple of times. Pretty hard."

"Why?" Cobb said.

"He came after me with a bottle."

"So you kicked the crap out of him and took the kid and left," Cobb said.

I shrugged. They looked at me curiously, like I was a museum specimen, something to examine from various angles. Then Cobb stood up and reached for the recorder. He clicked it off and the eye went black.

"So what is it you do at this newspaper, Mr. McMorrow?" he said, slipping the recorder into his jacket pocket.

"I'm a copy editor."

"Is that right?" he said. "What do you do if the writers spell a word wrong? Break their fingers?"

CHAPTER 31

They left, but said they'd probably be talking to me again. I said that was fine, but it really wasn't. After the door closed, and their cars crunched out of the yard and down the road, I went to the window and stood. Roxanne put their mugs down on the counter and came and stood beside me. I put my arm around her waist and we both looked out.

The wind had shifted to the north and the temperature was dropping. The trees were towering figurines with brittle glass branches. At the edge of the woods, the brush glittered in the sun. The tall grass was encased in crystal, like upended icicles poking from the snow.

"It's beautiful," Roxanne said.

"It's not right," I said. "This isn't the way I want it to be. Not for us."

I looked at her.

"All of us, I mean."

"I know."

"They think I caused her death."

"They don't know what to think. They're just asking."

"Or they think I'm some sort of pervert."

"That will work itself out," Roxanne said.

"I just want them to leave us alone," I said.

"They will, Jack."

"I suppose. But what if—"

"What if what?"

"What if I do get dragged into this thing somehow? This Rusty guy, if he really thinks that something I said put his wife over the edge, then I don't know. He could—"

"But you know that's not true, Jack," Roxanne said softly.

"No, I don't. I don't know what that note meant."

"Maybe it didn't mean anything. If she killed herself, it was a lifetime of, I don't know, sadness, frustration, mental illness. I don't know. But it wasn't you."

I looked out at the woods, the silver trees like knives against the blue sky.

"Yeah, I know. But you hate to think you were the one to give her the last little shove."

"You don't know that at all. Husband's a jerk, maybe abusive. She was sick, right? Son runs away. If someone was in severe depression, that could be more than enough."

"Sure, I know that. But her face. The blood just drained out of it, like you'd pulled a plug."

"Jack, you can't blame yourself."

Roxanne put her arm around me.

"These events were set in motion a long time before we ever even saw this boy," she said.

We stood and looked out at the porcelain woods, and we could hear the sound of the wind in the branches, the roaring of thousands of tiny snaps, building with the gusts and then receding like an ebbing wave.

"He's going to be crushed," I said. "He was close to his mother. He really was."

"It's sad."

"How could she do that?"

"Maybe she didn't," Roxanne said.

That silenced us for a moment and we stood there, thinking of this woman and who might have killed her.

"Rusty," I said.

"I'm sure that's the first place police will look," Roxanne said.

"And you know what's really sad?" I said. "I bet Rocky doesn't even know. If they don't find him, he could see it on TV, in the newspaper."

"That would be a terrible thing."

"Terrible piled on terrible."

I was headed for Stonington, for a story for the *Times* on the last fishing dragger there. I took the second shower, kissed Roxanne good-bye and waved as she pulled out of the dooryard. And then I called Tippy.

Her answering machine came on, telling me to leave a message if I was calling regarding stray or abused animals. I was, sort of, so I stayed on the line.

"Tippy, this is Jack McMorrow. I heard about what happened and—"

There was a clatter and Tippy herself said hello.

"Tippy. Jack. Listen, sorry about what happened with Rocky. I didn't think—"

"It's okay. There's a certain percentage of loss one has to accept if one is to do any good at all in the world, isn't that right? The girl was up at six, did her chores. She's really rather sweet, though I must say that thing in her face—it makes me ill just to look at it. But she was a good—"

"I need to talk to Rocky, Tippy," I said. "Or somebody does."

And I told her why.

"Oh, god," Tippy sighed. "The poor child."

"Yeah. It's sad. He wasn't close to his stepfather. Only child. It's going to be very hard."

Tippy talked about bad luck and the burdens placed on people and other creatures. I interrupted again and asked if Tammy was there. Tippy said she'd left, but promised to be back in the afternoon. I told Tippy to call me if she saw or heard from either of them.

"Call me if you hear anything. Even if it's from the police, that they've found him or—"

I paused. Heard a truck approaching. I went to the front of the house and looked out. A white van was coming up the hill fast, bouncing off the potholes and ruts. And then behind it, a pickup. A big one.

It was green.

Rusty.

"Gotta go," I said, and hit the button. Then poked the

speed dial. The van had pulled in. The doors were opening. Guys were jumping out.

Phone to my ear, I ran to the closet. The number was ringing. I yanked the door open, grabbed the rifle. Mary's voice.

"Mary. Jack. I need help. Tell Clair—"

A thump outside. The phone went dead. I ran for the kitchen, for the shells in the drawer. Clawed for the box. The door crashed open. Shells spilled across the counter.

"Get him," I heard.

I had one shell in, but they were on me. Gun yanked from my hands, fingers digging in my throat, my hair. I lashed out with my feet, but they pushed me back, pinned my arms back, and I fell to the floor, under a pile of bodies. The hand was squeezing my throat. I couldn't breathe. I tried to scream, but it came out a choking sound.

"Break his arms," someone was saying. "Break his legs."

"Kill the skinner. Cut his balls off."

"No, let Rusty do it. It's his old lady got killed."

"How tough are you now, skinner? Like the little boys? Like scaring little ladies? How's it feel now, skinner?"

They started punching my abdomen, and I tensed my muscles to protect myself. Then someone punched me in the groin, and I tried to double up but I couldn't, and the pain ran into my belly, down my legs.

"Like that, skinner? Won't be using that again, you scumbag."

Something, a rope, a belt lashed my face, but all I could see was jackets and arms, leering faces, and then the crowd parted and a guy—blond, big beard and gut—leaned down and yanked my head up and cinched a belt tight around my neck.

A noose.

CHAPTER 32

They pulled me to my feet and held me up, my arms pinned behind me on the countertop. My legs were kicked apart, and a guy stood on each bare foot. Boots ground on my insteps and I bellowed, and one of the guys on my feet grabbed my jaw in his hands and squeezed until I was quiet.

Rusty stood in front of me. He was bigger than I'd remembered, his eyes bleary. He took two long steps, turned like a pitcher, and punched me hard in the gut.

"Oh," I said. I felt faint. Thought I'd vomit. The room spun and I felt hot and clammy and started to collapse.

"Give it to him, Rust," I heard them say.

"Kick his skinner butt."

"Don't let him pass out, goddamn skinner pussy."

Rusty came into focus, close to my face, teeth bared, breath rank with alcohol.

"You killed my wife."

His words came slowly, each one seething with hatred.

"No, I didn't," I said.

No plea. Just a flat statement. Rusty took a step back, went into his wind-up, and punched again, same place, the blow collapsing me inward.

"Yeah," I heard. "Another one, Rust."

I couldn't breathe, couldn't gasp, the belt was choking

me. I started to panic, to thrash, and they held me tighter, twisting my arms back until that hurt, too, and someone laughed, a nervous high-pitched cackle.

Rusty leaned close.

"You killed her. You told her about the boy and it killed her. You messed with my boy. Now it's payback time."

His hand went behind him and came back with a knife, black and silver. He unclasped it, looked at me again, and then jammed the blade under my belt and yanked upward.

The belt was cut loose.

"He's pissing himself."

"He ain't gonna have anything to piss with."

"It's payback time, skinner."

The high-pitched voice. Singing the words.

I felt Rusty's hands digging at the waist of my pants. Heard the snap come undone, felt the fly unzip.

Oh, god, I thought. Oh, god in heaven, save me.

"No!" I shouted, and the hand grabbed my jaw.

A cold jab. The blade against my belly. Rusty's voice.

"Where's my boy?"

Where was his boy? Where was Rocky?

"I don't know."

The blade sliced and I felt it, not pain, but heat. White-hot, but not burning, something wet and warm. Blood.

"Where is he?" he said. "Where the hell is the kid?"

"Bangor," I gasped.

"Skinner's singing now."

"Where?"

That was Rusty.

"I left him with a friend last night. An old lady. She put him up in her house."

"What old lady?"

"Her name's Danforth. Tippy."

"Tippy? I think he's bullshitting you, Rust."

"Cut him some more, then we'll find out. Goddamn lying son of a bitch."

A jab. A prick. Pain this time.

"Where in Bangor?"

"Broadway. I don't know the number. A mansion. Big place."

Their faces, a couple filled with gleeful lust. One with hatred. One toward the rear, a long-haired guy, no expression at all.

"A mansion. Yeah, right. Go ahead, Rust. Give it to him."

"He's lying, Rusty."

"What color's the house?" Rusty said.

Color, I thought. What color?

"White. Right up from the downtown on the left. Ask anybody, they all know her."

But then Tippy crept into my mind, the house with the doors wide open, the house full of cats. Tippy telling Rusty that Rocky wasn't there, she didn't know where he was.

"But he left this morning," I said.

"See," they crowed. The belt around my neck jerked and cinched tighter. The guy pulling the belt leaned close and spat against the side of my head.

"Chicken shit," he said.

"So where'd he go?"

"Don't know. He's with kids in Bangor. They're easy to find. Street kids."

"Put his hand on this stove, Rust. That'll make him talk."

"You killed her, you son of a bitch," Rusty muttered. "You did it, you did it, you did it."

The last was a bellow and he swung again, and I tensed and the blow came, a crashing pain that spread like a flash fire. I doubled over, gasping. The belt guy jerked me back up and one of the guys on my feet reached for my jeans and started to yank them down. The other guy on the other side did the same and the jeans were at my knees, and the room fell quiet, and the hand reached and got the waist of my shorts and ripped them and I was exposed. Rusty leaned down toward my crotch with the knife. I screamed, "No," and the door blew open.

"Party's over, boys," Clair said.

They froze. Rusty turned. Clair had a shotgun at his hip, aimed at Rusty's face.

"I'd pump it like in the movies, but there's already a shell in the chamber," Clair said. "Four in the tube. You let him go or I start killing you."

He spoke with an odd, detached calm. This was a man who had killed many times before and everyone in the room sensed it. Rusty shuffled, backed a step toward me, knife behind him.

"This ain't your fight so why don't you—"

"He's got a knife in his right hand," I said.

"A three-count," Clair said to Rusty. "Then I cut you in half."

"Hey, easy," one of the guys said. "I didn't do nothing. I just—"

"You know guns, boys? This is a Remington 870 pump. Magnum. Number four buckshot. The way you're all bunched up, I'll bet I won't need five shots. It'll be like bowling."

"One . . ."

"Jesus Christ . . ."

They got off my feet, let go of my arms. The belt around my neck went slack.

"Two . . ."

"Don't shoot, man. Hey, I got my hands up."

Rusty still hadn't moved. Two of them raised their hands high. Three more started to sidle toward the door.

"On the floor," Clair barked.

They fell like they'd already been shot. Rusty still stood, staring at the gun barrel.

"Three," Clair said.

There was a moment when nothing happened. Just the word, its echo, hanging in the air. Clair's finger on the trigger. The knife in Rusty's hand.

And then he dropped the knife. It clattered, then was still. Clair lowered the shotgun, took three long strides toward Rusty, and in one quick, practiced motion cracked him across the face with the butt of the gun. Rusty fell backward and his head made a hollow, wooden sound as it hit the floor. His mouth was open, his eyes were half-closed. Blood spilled from his flattened nose, running down his cheeks in dark rivulets.

Clair picked up the knife, then looked at me, glancing at my crotch. I leaned down and saw drips of blood below my navel. Pulling up my shorts, I used them to dab at the cuts, then pulled my jeans up, too.

"How bad are they?"

"Not very deep," I said. "Little jabs."

"They all in on this?" Clair said.

He still was calm, but there was something chilling in the hardness of his expression, even to me.

"Yeah," I said. "Pretty much."

"Okay. We'll pick one."

They were on the floor all around us, like suspects at a drug bust. Clair glanced around the room, then went to the nearest guy, the one who had held the belt and spat on me. He put the barrel of the shotgun on the back of the guy's head, and the guy said, "Oh, no. Please, no. I didn't do nothin', I was just—" Clair raised the gun, took a step back, and like a football kicker, booted the guy in the side.

Three of them pleaded when the gun was put to their heads. Three were silent. They all groaned after Clair had punted them, one by one. One guy, the one who had laughed, said, "Oh, my ribs." Rusty, already punished, lay on the floor, his bloody hands held over his smashed nose and cheekbone.

"Okay," Clair said, standing over the group like a guard charged with a chain gang. "Now you can call the police."

It was a long wait. Clair had me hold the shotgun while he tried to call Mary, but the phone still was dead. I asked if they'd cut the line, and one of them nodded.

So I went out to the truck to call, first Mary, to say we were fine but Clair would be held up for a while, and then I called the sheriff's department. I told the dispatcher there had been a home invasion and an assault. He didn't perk up until I said the seven guys who had done the invading and assaulting were in my kitchen.

"They're still in the home, sir?" the dispatcher said.

"Yes, they are."

"Are you in any danger at this time?"

"No," I said. "Not at this time."

Still, it took most of the morning. A young deputy arrived first, then a state trooper, then a couple of guys from town who were paramedics and had heard the ruckus on the police scanners in their trucks. And then an ambulance, for Rusty and the laughing guy, who said he still couldn't breathe, and finally Divan and Cobb, all the way from Belfast.

"I think we should just attach ourselves to McMorrow

here," Cobb said, as we sat in his cruiser. "Establish one of those field offices. It'll save the state a lot of mileage money, don't you think?"

Divan half-turned to see me.

"You're keeping us pretty busy, McMorrow," she said.

"I'm not," I said. "He is."

I nodded toward Rusty, at the back of the ambulance. A paramedic was fixing some sort of splint on his face.

"Ask him."

"He says your buddy there busted his face up for no reason."

"He had a knife and he was threatening me and he wouldn't put it down. Clair could have shot him and still pleaded self-defense."

"Mr. Clement says he blames you for his wife's death and he just lost it. Says he didn't mean to hurt you, he just wanted to scare you."

"Yeah, right. You blame a guy for your wife dying, so you decide you'll scare him? Give me a break."

Divan looked at Cobb and I could tell she didn't buy it, either.

"Hey, mitigating circumstances. I can just hear his lawyer. Guy's wife dies, maybe a suicide. He's up all night. Grieving. Drinking. Fixates on you as the cause of all this. Drives over here in a rage with his crew."

"Six guys hold me down while he gets ready to—"

I hesitated.

"Cut me in a serious way. What's mitigating about that?"

"Good thing your friend was home," Cobb said.

I silently thanked god.

"This guy's a one-man goddamn battalion, isn't he? You said he was in the service."

"Marines. Force Recon they call it. Vietnam."

"That right?" Cobb said.

Divan looked over at Clair.

"Huh," she said.

"They'd be a hundred miles behind enemy lines in Vietnam. Laos. A handful of guys all by themselves."

"One mean mother, huh?" Cobb said. "Well, I guess that explains how we got three guys with broken ribs, one guy they say maybe has a collapsed lung. Guy in the ambulance said your friend there put that cannon to their heads and made them beg, then put the boots to 'em."

I didn't say anything.

"Reckless conduct with a firearm, McMorrow."

"Come off it. He saved my life. What was he supposed to do, reason with them? What about Rusty? What's he charged with?"

"I don't know," Cobb said. "Maybe terrorizing with a dangerous weapon. Assault. Criminal trespass. Criminal threatening. With the dead wife and all, D.A. may decide the whole thing's a little touchy, going after a guy while his wife's body's still warm."

"So he walks?"

"No, but he may bail. Just warning you."

"I'll be ready," I said. "And Mrs. Clement?"

Cobb looked at Divan. She didn't say anything, but her eyes flared, flickering some sort of warning.

"Yeah, well, that investigation is ongoing," he said.

He paused. Looked at me in the rear-view mirror.

"Unless you want to tell me any more about your last conversation with the deceased. You sure you didn't say something else? Maybe said you were gonna write something about this kid? How he was making it on the street. How he was turning tricks in Portland?"

I cursed him aloud.

"Hey, I'm just brainstorming, McMorrow."

"And I've said all there is to say."

In the mirror, I saw Cobb watching, watching, always watching.

The ambulance pulled away first, lights flicking but no siren. Then the locals in their pickups. Then one of the cruisers, with three of Rusty's buddies, the probation holds, hand-cuffed in the backseat. I overheard Rusty telling Cobb he couldn't go to the hospital because he had to go home and complete his wife's funeral arrangements. Rusty put his hands over his bandaged face like he might cry. When he brought his hands down he was looking at me, and he wasn't crying at all.

Cobb's cruiser pulled out, tires grinding in the snow. We stood for a minute and Clair looked up at the ice-coated trees. Blue jays hurried by overhead, like grousing com-muters, bound for my ice-bound feeders.

"Pretty, huh?" Clair said, like nothing had happened.

"Oh, yeah," I said. "Beautiful."

"You know in the jungle sometimes, lying there for hours with the bugs crawling over me, sweat pouring off me, I'd dream about ice storms."

"I'll bet."

"And then things would explode and you'd go into the other state, not thinking at all."

Clair paused, looking at the trees, but beyond them into the past.

"This was like that."

"I could see that," I said.

"I hope I didn't get you in any deeper."

"You got me out of it."

"I mean after. I couldn't just walk away."

We stood, and it was a little awkward, this glimpse of Clair stripped naked.

"There have to be consequences," he said. "There has to be something to tell the enemy that for every action they take, the reaction will be greater, so everything the enemy does is a net loss. Not them losing two, you losing one. A big loss. So they know everything they do carries a price."

"And the price here was . . .?"

"I'd say their boss won't be able to round up much of a posse next time," Clair said.

"Maybe he'll come by himself," I said.

"If he was gonna do that, he would have come solo today."

"But he wanted a show."

"Right," Clair said. "That was staged, to a point. But dangerous because it was out of control."

"But if you're going to kill somebody, or even hurt somebody, you don't bring six witnesses."

"No. But you do if you want six witnesses for some other reason."

I thought.

"To show you couldn't have killed her," I said.

"Beside yourself with grief," Clair said.

I pictured Rusty, the knife in his hand, fist balled up. His anger was real, but it wasn't crazy rage.

"You know what he wanted? I mean, before you got there?" Clair shook his head.

"He wanted to know where Rocky was. He kept asking me. Where was he? Where did I leave him?"

"He's hunting for him?"

"I guess. But there was this desperation to it. He had to know. Once I told him, it was back to the enraged husband."

"Maybe wants to tell him about his mom himself."

"Maybe," I said. "Maybe not."

CHAPTER 33

Marna lived in one of those complexes built in a dairy-farm pasture—drab gray-sided buildings that go up overnight like the builders are staking a claim. This was out by the Bangor mall; Marna's building was 6A, toward the rear. It was drab and bare, with a couple of shrubs and kids' toys frozen in the snow like stuff stuck in the ash at Pompeii.

I stood at the door and pressed the buzzer. Marna's voice came on, like someone taking an order at a drive-through. I said hi and she sounded surprised, a little flustered. She clicked the door open and I walked down a corridor where boots and sneakers were placed on plastic trays. One door opened and she popped her head out. Another head followed, waist high. A little girl peered at me and grabbed Marna around the legs.

"Jack," Marna said.

"Hey, there," I said. "Sorry to bother you."

"No bother. What happened to you this time?"

I touched the scuff marks on my face. Shrugged.

"I know. You walked into a door."

"Not exactly," I said.

"You don't have to explain, Jack."

"Okay. Can I come in?"

"An adult to talk to? Would I turn this down? Hey, if I offer you coffee in a sippee cup, please be understanding."

She opened the door wide and I followed her in. Marna was wearing gray sweatpants and a University of Maine T-shirt. Her hair was pulled up on top of her head in a big plastic clip. She was barefoot and I followed her into the room, wondering if I should take off my boots. I hesitated on the threshold and she waved an arm and said, "Just come in, on the condition that the state of this apartment doesn't leave this room."

The apartment was plain and white, with toys and children's books strewn everywhere on the carpet. There were scribbled drawings pinned to a corkboard, like pages from a Rorschach test. There was one stuffed chair and a small television on the floor. In the center of the room was a tiny table with tiny plates and a bowl. Dolls were seated in the chairs.

"Jack, this is Annie. Annie, this is Jack. He works with Mommy at the paper."

I said hello. She looked up at me, all big eyes and curly dark hair. She didn't resemble Marna and I wondered who her father was, and where.

"You have a big boo-boo on your face," Annie said.

"Annie—" Marna began.

"It's okay. You're right. I do. But it doesn't really hurt."

"Good," Annie said, bouncing to the table. "You came just in time for the tea party. It's the whole family. The mommy and daddy and the little girl and the little boy."

She propped one of the dolls up. I smiled but considered Tammy and Rocky, and wondered if the whole, happy family was something from a fairy tale.

"Are they hungry?" I said.

"Oh, yeah," the little girl said, and she took a cracker and crumbled it into the mouth of one of the dolls. Crumbs fell to the carpet. Annie stepped on them with her bare foot.

"Oh, well. Cleanliness is overrated," Marna said. "Another guilt trip foisted upon us by the vacuum-cleaner industry.

Come into the kitchen, if you dare, and I'll make you a cup of coffee."

I followed her to the end of the big room. There were dirty dishes on the counter, more scribbled pictures on the refrigerator door. Marna stretched her short square frame to get mugs from the cupboard, then a jar of instant and a box of store-brand teabags. She put water in a kettle and put it on the stove.

"So, Jack with the big boo-boo," she said, fixing her hair as she turned to me. "This is a surprise. How'd you find me?"

I shrugged.

"Oh, I know. You can find anybody. Everything okay, I hope. Tippy didn't hand out pink slips? Randall didn't decide to work nights?"

"No," I said. "I was on my way to the paper and I thought I'd stop. I need a favor. I didn't want to talk about it in the newsroom."

"Where the walls have ears. What is it?"

The kettle began to hiss like a drumroll.

"Well, I was just wondering. You know all the funeral directors, right?"

"Not intimately. Yuck. Can you imagine?"

"No," I said, smiling. "But you talk to them every day."

"Oh, yeah. They like me because I talk a lot. Unlike their customers."

"Think they'd tell you about a cause of death?"

Marna paused, the chatter subsided.

"Maybe. Why?"

"Well, I know this person who just died and people are saying it was a suicide. I was just wondering what happened, I guess. It has a bearing on some other things."

The kettle began to whistle. Marna turned and took it off the burner and poured.

"What's the name?" she said, her back to me. Annie pranced into the kitchen and Marna went to the refrigerator and took out milk and a Popsicle. She told Annie she could watch TV. Annie scampered back out.

"Flossie Clement. Might be a nickname. I don't know."

"Where?"

"Woodfield," I said.

"That's Savant. He handles that whole area."

"Think he'd tell you? If you asked in the right—"

"Jack, you know me. If there's one thing I can do, it's talk. And get other people to talk. I get talking and it's contagious."

I could tell Marna was warming to her task.

"Can you get them to chatter about a cause of death?"

"That's usually from the medical examiner."

"I know, but they'll probably take a while. I'd like to know now. This Savant guy, if he's seen the body, he probably has a good idea already."

"You mean what happened?"

"Right. The circumstances."

"A gun or pills or a hose in the exhaust pipe?"

"Right."

"When do you need to know this?"

"As soon as you can get it," I said. "You're off today, right?"

"Yeah. But they don't need to know that. I'll have Annie pound on a keyboard in the background."

"What would you tell them?"

"That somebody called, asking if we were going to run the Clement obit tomorrow. They were from out of state and they wanted to have a paper FedExed to them. I just need a heads-up."

"For an honest person, you lie awfully well."

"Only for a good cause," Marna said. "I assume this is one."

"Yes," I said. "It's important."

"Then I'll do it. I'll call you."

I gave her my cell phone number. She wrote it down with a purple crayon. Annie came charging back into the kitchen. She stopped in front of me and held out a small but perfect hand. She opened her fist and it held a cracker.

"Dollie's giving it to you," she said. "Because you're hungry."

I smiled and thanked her and she ran back to the tea party. Marna handed me the mug of tea. I sipped; she touched her lips to her coffee, leaned back on the counter, and crossed her legs.

"Marna," I said. "You're a mom."

"How observant. You must be a reporter."

"Nothing slips by me. And let me ask you something. As a mother, if your child had run away and was on the street, and you loved him very much, way more than his father or stepfather or whatever, would you kill yourself and leave him alone?"

"Well, I don't know," Marna said. "And I hope I never have to know. But I think I'd be in mom mode."

"Mom mode?"

"Yeah. If my kid was out there alone, I wouldn't be thinking about me. I'd be protective, thinking of how to keep him safe."

"And killing yourself, that would be the opposite," I said.

"I don't know, Jack. I'd feel like I was abandoning my own kid," Marna said.

"Unless you were the reason he ran away. And maybe got hurt."

"You'd really have to think there was no hope. That he was dead and gone or something. Run away to Australia or someplace."

"Or killed," I said.

Marna lifted the mug to her mouth, swallowed and looked at me. In that moment, her eyes were as big and wide and curious as her daughter's.

"Or killed," she said. "That would probably do it."

She paused, studied me.

"Does that help, Jack?"

I ran over it all in a single, dismaying instant. Flossie. The truck. The look on her pale, fragile face.

"Yes," I said. "And no."

CHAPTER 34

It was a little after one, lunch hour on Main Street, and people were strolling on the sidewalk, squinting in the sun like they'd just emerged from bomb shelters. I parked in a bank lot in front of a sign that read CUSTOMERS ONLY and started walking.

I wanted Rocky, of course, but mostly I wanted a kid, not just any kid, but one of the rural refugees who would be likely to know Rocky, maybe even know where he was. It was more likely that I'd get what was known in sales as a referral. One kid would point to another, that kid would point to somebody else. It was like reporting, but easier. I didn't have to take notes.

So I walked through the little city parks, past the statue

of Hannibal Hamlin, with his cold, stoical stare. I continued along the sluiceway of the Kenduskeag Stream, gurgling blackly on its way to the Penobscot River. Pigeons scattered, then wheeled back to squabble over scraps of a sandwich. I swung onto Main Street, where cars sloshed through murky puddles. As I walked I looked up the alleys, between the buildings. Up one side of the street, down the other.

In front of the bus station, a thin man in curled-up sneakers and a gray sweatshirt leaned against the wall. His gaunt face was right out of the Dust Bowl, a WPA portrait. I approached him and he looked up, alarmed, and slipped the brown-bagged can behind him.

"Hey," I said, not bothering to smile. "I'm looking for some kids. Teenagers."

He stared back, and I could see the hairs in his nostrils, the dirt in his pores, the crust in the corner of his eyes.

"You know. Dyed hair? Rings in their noses?"

Still he stared.

"Kids? Les enfants? Bambinos?"

The guy looked away.

Feeling sour and nasty, I asked everyone I could accost. A slow-track lawyer shook his head and scurried into his foyer. A secretary, shivering in her short skirt while she sucked down a cigarette, said she hadn't seen anybody, and flicked the butt past my head.

I ducked and continued on. The video arcade was closed until three. The Indian restaurant was open, but the waiter shook his head and turned his back.

If there had been any diners, I would have grilled them but there weren't so I walked down to the river. No one had been to the bridge abutments since the snow. The frozen Penobscot was cold and white and empty.

Turning back, I followed our route from the previous

night: across the tracks, onto the rubble and over the wall. A guy coming out of the back of a store looked at me suspiciously. I started to approach him and he went back inside and slammed the metal door.

I could have carried a vacuum cleaner and done better.

Then it was around that block of buildings, across the street and up the hill toward City Hall. I crossed with the light and hiked up the hill. Cars passed, and I thought of the cacophony of New York, the constant downtown din. There was a cold silence to this city. Nobody beeped their horns. Nobody talked to strangers. They were all Amish and I was shunned.

I continued on, past City Hall and into District Court, where I circled the long lobby. I saw deputies, closing in on retirement minute by minute, breath by breath. Two women, one crying on the other's shoulder. A couple of lawyers, carrying their briefcases like big black IDs. We aren't dirtbags. We work here.

But no Rocky. No Tammy. No kids.

Leaving the courthouse, I started down the hill, sliding on the sand. Picking my way, I kept my eyes on the sidewalk, then looked up.

They were hurrying toward me, in the shadows on the other side of the street. Two hooded sweatshirts, one baseball hat worn sideways. One with no hat at all. Jacket open. Belly showing white in the cold.

Tammy.

I crossed toward them at a diagonal.

"Tammy," I called.

She looked up, stopped and started to back away. The three boys looked back at her, then at me, then back at her.

"A cop?" the kid in the hat said.

She shook her head and he came off of the sidewalk

and started toward me, arms low, mouth hanging open.

"Tammy, I need to talk to you," I said.

Tammy hesitated. The two hoods stopped and waited. I strode past the open-mouthed kid and he did a little skipping step to stay alongside me but out of reach.

"What are you trying out for?" I said. "Alvin Ailey?"

He stopped skipping and stood there. Tammy hooked her thumbs in her pants, her at-ease position. The hooded kids peered out at me like monks.

"Have you seen Rocky?" I said.

"Nope. Not since he blew the animal lady's."

"Well, what happened there? Tippy was just doing him a favor. She wasn't going to turn him in."

"She started asking us where we were from, why didn't we go to school, did we have pets at home, that kind of stuff. Rocky just kind of like freaked. I go, 'She's just talking, partner. She's just, like, making conversation.' He got all jumpy. I think he was still messed up."

"Maybe I shouldn't have left him," I said.

"Who's this?" one of the hooded kids said.

"Twig," Tammy said.

"Oh," he said.

"You seen him today?" I said, throwing the question out to all of them.

The guys looked at Tammy. Tammy looked at me. She shook her head. They shook theirs, too.

"Come on, Tammy. You sure?"

This time she looked away.

"Nope," she said.

"Tammy."

"She said 'no,' man," the kid in the hat said. "Leave her alone."

I looked at him. A smattering of acne. Wisp of a goatee,

like dust from under the bed. Stud in his nose. Reckless, dumb expression. What if my child ended up like that? My child.

"Just shut up, will you?" I said.

"Hey, man, I could—"

"Tammy, I've got to talk to him. Something's happened to his mother."

Her expression changed.

"Like what?"

"Like something not very good. Something bad."

"Is she in the hospital?"

"Big deal," the kid in the hat said. "My ma's in the hospital like every other week. She's been through detox like twenty-eight times. Now they won't take her anymore at Eastern Maine."

"Tammy, this is serious," I said.

She fingered her eyebrow ring, the worry bead implanted in her face.

"He took—"

"The money. I know. That was stupid."

Tammy shrugged and her shirt rode up.

"He said, 'How far can I go with this money?' I said, 'What do you mean? On a bus?' He said, 'No, right now. In a taxi.' I said, 'Sixty bucks? Jeez. I don't know.' I said, 'Boston? Maybe Portland?' Twig said, 'No, I just want to go home.' And then he, like, scoops up four pieces of the pizza the lady got and he goes out the door. I said, 'Twig, this ain't good, man. You're gonna end up in MYC.'"

"I been there," the kid in the hat said. "It's no big deal. Cottage A, they treat you like shit, but—"

"So that's all, Tammy?" I said. "He just walked out the door?"

"Yeah," she said, but there was something too sincere about it, too wide-eyed and innocent.

"Let's walk," I said. "I'm cold."

I started down the hill, and Tammy fell in beside me, shuffling along in her Nikes. The two guys in hoods were in front of us, and the kid in the hat walked point. I slowed and let the boys move ahead.

"So you going back to Tippy's?" I said.

"Sure. She's a little whacked, but hey, who isn't? What the hell. I never seen a house like that before. It's full of these friggin' antiques and shit. Rocky shoulda stayed. He likes all that old stuff."

"But he left."

"Yeah."

There was a new vagueness in her tone. I slowed some more.

"So where is he really?" I said softly.

"He left. Like I said."

"Went home?"

"I don't know. I didn't go with him. I was watching TV. Rich lady like that and you know what? No cable."

I waited.

"So what is it?"

Tammy didn't say anything.

"If you want to help him, tell me."

She exhaled impatiently, and looked at the ground.

"He was in town this morning," she said, in a whispering mumble.

"Where is he now?"

"I don't know."

"Come on, Tammy."

"I don't know."

"Tammy. His mother."

She shook her head, disapproving, not of me, but of herself.

"OK. I don't know why I tell you shit but I do. You ever been to that history place?"

"What's that?"

"This old house, but it's like this museum. Full of old stuff with little tags saying where it came from. They give tours. These historical people. I call them the hysterical people."

"He's there?"

"I don't know. He might be. It's where he goes in the daytime. Normal people go to the mall, you know? Twig goes and hangs with these whacked-out old ladies. He's a friggin' trip, I'll tell you."

Our little platoon, Fagin and the gang, swung onto Main Street, past a tattoo place that did body piercing, an army surplus store with dusty mannequins in jungle fatigues. The kid in the hat made machine-gun noises, then leapt into a whirling karate kick. Another ninja who needed a good smack in the head.

There were more people now. The lawyer I'd tried to talk to before came out of his office and gave me a dismissing look. A twentyish guy with long limp hair and headphones looked Tammy up and down. She thrust her chest out and fixed her mouth in a sneer.

"In your dreams," she said as we passed.

At the corner of the next block, we slowed.

"You wanna go to Kmart?" the kid in the hat said.

"No way," one of the hooded kids said. "I get bagged, I'm going south."

"Come on, pussy," the kid in the hat said.

"They catch you again, you're gone," Tammy said.

"They ain't gonna catch me. I'm the flash."

I took a notebook from my jacket and wrote my phone numbers, ripped the paper out, and handed it to Tammy. She looked at it and stuffed it in the front pocket of her jeans.

"If you see him before I do," I said.

"His mother, huh?"

"Not good."

"Okay," Tammy said. The boys crossed the street, turned and yelled, "Come on."

"Ain't going," she shouted back.

"So where is this place?" I said.

"Up the hill, on the right. It's got this sign."

"You want to come?"

"I'm going back," Tammy said. "Old dippy Tippy has this cat that's gonna have kittens and she said I could have one. I want to watch."

"Good for you," I said.

"I want to see 'em come squirting out. You ever seen anything being born? My oldest sister, she's a flaming bitch, but she had her baby at home. We were there, waiting in the other room, which was bullshit 'cause my mother and my sister's boyfriend were in there with video cameras, and I don't know why 'cause my sister, she was screaming and yelling like they were cutting her up with a chainsaw."

I looked at her, chattering away, now that the boys were out of earshot.

"It was like this horror movie. She's bawling and then the baby's coming out and everybody's like, 'Oh, my god, oh, my god.' I'm in the other room, I'm saying, 'What's it got? Three heads?' You got kids?"

I shook my head.

"Not yet."

"Well, if you do, don't bring a video camera. That's all I can say."

And it was, because she skipped across the street, weaving through traffic like something blown in the wind.

CHAPTER 35

The museum was a brick Greek Revival place with an open-columned porch, and a sign: TOBIAS WELLINGTON HOUSE — 1834. HOME OF THE BANGOR HISTORICAL FOUNDATION. The public was welcome on Tuesdays and Thursdays from 1 P.M. to 4 P.M.

It was Wednesday. The place was closed.

I walked up the shoveled path to the porch and crossed to the big double door. It was massive and carved, with beveled and etched glass. It was locked.

The windows were dark but when I shaded my eyes with my hands and peered in, I could make out portraits on the walls, placards beside the portraits. There was a massive black marble fireplace and columns separating two of the rooms.

The house was still. The chandeliers didn't swing. The eyes in the portraits didn't move.

But Rocky did.

He came into the rear of the big room and went to the back window and peered out. As he turned, I stepped to the side and pressed myself against the brick wall, between two windows. I heard faint steps inside the house. They came closer, then stopped just to my left.

Rocky was looking out.

A truck rumbled past, then a string of cars, and then there was a pause in the traffic, and quiet. I listened for his footsteps again. I heard his voice, echoing faintly.

"The gasoliers we think were put in about 1848," Rocky was saying, in an odd sing-song. "This is the morning-glory pattern. This is a matched pair between the two. The black Italian marble fireplaces, we're not sure when they put them in. Did Wellington put them in when he built the house, or did Sidney put them in to make the house more elaborate? Most experts think Sidney removed the white marble because there were four white marble fireplaces upstairs. Now, originally Wellington had this as a double parlor with a partition and a door, like all of these old houses of the time. But Sidney wanted to have the grand salon of Paris—"

He pronounced it Paree. A chill went through me.

I heard his steps, squeaking on the wooden floors. His monologue went on.

"These are Corinthian columns, as opposed to the Ionic out on the porch. This is all hand-carved wood, all the leaves and the scrollwork . . ."

And then the voice was fainter and I couldn't make out the words. I leaned toward the window and peeked in, and saw Rocky at the other end of the house, standing in front of a portrait, arms raised, finger pointing.

"Note the detail," he said, and then he slipped from the room.

I stood on the porch, unsure what to do. Should I interrupt whatever play-acting Rocky was doing? Would it be like waking a sleepwalker? And why was it they said you shouldn't do that? I couldn't remember.

And how had Rocky gotten in? Was there a key? Was he a member of the historical society? How many times had he taken the tour?

The gasoliers. The grand salon of Paree.

I stood for a moment, my back against the bricks. Cars stopped for the light at the intersection and people looked over at me. The light changed. The cars rolled through. I eased my way along the wall, slipping past the windows and around the corner. Stepping carefully on the porch boards, I made my way to the rear of the house, and down a set of wooden stairs.

There was a short gravel driveway and a lot big enough for four cars. It was empty. There was a back door, and I tried to turn the knob. It turned. I pushed. The door was locked.

I stood there. Rocky could have locked it from the inside or he could have gotten in through a window. I continued on, over the snowbank at the end of the parking lot, behind the house, into an alcove between the main house and an attached ell.

Where there were footprints. One fresh set over old tracks. They led to a wooden bulkhead door, painted green and peeling. The door was down but there were chips of paint on top of the snow.

Rocky's entrance.

I looked around, eased one of the doors up, and saw that there were no stairs. The door covered a stone-lined space, three feet deep, probably originally used to deliver coal. The space ended with another wooden door that opened inward. I stepped into the hole and lowered the bulkhead door down over me. Crouched in the darkness, I felt for the inner door, scooched toward it, and pushed.

It swung upward and damp cellar smell billowed out. I leaned into the space and tried to see the floor, but it was too dark. The door was heavy and my arm started to cramp, so I held it with both arms and eased my legs over the stone lip of the little cairn. I peered down. Felt spider webs on my face, but I couldn't brush them off. I blew them away from my mouth, and poked into the darkness with my boot.

The foundation wall was rough stone. Finding toeholds, I eased my way down, and the door lowered. It swung closed. I stepped onto the floor. Wiped my face. Peered into the deepened blackness and waited for my eyes to adjust.

I took a tentative step. And another.

It seemed to be lighter at the far side of the cellar, and I shuffled forward again. Again.

Something clanged under my feet. There was a roar to my right, flames and light.

I jumped, then settled. The oil burner had kicked in. I'd tripped on a pipe.

I listened. There was no sound from upstairs. I waited, forced myself to count to fifty. Then, in the dim flickering light, I picked my way across the cellar, between brick columns and steel posts, and found the stairs.

At the bottom, I stopped. Counted to fifty again. Started up.

The stairs creaked, but just barely, not like in the movies. As I continued up, I could see the thin horizontal line of light at the bottom of the door. It was level with my head, and then I was above it, and . . .

Something clattered. Hit me in the face. I grabbed at it and it was cold metal, and I held on.

It was a pipe. It was attached to the vacuum cleaner at the top of the stairs. I cursed silently and propped the pipe against the wall. Listened again. Nothing.

I paused at the door, and then felt for a knob, but found a latch. I eased it up and it made a snap, and I waited and listened. Pushed gently. The door swung open.

The stairs led to a kitchen. I could see a brick chimney,

a fireplace hung with cooking utensils, and a black slate sink. There were cups and saucers on the sideboard next to the sink. Stacks of papers and books beside the cups and saucers.

Rocky's voice, then steps. He was coming downstairs. He was coming this way.

". . . four white marble fireplaces upstairs," he was saying. "Each bedroom had a walk-in closet, which was unusual."

He was coming closer. I stood there by the open cellar door. Should I hide? Should I call out and warn him?

"We're trying to restore the upstairs, too, but it's a long process. Note that we say restore, not renovate. There's a big difference and if you follow me into the kitchen, I'll explain—"

"Hey, Rocky," I said, smiling. "How's it going?"

He froze and said, "Wha—"

"It's okay, buddy. I just need to talk to you."

"No," Rocky said, and he ran from the room.

When I came into the hallway, I saw him running, then sliding into the front door. He fumbled with the lock, tugged at the door, fumbled some more.

"Rocky," I said, walking toward him. "It's okay. You don't have to run. I'm not going to—"

He whirled, his eyes wide, and ran for the stairs, to my right, leaping up them. I broke into a trot, and started up behind him. He went to the left, feet pounding. I followed, through one room full of plastic and plaster pails, and into another. I called, "Rocky, come on."

But he was clattering down another set of stairs. I followed and the stairway was narrow and steep, and I half fell at the bottom, and heard a clang and a crash.

The stairs led to a room behind the kitchen, and I turned and could see the cellar door, still open. I ran toward it and heard panting and then a moaning sound, and I reached for a light switch and hit it and looked down the stairs. The cellar lights were on. Rocky was on his side on the floor, trying to crawl, but clutching at his leg. The vacuum cleaner was upside down beside him. I went down the stairs, crouched beside him.

"You okay?" I said.

"Leave me alone," he sobbed, scrabbling along the floor. "Leave me alone."

"Hey, stop. Just stop."

"I didn't do nothin'. I didn't take it."

I put a hand on his shoulder.

"It's okay, Rocky. I don't care about any of that. Just stop. Just relax. What'd you hurt?"

He reached back and clutched his leg. He was crying, sobbing in short, quick pants.

"Hey," I said. "Take a deep breath now."

Rocky didn't, but the pants came more slowly and he rubbed at his knee.

"Is that what you hurt?"

He nodded.

"Can you move it?"

He did, wincing.

"You think it's broken?" I said.

Rocky shook his head. The silver paint around his mouth still showed faintly and tears had left luminescent trails on his cheeks. He reached under his glasses and wiped with his hand. His hand was dirty and it left a long dark streak from his cheekbone to his chin. He looked small and young and broken.

How could I tell him?

I helped him to his feet and he put weight on his leg and took a couple of tentative steps. At the stairs, I put my arm around his shoulders and lifted, half carrying him upstairs. In the kitchen, I let him go and he limped to the sink and stopped, facing the wall. I walked over and stood beside him.

"You okay now?"

Rocky shrugged, shoulders thin under his filthy T-shirt. When I stood close to him, I could smell him, smell his hair. He was dirty.

"You come here a lot?" I said.

For a moment he didn't respond, then he nodded.

"How'd you know?"

"Tammy told me."

He frowned.

"I told her I really needed to talk to you. It was important. She wouldn't have told me otherwise."

"I'll pay back your friend's money," Rocky said.

"That's okay. Don't worry about it."

"I didn't mean to take it. I just . . . I just did."

"Was it the paint?"

He scowled and shrugged.

"You shouldn't do that, you know. It's very bad for you."

"So?"

"So you shouldn't hurt yourself like that."

"Why not? It doesn't matter."

"Sure it does, Rocky. You're a good kid. You'll do some good things."

He shook his head.

"I'm not good. Nobody's good," he said.

"Sure you are."

"I'm shit. Everybody's shit."

"No, you're not. Don't talk that way."

He shook his head again and his scowl deepened. His glasses had slipped down his nose and he pushed them back up and sniffed.

"It's all shit," Rocky muttered.

"No, come on. What makes you say that? You're a good kid. You're smart. You like these old houses, don't you? Someday you'll work in a museum or something, but you're going to have to—" Get counseling, I thought. Get help. Get over this somehow. "—get back on track," I said.

"I'm not going back," Rocky said.

"Well, Rocky—"

I paused. He was right. What was there for him to go back to? A brute of a stepfather? He'd probably marry that waitress. She'd tell everybody at the restaurant how the kid played with Legos. They'd all have a good laugh.

"I'm not saying you have to go back. But there are better places than the street."

"I like it here. I'll stay here."

"Rocky, you can't hide here for the rest of your life."

"I won't hide. I'll work here."

"I don't think they'll let you do that," I said.

"Yeah, they will. They like me here. They say, 'Dave's our most dedicated member. He's—'"

"Dave?"

Rocky caught himself, looked almost bewildered.

"Yeah, well . . ."

He looked at me blankly.

"Dave," I said. "Not Rocky."

"No. Not Rocky. Rocky left because he had to . . . he had to go."

His eyes narrowed, as though he were reading the fine print in his own head. He frowned and shook his head. Something had eluded him, something had slipped from his grasp.

"He left 'cause—"

"Did something happen?" I said softly.

"No, but my mother said, 'Rusty, he doesn't want to go.' And Rusty said, 'We got one permit. The kid's. Do you understand that. I'll shoot the goddamn thing. He doesn't have to even pull the trigger.' And mom said, 'But he doesn't want to do it. He doesn't want to see you shoot it.' Rusty gets all mad, and he pounds the table and the beer spills and he says, 'See what you did, goddamn it,' but I didn't do it. But he grabs my arm and he twists it and he makes me take this towel and wipe it up, holding my arm really tight and going back and forth, back and forth, and my mom says, 'Leave him alone. Just leave him alone.' Rusty says, 'Wouldn't I like to, but I got this permit for the little puke. A hundred bucks for that goddamn moose permit and I don't care if the little pussy wants to stay home and play goddamn paper dolls, he's going. And I'll shoot it and I'll gut it out, and he can just stand there and goddamn watch.'"

I stood motionless and listened.

" 'Why don't you think about somebody other than yourself?' " Rocky's voice but higher, mimicking his mother, then low. Rusty.

" 'You leave him out of this.' . . . 'Turn him into a pansy fruit loop. I don't give a shit.' . . . 'Don't you talk that way in front of my son.' . . . 'I'm leaving. I don't need this.'"

Rocky paused, as though spirits had left him.

"And then the door, bang, smash. The truck starts, vroom. He's gone and my mother's crying, but trying to smile at the same time, and she can really do that, really do both at once. Cry and smile. And she always says, 'How 'bout we get a movie?' We always get these old movies, black-and-white and everything 'cause they're the movies we like. 'You like old things, don't you?' my mom says. 'I don't know where that came from.' Everything in our house is, like, modern and brand new. Rusty likes it really clean and no junk around. If I leave something out, it's gone."

Rocky paused, leaning against the black sink. I stood and waited and slowly he focused on me.

"So when did all this happen?" I said.

"What?"

"The moose permit?"

"Oh," he said, as though I'd brought it up. "I don't know. The fall."

"What made you think of it now, Rocky?"

He pushed at his glasses, wiped nervously at his face.

"I don't know. I just did. Sometimes things just kind of replay in my head. My mom says I have microphone ears 'cause I remember everything people say. Like I'm a tape recorder."

"She says that?"

"Yeah."

Rocky smiled, looked inward again.

"She's cool. She's a real nice lady. You'd like her. She, like, never says anything bad about people. She never gets mad. She'd never do anything to hurt—"

He stopped. Looked troubled for a moment.

"To hurt anybody?"

Rocky saw me again.

"She never would."

"I'm sure," I said.

"Really."

"I believe you."

"Really cool," he said.

"I know."

Rocky started, as though he'd been interrupted.

"You do?"

"Sure," I said.

"How do you know?"

"Well, you just told me."

"Oh," Rocky said. "Well, yeah."

I was off the hook, if I wanted to be. But it wouldn't be honest, and that left no choice.

"I met her once," I said.

He looked at me. The house popped and creaked.

"When?"

"A few days ago."

"My mother?"

"Yeah. Flossie. That's her name, right?"

He nodded, his mouth slightly open.

"How'd you—"

"I went to your house. I told her you were okay. She was very worried."

"What'd she say?"

"She just asked how you were. That was it, mostly. Were you all right? Where were you. And . . . and I told her about the truck. I'm sorry, but I thought I should."

"The truck?"

"That they thought hit you."

"She musta freaked."

"A little," I said. "She freaked a little."

He gave the glasses a poke. Wiped at his face. He seemed to be thinking furiously, calculating something. I waited a moment, then spoke.

"Did you go there last night, Rocky?"

He shook his head.

"Uh-uh."

"Because Tammy told me you wanted to take a cab home."

"No. I . . . I couldn't."

"So you still have the sixty dollars."

"No, I spent it."

"On what?"

"No, I mean, I lost it. It musta fell out of my pocket. But I can get some more money and I'll pay the lady back. You don't have to call the cops or anything. I promise I'll pay her back."

He was a very bad liar.

"That's fine, Rocky. Don't worry about it. So what did you do last night?"

"I came here," he said.

"You slept?"

"There's a sofa upstairs."

"Must've been tough getting through that cellar in the dark."

"No, it wasn't that bad 'cause I could see the line of the door. The light—"

Rocky caught himself. It hadn't been night. It had been morning. I knew. He knew. The taxi companies would know whether they'd taken a kid to Woodfield. And back.

He fidgeted. I looked away, tried to look blasé. So if he had come home, why had his mother killed herself? Her baby was back. Or had she been dead already? Had Rocky walked in and found her body?

It didn't appear so, though there was something odd about him. This sing-song recollection of conversations. He wasn't right. But if he had gone home, why would he leave again? He must have been exhausted. Hungry. No, he had the pizza. But why not stay? Why leave in the first place? Why was he hiding in a museum in a strange city? Why wasn't he home, where he belonged?

Where his mother had just ended her life.

"How 'bout some lunch, Rocky?" I said, smiling. "I'm starved."

He shrugged, then suddenly looked right at me.

"What'd you really need to tell me?"

I hesitated.

"Well—"

"That you saw my mom?"

"Well, sort of, but—"

There was a bang. Outside. The porch.

Rocky flinched, turned toward the hallway. There was another bang, and another. Heavy footsteps on the planks. I went to the doorway and looked out.

A figure stood at the front door, the silhouette tall through the frosted glass of the door. A man. He turned the knob and pushed but the lock held. He rattled the door. I turned back toward Rocky. He was standing in the middle of the kitchen, poised to run.

"They know you here?" I said.

"Yeah, but I don't have a key."

"Can we say the door was open and you came in and locked it?"

"I don't know. I'm not supposed to be here. We gotta hide. We can't—"

The silhouette left the door and I heard footsteps on the porch.

"He doesn't have a key, either," I said. "Stand in the corner, where you can't be seen."

He did, and I moved into the center hallway and looked into the parlor. I heard steps. A figure passed one window on the side of the house, but I saw only movement. The man was walking slowly. He stopped. I pulled my head back as he appeared in the window, opposite the doorway.

But I saw the face.

The bandage on the nose.

CHAPTER 36

"It's Rusty," I whispered.

"Oh, my god," Rocky said in a whisper, "He's gonna kill me."

And then I heard the cellar door opening, Rocky's sneakers on the stairs. His faint footsteps scuffed below me, then there was a muffled bang as the inner door to the bulkhead fell.

Rocky was going out the back, but Rusty was walking that way, along the porch, moving toward the back steps. I went to the top of the cellar stairs and hissed, "No, don't," but Rocky didn't answer. I went to the kitchen window and eased forward just far enough to see. Rusty was coming toward me, distorted in the leaded glass, and I backed away. He went past the window, off the porch, and up the stairs to the back door.

The wooden storm door creaked open. The inner door rattled. Rattled louder. Then there was a scraping sound.

Rusty was trying to pick the lock.

The bulkhead was ten feet from him, just around the corner. Could Rocky hear him?

"You little piece of crap," I heard Rusty say. "I'm gonna wring your goddamn neck."

And then tell him his mother was dead? Nothing like a shoulder to cry on.

The scraping continued and then Rusty said, "Goddamn

it," and slammed the outer door shut. I backed away from the window and waited for him to pass, but he didn't. Instead I heard him mutter, "You're dead, you little shit."

It was quiet. I breathed slowly, in and out. Stood motionless. Listened. Rusty must have been doing the same.

I waited. A minute passed. Then two more. Rusty was waiting, like a cat. Another minute and another. I stood, and so did he, on the other side of the wall. Rocky crouched like a stowaway between the two bulkhead doors.

Wait, Rocky, I prayed to myself. Just wait.

And then there was a faint scratching, the scritch of sneakers shifting on concrete. I heard Rusty step off the landing, then the sound of his boots crunching in the snow. Moving away.

Moving toward the bulkhead door.

I went to the back door. Turned the bolt and yanked the door open, and pushed through the wooden storm door and stepped out onto the landing. I stood there as Rusty turned, saw me, and stopped.

"What the—"

"A history buff, too? You're a real Renaissance kind of guy. But sorry, the Greek Revival discussion group doesn't meet until tomorrow."

He started toward me, muttering obscenities. I had my hands on my hips and a smile on my face, but my weight well forward.

"You don't have your buddy now," Rusty said, coming toward me.

"At least I only needed one. You had to bring the whole garden club."

He leapt for the landing, both arms outstretched. Banging me backward, he grabbed me by the shoulders, but I got my arms between his and both hands around his throat. We leaned into each other, like elk during rutting season, him looking down and me looking up, and he was grunting, trying to drive me off the stairs. I held my ground and pushed back and he wasn't as strong as I'd expected. He gave ground, his boots sliding on the ice as I squeezed his throat. He kicked for my groin and I twisted and took the blow on the thigh, and when he kicked again, I rammed into him as his leg was off the ground, and he fell back against the door. I got a leg behind him and thrashed and shoved until he tripped and slid and landed on his side, his head down over the first step.

His throat was bare, his neck bent back like something ready for sacrifice. He writhed and I jumped on him, pinned him again, his left arm under my knee, my forearm against his throat.

He gurgled. Choked. His right arm was moving down by his side and I got my knee up and pinned his hand to the boards. Reached back and felt his hand, clawing at me, then the knife, still in the sheath on his belt, but him fumbling with it and the blade coming out.

I leaned down and yanked it from his hand, then pressed the back of the blade against his throat.

"Where are your boys now? Who's gonna hold me down, huh? Gonna cut me again? Huh? Huh?"

I pressed his throat harder, felt the vertebrae against my arm. He coughed. Gurgled again. His face was distorted under the bandage, his eyes bulging and I was smiling, the sweet rage bubbling over inside me like syrup. And then I thought of the baby, my baby. I thought of Roxanne. I thought of Clair, his cool grace under fire, and the smile left me. I let up.

And then there was a bang like a door slamming.

The bulkhead.

Rocky.

The sound of footsteps in the snow and then he was gone. We both knew it.

I eased back on Rusty's neck, and he gasped and coughed and gasped again. His mouth gaped open and I could see a white film on his tongue, the silver fillings in his teeth, the red tadpole at the back of his throat. I kept the point of the knife against the jugular side of his neck and droplets of blood formed. I eased back on the knife and he jerked and my hand brushed against the blood. I wiped it on my shirtfront.

"You're dead," he wheezed.

"And he's a dead boy? Why do you want to kill your own stepson? What the hell is your problem?"

His breathing was an asthmatic rasp. Still straddling him, I took him by the throat again.

"What's wrong with you? What do you have against him? Just because he doesn't play football? Won't shoot a moose?"

I pressed the knife point.

"So you pick on him? In front of your friends? Treat him like dirt? What the hell's the matter with you? What the hell is it?"

I pressed with my foream. He coughed and I let up.

"Gonna . . . kill you . . . slow," Rusty rasped.

As he said it, he smiled.

"That's not what we're talking about. We're talking about Rocky. I heard you. I heard you out here. 'Gonna wring his neck. He's dead.' Why? 'Cause his mother killed herself? What the hell is it?"

Rusty still was smiling, his cockiness returning with his breath.

"She didn't kill herself. You killed her," he said.

"That's crap and you know it."

"You don't know shit."

"What don't I know?"

"I did everything for that kid. Everything. Took him in the truck with me every place I went. Tried to teach him to hunt. I got him his own snow machine. His own four-wheeler. But it was too late. He's a momma's boy. If it weren't for me, the kid would be a goddamn girl. He'd be wearing a dress. No boy of mine is gonna be like that. My old man, he was alive, he'd beat the girl outta him."

"So you come from a long line of sadistic bullies."

"My old man could chew you up and spit you out."

"Made you what you are today? Well, there's something to be proud of."

"Kiss my—"

I pressed the blade point.

"Why's this boy threaten you so much? Why does he scare you?"

"I ain't scared of nothing."

"I think you're scared of him. Otherwise, you'd let him go."

"Kiss my ass."

"You're shaking in your boots. What does he have on you? What does he know?"

Rusty smiled up at me, blood oozing from his swelling lip.

"He don't know shit, except for what you taught him. What'd you teach him to do, skinner?"

I pressed the blade harder and he coughed. I felt an urge to slice with the knife. To hammer his broken nose with my fist, hammer it back into his skull. But he was goading me. He wanted to drag me down, suck me into the sordid mess that was his life.

And he wanted Rocky. And I was going to find out why.

"Why don't you just let him go?" I said. "Why are you chasing him?"

Rusty looked at me, his eyes narrowing and crinkling the white tape on his cheekbones.

"Because he's family," he said. "Why are you?"

I flung myself off him and backed away, dropping the knife into my jacket pocket and trotting across the backyard of the house in Rocky's tracks, leaving Rusty on his knees. Tracks went to the street and disappeared, and I hurried up the block but Rocky wasn't in sight.

I loped up the hill, the big old houses perched above me, the roofs of the old downtown below. At the corner of the next block, I turned and looked back. No Rocky.

I turned right on a cross street, hopping a snow bank and trotting along in the street. People in passing cars looked at me curiously. A guy in a pickup honked his horn and swung wide, as though the road were mined ten feet all around me. I kept running, looking down the driveways, between the houses and garages. The street zigged and zagged and popped out on another main drag, where I paused on the curb.

The police station was somewhere nearby. I could just go there, tell them.

The traffic broke. I kept running.

I moved in a fast trot back down the hill, slipping on the ice and snow, skipping between the cars, looking ahead and on both sides for the red plaid jacket.

Rusty's truck passed.

He was going up the hill, the way I'd come, but the brake lights went on and he pulled the truck into a driveway and started to back out. I didn't want to find Rocky now, I'd have to wave him off. Say, look out, your dad's on my tail.

And he was, the diesel clacking as the truck pulled back into traffic. I ran along the sidewalk, faster, leaping over snowbanks, slipping and falling once, but then back on my

feet. But what could he do, shoot me at midday in downtown Bangor? Jump the curb and run me over? Or lay back
and try to follow, hope that I'd lead him to Rocky?

Rusty did just that, once he had me in sight. I needed to
shake him and get to my truck and get on the road, because
I had a feeling that was where Rocky was now, walking
backward with his thumb out. When he ran, he hit the
highway. But if I was quick, I'd get there before somebody
took a chance on the skinny kid with glasses.

I could hear the diesel behind me as I approached the
next cross street. I slowed to a walk, then took a right, walking faster on the plowed sidewalk. Rusty followed, idling. I
took another right, and started to circle back. The street was
narrow, with big Victorian houses chopped into offices. I
walked along, then cut up a driveway, through a snow-filled
yard behind a dentist's office, and over a short chain-link
fence strung with vines.

The green Dodge roared ahead to get around the block,
and I jumped back over the fence. A face poked out from behind a shade in the office, and I followed my own tracks
back to the street, up another driveway, into another yard,
where a dog looked up, startled. He woofed, the chain ran
out like line on a fishing reel, and I went over the fence with
the mongrel slashing at my legs.

He ripped my pants. I ran on.

I was a block over now, and couldn't hear the diesel. Looking up and down the next side street, I took another right,
looked for an easy cut-through. There was a beehive apartment house, with a double lot for tenants' junk cars, and I
slipped through it, pulling my jacket off as I ran, and turning
it inside out. It was copper-colored quilting now. In the trash-
strewn lot, there was a shredded baseball hat embedded in the
snow, and I kicked it free, shook it and stuck it on my head.

And walked.

Main Street was the next main drag, and I took a right, strolling along close to the edge of the buildings. In the distance ahead of me, at the top of the hill, the Dodge turned right and headed my way. I walked into a car lot, and bent to check the stickers.

I waved and continued to work my way up Main Street. Rusty swung back and I walked through a fried-chicken place, in one door and out the other. The truck passed. I crossed the street, cut through to the waterfront, and followed the railroad tracks. When I came back up over the concrete wall, I was fifty yards from the bank parking lot. I hurried over, dumped the hat, peeled off my jacket and put it back on, started the truck and drove.

Rusty had passed me heading south, and I drove west, out of the downtown, in the general direction of the interstate. How long did it take to hitch a ride in Bangor, Maine, in the middle of the day? I supposed it could take two minutes, or it could take two hours. A scruffy kid with paint on his face? I figured I still had time.

I drove fast, past schools and tenements, into the suburban spread, where the houses had garages and the driveways had been scraped clean by plows, like finger swipes through white frosting. The snowbanks narrowed the road and a hitchhiker here would have to have one foot in traffic.

And Rocky did.

He was walking fast, with his hunched back to the passing cars, his left arm out, thumb extended. Every few steps, he'd break into a trot. I pulled the truck alongside him, leaned over and swung the passenger door open. Rocky stood there for a moment. The car behind me stopped, then pulled around me, the kid at the wheel turning and shouting an obscenity as he passed.

I gave him the finger. Turned to Rocky.

"Get in," I snapped.

Rocky still stood there.

"Or you can wait for your dad," I said.

Rocky hesitated, then grabbed the door. I shoved books and a wrench and notebooks and newspapers onto the floor, and he got in. I started off, ramming through the gears, and then we were away.

"He isn't my father," Rocky said.

"I noticed," I said.

CHAPTER 37

For miles, we rode in silence. We took the back way, south to Hampden and then west, and soon the tract houses gave way to grown-over farms, with gangrenous barns and farmhouses collapsing slowly into their cellar holes, clapboards bare as bleached bones. Next to the houses were trailers, hunched on snow-covered slabs, and then the trailers gave way to woods, with only an occasional driveway winding its way into the trees, the NO TRESPASSING signs stating the obvious.

Climbing the hills of Dixmont, I finally spoke.

"Where you headed?" I said.

Rocky shrugged. "Where you going?"

"Portland," I said.

"That's fine," he said, as though it didn't matter.

Portland, Maine. Portland, Oregon.

"Where you want to go in Portland, Rocky?" I asked him.

His shoulders did their rise and fall. Rocky looked out the window at the view of far-off ridges to the north.

I didn't want to dump him in Portland. I wanted to hand-cuff him to the truck and drive him to the Waldo County Sheriff's Office in Belfast. I'd hand him over to Divan, say, "Here he is, deputy. All yours." I glanced over at him, and saw him blink slowly. He was drowsy, probably having slept very little the night before. If he dozed off, I could turn off in Dix-mont, head south through Brooks and on to Belfast, on the coast. I could turn this kid in, continue on to Portland and start making plans to take care of my own. I'd have to tell Di-van that Rusty had threatened to kill the kid, that something was seriously wrong there. She could pass it on to DHS, and maybe make sure they stuck him in a safe house. Rocky could tell them I hadn't touched him, and I'd be free and clear.

I looked over. He closed his eyes, then opened them. I turned up the heat, turned on the fan. We'd crossed the peak of the ridge and were coasting down into Dixmont Center. The turn-off to Belfast was a mile away. The heat billowed through the truck cab. Rocky's eyes closed, then opened, then closed again, then opened but just barely.

The Belfast sign passed, the arrow pointing left. I slowed, but gradually. Rocky's head was starting to make tiny circles, and his mouth had fallen open. The intersection was in sight. I slipped the truck into neutral, touched the brakes. I'd just roll gently around the corner, and we'd be in Belfast in twenty minutes, and then—

The phone rang.

Rocky jerked awake, alarmed.

I braked just before the turn-off, pulled over on the

shoulder and grabbed the receiver from between the seats.

"Hello."

"Hi, is this Jack?" a woman's voice said. It was fuzzy and distant.

"Yeah."

"Jack, this is Marna."

"Oh, hi."

"Can you hear me?" Marna said.

"Yeah. Not great but I can hear you."

"Well, you said to call."

"Right."

"If I talked to the funeral guy, I mean."

I looked at Rocky. He was listening, eyes narrowed behind his glasses.

"Right," I said, my voice brightening.

"So I got it," Marna said, as though I still didn't.

"You did?"

"Yeah."

"You mean—"

"The cause," she said, her excitement coming through the static. "I mean, the circumstances and everything."

I looked at Rocky. He was staring intently at me. I smiled and looked away.

"I called Savant, he's this old guy who comes into the newsroom. You've seen him. Wears black clothes and never smiles? Anyway, he wasn't there, but this woman was, who I've talked to a couple times when I called with a question about an obit. She's real nice, and we started talking and I knew she didn't work there all the time, you know? Well, she doesn't 'cause guess what."

"What?"

"She works for the medical examiner's office. Part time."

"Really."

"Yeah, and I'm like, 'This is too perfect.'"

"So she talked to you?"

I forced a smile again.

"Well, yeah. I mean, I had to—I don't know if you're supposed to do this. I'm not a reporter—but I kind of fibbed a little. Well, I didn't really. But I was talking to her and I was asking her about what she did and did she like it and all that, and she said she's not a doctor, she's like a technician or something. And I'm saying I'd like to get out of this dead-end newspaper job. I mean, I'm not a reporter. You try typing briefs all day."

"That's okay."

"So anyway, I act like I'm all interested, and I was, sort of, but it turns out she fixes up the bodies for the funeral homes, if they've been run over or mangled or whatever, she kind of makes them look normal again. So they can have the casket open at the wake and everything."

"No kidding."

"No. And you know who she just worked on?"

"I can guess."

"I'm saying, 'Yes!' I mean, she said self-inflicted gunshot wound. A woman. Blonde. Did you know they have to wash the hair?"

"No," I said.

The smile was becoming a strain.

"Oh, yeah. If it has blood in it or something. But anyway, I'm asking questions, you know, Miss Innocent. And she says sometimes it's not easy, making the people look presentable. She says—I wrote it down—she says this lady was really pretty but she shot herself in the mouth."

The motor ticked. A loaded log truck lumbered past. Rocky watched only me, his gaze flickering from my eyes to my mouth and back.

"That's interesting," I said cheerily.

"Well, I guess. And that's not all. She says the hard part is the bullet took off a little piece of her lip. So get this. She has to fill in the missing part with this waxy stuff, then cover the whole thing with lipstick. 'Cause if there's a wake, you know people are gonna be kneeling and staring right at the lady's face."

"If there is. Did she say?"

"Oh, shoot. I didn't ask that. I was so wrapped up in this death stuff," Marna said. "So. How'd I do?"

"Good. Great. I'll talk to you about it more."

"She said the woman shot herself in the mouth, but it was harder for her—her name's Gretel—because the lady held the gun, like, close to her mouth but not in it. You know how they put the gun right in their mouths, like on TV?"

I felt Rocky's stare and suddenly felt very, very sad.

"Yeah. Well, this time the gun was in front of the face and the mouth was open. But the bullet sort of caught the lip. Nicked a tooth on the way in, too. Did I tell you that?"

"No," I said.

"And listen to this. She said it was very unusual for a woman to shoot herself. It's more of a guy thing. And even more unusual for a woman to shoot herself in the face. Women are vainer, I guess, and this woman was quite pretty. They don't want to mess themselves up. They usually use pills. Or they jump. Did you know most jumpers are women?"

Marna paused.

"I'll be off in a minute, honey," she said, away from the phone.

"But was there any question?" I said.

"Oh, sorry. About what? Whether she did it?"

"Yeah."

"Well, she didn't say that. She said it was sort of different, the way it was done and everything, but mostly she was talking about what she has to do. I was saying, 'Oh, really. Now how long do you have to go to school for that? Gee, what an interesting job.' Do you think I shouldn't have done that? 'Cause now she wants to have lunch and talk about it more. I might, even if you don't care about it. I think it might be kind of interesting."

I glanced at Rocky. His expression had turned into a glum sort of scowl. I managed to smile but he wasn't buying it, and his scowl deepened. He knew I was hiding something. I prayed he didn't suspect what it was.

"Sure," I said. "It could be. But listen, there really wasn't any other possibility?"

"You mean, that she didn't shoot herself?"

"Yeah."

"No. I mean, I didn't ask. There was the part about it being unusual. For a woman, I mean. And the tooth, and the lip. And then the gun being outside her mouth, not right in her mouth, but other than that . . ."

"And that's what it was?"

"What what was?" Marna asked.

"What the decision was?"

"You mean suicide?"

"Yeah."

"That's what she said. Self-inflicted gunshot wound."

"How do they know that she—"

"She what? Was holding the gun?"

"Yeah."

"I don't know. I mean, don't they find it in their hands?"

"That and other things," I said. "Things about the person's life. Other things."

"Well, was this person upset about something? Depressed?"

I looked at Rocky. His thin legs pressed together, his oversized sneakers, the little boy's face stuck on a half-grown frame, the glint of silver above his lip.

"Yeah," I said. "She was."

And then Marna said she had to go because something had spilled. I thanked her and said good-bye and hung up. When I looked up, Rocky still was staring, his chin jutting out in defiance.

"That was about my mother, wasn't it," he said.

I looked at him, tried to muster a denial, but couldn't.

"Yeah," I said.

He turned to face forward, folding his arms across his chest.

"Well, I don't care what anybody says," Rocky said. "She didn't do it."

CHAPTER 38

"*What makes you* say that?" I asked, as gently as I could.

Rocky stared through the windshield and didn't answer.

"You don't want to talk about it?"

He stared. I put the truck in gear, put the blinker on, and turned left, headed south. I could see him tense.

"Where we going?"

"Belfast," I said, easing the truck through the gears.

"I thought we were going to Portland."

He was suddenly panicky, his dirty fingernails clawing at his jeans.

"This is serious, Rocky. I think we have to talk to the police. There's a sheriff's deputy who's been looking into this, and I think we ought to—"

"No, he'll kill me," Rocky said, reaching for the door.

It popped open and there was a wind-tunnel blast of noise and cold. Rocky swung his feet out and I said, "No," and reached for him. The truck swerved as I fell toward him, my feet coming off the pedals, one hand gripping the steering wheel. I groped for the brake pedal with my foot, grabbed the back of Rocky's jacket. He was poised at the edge of the door like a skydiver.

"No, don't," I shouted, and the jacket started to pull free. The truck swerved left and right, crazily, still going forty or fifty, still too fast. Rocky had one hand on the door frame, started to pull himself out of the seat.

"No," I said, and my foot hit a pedal but it was the gas, and the truck accelerated and the door started to close, and then I found the brake and pressed and the truck whipped to the right, sliding sideways. Rocky fell back into the cab, on top of me, and I let go of the steering wheel and we were sliding backward, then forward, spinning around and around until there was a crunch and I came off the seat, and Rocky did, too.

I was wedged between the seat and dash, my legs tangled in my seat belt. The truck had stalled, but the seat-belt chime was ringing like an alarm clock, telling me it was time to get up. I tried, but I couldn't move with Rocky on top of me.

"You okay?" I said.

He didn't answer, but suddenly started flailing, his legs and arms jabbing me in the face and belly. Then he was off me and out the door, and I kicked my legs free and squirmed after him, flopping out onto the snow. The rear of the truck was jammed in a snowbank. Rocky was running up the road.

I scrambled to my feet, saw a yellow trailer just off the road to my left. A big heavy woman was standing in the dooryard, and a man was coming out the door. Rocky kept running, past their driveway, and the man, wearing a baseball hat, turned and trotted back inside, probably to call the cops.

"Goddamn it," I sputtered, then called, "Rocky, stop."

The woman took a couple of steps toward me.

"Leave the boy alone," she shouted.

I ran past the woman and the driveway but my belly hurt and my knee, too. Rocky was sprinting up the road, his plaid jacket whipping behind him. I hobbled to a halt and turned back. The woman had come out into the road, her hands on her hips, her belly hanging over the waist of her gray sweatpants. The front of her sweatshirt said, LAS VE-GAS, and she was wearing white basketball shoes, unlaced.

"He your kid?"

I shook my head.

"Then why you chasin' after him?"

" 'Cause I'm his goddamn guardian angel," I said over my shoulder.

"Goddamn drunks and druggies," the woman called. "Why don't you go back wherever the hell you came from?"

By the time I got to the truck, Rocky wasn't in sight. With the woman still watching from the end of the driveway, I looked the truck over.

The rear end was jammed in the snowbank so that the rear wheels were off the pavement, the right more than the left. I got in and turned the key and the truck started. As it idled quietly, I got out, locked in the front hubs and climbed back in. With the door open, I put the truck in four-wheel low and eased out the clutch. The rear wheels spun, the front wheels, too, and there was a grinding whine. Then the front end grabbed and the truck lurched forward and rolled.

I shifted out of low, into high, and slammed through the gears as I sped up the road. The woman glared and I saluted, and drove fast until I reached the point where I'd last seen Rocky. Then I slowed and, driving on the left side of the road, looked for his tracks in the snow.

The snowbank was hard and too high to see over from the truck. I stopped and got out, and climbed the bank and looked up the road. The snow between the bank and woods was coated with ice, an unbroken candied surface as far as I could see. I got back in the truck, drove another fifty yards, and stopped again.

"Rocky," I called.

From the woods, there was no answer.

An empty pulp truck passed, southbound, reminding me that Rocky still could catch a ride and be gone. But he'd vanished so quickly, I thought he had to be in the woods. I ran along the top of the snowbank, sure that if he went over on this side of the road, I should be able to see . . .

Tracks.

They were twenty yards ahead, breaks in the sheen of the snow that showed Rocky had plunged straight into the woods, knocking the ice and snow off the spruce curtain as he went. I ran back for the truck and drove back to the tracks. Parking the truck, I tucked my jeans in my boots and laced them tight, and put on insulated gloves. Then I went over the bank and started to follow, but stopped.

What if he'd just made a loop in the woods and then had come back to the road? Or crossed over the road?

I ran along the snowbank for thirty or forty yards, eyes on

the woods. There were no breaks. I turned and went back, and, shrugging through the trees, followed.

The tracks went through the spruce curtain, and then into the second-growth hardwoods that grew densely behind them. This had been pasture, twenty or thirty years ago, and maples and birches had filled the high ground close to the road. Rocky's tracks threaded through the trees, first veering to the right, then to the left. His feet had punched through the crust like fists through windows, leaving jagged pieces of ice on the hard surface of the snow. The snow was a foot deep near the road, but then deeper, and the leading edge of the crust slashed at my shins. A hundred yards into the woods, he had climbed a knoll and then plunged down, and on the far side of rise, the snow was deeper and Rocky had fallen, leaving his outline in the crust, like a chalk outline at a death scene. I stepped through it and continued on.

"Rocky," I called out.

I listened. The treetops crackled in the wind. A chickadee called in the distance, oblivious to the mess the humans had made.

Rocky didn't answer.

I plunged on, down into a hollow where there were old dead pines and cedar huddled in patches. This was lowland, and there was a faint indentation in the snow that looked like it might be a streambed. Rocky had crossed it, and I followed, skipping over his tracks to try to stay on the higher points that might be rocks or logs or stumps. At the center of the streambed, I hesitated, then leapt over three of Rocky's prints, now filled with icy gray water.

He'd broken through. His feet were wet.

But he'd climbed away from the stream, away from the road, deeper into the woods. I stopped and listened, thinking I might hear the sound of his footsteps, but I could only

hear the rattle of the wind in the trees. I continued on, starting to sweat under my jacket. It was uphill now, and there
were blowdowns, shallow-rooted hemlocks and spruces that
had been upended by a storm. They all had fallen in the direction of the wind, limbs driven into the ground like
stakes, making these woods an almost impassable tangle of
trunks and branches.

Rocky had crawled under one tree, toppled over another.
I followed his route, saw where he had backtracked, where he
had climbed a trunk and then had fallen, breaking branches
and landing hard in the snow. He left his imprint and,
where his hands had been, a stain of blood.

But then he had gotten himself up and moved on, and as
I did, too, the woods fell into shadow. I looked to the northwest and saw gray clouds covering the sun. The temperature
dropped almost instantly, and I felt a chill where I was
damp with sweat.

I called his name again and again heard only the wind.

CHAPTER 39

The tracks were moving steadily uphill, but veering left
and right around blowdowns, into blind openings that led
to dead ends. I'd been walking for an hour and now Rocky
was stumbling often, and I saw another smudge of blood in
his handprints. Then, as he crossed a shallow ravine where

I plunged into the snow nearly to my hips, I began to see blood in his right footprints.

The shattered crust was sharp as broken glass, and I could feel it sawing away at my shins. The legs of my jeans were wet, and snow had worked its way down inside my left boot. Rocky had sneakers on. His feet were wet, and we were a half-mile or more from the road, still moving deeper into the woods. We'd have to backtrack out, so I could double every step I took. And Rocky was weaker and colder.

His return trip was going to be tough.

The clouds had moved across the sky in a dense gray wall, and the wind had picked up. The trees swayed and snapped, and icy snow blew from the treetops like sleet. I trudged on, calling Rocky's name into the wind, and then the snow began to fall. It was a sudden squall, and the snow was immediately dense, and the distant trees receded into the white smoke like masts in fog. I walked with my head down and my collar turned up, stepping from print to print, still catching an occasional glimpse of blood.

And then, at the crest of a ridge, a fallen figure in red.

Rocky had stumbled down a steep pitch, into a snow-filled hollow, and collapsed. I kicked my way through his tracks, smashing the crust as I slid down the incline, and bent to roll him over.

He was in a fetal position, his hands between his legs. I turned him over and he looked at me. His lips were gray-blue. His teeth were chattering uncontrollably.

"Sorry," he said, the word shivering slowly from him.

"We've got to get you out of here," I said.

His shirt was open and his T-shirt was wet. His neck and chest were a pale gray. I took my gloves off and took his hands from between his legs. His fingers were white and stiff, his fingernails blue. I held his hands in mine, blowing warm air on them, like it was mouth-to-mouth resuscitation. After a minute, I felt his socks. They were hard, frozen on his feet. His sneakers were unlaced, filled with snow. His shins were scraped and the scrapes were dark gashes against skin the pale color of death. His legs were thin.

I had to figure out how to get him home. Or should I build a fire and warm him here? Three miles to the road—if he could walk at all, it was a toss-up. The truck would be warm. Here, it was snowing harder, and there was no shelter. Even with a roaring fire, we'd be wet, his clothes would be sodden.

"Let's go," I said.

I reached down and took him under the arm and lifted. On his feet, he leaned against me, his whole body shaking. I bent his fingers into fists, and took my gloves and pushed and prodded his hands inside them. Then I put my arm around his shoulders, my hand under his right arm. I could feel his ribs, the bony fins of his shoulder blades.

"God almighty, don't you ever eat?" I said.

He shivered.

"Here," I said. "I'll help you."

I set off up the grade, slogging through my own tracks, breaking the crust with my knees. Rocky staggered and I dragged him, and between us we reached the crest of the slope. We paused, and I looked at him. Snow-covered hair. Blue lips. Chattering teeth. White blotches on his cheeks, where the blood had drained from the tissue, retreated inward to protect the vital organs.

We had to keep moving.

"Come on," I said, and we began to backtrack, following the meandering path down from where Rocky had led me. It twisted right, veered left, slipped between trees and through the scourges of blackberry canes. I turned my shoulders to protect him from the thorny whips, but one or two slipped past me, and slashed at his face, leaving bloodless scratch marks, like the etchings in the glass at the house in Bangor.

Rocky didn't cry out, didn't put up his hands to protect himself. I held him by the arm, fending him off as we slid down the sides of ravines, pulling him up as we climbed. The wind had died, at least in the woods, and the snow fell steadily, building up on Rocky's head. Every few minutes, I reached over and brushed his hair off, wiped the snow from the back of his neck where his thin jacket gaped open.

"A little cold isn't going to bother a couple of rugged guys like us, is it?" I said.

"I'm not rugged," Rocky said weakly.

I looked at him. It sounded like something he'd had to admit before.

"I'm not, either," I said, smiling and patting him on the back. "But maybe between the two of us we'll add up to rugged. You know. The whole is greater than the sum of the parts."

"That's not how it goes," he said.

I took him by the forearm and started walking again.

"You're right. I've never been very good at those sayings."

"Aphorisms," Rocky murmured.

"Right. Adages. Addage and subtractage. Are you good at math? I figured you would be. That was never my strong point. I figure that part of my brain has atrophied and is now the size of a raisin. And inside that raisin is everything I still remember about trigonometry, analytic geometry, and calculus. Maybe it's not a raisin. Maybe it's smaller than that. What's smaller than a raisin but still wrinkled and dried up? A currant, maybe . . . Well, it's probably the size of that. . . ."

And so I chattered away while we walked. I couldn't tell whether Rocky was listening but I hoped my babble gave him something to think about other than the next frozen step. And the next. And the next.

I followed my old tracks, and sometimes his, weaving like a fox coursing for scent. But it seemed colder and Rocky began to plod more and more clumsily, his snow-covered sneakers catching the crust as he lifted them, sending jagged pieces of ice skittering across the top of the snow.

Each of those missteps used energy and calories and heat, and the blotches on Rocky's cheeks seemed bigger and whiter. I stopped and brushed him off and then I listened.

In the distance, I heard the drone of a truck. Then a pause, and then the drone was higher pitched, as the trucker downshifted. The sound came from my left, which meant the road probably was in that direction and our path took too soft an angle. I grabbed Rocky firmly by the arm and said, "Come on."

I plunged down an incline, stomping the crust as I went. There were bigger hardwoods on the opposite slope and I grabbed the trunks, swinging my way up with Rocky in tow, until I lost my grip and he fell back on his seat in the snow and just sat there, shaking, his arms folded across his skinny little chest.

"Get up," I said, and I lifted him from the armpits, and then started dragging him through the trees. Branches raked my face, but I didn't care because I could sense the road ahead, the light beyond the trees.

"We're almost there, buddy," I said, heaving Rocky after me. "What'd I tell you? Maybe we can start a guiding service, you and me. Jack and Rocky, registered Maine guides. How's that sound?"

It sounded like Rusty, with his moose permit, and I caught myself.

But then I could see the dark druid shapes of the spruces that lined the road, and I drove ahead with a surge of energy, towing Rocky behind me.

"We're there, Rocky," I said. "We're gonna get you thawed out. How 'bout hot chocolate and hot soup and a hot bath and—"

A car passed. I could hear the drumming of tires on ice and pavement, and then I couldn't hear it. The car had stopped. I crunched a few more steps toward the dark hedge of trees, and then I heard a car door open. The trees were there, ten feet away, but the maples were dense and I had to shove them aside and pull Rocky through, step and pull, step and pull, and then I heard it, a cracking snarl.

A police radio.

"No," Rocky gasped.

I stopped. He fell back in the snow, crouched there and was still. I was, too. Through the gaps in the snow-covered spruces, I could see a blue car. Hear it idling.

"Rocky," I said softly. "What is it? They'll help you."

His hands were over his mouth and the shivering made them tremble.

"No," he quavered.

"Rocky."

"I'll stay here."

"But you'll freeze to death."

"I'll stay here," he said.

"You can't."

He didn't answer.

"Come on."

Rocky shook his quivering head.

"No," he said. "Don't make me."

"I can't leave you here."

"Don't make me."

"You're freezing."

"No, please."

"Why?"

Rocky rocked on his knees.

"He'll kill me," he said, the words shaking from him like pennies from a bank.

"Who, Rusty? Why?"

Rocky sat there, his head doing its jackhammer jiggle.

"Why, Rocky?"

"Can't talk," he said. "Because of my mom."

I looked at him. Heard the police radio spit again, the metallic garble muffled by the falling snow.

"Rocky," I said softly. "What is it?"

He shook his head, like a mechanical doll.

"My mom," Rocky said. "Can't hurt my mom."

Hurt what, I thought. Her memory?

I stood over Rocky like he was a gutted deer I'd dragged from the woods. The police radio blurted and then there was a message that came through more clearly.

"Augusta, three thirty-eight."

It was a state trooper, getting a call back from the Augusta dispatcher.

"Red eighty-eight Toyota pickup. Registered to Jack McMorrow, P.O. Box, Prosperity. Expires eleven, oh-four. One prior, speeding, ninety-nine. No warrants."

"Save that for me," the cop said, more distant.

I hesitated. He was at my truck, running the plate. His cruiser was warm. Rocky was nearly hypothermic, half-frozen. I reached down and touched his cheek. It was cold and hard. I looked at his eyes, staring rigidly.

He was paralyzed with fear.

If I marched Rocky out of the woods, the cop would get him in the car, maybe call an ambulance and take him to the hospital. They'd thaw him out, check for frostbite. And then they'd—

"Three thirty-one," the radio voice said. "Additional on that. There's a file six out of Waldo S.O. Jack McMorrow, D.O.B. eleven-eleven fifty-six. May be in company of a juvenile. Rocky Doe, D.O.B. one-eighteen-ninety-one. White male, brown and blue, five-foot five, one-hundred five pounds. Stop and hold for fifteen eighty-six, Waldo S.O. Parent will go for juvenile."

"No," Rocky pleaded, closing his eyes.

I stood behind the trees as the cruiser idled. Heard the cop open and close the doors of my truck. I knew I should just step through the trees and, like some bounty hunter, turn in my runaway, send him back to his master.

Turn him over and go home.

Now I could see the cop, walking to his car. He was very tall, very young, hair shaved past his ears, and a blue Smokey the Bear hat perched on his head. He stood by the driver's door of the cruiser and began to talk.

"I've got that subject's vehicle on Route 7 in Jackson. Subject has apparently gone into the woods. Resident here said vehicle went off the road and a male juvenile fled the vehicle. Like I said, the truck is here, but nobody's around. I can stay here and wait, unless you've got anything else."

The trooper waited. I waited. Rocky huddled at my feet, snow beginning to cover him like a battlefield casualty.

"Augusta, three thirty-eight," the radio voice said. "If you can clear there, we've got a two-car accident, Route 9 in Newburgh. One vehicle is blocking the roadway. Unclear on injuries at this time."

"Ten four," the cop said.

The car door slammed. The motor roared. The trooper drove off.

"Yes," Rocky said, teeth chattering, turning the word staccato.

I hauled him to his feet.

"Let's go," I said.

"Where?" he asked.

"I don't know," I said.

"Not Rusty?"

"No," I said. "Not Rusty. If I can help it."

CHAPTER 40

"Jack," Roxanne said from the kitchen as I pushed through the door to her house.

I heard the sharp tap of her heels and then she came around the corner, still in her work slacks, arms outstretched, smiling as though she loved me more than life itself.

And then she stopped.

"Roxanne," I said. "Roxanne, you remember Rocky. Rocky, you remember Roxanne."

"Oh," Roxanne said, her eyes showing only a flicker of surprise, a twinge of disappointment. "Hi. Good to see you again."

"Hi," Rocky said glumly, as though he didn't believe there was anything good about it at all.

"You remember Roxanne, don't you? From here in Portland?"

He looked at her more closely.

"Oh, yeah," Rocky said.

"She's the one who helped get those kids off of you, down behind the square."

"Yup. I mean, thanks a lot."

"You're welcome, Rocky," Roxanne said, and then she looked at me and smiled. It was her eyes that said, "What the hell is this?"

"Rocky had kind of a cold afternoon," I said. "He spent some time in the woods and got a little frostbitten, I think. Needs a good warming up."

"Oh," Roxanne said. "Well, that we can do, Rocky. How 'bout some hot chocolate. I have vegetable soup. You like that?"

He shrugged.

"Yeah, sure."

"We stopped in Unity and had hot chocolate and pizza," I said. "I think what he needs is a hot shower and then maybe something to eat. How's that sound, Rocky?"

"Okay," he said.

"Fine," Roxanne said, smiling at him gently. "You follow me and I'll show you the bathroom and get you towels and all that."

She turned and started for the stairs. Rocky still stood there, his big sneakers leaching puddles onto the hardwood floor.

"Go ahead," I said. "Go with her."

He did, but reluctantly, clomping up the stairs. I followed, and while Roxanne showed him the linen closet where the towels were kept, I went into the bedroom to find him some clothes. I heard the bathroom door click shut.

Roxanne came into the bedroom and that door clicked shut, too.

"Sorry," I said.

"What's going on?"

"I didn't know where else to take him. He—I tried to call you, Rox, but I never got hold of you."

"I haven't been home."

"I tried your office."

"I was on site visits."

"I tried the car."

"I was mostly in people's houses."

"Well—"

"What's the matter?"

"He's just absolutely petrified of his stepfather, and I guess I can see why."

We sat on the edge of the bed, and I told her about Rusty at the history house, and at my house. I told her about the cops, and I told her about Marna, and I told her about the woods.

"My god, Jack. Are you okay?"

Her eyes dropped to my groin.

"Fine," I said. "Well, some little nicks, but nothing . . . nothing vital."

I managed a smile and took her hand.

"How are you?"

"Good. Fine."

"Felt any kicks or anything?"

"A couple."

"Great," I said.

"Thank god for Clair," Roxanne said.

"I did."

"If anything ever happened . . ."

"It didn't."

"It can't," Roxanne said, taking my hand. "Not ever. Not now."

"It won't."

"So, what do we—"

"What do we do with him? I don't know. If I hand him over to the cops, they'll give him to Rusty. They have to, don't they?"

"They don't have to but they will. There's no evidence that he's done anything to the boy, or that the home is unfit or anything like that. But Jack—"

"I know. You can't have him here. I'll find another place, but right now, I just didn't know where else. The guy'll look for him at the shelters, I would think, and—"

"No, that's not what I was going to ask you."

I waited.

"Jack," Roxanne whispered. "Does he know?"

I looked at her.

"I don't think so. He said she didn't do it, but I think he's talking about something else, not suicide. He wouldn't say any more, but if he knew she was dead, he'd be upset, hysterical, I think. And he's not at all."

"Oh, god," she said. "Somebody's got to tell him."

"I know. I just couldn't bring myself—"

"Well, we'll have to. What if there's a funeral or something and they can't find the son? That's just not right."

"Nothing about this is right, Rox," I said. "Nothing."

"But he can't just not know."

"I know, but you should hear the kid talk about his mother. It's like she was his closest friend. He just doesn't have anybody else. The stepfather, saying he's going to wring his neck. I heard him."

"But I can't have him here. It's against everything—"

"I know. And I've got your northern counterpart there, on my trail."

I put my arm around her shoulder.

"Oh, Jack. What about us?"

"We're still here. That hasn't changed. I'm sorry to drag you into this."

"You didn't drag me. I came willingly."

She kissed me, then held on. And then we heard the bathroom door open.

"So what do you—"

"Oh, Jack," Roxanne said. "I've got to think about this one."

Rocky was standing in the hall in his dirty clothes. I told him I'd find him something clean, and I went to the bedroom closet and came up with black soccer shorts, gray sweatpants, a red Adidas T-shirt, and white socks. I didn't tell him they were Roxanne's.

She showed Rocky to the guestroom and left him to change. I set the table for three and then took a Sea Dog pale ale out of the refrigerator and opened it. Roxanne stirred the soup and put French bread in the oven to heat. I stood in front of the window and looked out on the lights of Portland and drank. The ale went down in three gulps, and I went to get another. Opened it, and lifted it to my mouth and stopped.

I went to the table and put the bottle down by my glass. Two would be the limit, because this was no time to get sloppy, no time to check out. This was only a reprieve. They were all still out there—and Rocky was here.

Five-five. A hundred and five. Brown and blue. Parent will go for.

So we fed him by candlelight, because that was the way we ate, and if Rocky thought it was odd, he didn't show it. He didn't show much, didn't say much, either. But he ate slowly and steadily, taking the bread when it was offered, a second bowl of soup, another glass of milk. Roxanne talked to him, but didn't interrogate. Instead, she chatted about living on the harbor, and how she'd learned to tell the ships by shape and route. Tankers and tugs and fish processors and Navy ships that used the Bath Iron Works drydock. Rocky listened and looked out the window at the lights of the Portland skyline.

"Jack loves the country," Roxanne said, "but I need my city fix. The buildings and people and just the whole hum of it all. Jack lived in New York City for a long time and he says he doesn't miss it, but I would. A city is so, I don't know, so alive."

"So indifferent. Anonymous."

I smiled.

Rocky looked from me to Roxanne and back.

"We agree to disagree," Roxanne said.

"Huh," Rocky said, puzzled but intrigued. A disagreement that didn't end with a drunken shouting match? A disagreement that didn't end with me storming out of the house?

How novel.

But still Rocky was quiet. He answered in monosyllables, said please and thank you and not much more.

Finally, when Roxanne couldn't talk about ships anymore, we lapsed into silence. The beacons on the bank towers glowed red from across the harbor. Cars flowed across the bridge, like bubbles in a water-filled tube.

"Pretty, isn't it," Roxanne said.

"Yes, it is," I said. "I admit it."

Rocky sat there, silent and passive. What was this? Some Zen thing? Had his eruption in the museum house been some sort of side effect of huffing paint? Kills brain cells. Can lead to death. Also can cause user to become uncharacteristically chatty.

I looked at him, then at Roxanne. She raised her eyebrows, and got up and began to clear the table. Like it was reflex, Rocky got up, too, nearly upending his chair but reaching back and catching it before it toppled. He took his plate and glass and followed Roxanne into the kitchen, then came back and collected the soup tureen and the bread basket.

Someone—Flossie presumably—had taught Rocky some manners. Now that someone was dead, a bullet plucked with tweezers from the base of her brain. She wouldn't be teaching him anything ever again.

He came back into the dining room and looked out the window, his back to me. Dishes rattled in the kitchen.

"You want to go online, Rocky?" I asked. "Watch television?"

He shrugged. I pointed to the remote, on the table in the adjoining room. Rocky walked that way, padding along in his socks, stiff and noncommittal. I went to the kitchen and put my dishes on the counter. Roxanne was bent over, unloading the dishwasher. I touched the bare band of her waist, and she stood and put her arm around me.

"Not the way we planned it, is it?" I said.

"Is it ever?" she said.

"Once in a while. Purely by chance."

"It wasn't my first choice," Roxanne said.

She smiled, a little ruefully, and I pulled her close.

"I thought we'd lie in bed and talk about our baby," she said. "Plan a trip to someplace where we can lie in bed and talk about our baby some more."

"Where would we do that?"

"I've got it narrowed down to Barcelona, Wales, or Bruges in Belgium. It's supposed to be sort of a miniature Venice."

Roxanne smiled as I reached out and touched her belly.

"Can you believe it?" I said.

"Yeah," she said. "I can."

I kissed her on the cheekbone, which was hard but silky. She turned her face and we kissed again.

And the television blared on.

Roxanne gave me a peck on the lips, then bent to the dishwasher again. When she rose, she put clean plates on the counter and said, "Well?"

"Well, what?" I said.

"Well, I think somebody should tell him."

"Us?"

"I don't know. But it's got to be done."

"God, does he have a worker or anything? Like you, I mean?"

"Yeah, maybe, but only nominally. I don't think he's stayed in one place long enough to have any real contact with anyone. Certainly there's no relationship there."

"What about a counselor type?"

"Sure. Police might recommend he have one."

"When they hand him back to Rusty."

"Yeah," Roxanne said.

"Then who does that leave?"

She looked at me.

I took a deep breath and exhaled, then started putting the dirty dishes on the racks. From the other room, we could hear Rocky blipping through the channels. I stepped back and looked out and could see him, standing there in the blue light, the only movement in his right thumb.

"I don't know what the answer is," Roxanne said quietly.

"Sometimes there just isn't one."

"I think we need to turn him over to the police."

"But—"

"And we stress that he needs to be evaluated, and maybe shouldn't go back to that house to live."

"Who decides that?" I said.

"A district court judge."

"When?"

"As soon as they can find one."

"And in the meantime, Rusty says, 'He's my kid. I'm taking him home.' The guy, if you'd seen him, you'd know. He's determined. There's something very wrong—"

The phone rang.

Roxanne went to the end of the counter and picked it up.

"Hello," she said.

"Hello," she said again.

She paused and hung up.

"Somebody was there. I could hear breathing."

"You're sure?"

"Yeah. And a car or something. I could hear a motor."

"A cell phone?"

Roxanne nodded.

"Strange," she said.

"Maybe it was just a random thing."

"Maybe."

She sounded doubtful.

The phone rang again.

"I'll get it this time," I said.

"No," Roxanne said.

She picked up the cordless receiver, and brought it slowly to her mouth.

"Hello," she said, listening intently.

"Are they there?" I whispered.

"Hello," Roxanne said once more.

And took the phone from her face and pushed the button to disconnect.

"Same thing?"

"Yeah. Breathing. Traffic noise."

"Let the machine answer it," I said.

"I just thought, well, the number's unlisted and I've got some moms I've given it to lately in case, you know, things get real bad at home, or they feel they're going to lose it with the kids. And I called a couple of friends to tell them about the baby, so I thought—"

"You haven't been bothered lately?"

"No, not at all. Not here. A couple of big-mouths but they were all talk. And that was weeks—"

The phone again, the ring cutting through the silence. We stood and looked and waited. After four rings, the machine intervened and after a couple of clicks, the light showed that a message was being left. The light stayed on. Roxanne touched the screen button and we listened as a woman's voice came from the speaker, speaking quickly and quietly.

"Hi, this is Marna from the newspaper. Calling for Jack. Jack McMorrow. I hope this is the right number, but, um, Jack, I think you need to know what's going on up here. That's extension 298. I guess you know that."

I picked up the receiver. Marna had hung up.

"What do you think that's about?" Roxanne said.

"I don't know."

"She sounded—"

"Nervous," I said. "Something's wrong."

I dialed the newspaper, and the call went through to the newsroom. Miss Child answered. I hesitated and handed the phone to Roxanne.

"Extension 298, please," she said.

Marna's voice mail kicked in. I told it to have Marna call me back. The television blared. Rocky stood in its flickering glow, the remote control low at his side like a weapon.

"What do you think it is?" Roxanne said.

"I don't know. Maybe they're thinking of firing me. Maybe Duguay stopped in again. Maybe something with Tippy."

The television suddenly went silent. We both looked over as Rocky tossed the remote on the couch, then thought again and picked it up and placed it on the table. He stood in his stocking feet, with his hands in the waist of his sweatpants, then rubbed his hair wearily. He turned toward us. I walked toward him and Roxanne followed. Rocky looked at us, searching our faces for some hint of our intentions.

"There wasn't anything on," he said.

"There never is," I said.

"We disagree about that, too," Roxanne said, and smiled at Rocky.

"She means she likes to watch TV sometimes," I said.

"Yeah, my mom does, too."

I swallowed hard. Roxanne smiled gently at Rocky. He looked away, at our reflection in the window. The three of us stood there like we were at a bad cocktail party.

But it was my party. I had to be the one to break the ice.

"Rocky," I said. "We need to talk."

He looked at me, his mouth twisting, starting to quiver. Did he know?

"Your mom, she—"

I hesitated. Right in front of me his face was melting, his mouth pursed, eyes closed behind the glasses. His hands were out of his sweatpants and he was clenching and un-clenching his fists. Roxanne put her hand on his shoulder.

"It's okay," she said softly.

"She didn't do it," Rocky cried, then sobbed. "She didn't."

"It's all right," I said.

"She didn't. She's a good mom. She's a great mom."

He sobbed again, started to rock in place. I looked at Roxanne but she was rubbing his shoulder and telling him it was okay.

"Rocky," I began.

"I know she didn't. I know it."

"But the—"

"The note. It didn't mean nothin'."

I thought. Had Flossie left a note? Had she already been dead when Rocky had stopped at home?

"It didn't mean she did it," Rocky said, his voice cracking. "She wouldn't do that. She was really nice. She wouldn't've."

"No?"

"But you're gonna tell, aren't you?"

He looked at Roxanne. Slid a finger under his glasses to wipe away tears. Sniffed and wiped at his nose. Roxanne glanced at me; we both were puzzled.

"She's gonna tell 'cause she works for the state and they have to tell everything, right? They have to, so she'll tell and everybody'll know."

I glanced at Roxanne. She was listening intently.

"Well, not everybody, Rocky," I said slowly.

"And they're gonna put her in jail but she didn't do it, she couldn't've. She's just saying that. Goddamn stupid note. Goddamn kitty. Goddamn stupid lady."

He had stopped sobbing, but the tears were running down his flushed cheeks as fast as he could brush them away.

Kitty, kitty, kitty. How can you live?

"Your mom didn't do it?" I said.

Rocky shook his head, slowly, then quickly, like a dog with a rat.

"No," he said.

"Because she couldn't do that, not something like that?"

He shook his head. Roxanne looked at me, then shook her head, too. I blindly pressed on.

"Well, then who did, if your mom didn't? Who could do that?"

Rocky turned away from me. Roxanne glared, mouthed the word, "no." I waited.

"He could," Rocky said, the words low and raspy, coming through clenched teeth.

"Who?"

Rocky raised his hands to wipe his face. Roxanne still had her hand on his shoulder. I waited.

And the phone rang. Once. Twice.

Roxanne hesitated, as though she didn't want to leave Rocky alone with me, then walked to the kitchen and picked up the receiver. She said hello, and listened, and then said, yes, I was there, and walked to me. I took the phone and answered.

"Jack. Sorry to bother you," Marna said. "I mean, I wouldn't if it weren't something that seemed important. I mean, I'm dialing from your phone 'cause I knew you had Roxanne's number on speed dial and I hope you don't mind or anything but I just thought you'd like to know."

"Know what?" I said.

"The police were here."

"Yeah?"

"Looking for you."

"Why? What police?"

"These detectives. Two of 'em. They came here looking for you, and Randall said you weren't scheduled to work."

"What'd they want?"

"Well, I didn't hear that part because Randall sorta took

them out of here and went down to the conference room, but, um—"

"But what?"

"But Lori, she's working on this story and—"

"What story, Marna?"

She didn't answer for a moment.

"Somebody got killed. Down by the river."

"Who? Who was it?"

"Jack, it was a kid."

I felt like the floor was sinking away.

"Yeah?"

"Jack," Marna said. "You know that girl, the one who came in here?"

"Oh, no," I whispered.

"The one with the cigarette. The one who came in here to see you? Lori said she's the one who's dead."

CHAPTER 41

I stood there, unsteady.

"What's the matter?" Roxanne said.

Rocky was staring at me, expectant. I looked beyond him, saw Tammy, sitting at the restaurant table, her lipstick smudged with cocoa. I sighed.

"What?" Roxanne said.

Rocky scrutinized me, trying to intuit the news. I started

to tell them, said, "The girl—" But then I was startled by Rocky's intense gaze and I stopped.

"I've got to make a call," I said, and I moved away, but only as far as the kitchen, where I dug a phone book out of the drawer and looked for the state police number on the inside of the front cover. It was toll free. I dialed, and a dispatcher, a man, answered. I told him my name and said I understood there were detectives looking for me in Bangor. He asked me if I was in Bangor, and I said, no, I was in South Portland, Unit 120, Harbor View. He called me sir, and asked me to stay on the line. I did, as Roxanne and Rocky watched from the dining room. I heard police-radio crackle, and then the dispatcher talking to someone he addressed by call number. And then he was back.

"Mr. McMorrow. Detective Cobb is on his way to see you," the dispatcher said. "He'd like you to stay at that location."

"I'll do that," I said.

I hung up and Roxanne walked toward me. This time it was my shoulder she took, as Rocky watched.

"What is it?"

I hesitated, then mustered a smile and called to Rocky.

"A family thing," I said. "We'll be right back."

I took Roxanne's hand off my shoulder and led her up the stairs. In the bedroom, I shut the door and told her what Marna had said, that the police were on their way.

"I was with her today."

A shimmer of alarm crossed Roxanne's face.

"On the street. I was looking for Rocky. She's one of his friends. Maybe his only one on the street. I walked along with her. She was with some other kids. Boys. She was fine. She was a nice kid. She was just talking. She was talking about her sister having—" I paused. "—a baby. Oh, god."

"Jack, I'm sorry."

"Yeah."

"Do they know what happened?"

"Maybe. I don't. I mean, Marna just said she was killed. 'The girl in the office with the cigarette,' she said. She blew smoke on Randall. She was working, sort of, for Tippy. She was happy, she was fine."

"And they're sure it was a murder?"

"I guess. I don't know. Killed. I guess that means—"

There was a sound behind the door, a faint scratch. I kept talking as I reached for the knob.

"So I don't know what to tell you, Roxanne. It could be—"

I yanked the door open. It was Rocky, but he didn't flinch, just stood there, square to me, defiant.

"Somebody's dead?" he said.

After a moment, I nodded.

"Yeah," I said.

"Who is it?"

"I don't know," I lied.

"Yes, you do. You're just not telling me."

"All I know is it's a girl. In Bangor. I know it was down by the river. But nobody told me a name."

"How did she die?"

"I don't know."

"How do you know that it's a girl?"

"They're doing a story at the paper," I said.

"And they don't know who it is?"

"I don't know. The person had heard secondhand, but she's not a reporter."

I waited. Rocky was still in the doorway, blocking it. There was something faintly threatening about him, his presence here on the threshold of the bedroom, with the bed

neatly made, Roxanne's pumps on the floor by the closet
door, the smell of her perfume in the air. A wave came over
me, a feeling that Rocky didn't belong here, in this room, in
this house, in my world, with my baby. That murder didn't
belong in our house.

"So why don't we just go down and—"

"I know who it is," Rocky said suddenly.

For a moment I didn't say anything. I heard Roxanne
breathing. Rocky scratched his nose, and I heard that, too.

"You do?" I said.

"Yeah. It's Tammy."

I swallowed slowly. Roxanne looked at me. The phone
rang in the bedroom. I went to the table by the bed and answered it.

"Jack, it's me," Marna whispered.

I watched Rocky. He took a step into the room. Roxanne
stood tensely, five feet from him. I held the phone and listened.

"I just thought I'd let you know what's going on. The
girl, the one who was killed. They're saying she was
stabbed."

"I see."

"And Lori, she's been trying to call you at home. She's
trying to find out about the girl, more about her life."

"It was short," I said.

"I guess. But the *Bangor Daily,* they've got, like, three reporters working on this story and Lori is all alone on it. So
she's looking for some different angle. She's left messages at
your house. I don't know if you want to talk to her about it,
but I thought—"

"Not now," I said, watching Rocky watch me.

"Oh," Marna said. "Sorry. I mean, I didn't mean to interrupt—"

"No, that's fine. Maybe I'll talk to her later."

I hung up and moved toward Rocky and Roxanne.

"So what makes you say that?" I asked him.

He smirked, a bitter, defeated expression.

"You know I'm right. She liked me. And anybody who likes me has bad things happen to them."

He shook his head and gave a sad sort of snort.

"Is that true?" Roxanne said.

I waited.

"Sure. Tammy, she liked me. She stuck up for me. She even got in a fight for me once. And there was this kid in fifth grade, we were friends and he came over to my house and everything, and he got this infection and he died. I'm like, what's that guy with the hood and the big knife thing?"

"The Grim Reaper," I said.

He drifted off in thought for a moment but I brought him back.

"Is that all, Rocky? A friend in fifth grade and a friend on the street now? That doesn't seem like so much."

He looked at us, first one, then the other. And then he pushed his glasses up and dug at his nose again.

"Well, there's my mom," Rocky said.

He paused. We waited. I wasn't breathing. Roxanne's lips were pursed, her arms crossed.

"She likes me and it's made her life pretty crappy."

I exhaled silently. Roxanne wet her lips. Rocky smiled, an odd, unsettling grin.

"So," he said. "Why are you guys letting me hang around?"

With that he turned and bounded down the stairs. I glanced at Roxanne and followed, and found him by the front door, holding his soggy sneakers.

"My shoes, they're all wet inside. The snow melted and now they're, like, soaked."

"We can dry them with a hair dryer. I'll get it for you."

"Naah."

"Suit yourself. But wet feet are no fun in the cold."

"Well . . ."

"I'll get it," I said, and I went back up the stairs to the bathroom. The hair dryer was on the counter, plugged into the wall. I yanked the plug out and Roxanne came in.

"You're going to let him go?"

"Should I tie him to a chair? They'll get me for that, too."

"I don't know. Let me make some calls. Maybe I can get a blue paper for him. He's not right."

"How long will that take?"

"I don't know. I can get the city police over here in two minutes."

"You think he's nuts enough for them to take him in?"

"Involuntary? I don't know," Roxanne said. "It's a judgment call, but you heard him. He's scary."

"And then even if they do take him, what then?"

"Jack," she said. "Would you rather have him here?"

I looked at her. Eyes full of worry, arms crossed protectively over her breasts. It was decision time, the first of many to come. This kid or my kid? Who will it be, Peter Pan?

"No," I said.

"What do you think the detective is going to say when he sees him here?" Roxanne said.

"I think he's going to have some questions for him. And then they'll take him away."

I looked at the hair dryer.

"Is there a way to make this thing just blow cold air?"

There was, and I alternated between that setting and the warmer one, pulling the nozzle out of the shoe every few minutes and checking the soggy lining. Roxanne was by the kitchen sink, grimly picking dead leaves off a house plant. I was sitting in a straight chair in front of the big window, and Rocky was perched on the edge of the couch, watching me.

Rocky didn't ask about Tammy and I didn't bring it up, either. A light tanker drifted by, its navigation lights slipping through the blackness as it moved out into Casco Bay. I talked about working as a merchant seaman or a fisherman in the winter and how tough it must be, out there in the vast Atlantic, an ice-cold ocean as deadly as boiling oil.

"They have to go out and chop ice off the railings and deck, and they can have storms with forty-foot waves. My dad was in the Navy in World War II and he used to talk about waves towering over his ship, which was towering in itself. Way up there, this wall of water, and then it comes crashing down. Ba-boom."

That killed five minutes, which meant Cobb was five miles closer, probably more. It was one hundred and thirty miles from Bangor to Portland, less if he had been anywhere to the south. If the interstate was clear, he'd be in the passing lane doing the cop's customary eighty. I figured it would take him another hour and fifteen, anyway.

The hair dryer kept blowing. I kept talking. Rocky watched me, holding one sneaker while I worked on the other. Before I switched them, I'd turn up the heat for a few seconds, so the shoes were hot, like cookies right out of the oven.

Roxanne finished one plant and started on another. The tanker moved out of sight, and only the lights of Portland showed, with headlights moving like orderly columns of fireflies. I asked Rocky if he thought they looked like fireflies and he shook his head glumly.

"A torchlight parade on a mountain," Roxanne chimed in.

"She skis a lot," I said. "You ski?"

Another shake of the head.

"Me neither. I snowshoe. You do that?"

"Uh-uh," Rocky said.

"You see a lot more. Snowshoe hares. I saw a snowy owl this winter. Ever seen one?"

He shook his head, lost in thought.

"Beautiful birds. They come down from Canada when prey is scarce. This one stayed near this clearing in the woods near my house for about a week. I went out there with my binoculars and a folding chair and watched him."

Rocky didn't respond. I continued.

"You know what they think it was eating? Cats."

"Oh, god, Jack," Roxanne said.

"Yeah, it was there a week and my buddy, Clair, he started out with seven or eight barn cats, and in a week, he only was seeing three or four. The lady across and up the road from him lost a pet one, though. Kind of sad. She'd be out there on the steps, yelling, 'Here kitty, kitty, kitty.' "

Rocky flinched. Roxanne looked up.

"You know, Rocky, we never did talk about that," I said softly.

He got up from the couch and picked up the remote. Pointed it at the TV and it flickered on. The scenes spun by like a newsreel.

"Yeah, well . . ." Rocky said.

"So what's the deal?"

He stared at the screen. I felt Roxanne listening. I waited. Rocky didn't speak. I turned the hair dryer off. And the phone rang.

Roxanne answered it. She sad, "Yes," and "Okay," and then turned away and started giving directions to the condo.

"Yes, it is," Roxanne said. "Yeah. It's a Ford Explorer. It's green. Yeah, it's right out front. Uh-huh."

I listened, but watched Rocky. The TV channels whirled—a flooded trailer park, a hockey game, two cops with guns drawn—but he was listening to Roxanne, too. I turned the hair dryer back on and Roxanne hung up.

"Somebody coming over?" I said.

"Yeah," Roxanne said.

I could see Rocky tense.

"Tomorrow," she said. "Somebody from work."

"They know the way?"

"I told them."

She went around the corner and I heard the bathroom door shut. I got up and held the shoe and hair dryer out to Rocky.

"Here," I said. "I'm not your manservant."

He turned from the TV and took the shoe and held the dryer in it, still holding the remote.

"I'll be right back to spell you," I said.

I went around the corner to the bathroom. The door was open a crack, and Roxanne was standing in front of the mirror.

"A half-hour," Roxanne said.

"Cobb?"

"No. Another name. A man. From Bangor."

"Bangor police?"

"I guess so."

"You tell him about—"

She shook her head.

"No. I just gave him directions."

Roxanne peered in the mirror and brushed at the skin under her eyes. She frowned.

"I look like hell," she said.

"No, you don't."

"Yes, I do."

She turned to me, frown still in place.

"And I want him out of here. I spend ten hours a day dealing with kids. I talk to their mothers and their fathers and their stepfathers and boyfriends and girlfriends and—"

And then I felt a chill, a draft.

I backed from the bathroom, rounded the corner, and walked into the room. The TV was on. The hair dryer was running. It was on the table beside the remote control. The sliding door was open a crack. The sneakers were gone and so was Rocky.

"Shit," I said.

I slid the door open and walked out onto the deck, my socks catching on the snow. Rocky's tracks crossed the deck to the stairs. I walked over and looked down. He'd taken a left and hugged the building, heading in the direction of the street.

"Fine," I said aloud. "Go freeze to death. Get your throat slit and your head pounded in."

And then I heard myself and didn't like the sound of my own words. I cursed and padded back to the door and inside. Roxanne was leaning over the table to turn off the hair dryer.

"Gone again?"

CHAPTER 42

The car was a dark blue Crown Vic, unmarked. I watched from the bedroom window as it pulled into the space between Roxanne's Explorer and my truck. The headlights went out and I could see two men inside. They sat for a moment and then got out. The one on the passenger side was Cobb, and as I watched, he reached back into the car and took out a flashlight and shined it inside the cab of my truck. The other detective, a younger guy in a black leather jacket, came around the car and my truck and played his light in from the passenger side, toward the back of the seat, the gun rack. Then both lights went out and the detectives walked quickly toward the door.

Roxanne let them in.

"Hello again," I heard Cobb say as I came down the stairs. "This is Detective Bruno of the Bangor Police Department. Is Mr. McMorrow—"

I appeared and Cobb paused.

"Hi," I said.

"Hello," Cobb said. He smiled and introduced the other detective again. He nodded at me, his black eyes searching my face. I could smell cologne on him, which seemed out of character. Roxanne turned toward the kitchen and he reflexively looked her up and down, then turned back to me.

"Hey, listen, Mr. McMorrow," Cobb said, sounding agreeable. "We don't want to bother Ms. Masterson here. I'm sure she's got things to do. So how 'bout we run over to Portland P.D. so we can talk?"

I considered it for a moment. They were taking me in, voluntarily. I flashed back to New York homicide cops. I could still hear them:

"You don't say the word suspect 'cause that means Miranda rights . . . . You always try to take them easy first, McMorrow, 'cause a guy isn't gonna say shit after you've banged his head on the car . . . . This ain't TV, you know what I'm saying?"

So what was this? I searched my memory for the term.

"A noncustodial interrogation?" I said.

Bruno's eyes narrowed.

"Jesus, McMorrow," Cobb said. "What you doing? Going to the criminal justice academy or something? We're just cops. We forgot all those big words, isn't that right?"

Bruno nodded. A lie.

Cobb said. "Hey, I'll drive. We'll bring you home."

He made it sound like we were going for beers. The three of us. Buddies. I turned toward Roxanne, saw the concern in her eyes, concern for me, for us, for all of us. I turned back to the cops.

"But there's something I should tell you," I said.

Cobb had moved toward the door, but he stopped. The Bangor detective hadn't taken his eyes off me.

"Rocky was here," I said. "But he just took off."

"How much lead time?" Cobb said.

I told him.

"Shit," he said.

"Right," I said.

I grabbed a leather jacket, told Roxanne to lock the doors and out we went. Down the steps and all the way to the car,

Bruno stayed to my right and Cobb to my left. As we reached the car, Bruno took a radio out of his jacket pocket and called Portland P.D. He gave his call number and Cobb's and asked Portland and South Portland to look for Rocky. Bruno knew his name, his age. When he paused, I added the glasses, the sweatpants.

We waited, then heard the call come over. An ATL for area units, with name and description. Stop and hold for S.P. three thirty-one and Bangor P.D. Juvenile wanted for questioning in connection with ten forty-eight, Bangor this date.

A ten forty-eight was a homicide.

Cobb smiled and opened the back door of the car. I started to get in, but Bruno put his hand on my shoulder.

"Hey, Mr. McMorrow," he said. "I noticed you've got the gun rack and everything in your truck. You carrying anything you shouldn't be?"

"No," I said.

"You're sure?"

"Yeah."

But as I leaned toward the car again, I remembered. Patted my pocket. Felt the weight of it against my hip.

I stood again.

"There's a knife in my right jacket pocket," I said.

"Okay," Bruno said, moving close behind me. There was just a hint of tension in his voice, more than a hint in mine.

"Why don't you just kind of empty your pockets, sir," he said.

"The knife's not mine," I said.

"Is that right?" Cobb said.

"It's Rusty's. I took it from him."

"Uh-huh," Bruno said. "Let's see it. Right on the roof of the car there."

"He tried to use it on me."

I fished it out and placed it on the car roof, where it rocked like a teeter-totter on the curve of the snow-dusted metal.

"Oh, yeah?" Cobb said.

I followed the knife with a sheaf of folded bills. Some change. A crumpled receipt. My wallet and my keys. On the key ring there was a thirty-ought-six cartridge, a gift given me by Clair when I'd finally learned to shoot straight.

"It's a dummy," I said. "My friend's a Marine."

"Right," Cobb said. "Rambo, there. McMorrow's got this friend who's some kind of Green Beret or something. He's the one busted the logger guy's nose. A real bad-ass but with gray hair."

"Silver," I said.

"Hey, who's telling this story, McMorrow?"

Cobb was smiling again. Bruno wasn't.

"That it?" he said, when my pockets were empty.

"Yeah."

"Would you mind if I checked, just in case you missed something?"

I turned and put my hands on the top of the car. Bruno patted me down. Neck and underarms, waist and crotch, boot tops, left and right. Cobb leaned into the front seat and came out with a small paper bag and a surgical glove. He put the glove on and used that hand to pick up the knife by its ends and drop it into the bag.

"You're probably gonna find blood on it."

"Is that right, McMorrow?"

"Rusty's," I said. "He got cut a little when I took it away from him."

"No kidding," Cobb said, and then to Bruno. "See, I told you we'd have something to talk about. I mean, for a newspaper guy, McMorrow here is a very interesting person."

CHAPTER 43

We parked in the garage that was part of the building, a big modern place with a glass-fronted entrance that let you look in at the people, sort of like an ant farm filled with cops. Cobb and Bruno flashed their gold badges to the dispatcher in the window and she buzzed us in, Cobb first, then me, and Bruno bringing up the rear. A detective coming down the stairs, a short muscular guy in jeans with a nine-millimeter on his hip, knew Cobb and they said hey and hello and hit each other on the shoulder. Then Cobb introduced Bruno while I stood there like somebody's tagalong little brother.

Except I wasn't part of their brotherhood, and the Portland cop knew it. He looked at me, then at my hands, to see if they were cuffed.

We went past the dispatcher's counter and into another room, and the Portland cop came back with a key on a plastic tag. He led the way up the stairs and down a hall, and opened the door. The detectives said, "Thanks." I didn't bother.

The room was white with white plastic chairs and a white-topped table. Cobb motioned for me to sit and I did, and he and Bruno did, too. Cobb's black tape recorder went in the center of the table, with Bruno's black-and-silver one beside it.

"There," Cobb said, smiling. "Stereo."

"Okay, Mr. McMorrow," Bruno said, very seriously

as if to offset Cobb's banter. "Tell us about your day."

I took a deep breath and folded my hands in front of me on the table.

"It's been a long one," I said.

"We got time," Cobb said.

So I started off, as the little red lights flickered in front of me. Cobb paced and listened. Bruno, his hair just so, teeth very white, sat and took notes in a small coilbound pad. When he wrote, he stuck out his tongue.

I started with the visit from Rusty and his buddies, and Bruno looked up when I got to the part about the pants coming off and the knife coming out. But he didn't say anything, and Cobb didn't either. I'd expected Cobb to rush things along because he'd heard it before, but instead he asked some of the same questions he'd asked that morning. He even asked me to back up to my conversation with Flossie.

"What was it you said to her?"

I told him again. About Rocky. About Kitty.

"But it's not a cat?" Cobb said.

"I don't think so. I think it's a person. A woman or a girl. Like I told you, there was a woman killed in a hit-and-run."

"Yeah, right, and her name was Kathy or something," Cobb said.

Bruno looked at him.

"Begins with a K," Cobb said.

Bruno looked puzzled.

"An old case," the older detective said. "McMorrow's idea, not mine."

And then he told me to keep going. I did, recounting my visit to Bangor to search for Rocky. I told them about finding Tammy and talking to her on the street. When I got to the part where she told me Rocky was at the museum, Bruno told me to back up and start again, because he couldn't keep up with me. That was transparent, but I did it anyway.

Before I talked about the museum, Cobb went and got three coffees from a machine. I didn't drink mine and Bruno didn't, either. Cobb slurped and said, "Go ahead," and I did. Rocky in the museum. Rocky giving the tour. Rocky denying he went home that night, the night his mother died, but slipping up when it came to the part about the light in the cellar. Rocky saying his father was going to kill him. Rusty saying he was going to wring Rocky's neck.

"A lot of parents say that, don't you think?" Cobb said.

"Not like that," I said. "This was meaner."

He shrugged, and then I talked about grappling with Rusty, how I felt he'd threatened Rocky, how he tried to use the knife on me when I had him down.

"He says you jumped him and pulled a knife on him so the kid could get away," Cobb said.

"That's not true," I said.

"What's that on your shirt?" Bruno said.

I looked down. Near my waist, there was a brown stain in the denim.

"I think it's blood. He jerked around and the knife cut him."

"We're gonna have to take that shirt," he said.

"Whatever," I said.

So then there was the chase on the streets, and the ride in the truck. I told them about Rocky saying things like, "She didn't do it," and "They'll put her in jail."

"For what?" Bruno said.

"I don't know," I said.

"Like she's alive?" Cobb asked.

"Yeah. He said something about not hurting her. And when he figured out I was trying to turn him over to the cops, he said, 'He'll kill me,' and tried to jump out of the truck."

"Who'll kill him?" Cobb said.

"Rusty, I think."

And on it went, how we got to Roxanne's and Rocky was outside the door and he guessed it was Tammy who was dead. The talk about "stupid kitty," and more about his mother going to jail.

"What did he say? Exactly?" Cobb said, finally taking a seat.

"I don't remember exactly. Something like, 'She couldn't've done it. She's just saying she did.' And I said something like, 'Who could do it?' And Rocky said, 'He could.' "

"Could what?"

"I don't know. Were you going to put her in jail for something?"

"Not that I know of."

"And you would know, right?"

"You would think so," Cobb said.

"Jesus," Bruno muttered.

They paused. The black recorder clicked as the tape ran out. Bruno flipped the cassette.

"So," Cobb said.

"So he guessed who was dead," I said. "He guessed it was Tammy. After I heard about it, I was talking to Roxanne. He was listening. Through the door."

"How'd you hear?" Bruno asked.

I hesitated, then told him.

"Newspeople stick together, huh?" Cobb said.

"Like cops," I said.

"What'd he hear? Rocky, I mean," Bruno said.

"Through the door?"

"Right."

"I don't know. That somebody was dead. That it was a kid, a girl. Maybe that I'd just talked to her."

"Would that be enough?"

I thought, my head in my hands, my elbows on the table. The recorders made a very faint hum. I looked up suddenly and caught Cobb staring at me intently, the offhand facade peeled back.

He looked away.

"I don't know," I said. "Maybe. He knew I'd spent some time with Tammy. She was the only street kid I really knew, except for him. He knew I'd set her up with Tippy Danforth and all that."

"The cat lady," Cobb said.

"But not the same one," Bruno said.

"No," I said. "Because the other one's dead."

"Since when?" Cobb asked.

"1987," I said. "The date on the note."

"And what's the connection?" Bruno said.

Cobb answered.

"The kuh sound," he said.

CHAPTER 44

But that was only the beginning. I talked and they listened intently. Noted every change of my expression, searched for meaning in every pause, every swallow, every rub of my nose, scratch of my head. No one gets more complete attention than a witness in a murder investigation, unless, of course, it's a suspect.

Maybe I was a little of both.

They wanted to talk about the time I spent with Tammy. I recounted our conversations, described the boys she had been with before she went for a walk with me. I tried to remember everything she'd said about her family, her home. At nine forty-five, Cobb left the room and when he came back, he had Divan with him, from Waldo County.

Jack McMorrow. This is your life.

"Hi, there," I said.

"Hello, Mr. McMorrow," Divan said.

"You know each other?" Bruno said.

"We go way back," I said. "A couple of days. Seems like years."

Divan gave me a noncommittal smile.

"You don't mind if Officer Divan joins us at this late date? She's assisting in the investigation," Cobb said.

"What investigation?"

He hesitated, then smiled, his defensive reflex.

"You've got a suicide in Woodfield, a homicide in Bangor," I said.

"So what's the connection?" Bruno said.

Bruno glanced up at Cobb. Divan looked at him, too. Cobb stared at me, and then the grin kicked in.

"I'm looking at one of them," he said.

"True," I said. "And don't forget you've got a runaway, too. What's the connection there?"

"We'd like to find him," Cobb said, "but every time we show up, you've turned him loose."

"I didn't turn him loose. He bolted."

One smile. Two cold stares.

Cobb brushed at his bald spot and turned. As he started to pace, he asked me if I had any idea where Rocky might have gone. I said I didn't, really. Monument Square. A shelter. The mall. But if he made the highway and stuck out his thumb, he could be anywhere.

They wanted to know about the fight, again.

I told them.

They wanted to know what I said to Rocky in the museum, what he said to me.

I told them.

They wanted to know what Rusty said at the museum.

I told them.

They wanted to know everything that happened on the ride from Bangor. The time at Roxanne's. They wanted to know what I'd said to Roxanne in the bedroom.

I told them that, too.

They wanted to know what I thought of Tammy, about the Indian restaurant, again. Tippy again. The part about the taxi. Everything, again and again.

At ten forty, I realized what made Cobb a good detective. Bruno and Divan looked pale and drawn, but Cobb didn't tire. In fact, as the night went on, he became more animated, more focused, more intent on my every word. He paced the room, pawed at his bald spot, gestured with his hands. It was like we were screenwriters collaborating on a script.

"Now tell me again why you think Rocky is afraid of his stepfather. . . ."

The coffee curdled and the tapes stacked up, carefully labeled in Bruno's left-handed script. And then Cobb suddenly smiled and said, "Well, I hate to cut this short."

He smiled. Bruno looked relieved.

"But we need your clothes and your boots."

"Okay."

"And we need your truck."

"Yup."

"And we need to talk to your girlfriend."

"Now?"

"As soon as she can get here. Can she bring you some clothes?"

"Yeah," I said. "You want me to call her?"

"We'll take care of it," Cobb said.

"How long will she be? She has to get up in the morning and she's pregnant."

The investigation halted for a moment of awkward silence. The business of violent death had been oddly interrupted by news of impending birth.

"Hey, this is gonna sound funny, coming right now, but would you mind giving us a blood sample?"

I shrugged.

"Just to sort of nail things down for us."

"Nail things down which way?" I said, looking up from the table.

I waited for an answer. It didn't come.

It was eleven thirty-five, way past her bedtime, when the police cruiser drew up in front of the door. A cop came around to open the car door for her. She was pale and worried, like an indicted celebrity in a newspaper photograph. She swung her legs out of the car and visibly steeled herself and started for the door, a small duffel in hand, the cop at her side.

The glass door clicked and opened and Roxanne strode through. When she saw me, she hurried toward me, her eyes searching for a clue to my status, my state of mind. I smiled and she came to me and took my hand. I took the bag and Divan appeared from the dispatch room to my right and Roxanne gave my hand a squeeze, and Divan said hello and I said, "I'll be here," and Divan led her through another door and she was gone. I stood there for a moment, and then Bruno materialized, holding a grocery bag. He took my bag and unzipped it, and rummaged through it.

"She bring the Uzi?" I said.

Bruno looked at me, startled. Then he got it, but he didn't smile, just told me to follow him down the hall to an interview room, where I stripped and handed my clothes and boots to him through a crack in the door. Then I closed the door and glanced at myself in the mirror. I looked old, face drawn and lined, my skin a stubbled pale gray in the fluorescent light. But the mirror no doubt was one way, so I turned and put on the shorts and jeans, shirt and sneakers.

Roxanne had forgotten socks.

So with bare ankles, I waited for her. From my chair, I could hear the radio chatter, the dispatchers talking to people who had called on the phone. "Is he conscious now, ma'am? . . . Does your boyfriend have the weapon at this time? . . . Just stay put, sir. We'll send someone over to talk to your neighbors. . . . What was your daughter wearing, ma'am? Ma'am, we'll do our best to locate her. No, there have been no accidents tonight. She's probably fine, ma'am. . . ."

I wouldn't be so sure.

I got up and stretched, looked toward the door through which Roxanne had disappeared. I'd tried to protect a kid, and Roxanne had found herself having to protect me. From whom? From Rusty? Or was the common denominator here a skinny little kid who called himself the Grim Reaper?

A shudder ran through me as I sat there. Rocky in my house. Rocky taken in by Tippy, trusting Tippy. Rocky standing silently outside Roxanne's bedroom door. Was there a pathological pattern? Did Rocky slash the hands that fed him? Had this Kitty tried to help him? Was that why there was a question?

How could she live?

*   *   *

And then the door behind me clicked, and I turned as Divan thanked Roxanne for coming in. A patrol car pulled up and I looked to Divan and she said I could go, they were all set.

We rode in silence, me and a blond woman cop. From the bridge, the harbor waters and the bay were black as space. And then we were off the bridge, and turning into the condos, where the day ended as it had begun, with flashing lights outside my door.

This time it was a Portland P.D. ramp truck that had rolled into the parking lot at Roxanne's building. The ramp-truck driver was a young guy who leapt from the cab as Roxanne's neighbors watched from their windows. I stood with the cop and watched, too, as the wrecker driver wrote the truck registration number on a form on a clipboard. Roxanne went inside.

"I need to sign anything?" I called to the driver.

"No, sir," he said. "And everything in the car stays."

"Cell phone?"

"Everything."

And then from the cab of the truck, the driver took a pole with hooks on both ends, and used it to pop open my truck door. Leaning in, he pressed the clutch pedal down with one end of the pole, and hooked the shifter with the other. Then he eased his way out, closing the door with the pole, too. The hydraulic rams lowered the ramp, and he hooked a cable to the truck's rear axle. The motor revved and in the flashing yellow lights, my truck rolled up the ramp, which then tipped back into place. The driver chained the Toyota down and then the ramp truck and the police car were gone.

The wheels of justice don't always turn slowly.

CHAPTER 45

When I came in, Roxanne was already in bed. The light was out, and she was lying on her back. Her eyes were closed but she wasn't asleep. I sat on the edge of the bed.

"Sorry about all this," I said.

"It's okay."

"Was it difficult?"

"No. It was just late."

"What did they ask?"

"About you. All kinds of questions about you."

"What'd you tell them?"

"The truth."

"Did they believe you?"

Roxanne put her hands over her eyes, ran them down her cheekbones to her chin.

"I don't know. Who knows? I'm just—"

"Tired," I said. "I know. I'll let you sleep."

"Jack, I'm so tired I feel sick. And I can't do that. It's not good for me, for us."

"I know."

"I have to be at work at seven."

"So call in sick."

"I can't," Roxanne said. "Jack, I just need to sleep. We'll talk tomorrow."

"Okay," I said, and I kissed her on the forehead. She gave my hand a squeeze and then closed her eyes. I eased off the bed and left the room and went downstairs.

The house was quiet, but not silent. The refrigerator hummed, and the microwave beeped, telling Roxanne the hot water for her coffee was ready. It had been ready for hours, but the machine beeped patiently, a faithful servant. I turned it off and the kitchen light, too, then the light in the hall. When my eyes had adjusted to the dark, I went from window to window, door to door, turning the locks and peering out into the cold stillness. Nothing moved under the parking lot lights. Nothing showed against the glow of the city, across the harbor. The bridge lights glowed red in the sky like the lights of motionless airplanes. I watched for a few minutes, eyes narrowed, looking for some clue in the blackness, some reason for a girl's life to end in this lonely way, for a woman to live with such sadness that she would choose death over the son she loved and who loved her.

A life conceived, two lives extinguished. And the lives gutted and tossed aside seemed to somehow diminish the value of the one life we'd created. If those lives were cheapened, so was this one. If no explanation were offered, all of our lives were made cheaper still. If the explanation involved me, my baby would be sullied. And I wanted its slate to be oh so clean.

So I stood and watched. Waited, but no clue appeared. Nothing showed, except the lights and their reflections on the black, beguiling water. I considered going out, looking for Rocky, but I'd done that and even with him in hand, had come up empty. It was time to move ten feet and dig a new hole. I turned away from the window and walked to Roxanne's desk and fumbled for the button in the dark.

I found it.

The computer turned on.

It burped and whirred and clicked, and the screen glowed blue. I sat there in its wash and half-grudgingly clicked on the little pictures.

I went to a people-finder site, typed and hit the enter key and the machine did its thing. Sitting in the blue haze, I waited while the machine rounded them up.

Sandra Bakers. Three-hundred ninety-one of them.

Downey, California. Delray Beach, Florida. Sun City, Arizona. Newport, Vermont. St. Paul, Minnesota and Bryn Mawr, Pennsylvania. I scrolled through quickly and the Sandra Bakers marched across the screen. There were dozens of Sandra L. Bakers, even more listed under Sandra M.

If my Sandra Baker had left the state, this would be no help at all.

But odds were that she had stayed, so I narrowed my search to Maine. The computer scuttled here and there and rounded up only three Sandra Bakers with Maine phone listings. None lived in the Somerset County town of Scane-sett or in Somerset County at all. One was in Searsport, southeast of Bangor, another in South Portland. The third was in Eastport, way downeast. That did not include Sandra Bakers who didn't have phones in their names, or didn't have phones at all, or lived with their daughters and sons-in-law. Or Sandra Bakers who were listed under the initial S. Or had married or remarried. Or who were dead.

Always a possibility.

Sitting there in the quiet, I searched for S. Bakers in Maine. There were five, scattered from Ellsworth to Auburn, none in Scanesett. I started to reach for the phone, but then remembered it was one in the morning. I put the phone back down. It was just the computer and me. I put it to work.

Getting my date book from the counter, I dug out the

microfilm page with the hit-and-run and double-checked the first name of the investigator, a David Turgeon. I'd never heard of him, so I ran him, too, and got the scattered list. Forty-three of them around the country, four in Maine. If he was a detective in 1987, there was a good chance he was retired. There were five David Turgeons in Florida, including one in Pompano and another in St. Augustine.

Or he could be patrolling in Aroostook County. I'd find him in the morning.

It promised to be a day's work, but no more. At the *Times,* I'd once done a story revisiting the relatives of victims of a serial killer ten to fifteen years after the murders. Some were easily found, just by opening the phone book. Some took calls to other relatives, neighbors, phone operators, town offices, and tax assessors. As long as each encounter yielded a single new clue, the trail meandered on and the person eventually could be located. Even in the vast reaches of the country, even in the teeming cities, it is very hard to truly disappear.

If Sandra Baker was alive, I'd find her. I'd find her if she wasn't.

I shut down the whirring machine, with its blue Cyclops eye, and made one more round of the perimeter, as Clair would have called it. Portland was a city that, unlike many, actually slept, and the harbor was black, the skyline dimmed. Roxanne's neighbors were snug in their beds, resting so that in the morning they could once more sally forth to earn their mortgage payments. I padded quietly up the stairs and went into the bedroom, pausing to look once more from the darkened window. As I watched, a car turned in from the road and coasted through the lot.

It was an unmarked cruiser. As it slowed behind Roxanne's car, I could see the head turn in the driver's seat. They were looking for Rocky, and making sure they didn't lose me.

There was no chance.

I fell asleep with my arm draped protectively over Roxanne, my face against her hair. I awoke to the sound of her hair dryer in the bathroom. It still was dark, a blue-black dawn. The bathroom door opened and the light spilled out and I squinted as she came over. She was wearing a wool skirt and dark tights and a big sweater.

"Is that one of those maternity outfits?" I said.

"Jack, I've had this sweater all winter."

"Oh. It looks different."

"You look at it differently."

"Sorry."

"You don't have to be sorry. I'm glad you do."

Roxanne leaned over and kissed my forehead.

"But I've got to go."

"What time is it?"

"Six thirty."

"What do you have to do? Make the doughnuts?"

"Get my act together for today."

"At six thirty?"

Roxanne hesitated.

"While you were gone last night, I got a call from the district manager. I've got to meet with him at seven."

"About what?"

She paused again.

"Well . . ."

"About Rocky? About me?"

"It's nothing. He just needs to know what's going on. I guess he got a call from the police last night."

"Sorry," I said. "You need me?"

"No, it's nothing," Roxanne said. "Routine."

But there was an edge of apprehension in her voice.

"I thought we might talk," I said. "You know, about things. Like, I haven't told anyone about the, well, the—"

"Baby."

"Right. The baby."

"And you want to see Clair and Mary."

"I don't know. Don't you? It's a big deal. But you can't come up?"

"Not until Saturday."

"I'll come back."

"You don't have to," Roxanne said.

"I know, but I will anyway. Late. I've got to be at work at three, but I don't think I'll be late. Something tells me they may not need me."

"How are you going to get there?"

I'd forgotten.

"Oh, yeah. I'll rent something. You think insurance covers a rental when the police take your car in connection with a murder investigation?"

Roxanne didn't laugh.

"Are you going to talk to those detectives again?"

"I'm sure. I want to know if they found him. And they want a blood test and they said something about a polygraph."

"Jack—"

"It's nothing. Routine, as long as you're not lying."

She kissed me again.

"You've never lied in your life," Roxanne said.

"Just a few white ones," I said. "But not to you. You know, I'd rather you weren't alone tonight."

"I'll lock the doors."

"Leave the outside lights on."

"Okay."

"Have somebody over."

"I just want to have you over."

"I know, but I'd feel better if somebody else were here earlier. How 'bout Skip next door?"

"He's in St. John, the Virgin Islands. He and his new flame, this stockbroker guy named George. They chartered a boat."

Roxanne squeezed my hand.

"Jack, I've seen worse than Rocky and his father."

"Maybe not the worst of them."

"I'm a big girl."

"I know you are. But now—"

"Worrying for two, Jack McMorrow?"

"Yes," I said. "I am."

"And I love you for it," Roxanne said. "But I'll be fine."

I stayed in bed and listened. The almost musical tap of her heels on the floors. The door opening and closing. The sound of the Explorer starting, and the sound of her scraper on the iced-over windshield. The motor revving, then the car crunching on the ice, and Roxanne fading into the distance.

I was alone, a chronic condition.

After a minute, I got up and showered and shaved, and looked at my tooth in the mirror. It seemed to be turning gray, but I told myself it was the bathroom light. White lie number one. After toast and tea, I called the car rental place at the Portland Jetport and asked if they would deliver a car to me. The young woman on the phone said they didn't do that, so I said I had to be in court in Bangor. Still no dice. I hung up and called a cab. At the cab company, another woman told me it would be a half-hour. I told her I was in no hurry; it was just the typical American male's innate fear of being without a motor vehicle. She said it would be an hour. I said actually even ten o'clock would be fine. She said that would be finer.

So with the taxi scheduled, I went to work. It was too early to start on Sandra Bakers, so I called Tippy Danforth, who'd be out cleaning the pens. The tape began to play, but then she picked up. I said hello.

"Oh," she said, as though not sure how to react.

"I'm sorry about everything."

"Well, I am, too. Terribly sorry. It's—"

She caught herself again, and I knew. She wasn't sure how much she could say, wasn't sure exactly what I was. Copy editor or pervert? Good Samaritan or psychopath? It made a difference.

"You've talked to the police, I assume," I said.

"Well . . ."

"Whatever. I'm just calling to say I'm sorry that you got involved, with Tammy and all this. I was just trying to help her and you were, too. And it's all gone to hell."

"Yes, it has," Tippy said.

"And this is the other thing. Rocky, I'm not so sure you should be around him. If he comes back, I mean. He was here last night—I'm in Portland—and he was acting pretty strange and then he took off again. I don't know if the cops have picked him up, but if he turns up at your place, or in Bangor at all, I'd just call Bangor P.D."

"I certainly will do that."

Her voice had softened.

"So I guess that's about it. I don't know. That and maybe what Tammy said. I saw her yesterday on the street and we talked and she told me how much she liked being at your house and working for you. She said she was going back to see kittens born. She said you were going to give her one to keep. She was happy about that."

"That's true. I told her she could keep it here. I didn't want her carting it around on the streets. The boy, too."

"The boy, too, what?"

"I said he could have one."

"A cat?"

"A kitten," Tippy said. "These kids are so alone. You know, I think they just need a companion that doesn't question them, interrogate them. Something that will just love them."

"That could be."

"But you're right about him behaving strangely. Because when I said he could have one of the litter, too, his reaction was quite odd, really."

"What did he do?"

"Well, I just said, 'How would you like a kitten?' and he just stopped talking, just withdrew. Never said another word in my presence, and, of course, when I got up he was gone."

"That's all you said?"

"Yes. Do you think I offended him? I'm not around children, so I don't know quite how they think. Not like I know cats and dogs. Maybe he thought I was treating him like a baby or something. But that's just the way I refer to them."

"To whom?"

"To the cats. I call them my kitties. I said, 'You can have a kitty, too.' "

"Kitty, as in Katia?" I said, half to myself.

"What?" Tippy said.

"Nothing," I said. "If you see him, or his stepfather, call the police. Call me, too."

Tippy may have hung up puzzled but I didn't. It was almost eight o'clock; I made another cup of tea, and with barely a glance at the harbor skyline, went to the desk and picked up the phone book. I opened the inside of the front cover and went down the list of emergency numbers. This wasn't one, but there was a business listing for the Maine State Police in Augusta. I dialed. Waited.

A man answered, and I asked for Detective Turgeon. He said there was no detective by that name with the Maine State Police, could somebody else help me? I said I wasn't sure, but had Detective Turgeon retired? He said he didn't know but he'd check.

He put me on hold. I waited, and he came back. He said Detective Turgeon retired some time ago. I asked where Turgeon was now and he said he had no idea, as though the detective had been lost at sea. And then I asked, as he was about to hang up, whether a ten-year-old death, a hit-and-run, would still be under investigation.

He said it would be active until it was solved. I asked if it would be on the bottom of somebody's case list. He said all active cases are under investigation, but some may not get daily attention. In other words, when David Turgeon packed up his desk, the case of Katia Poulin went with him.

So I took my Turgeon list and started calling. In Orland, Maine, on the coast, I found a David Turgeon who had been sleeping until the phone rang. I asked for David Turgeon, the former police detective, and this David Turgeon said he worked nights at a supermarket. Before I could apologize, he hung up. A David Turgeon in Kennebunk, Maine, had left an answering machine message in which a lisping toddler said, "Dave and Jessica and Chelsea and Matthew aren't home. Oh, yeah. Leave a message after the beep-beep."

I didn't. Instead, for some reason, I moved directly to St. Augustine, where a woman answered.

I made my pitch. She asked who I was. I told her and asked if I had the right place.

"Well, yes and no," the woman said.

All right, I said to myself, pumping my fist.

"Yes and no?" I said.

"Yes, my husband was a detective with the Maine State Police."

"Could I speak with him?"

"You're going to need a mighty long phone line," the woman said. "Mr. Turgeon passed away in 1994."

I said I was sorry. She said she was, too, and sorry she couldn't help me, but if I would excuse her—

"Not to keep you, but did your husband ever talk about a hit-and-run case? A woman killed in Newport? I don't believe it ever was solved."

In the movies, this would be the serendipitous moment. Some cases he put behind him, but that hit-and-run case gnawed at him, she would say. He went to his grave hoping the perpetrator would come to justice.

"You don't mean the shooting in Rockland?" Mrs. David Turgeon said. "That one bothered him."

"No, this was a woman run over and killed. In Newport."

I waited as she considered it.

"No," she said. "I don't know."

"Woman might have been called Kitty? Kitty Poulin? Katia Poulin?"

"No," the detective's widow began, and I could feel myself sag. "You sure you have that right? That name to me is a cocaine name. It was everywhere back then, just like people used to have martinis."

"And that's what you think of when you hear her name?"

"I'm probably wrong," Mrs. Turgeon said. "But I think of Dave saying, 'Another life down the tubes 'cause of that poison.' He said that a lot. You know, they sold it in the bars like it was peanuts. Terrible thing. And now I really do have to go."

So she went, just like that, just like Katia Poulin had gone, quietly and without fuss or bother. A week of investigation. A bunch of dead ends, and perhaps Detective Turgeon had been weary after twenty years, and his caseload was heavy and there were only so many hours in the day. And then perhaps there had been a live homicide, one with real clues and real suspects and a chance of a quick and just solution, and Katia Poulin slipped away, lost in ever-growing stacks of paperwork.

Like the papers in front of me.

I spread out my lists of Sandra Bakers. Like a salesman with mouths to feed, I started calling.

I started with the Sandra Bakers in Maine, considering the three. Searsport, Portland, and Eastport. Katia's obituary had listed only Scanesett as a Maine connection. Lubec seemed least likely, Portland and Searsport about equal. But in Maine, like most poor rural states, people tended to drift downstate toward the cities. Like something washed downstream, they caught in the logjam of jobs and welfare that cities offered. Caught like Rocky.

So I tried Portland's Sandra Baker first. The number rang, and a recording began. The number had been changed. The new number was . . .

I dialed again. It rang four times and a man answered. I asked for Sandra Baker. He said, "It's for you. Somebody selling something."

"Just hang up," a woman's voice said.

"You do it," he said.

The phone clattered and then a woman said, "Yeah?"

"Hello, is this Sandra Baker?" I asked, not too brightly.

"Who's this?" the woman said.

"This is Jack McMorrow at the Bangor *Clarion* newspaper. I'm trying to locate the Sandra Baker who is the friend of Katia Poulin?"

I paused.

"Is this the right number?"

"Who is it?" the man said in the background.

"Some christly newspaper in Bangor."

"Tell 'em we already get the Portland paper. What the hell we want the Bangor paper for?"

"Did you know Katia Poulin?"

"Who?" she said and she hung up.

I dialed again.

The Sandra Baker in Eastport wasn't home but a little girl was. She answered on the first ring and said her mother was at work. The girl sounded about six, and I got the impression she was home alone.

"When will your mom be back?" I asked.

"She gets done work at two," the girl said. "I get the bus at eight-nineteen."

"Have you ever lived near Scanesett?"

The phone went dead.

So I dialed over and over. No answer in Searsport. S. Baker in Hallowell was Steve. S. Baker in Oquossoc was disconnected, probably a summer camp. In Waterville, I left a message on a machine. In York, no answer. In Hollis Center, the woman who answered was deaf, which raised the question of why she answered at all. At nine o'clock, my Sandra Baker still was at large.

I sipped cold tea and leaned back, then called directory assistance. An electronic whisper, then a real person, a guy, came on the line. I pictured him rustling through pages but probably he was peering at a screen.

"There's no Sandra Baker listed in Portland, sir."

"Oh. How 'bout Lewiston?"

He paused.

"No. I don't see—"

"Could you try Bangor then?"

"All right."

He was losing patience, so I told him I really appreciated his help. He didn't answer, but then he said the number was unpublished.

"In Bangor?"

"Yessir, but that number is—"

"Is this the Ohio Street or Broadway listing?"

"Neither, but I really can't say any more."

"Thanks," I said. "You've been a big help."

He hung up, and I did, too. Another Sandra Baker. Scanesett to Bangor? Forty miles, from a small town to the nearest big city? It made sense, as much as anything did. All that remained was to find her and ask her about Katia and Kitty, why Rocky was running, why he carried that date in his pocket, why he thought everyone he touched turned to dust.

CHAPTER 46

The mini-van I rented at the Portland airport was black, with those smoked windows the car people call "privacy glass." It was big and cushy and quiet, and I turned in the driver's seat and looked back, trying to picture a kid in a baby seat, and a playpen stowed in the stern. But that image was replaced by one of Clair, sitting inside the sliding door with his shotgun. The Clair image came easier.

What was wrong with that picture?

I took 295 into the city, whipped off the highway onto Congress Street. I slowed and began scanning the sidewalks: students from the university or the art school, shuffling along like Sherpas under their backpacks. A few more of the lost souls, who gladly traded their dreary rooms for the biting cold. In the lot of a convenience store, an old man in red rubber boots and a woman's knit hat shuffled along, moving his feet like unfeeling stumps. He was accosted by two younger men, unshaven sidewalk jocks in baseball hats and curled-up sneakers. I slowed as I passed. One of them gave the old man a cigarette. I turned hard and pulled in.

The store was open twenty-four hours, a place to thaw your feet and hands as you dawdled as long as possible over a paper cup of coffee. On a cold night, this place was a sanctuary.

I shut off the van and got out. The two guys in the hats and the old man in the red boots still were huddled down near the street. I approached them, and one of the guys looked up.

"Hey," I said.

He nodded, disheveled and wary.

"I'm looking for a kid. A young kid."

The guy grinned, and the inside of his black-toothed mouth looked like something out of a corpse.

"Who ain't?" he said.

The other guy laughed, but it turned into a tubercular cough. I waited for the hacking to cease.

"I ain't. Not for that reason. I'm looking for a kid named Rocky. Fourteen and little and skinny. Big glasses and a red plaid jacket."

They shook their heads, first one, then the other. The old

man dragged on his cigarette and squinted at me through the smoke.

"You a cop?" the second guy said.

I shook my head.

"Friend," I said.

"There a reward?" the first guy said.

I considered it, then took a notebook from my parka. I wrote my number in Prosperity.

"Yeah, there is," I said.

"How much?"

I considered that, too. How badly did I want Rocky, what bounty should I put on him? How badly did I want this to be over?

"Hundred bucks, cash."

The baseball hats looked at each other, the greed passing through them like a jolt of adrenaline.

"But he's got to be fine. If something happens to him, we've got the opposite of a reward. You know what I'm saying?"

They all looked at me. I didn't flinch and they looked away.

"Really, information as to his whereabouts would be good enough."

I scrawled the toll-free number at the *Clarion.*

"Make sure you ask for Jack. If I'm not there, leave a message on my voice mail."

They looked at me like I'd asked them to write software.

"It's just an answering machine. You know, talk after the beep?"

I wrote "red plaid jacket" and "Rocky" and "skinny with glasses" and held out the paper. The first guy, the alpha male, snatched it like it was the hundred-dollar bill itself. He glanced at it, then folded it small with reddened dirty fingers and put it in the front pocket of his jeans.

"He's on the street?"

"Yeah, I think so."

"Turning tricks? Shooting up?"

"No."

"No gang shit? I ain't messing with them little bastards."

"No, nothing like that," I said. "He's just a kid. A nice kid."

They looked at me like they thought that highly unlikely. I thanked them, started to turn away, and the first guy said, "Hey, buddy. How 'bout a couple bucks up front?"

I turned back and fished a five out of my pocket. The first guy grabbed it and I left them bickering over it like jackals over carrion. I continued on.

Inside the store, I made my inquiry but got a blank shrug. I bought tacks and tape and made my way up Congress, leaving my messages outside a tattoo parlor, at a news stand, in front of a karate school. I asked my questions, ripped out my pages. Nobody admitted seeing Rocky. At a tattered bulletin board where Portland's underground cryptically surfaced, I wrote "Rocky. Call Jack" and the *Clarion* number on a piece of paper and tacked it up.

At Monument Square, I hit another bulletin board, and tried to talk to two bulky young women and a misshapen man leaning against the wall of a vacant storefront. I was giving my pitch when a couple of kids came out of a restaurant and started over. One of them was the girl from the alley fight, the one with the black lipstick who'd tried to bite me.

"Hey, I know you," I said. "You seen Rocky?"

"This guy's some kinda cop," she said, her eyes fixed on me. "Beat the shit out of my friend."

"I don't think so—" I started to say, but they were already backing away, five people retreating in five directions. They didn't make crosses with their fingers, but close to it.

I followed the girl and she broke into a run and slipped through traffic and I gave up.

I walked back to the van, sat for a minute in the warm velour, and drove around the block to the shelter. It was closed and the children had been turned loose to range for food, like organic chickens. There was a message board there, and I left mine with all the others.

Rocky, call Jack at the office. . . . Tanya M., we love you. Please call home. . . . Laney, call Michael at DHS. . . . Damian T., your mom isn't mad. Everything's fine. . . ."

Sure it was.

So the traps were set, the weir in place. If Rocky had stayed in Portland, perhaps he'd let himself be caught. If . . .

I went back to the van, double-parked on Free Street, and circled the block. At the far end of Congress, outside the *Portland Press Herald* building, I stopped and went to a phone booth and called Roxanne. Fumbling with the quarters in the cold, I left messages at her office and at home. I told her I was on my way to Prosperity and Bangor, that I really didn't want her to be alone. I was about to tell her I loved her when the answering machine beeped and hung up.

At noon, I was on the outskirts of Augusta. An oncoming city cop flashed his lights at me to warn me to slow down. I did, until the cruiser disappeared from view in the mirror, and then I gave the van its rein and continued east, through Vassalboro, South China, the town of Palermo, which had nothing to do with Sicily. I passed mobile-home churches with signs that promised salvation, used-car lots that promised the same, no money down. And then the Waldo County hills grew steeper, with spruce-green spills amid the hardwood browns, and the landscape, with its staggering barns and grown-over pastures, took on the poignant bleakness that I for

some reason found so reassuring. There was solace in the lone-
liness of these ridges, a pathos that was almost invigorating.

Roxanne said I took comfort from obscurity, but I said I
had tasted obscurity on Manhattan sidewalks, and there was
something stark and noble and timeless in these sleepy,
drunken hollows. She said she enjoyed the woods, in small
doses, and I said the same of cities, even the small one in
which she lived. I found the city smugness too laughable;
she found the country poverty and isolation too hopeless.
We would have to compromise somehow, five months from
now, but in the meantime, I turned from Route 3 and
wound my way toward my personal patch of oblivion. I
turned off at Prosperity, turned again at the big oaks, and
then onto my road.

There were tire tracks in the snow and I followed them
up the rise and past the college girls' house, still deserted,
past Mrs. Soule's, and up to my house, where the car or
truck had turned in. It had sat there, but there were no footprints in the crusty dusting. The car had then backed out,
and continued on. I did the same, following it up the road
to Clair's where it had turned into the yard and driven up
the ramp and into the barn.

I pulled in and parked in front of the rolling barn door
and sat there with the van motor running. The little door
inset in the big barn door opened and Clair came out. I
buzzed the window down as he walked over, tugging at his
hat and looking the black van over.

"What'd you do?" he said. "Rob an undertaker?"

"My new career. There's money in stiffs."

"Sure there is, if you don't mind working up to your elbows in gizzards."

And then I thought of Tammy, that little girl dead on a
table somewhere, stabbed and then quartered by the process

of autopsy. I stopped smiling and shut off the motor. Clair leaned close to the window and looked in.

I smiled.

"So where's the second-grade soccer team?" Clair said.

"It's a rental."

"Where's your truck?"

"In a garage, I hope. Police took it."

He looked at me.

"We need to talk," I said, and I followed him into the barn.

There was a kettle on the woodstove and I poured a cup of tea. I stood by the stove, mug in hand, while Clair bent over a chainsaw, the bar of which was held by a bench vise. He filed the chain. The file made a scritching sound and Marion McPartland played piano in the background, the music echoing through rafters. The woodstove ticked and popped.

"How's it going?" I said.

"Fine, so far," Clair said. "Of course, you just got here."

"Anything happening today?"

"A couple of trucks went by slow early this morning."

"A big Dodge diesel?"

Clair shook his head.

"Red Ford with a fuel tank in the bed. One-ton rack truck with chainsaws."

"Rusty's crew?"

"Could be. Looked like they worked in the woods."

"So does half the county," I said.

"Half the county doesn't circle this road twice in twenty minutes."

"Half the county doesn't know this road exists."

"That's right. And they gave your place a good look," Clair said. "Slowed down here but got a look at the Mauser and changed their plans."

"Where was the rifle?"

"I was holding it."

"Where were you?"

"Standing in the middle of the road. They had to back up 'bout a quarter of a mile. I figured I'd let them know the fire zone here extends some distance."

"What? About three hundred yards?"

"More like four. I got the scope on."

"It is rabbit season," I said.

We paused. Clair moved the chain up a link and filed. I asked for Mary and he said she went to the Maine State Museum with the Philathea ladies. A talk about prehistoric Maine.

"Sounds fascinating. Why didn't you go?"

"The bus ride with the ladies is a killer," Clair said.

A killer. I sipped my tea.

"You hear about the girl in Bangor?"

"Yes. A shame."

"That was Tammy. She was the one who helped Rocky."

"Saw it on Channel 5," Clair said.

"Somebody stabbed her. She was a nice kid. Very funny, in this naive but tough sort of way. I got a real kick out of her."

"That's too bad."

"I just saw her yesterday morning. They found her body at six."

"Cops have any ideas about who?"

"Yeah," I said. "They do."

"Who?"

"Me, for one."

Clair kept filing, peering at the chain. After a few strokes he said, "Are they serious?"

I shrugged.

"They're homicide detectives," I said. "They tend to be."

CHAPTER 47

Clair listened as he washed his hands with the pink soap from the dispenser above the work bench, then toweled them dry. I told him about Tammy on the street, Rusty at the museum, Rocky at Roxanne's. He opened the woodstove and tossed in a chunk of maple, then reached for his coffee and turned to me.

"So that's where it stands. I don't think I'm a strong suspect."

"A lot of weak suspects are sitting in prison," Clair said. "And the knife doesn't help."

"No."

"So what's your plan?"

"Find Sandra Baker, the woman who may know why the boy is running. The one I think was connected to the note in his pocket."

"What about the outlaw logger?"

"He's kicking around, I'm sure."

"Want some company? I was gonna run up to the John Deere place in Brewer, pick up a coupling or two for that power take-off shaft. Snapped my last one yesterday."

"Leave you alone for one day and things go right to hell."

"I was just saying the same about you. I'll follow you up. Gotta be back in time for the missus."

Ordinarily, I might have kidded him about that. Not now.

"Yes, you do," I said. "Roxanne's not going home until I get there."

"But you have to work?"

"Yeah, but I won't be there long. Something tells me they have a policy about murder suspects in the newsroom."

"If they didn't before, they may now."

Clair, rumbling along in his big Ford, had waved to me on the highway and continued on across the river to Brewer, for his tractor parts. I'd told him we'd meet in front of the *Clarion,* give me an hour. That turned out to be generous.

When I walked into the newsroom, heads turned away, hands reached for phones and files, dug through drawers. Randall wasn't at his desk. Marna was at hers, and only she said hello.

"Hello," I said back.

"You okay?"

"Fine," I said. "How 'bout you?"

"Good, but—"

She turned away and spoke softly.

"Police were here again this morning."

"About Tammy? Good. Maybe they'll actually catch somebody."

"Yeah, well, Randall was ballistic. He's afraid TV's gonna get it."

"Get what?"

"That they were here. You know—"

"Investigating? That's how they catch people."

"Well, he's afraid it's going to make the paper look bad."

"Hey, there's a guy with his priorities straight. Find a murderer or protect the reputation of a two-bit little newspaper."

I looked at her.

"Sorry. It's not so little. Who's doing the story? Is there a follow today?"

She flicked her eyes toward Child. I looked her way. Child saw me look and looked away. A reporter with better instincts would be hauling me into a room to talk, but she was fussing with something on her desk. Maybe Randall had told her to stay away.

Marna's phone rang and I sorted through my messages. Sticky notes said Cobb had called, and Bruno from Bangor P.D., too. Randall had written *See me ASAP!!!* and stuck the message to my computer screen.

I sat down and signed on at the computer. My password hadn't yet been revoked and the directories tumbled onto the screen. I scrolled through the city-desk queue, and quickly copied a file slugged MURDER2 CITY and then moved across the system into the file slugged OBITS. I copied that, too, and then slipped back into my queue.

The two files rested on top. I looked around the room.

My screen was visible to Marna and two other copy editors, neither of whom was at his desk. Behind me, Marna still was on the phone. "I understand, sir," Marna was saying, "and I would be frustrated, too. . . ."

I opened the murder story, unedited and incomplete. Child had written six predictable inches. Police had identified the victim as Tamara Weymouth, from the town of East Corning, forty miles northwest of Bangor. She was fifteen and a runaway and had been living with friends and in shelters for at least a year. The cause of death was a single stab wound to the neck; the knife had sliced a major artery and she'd bled to death.

"She was a nice kid," a shelter worker was quoted as saying. "She just didn't get many breaks in life."

Put that on Tammy's gravestone.

The rest of the text was garbled notes, typed as Child interviewed people on the phone. I wondered why she was doing the story from the newsroom and not from the streets of Bangor or farmhouses of East Corning, but at this point, what did I care?

Bruno had said that police were talking to people who knew the victim, both in her hometown and in Bangor. Police had not ruled out robbery because there was no money found on the body, but the victim was a transient and "she may not have had any on her." Reflexively, I started to paraphrase the awkward quote, then caught myself and read on, scrolling through the notes.

Police were confident the killer would be brought to justice. East Corning was a small farming community. The Weymouth family declined to comment. The local middle school principal said Tamara quit in the middle of the eighth grade, but the principal wasn't at liberty to discuss the student's record or character because of "issues of confidentiality."

And then there was some garble, and that was it. No mention of me. No mention of Tammy's association with Tippy, no doubt per Randall's instructions. When it came to the principles of good journalism, he never forgot who signed his paycheck.

I closed the story and quickly opened the obituaries. I scrolled down. A millworker. A homemaker. A dairy farmer. A guy who was in insurance and the Rotary Club. A woman who had been in the logging business with her husband, Rusty Clement.

Even in his wife's obituary, Rusty managed to do all the talking.

She'd died suddenly. She'd attended Woodfield Academy, where she was homecoming queen. She married Rusty Clement when she was twenty, and worked with him in his business for several years, seeing Rusty Clement Logging grow to one of the state's biggest independent logging contractors. She was predeceased by her parents, Lester and Marion Cayford. She was survived by her husband and one son, Arthur "Rocky" Doe.

There would be no public services. Burial would be in the spring.

That was it. No donations to the cancer society. No summation of her interests or loves. Even in death, Flossie Clement was brushed aside. And in the morning, her hollow tribute would be in print for everyone to read.

Including her son.

More likely, he'd be told. Or maybe he'd go for days, knocking around in places where nobody read the daily newspaper, or if they did, they didn't know his name. Or did the Grim Reaper have intuition?

I felt that odd chill again, that tremor that had run through me when Rocky had been in the bedroom, speaking in that forlorn, faraway voice. I felt I didn't know what powers of intuition he had. I felt I didn't know what I was into. I only knew that for my sake, for Roxanne's sake, for our baby's sake, I wanted out.

I saved Flossie's obit, created it as a new file, and sent it to the newsroom printer, along with the murder story. The machine, on a table near the reporters, whirred to life and I went and stood in front of it, blocking the view. It didn't matter; they all turned away.

Printouts in hand, I went back to my desk and dug out a *Clarion* phone list and got the extension for advertising. Then I hunched over the phone and dialed. The police scanner conveniently squawked.

"Hi," I said cheerily when a woman answered. "This is Jack in the newsroom."

"Hello, Jack in the newsroom," she said.

"I have a question for you."

"I'll try to answer it, Jack in the newsroom."

"We're looking for an address for a person who sometimes places 'In memoriam' ads. Would you keep a record of that?"

"Well, we might. Depends on how long ago. Whether she paid cash. What's her name?"

"Sandra Baker. Or Sandy. Something like that."

"When were the ads?"

"Last one was April 7."

"Last spring?"

"Right."

"Well, Jack in the newsroom," she said. "Let me look."

As I waited, Randall strode past, then stopped abruptly at the sight of me. He pointed a finger. I pretended not to notice. He waited. I started to talk.

"Okay, so what's the change? Corinna Cub Scout Pack 134 will meet when? Sure, I can find it. I know . . ."

Randall glowered, then waved to get my attention. I concentrated on the phone, and scribbled on a pad.

"Activities will include animal track identification, Native American storytelling . . ."

Randall strode off. The woman in advertising came back on the line.

"You got lucky," she said. "She pays cash, and the address is just a post office box, but last time she came in late and there was a question about getting it in, and she left a number. What's it worth to you?"

"A lot," I said.

"You're the guy who sits next to Marna, right?"

"Right, and you are—"

"Angelica. Who sits closest to the door."

I pictured her: sort of handsome, with silver-streaked hair and big glasses. She always said hello when I walked through.

"You can buy me lunch," she said.

"Deal," I said.

"You doing an article on people who place these ads?"

"Something like that."

"Here's the number, but you didn't get it from me."

She read it off. I took it down. It was a Bangor exchange.

"And what's the box number?"

It was 1281. I thanked her.

"That'll cost you a drink," she said.

"Done," I said, but I wasn't. I was only beginning.

CHAPTER 48

Randall's private office was a glass-walled cube he'd had erected after he saw *All the President's Men.* I left the door open and sat down and crossed my legs. Randall got up from his desk and walked over and closed the door. I perused the shelf of framed certificates from newspaper seminars, which Randall never missed.

"How's it going?" I said.

"How's it going? It's going just great, if you like being awakened by homicide detectives at one in the morning. My wife answered and she practically had a heart attack."

"Why?"

"Because unlike some people, we aren't accustomed to being called by cops in the middle of the night."

"Some newspaper editors would welcome it. At the *Times,* I worked with a great metro editor who had more sources than—"

"I don't care about the goddamn *Times,*" Randall hissed.

"Since when? I thought you loved stories about the big time. Living vicariously and all that."

"Since when? Since I had detectives investigating a murder by traipsing around my newsroom."

"The victim was in here. What else are they going to do?"

"She was in here because of you."

"So?"

"And they're asking about you, McMorrow."

"They have to do that, too."

" 'What was his connection with this girl? How long has he worked for you? What do you know about him?' "

I nodded.

"Those sound like the right questions to me."

"They're not the right questions. They're the wrong questions when they're asking about a *Clarion* employee. I'm going to presume you had nothing to do with this girl's death, but a *Clarion* staff member shouldn't be associating with some urchin, some trailer trash off the street."

He was leaning forward across his desk, teeth bared in a smug little sneer, blue oxford cloth sleeves folded precisely, a silver pen clutched in his soft little hand.

"That come with a spoon?" I said.

"What?"

"Never mind. You know, I've always hated that trailer-trash label. It implies some sort of phony class superiority, don't you think? Tammy was really a nice kid, and for people to assign her to some lower caste just isn't right."

"McMorrow?"

Randall's mouth opened and his eyes bulged.

"You also have to wonder about people who feel a need to draw class lines like that. I've always figured it comes from raging insecurity or fear. Which do you think it is? Or maybe it's both. I think some people need to constantly prop themselves up. Inside they're afraid that they're losers, so they reassure themselves by making somebody else inferior. Probably goes back to how they were raised as children and—"

"Do you know who you're talking to, sir?"

"I thought I did, but all this trailer-trash talk makes me wonder."

"Goddamn it, McMorrow, you arrogant son of a bitch. Consider yourself hereby notified that you are on administrative leave. You're not to set foot in this building without my express written permission."

"Is that paid?" I said. "I have to know what to tell my lawyer."

"From what I hear, you might one need one."

"That's right. One that handles slander suits. The *Clarion* policy cover you for that or just for libel?"

He leapt from his seat. I looked up at him and smiled.

"Want me to ask Tippy for you? Or don't you associate with people who have 'trailer trash' in their house?"

"You may leave the premises, sir."

At that moment, the phone rang. I slowly unfolded my legs, while Randall stood with his little hands on the desk. As I stood, he finally reached for the phone.

"Yes," he snapped, and then paused and said, "No, I am not available to talk to anyone at Channel 5. What do you tell them? You tell them, 'No comment.' You work at a newspaper, don't you?"

"Pretty to think so," I said to myself, and turned and opened the door and left.

I walked through the newsroom, where the heads bowed in deference. At my desk, I grabbed the printouts of the obit and story, and then waved to Marna, who was taking dictation over the phone, the receiver crooked against her neck.

"See you later," I mouthed.

Her eyes opened wide in what seemed to be some sort of expression of regret and affection.

"I'll call you," I said, and smiled.

I turned and started for the door. At Child's desk, I stopped. She was peering at the text on her computer screen like it was the Rosetta stone.

"Just tell the story," I said.

Child looked up, startled.

"I gotta go, but two things. One, Tammy was a nice kid. Very kind. Very smart. She had a lot of potential and her death is a terrible tragedy."

She still looked up at me. Her mascara showed in little lumps and I could see where she plucked the eyebrows between her eyes.

"You can write that down, if you want."

"Quote you?"

"Sure. Attribute it to Jack McMorrow, a former *Clarion* copy editor who met the victim on the streets of Bangor."

She scribbled in a notebook, and then she stopped and looked up again, her pen poised. As I spoke, she started to take it down.

"And two, you could go somewhere in this business, but you've got to get out of here. This place is the kiss of death."

It was. In more ways than one.

*   *   *

Clair wasn't in sight, so I zipped my parka and walked up the block to the post office, which took up a big chunk of the federal building on Harlow Street. I crossed the wide expanse of sidewalk and went through the double doors. The courts and marshals and the rest of the feds were protected by a guard and a metal detector. The postal workers, to the right, were not, and I strode into the lobby, which was quiet in mid-afternoon, wide open to anyone who had a problem with the price of stamps.

From behind the walls, I could hear people talking and laughing, but there was no one at the counter. I scanned the mailboxes until I came to the twelve-hundreds, then looked for twelve eighty-one. It was head high, all the way to the left. I could see that it was full of mail, and I peered through the glass door for a closer look.

With the rush over, the clerks had unloaded the junk mail, and I could see advertising circulars, addressed to "Boxholder." Underneath the circulars were catalogues or magazines and at the bottom was an inch-high stack of actual letters. I squinted and cupped my hands against my temples. I could see the "Sa—" of Sandra on a letter from a Bangor bank. But banks needed a street address, because checks needed a street address.

I thought for a moment, then went to a vending machine and bought a stamped envelope. From the trash can at the far end of the lobby, I pulled out some discarded mail—credit card offers, magazine subscriptions. When I had a thick wad of paper, I stuffed my envelope until it was bursting, then licked it and sealed it, pressing it down like an overstuffed suitcase. Then I addressed it to Sandra Baker, and made up a return address—12 Maple Street, Searsport, Maine. I looked over to the counter.

Two clerks had appeared, one a thin serious-looking man

with a crisply ironed uniform, and the other a big older woman with wild red hair. She was whistling, pausing to call out to someone I couldn't see. She laughed and then continued sorting through a drawer. I waited a minute and the thin man left, and I went to the counter.

"Hi," I said.

"Good afternoon to you," the woman said.

"I need to mail this," I said, "and I wondered if it could get there today."

I handed her the envelope.

"Today?"

"Well, it's her birthday. She's my sister, and I know she's going to be in later to get her mail, but she's leaving at six tomorrow morning for a week and I just thought maybe . . ."

I gave her an imploring smile.

"Twelve eighty-one," she said. "Well, you know, we're not supposed to divert from the normal procedures, which means this would be delivered—"

"But it's right over there," I said, pointing to my left. "It's fifty feet away."

She looked at the letter some more.

"You know this is gonna need more postage."

"Fine," I said.

The woman flipped it onto a scale, read the meter.

"Another thirty-two cents."

I smiled as I handed her change.

"So do you think you could, just this once, for her birthday?"

"Well, how old is Sandra going to be?"

"Fifty," I said. "The big five-oh."

"You don't have money in here, do you?"

"Well . . ."

I gave her a sheepish grin.

"She's going to Vegas. I told her to take this lucky money. It's only fifty."

"Fifty dollars cash?"

"A dollar for every year."

"Oh, jeez. What do we do with this guy? You're a good brother, you know that? My brother doesn't even know when my birthday is."

"We've always been close."

"That's nice. You know, this should be mailed registered, if it's of value."

"But then she has to sign for it?"

"That's the idea," the woman said.

"But she might get here late. Isn't the lobby open later than the windows?"

"Yeah, but—"

"Well, then she could get the notice but not the card."

I looked at her plaintively.

"Please?"

The woman looked around. She looked at the letter, then looked around. Suddenly, she opened her drawer and scooped out change.

"Eighteen cents, sir," she said, in her official voice.

I took the money. She took the envelope, slammed the drawer shut, and went through a door to her right, my left. Through the little glass-doored boxes I could see her walking. I moved toward the box, watched as she tried to stuff the envelope in, then stopped and pulled the sheaf of mail out. Shuffling it into a bundle, she stuck my letter in first, pressed the bundle flat, and slid it in. It stuck and she pulled half the stack out.

"Tell your sister she ought to come in more often," the woman said, fitting the envelopes back into the box.

"I'll tell her when I see her," I said.

As I peered through the glass, I tried to read the addresses before they were covered. I missed once, twice, then there was an envelope with the address hand-lettered. It showed only for a second but that was enough. "P.O. Box 1281, 484 Hope St."

I glanced up. For a moment, the red-haired woman and I were nose to nose. I gave her a thumbs up. We both smiled and she was gone.

CHAPTER 49

Hope Street was in the north end of the city, a mile back from the river. It ran through a quiet neighborhood of nondescript houses, forty years of forty-hour weeks and a paid-for bungalow over which the children would someday bicker. The houses were the kind you could find anywhere, Maine or Michigan, Massachusetts or Montana. They were monuments to quiet diligence, nothing more, and oddly lifeless on this cold afternoon.

Clair drove slowly and I looked for house numbers, which ran into the two-hundreds before the houses grew more scattered. We sped up past the woods that guarded the hospital, and then there was another house and another, in the low three-hundreds, and then, a few hundred yards further, a house with no number at all. Across the street there were scrubby woods, and no other houses in sight.

I looked as Clair pulled the truck to the side of the road

just beyond the house and stopped. The house was low and faded red with white metal shutters and a big screened porch on the far side. There was a newish Toyota Camry in the driveway, and the driveway had been plowed, but not recently. The drive and the car were snow covered, but both were black and the sun had melted the snow to a thin, icy veneer. There were no fresh tire tracks.

"Looks deserted," I said.

"Did you see the light?"

"Where?"

"In the car. Dome light's on, but weak."

"You've got good eyes for an old guy."

"Used to do this for a living. Think this is it?"

"I don't know," I said. "If we were cops we could run the plate."

"If we were cops we could kick the door in."

"Only with probable cause. Let's go knock."

"We have probable cause for that?"

"If it's Kitty's friend?" I said. "Yes, I do."

He backed the van to the end of the drive and shut the motor off. Chimes rang as we opened the van doors, stopped when we closed them. I walked slowly up the drive until Clair said, "Wait."

"What?"

"Don't walk there. Walk off to the side. I want to see the tracks."

"I thought you only did jungles."

"It's all the same," Clair said.

He walked up beside me and looked down. I could see faint snow-filled outlines, like craters on some planet, photographed by a satellite.

"See? It looks like two sets. She turned and went in the side door, and the second person went in behind her."

"Man? Woman?"

I paused.

"Boy?"

"Hard to say," Clair murmured. "They're so washed out. But this second person came across the driveway. Didn't get out of this car."

"It wasn't the mailman," I said. "She has a box at the post office."

"It was somebody."

"Maybe it was her husband."

"Or not," I said.

I looked in the car. There were two bags of groceries on the backseat, and I said, "Clair," and pointed to them. He glanced and nodded, and we approached the door, which led to a breezeway connected to a two-car garage. I peered in the garage window and saw another car, an old MG or Triumph, dusty with boxes piled on the hood. When I turned, Clair was pulling the storm door open with the blade of his knife hooked through the handle. He held it open with the point and looked in. His eyes narrowed and he frowned.

I stepped past him and up into what served as an entryway. There were two pair of women's sneakers and a pair of fleece-lined moccasins lined up on the floor.

This was where she took off her boots. There were no boots in sight. There were no men's shoes, either.

The entryway had a couch, a table with a lamp, and a bookshelf full of TV magazines and romance paperbacks. There were wooden pegs on the wall for jackets, and several of them hung there. Most were colorful and out of season. Opposite us was a door that led to the backyard. At the rear of the room, to the left, was another door that led into the main house. The keys were hanging from the lock, and the door was closed, but not latched.

"Hello," I called.

We stood and listened. A blue jay called from outside but the house was silent. Then there was a scratching sound from the back door. Then another. I walked slowly over and peered out the window. A gray tiger cat looked up at me and mewed.

I turned back.

"Cat," I mouthed.

Clair nodded.

"Hello," I called again. "Anybody home?"

There was no answer. I leaned close to the door and peeked through the crack, squinting with one eye. I glimpsed part of a kitchen table, then another grocery bag, tipped over, with food spilled out.

Lean Cuisine. Diet Pepsi in a two-liter bottle. A carton of cigarettes. Newports.

"Maybe she's in the bathroom," I said.

"Time to go. Maybe call the cops. Something isn't right here."

"Nothing's right," I said. "Hasn't been in a long time."

CHAPTER 50

We backtracked out of the place, past the car, down the driveway and back into the truck. A couple of cars passed as we were pulling away, and Clair followed them until we reached the next house, a quarter-mile down the road. Clair pulled into the driveway and backed out and we drove past the red house and back into the city.

"They're probably looking for me anyway," I said.

"You want to stop at a house?"

"Let's just keep going. We'll find a phone booth."

"You know, I've got to get home," Clair said. "Nothing personal, but I don't want Mary coming home to a dark house, with me tied up with cops or something."

"Getting to be a habit, isn't it?"

So Clair drove down the hills to the old downtown, stopping in front of the *Clarion.*

"Careful," he said.

"Always," I said.

"Give me a ring."

"The minute I know something."

"Don't wait that long," Clair said, and I hopped out and gave him a wave and the big truck rumbled off.

Hunched in my parka, I started down the sidewalk in search of a phone. It was after four, and between the brick-walled buildings the winter dusk already was turning to darkness. The passing cars had their headlights on in the slow procession that constituted a rush hour in Bangor, Maine, and I squinted against the glare as I walked. There was a bank up the block, and it seemed I had seen a public phone there. If not, the bus station was a block over toward the river, and I'd just run over and—

I saw them in silhouette. The ninja was out in front, swaggering into the line of cars, arms jerking, legs lashing out. Then another figure, hooded, ignoring the honking horns as he followed the ninja, then two more, with baseball hats on backward, and behind them a bigger guy, his long hair under a baseball cap, a paper bag under his arm.

Crow Man and the boys. The platoon on patrol.

I hurried down the sidewalk, breaking into a trot. At the corner, the light changed against me and the cars streamed past. I stood in the gutter and peered across the traffic, trying to keep the band in sight. They'd gone up the block, then slipped into an alley. I saw the last figure disappear. Was it Rocky?

The light changed, but it released another stream of cars and trucks, this one coming around the corner from my right. I stepped out into the street, gauged the distance, then broke between the cars, leaping to the sidewalk as the horns honked and someone shouted. Running along the sidewalk in the shop lights, I reached the alley and saw two of them turning onto the next street, moving toward the river. They disappeared around the corner, and I ran after them, tripping on something in the darkness and staggering, then rounding the corner myself.

They were across the street, moving in single file, the ninja kid still pirouetting in front. I waited for one car, then crossed diagonally behind them, catching up with the trailing kid as the rest of them started across a parking lot toward the railroad tracks.

I drew ahead of the kid, then turned in front of him.

"Hey," I said.

A pale white face turned to me, a face with glasses and for a moment I thought I had him.

But it wasn't him. It wasn't Rocky.

The kid didn't say anything, just jerked back warily and put up his arms.

"Leave me alone, I didn't do nothing to—"

"It's okay. I'm just looking for Rocky. Twig. You know him?"

He shook his head, his street-kid reflex.

"Come on. I'm a friend of his. He's looking for me, too."

I was walking backward. He gave another shake, followed by a feint, as he tried to get past me to rejoin the group.

"Have you seen him today?"

"I don't friggin' know him so leave me alone, man."

He dodged again, but I deliberately cut him off, pinning him against the brick wall.

"Hey, get the hell away from me. Hey!"

He shouted and the next kid heard him and turned. He called up the line and there were more shouts and then the sound of feet on the pavement. I watched as they approached and slowed, wary as hyenas. They spread out, one kid moving into the street and working his way up behind me, and then the ninja kid drew up and recognized me.

"That ain't no cop," he said. "That's that guy who was with Tammy."

Crow Man moved through his minions, paper bag under his arm. I moved aside and let the kid against the wall slip away into their ranks.

"That guy wouldn't let me go," he said. "He had me and he was asking me about Twig. He's looking for Twig."

The ninja kid moved around me until he was on my right, ten feet away. Crow Man walked toward me. He was scowling and he did not appear to be as drunk as the last time we'd met. I couldn't yet tell whether that was good or bad.

"Hey, buddy," I said, smiling. "How goes the battle?"

His eyes narrowed under his hat.

"I've seen you before."

"Mind like a steel trap," I said. "I'm looking for my friend, Rocky. You seen him?"

"You the guy climbed up? Under the bridge?"

"Doesn't sound familiar."

He looked at me more closely, and I could picture the

neurons bouncing around his tattered brain. I was giving silent thanks for alcoholic blackouts when I felt the ninja kid drawing closer. I turned.

"Back off," I said.

He stopped, mouth open, swaying on the balls of his feet. A car passed but didn't slow.

"You kill Tammy? 'Cause Tammy was a friend of mine," Ninja said.

"She was a friend of mine, too. And no, I didn't kill her. You have any idea who else it might have been? Who else was she with that day?"

"You ain't a cop," the ninja kid said. "You work for the goddamn newspaper. We don't have to tell you nothin'."

"You a reporter?" Crow Man said, moving closer.

"Yeah," I said. "And I'm looking for Rocky. Twig."

"What're you gonna do, interview him?" he said.

Crow Man said it as though it were something dainty.

"Maybe," I said. "But I have to find him first. Last time I saw him was in Portland yesterday."

"I think he stuck her," Ninja said. "He was talking to her."

In some circles, one would not logically follow the other. Not in this one.

"I can see why you'd think that, but it's not true," I said.

"You want to interview me?" Crow Man said.

"Maybe another time."

"Hey, I gotta story you wouldn't believe. Beat on from the time I was a little kid. My old man was a drunk. My mother was in the loony bin. Old man used to beat the crap outta me with a goddamn shovel handle. Hey, I could tell you a story."

"I'm sure."

"You pay for stories?"

I smiled, started to shake my head. Then stopped.

"I'll pay for Twig's story."

"No, I mean my story. You buy me a bottle of Jack, I'll tell you a story that'll knock your socks off."

"I'll buy you six bottles for Twig."

Crow Man swayed in his sneakers, taken aback. The other kids looked from me to him and back to me again.

"Bullshit," he said.

"Try me," I said.

I slipped a hand into my pocket and Ninja readied himself to spring.

"Cut the crap," I said.

He settled back onto his feet, and I dug out a twenty-dollar bill and held it out in front of me. In the streetlight, it fluttered. Crow Man's eyes fixed to it like a junkie's on a loaded syringe. He stepped forward and started to reach. I jerked the bill back and his dirty hand clawed at the air.

"Give it," he said.

"Uh-uh. But it's all yours and four more like it if you bring me Twig."

He still was staring at the bill, which meant a bottle, which meant another night of oblivion, if not bliss.

"We gotta take him, Crow," Ninja said. "He killed Tammy."

"You don't know that," I said. "You don't even know who I am, or what I really do."

I put headlines on news briefs. What they didn't know . . .

Ninja looked ready to try it. Crow Man still was looking at the bill. The other kids, opportunists all, waited patiently. I tried to look calm and self-assured. Ninja crouched and came off the ground.

His arms started churning as he hit me, knees on my chest, open palms thrashing at my face. The kids started yelling and I could hear him grunting and spitting as he swung and kicked and I backed away, trying to protect my

face, my groin. I stumbled but kept moving, and knew that
if I fell they'd be on me, all of them, stomping and kicking
and then it would be over, maybe really over and I had a
flash of Roxanne and the baby, this baby I'd never know, and
I wrapped my arms around the kid's shoulders and spun and
ran hard at the brick wall.

My arms hit first and then his head hit the wall and made
that coconut sound and he started to go limp, then thrashed
again but weakly. I slipped my arms out from behind him
and got him by the armpits and put him up against the
wall again, but this time more gently.

His eyes were unfocused and his mouth was open, his jaw
slack. His arms fell to his sides as I felt the back of his head,
then looked at my hand in the dim light. There was blood.
I looked into his eyes, hoping and searching for life.

After all, he'd meant well.

"You all right?" I said.

Ninja closed his eyes, then opened them and stared at
me. Then squinted to focus.

"I think maybe he needs an ambulance." I said to the Lost
Boys, now talking quietly among themselves. Suddenly they
stopped and there was a pause, a moment of silence broken
when Crow Man stepped forward.

"Ah, he's fine," he said. "But I was wonderin'. You got
that hundred bucks on you?"

CHAPTER 51

The negotiations were momentary, the agreement sealed without a handshake, but made in good faith, or at least as good as it got on the street at night in the cold. They'd deliver Twig to the Hannibal Hamlin statue by seven o'clock, unharmed. I showed them the hundred dollars, saw the yearning in Crow Man's eyes, and watched as he led the little band off down the street. Ninja was unsteady on his feet but Crow Man didn't wait. He was truly a man with a mission.

And then I turned back. I had one, too.

I walked up a block and through a brick-walled alley and out onto the street. It was after five and the stores and offices were closing, the street already emptying in the late afternoon. I walked up the hill, rubbing my arms, which were sore where I'd hit the wall. The tussle had done something to the cuts on my belly and I felt something warm dripping down to my groin. Back in the van, behind my privacy glass, I opened my jacket and undid my jeans and looked. My shorts were bloodstained and there were streaks of blood below the cuts, but they already were scabbing over.

The human body was a very resilient thing. Sometimes.

As I pulled away, the plan was to find a phone, call the police about Sandra Baker, if that was her house. Maybe grab some dinner and then head back to the riverfront to wait. And if they had Rocky? I'd childproof the locks, bundle him in the van, drive him to the police station, hand him to a cop, say, "Here he is. The Grim Reaper. He's all yours."

So I swung around the block, and there was a phone, against the wall outside the bus station. I pulled over and parked, and leaving the van running, went to the phone. There was gum pressed over the mouth end of the receiver and it had hardened like concrete in the cold. I picked most of it off, put a quarter in and dialed.

The number rang. Once, twice . . .

Roxanne answered. Or a reasonable facsimile.

"You've reached Roxanne Masterson at Child Protective Services. I'm away from my desk, but if you need to talk to someone tonight, call the following number."

I waited as she gave it.

"If you want to leave a message, you may do so after the tone. If this is J.M., I'm all set until eleven. Call the car between seven and seven fifteen."

On the phone, I heard her breathing. I listened until there was a last breath. Then a click, and the tone.

"I love you, too," I said, and hung up.

As I stood there, on the sidewalk of the deserted street, I knew what I would do. Like a smoker saying they would only have one cigarette, a drinker saying just one more drink, I told myself I would just drive by. Take one more look. Not even get out of the car.

CHAPTER 52

And I didn't, not right away. At first I just sat by the side of the darkened road, with the parking lights on, the motor running, and watched.

The light still was on in the Camry. There was one light on in the house, in the basement. I sat for fifteen interminable minutes and nobody came or went. Two cars passed on the road, one swerving wide around the van, the other a pickup that sped past headed out of town, and I pulled ahead to a wider part of the shoulder, the kind of place where deliverymen pull off to eat lunch. I shut off the motor and lights, and it was still and quiet and cold.

I took the flashlight from my bag and tested it, but it didn't work. I gave it a sharp rap and it did, and I turned it off and looked up and down the road. There were no cars in sight, and I got out, and, crunching through the crusty snow, crossed the road.

As I approached the driveway, headlights showed in the distance. I hurried past the Camry, stepping clear of the frozen tracks, and huddled in the shadows near the side door until the car passed. It did, and I slipped the flashlight into my parka pocket and took out a pen. I pressed it against the yellow light of the door bell.

Pressed again.

I waited a minute, then forced myself to wait a minute more. Then I counted to ten. Took the pen and pulled the storm door open, and slipped inside.

Listened. Looked. Turned on the flashlight and played it over the room. It was the same: shoes, jackets, keys in the lock in the inner door. I went to the crack and peeked. The food was on the table. I swallowed. Breathed slowly and silently. Inside, there was a click and the refrigerator started to hum.

"Hello," I said, and it was jarring as a scream.

I waited. There was no answer. I said it again. Waited some more. Used the pen to push open the door.

It swung but didn't creak. When it stopped, I could see the groceries, a brown leather pocketbook hanging by its strap on the kitchen chair. I called out again. No answer. I stepped into the room.

My boots made gritty footsteps on the tile floor, and I fought off an impulse to wipe the prints and get out. I told myself I only wanted to know if this was Sandra Baker's house. I didn't want to know that she was asleep on the couch.

I crossed the kitchen and stood in front of the refrigerator, moved the flashlight beam over it. There were notes stuck to it, pink and yellow and green. One was the number of a travel agent. Next to it was a newspaper article about a cruise: Miami to St. John to St. Croix and home. Someone had circled the phone number to call for information.

If it had been Sandra, she had some money.

There was a postcard from Atlantic City, showing the casinos, another from Greece, showing the Parthenon. The appliances were new and top of the line. There was a fishy smell from the grocery bags and I peeked in and saw a bag of shrimp, a jar of cocktail sauce, a twenty-dollar bottle of wine.

No screw tops here.

I listened. No sign of life, either.

Another door led to the rest of the house, and it was slightly ajar. I hesitated, then walked over.

"Hello," I said again. "I'm Jack McMorrow. I'm looking for Sandra Baker. Ms. Baker, this is a long story but I really need to talk to you. Do you know a boy named Rocky? Rocky Doe?"

Silence.

With the pen, I pushed the door open. It caught on the carpet in the hall and stopped. I pushed again, and it made a soft shush. There was an odor. A toilet odor. A rancid smell. I called, but my voice was hushed, too. I walked into the hall, the light leading the way like a dog on a leash.

To the right was a bathroom, and I flicked the light on and sniffed. The bathroom was neat, with matching flowered hand towels on the rack. The vanity had a white marble top. There were pink fluffy slippers on the floor by the tub, and I could smell deodorant. Perfume. The bad smell wasn't coming from there.

"Hello," I said again, but this time it was a whisper.

No one whispered back.

I moved along the hallway until I came to another doorway to my left, another door straight ahead. The doorway led to a living room, with white carpeting and two rose-colored overstuffed chairs that matched an overstuffed couch. They were empty.

The door was closed.

I pushed with the pen. It didn't open. I took a twenty-dollar bill from my pocket, wrapped the bill around the knob. Turned. The door opened. The room was dark. The smell was much stronger.

The light searched as I stood in the doorway. There were

boots on the carpet in front of me. Women's boots, one upright, one on its side. Then a liquor bottle, also on the carpet. Absolut Citron. A pill bottle. Pills, yellow and pink, scattered about the floor like tiny Easter eggs.

Dangling from the bed was a woman's foot.

CHAPTER 53

She was wearing socks, tweed slacks, a white sweater on which she had vomited. Her hair was orange. Her mouth was open and her eyes were closed. Her skin had taken on that shading that medical people call lividity, which I'd always thought an odd term because to me it implied emotion. It meant anything but.

Lividity meant the woman's blood had settled after she'd died. I could see it in her neck, a coloring like that rust-colored paint they put on the bottom of a boat's hull. Her face was blotchy and drawn. Her jaw was slack as though she were terribly exhausted. Perhaps she had been, when she'd drawn her last breath.

There is something mesmerizing about a corpse, this irrefutable evidence that despite all our efforts to believe the contrary, we are about as enduring as ripened fruit.

And for a long time I stood in the doorway and stared, drawn inexorably to the sight of her. Was this my Sandra Baker? Was this the woman who wouldn't let her long-dead friend die? Where was the explanation now? What had happened, that she had died before she could even unload the groceries? Why such a wide swath of death? Kitty, Flossie, Tammy, and now Sandra Baker. Where was my Grim Reaper now? Had he already come and gone?

There was a sound and I started. A humming, ticking sound. The heat kicking on.

As the water gurgled in the pipes, I backed slowly from the room, as though she might jump me if I turned my back. I turned in the hallway and made my way to the kitchen to find the phone. With the light slashing at the dark, I found the base of a cordless phone on the counter. The phone wasn't in it, and I played the light down the counter, across to the table. There was no phone but the pocketbook was hanging there. I peeked in with the light.

There was a wallet, the kind held together by a strap and snap, but the strap was undone. I took the pen and pushed the wallet open, and Sandra J. Baker stared me in the face, eyes open, mouth closed. It was her driver's license photo, and she looked almost merry, at least by comparison.

The wallet slipped aside and I picked further. A large package of sugarless gum, a pack of cigarettes. Kleenex, in a plastic wrapper. Matches. Lipstick and eyeliner pencil. Hard candies and yellow sticky-notes. Crumpled gasoline receipts that said "Bangor Mobil." Two keys on a metal ring. I gave them a poke.

One said Toyota. The other said "U.S.P.S. Do not duplicate." I thought for a moment, then moved to the door, where the keys still were hanging from the lock. I looked at them, saw another Toyota key, another post office key. The keys in the bag were her spares. I paused. I wanted to know more, but I couldn't stay here. But the mailbox, the one with my phony letter.

My fingerprints.

Leaning over the bag, I fished the key ring out with the pen, and put the pen and the keys in the pocket of my parka. Turning off the light, I let myself out.

CHAPTER 54

The road was dark when I left the house, and I didn't meet another car until one passed as I crossed into the city limits. I slowed at houses where there were lights, half-intending to stop and knock on the door and ask whoever answered to call the police.

But before I knew it I was back in the downtown, driving down Broadway, past Tippy's house, which thankfully was dark. Then I took a right, cut through to Harlow Street, and there was the post office.

The lights in the lobby were on.

I drove past the federal building, parked on a little court, and got out and walked back. The court side of the building was deserted, the door locked and the guard nowhere in sight. But the door to the post office was open, the service windows closed. I went to a section five feet over from Sandra Baker's box and leaned low, fiddling with the key and peeking through the boxes into the post office. I could hear the voices of the mail clerks, calling back and forth, but they were distant. I turned. There was no one approaching.

I rose quickly, went to box 1281 and popped it open.

The sheaf of mail slid out easily. I tucked it under my arm, closed the box and yanked out the key. At the door, I checked the sign. It said box lobby hours, 8 A.M. to 7 P.M. I'd scan the mail and return it. I had fifteen minutes.

Gloves on, in the dark, with the flashlight resting on the passenger seat of the van, I sifted through it. There were bills for credit cards, offers for still others. Something from a dentist in Orrington, an insurance company in Virginia. A renewal notice for *Newsweek,* and a bill from the *Bangor Daily News.* A postcard from a casino in Connecticut, signed by Myra, who had won one hundred and eighty-eight dollars and wished Sandy were there. Flyers from discount stores, a brochure for the new Toyotas. My letter and a letter with no return address, with the name "Sandra Baker" scrawled quickly.

And a Woodfield postmark.

I turned on the dome light and held the envelope up. The light showed what appeared to be a piece of paper torn from a spiral-bound notebook. There were words, but I couldn't make them out. I turned the envelope, turned it again. Took the flashlight and held it up, with the envelope against the lens. Two words showed, big and bold but backward. I flipped the envelope over and read.

The note said, "No more."

I examined it, but that was it. Two words. "No more." No more what?

I sat back for a moment, looked at my watch. It was seven minutes of seven, and I didn't want to meet a guard in the lobby locking up. I did want to meet Crow Man and the boys. I did have to make the call.

Gathering up the mail, I left my stuffed envelope on the seat and got out of the van, locked it, and started walking.

Putting the van key in my left parka pocket, I felt for the box key in my right. Felt again, then slipped off my glove. Stopping on the sidewalk, I dug in my parka pockets, then checked the pockets of my jeans. Went back to the van and looked in the seats, on the floors, in the gutter.

"Shit," I said.

I checked the van again. My pockets again. I dug in my pockets, patted my jeans, fished in the seats. Checked my watch.

It was four minutes of seven.

"Goddamn it," I said.

I'd done it now. I was being eyed for one murder, and had failed to report what could very well be another. I'd lifted evidence from the scene, probably committed a federal crime by taking someone's mail. Who investigated that, the F.B.I.?

It was two minutes of, and I turned and started up the sidewalk, intermittently turning the light on and playing it on the pavement. They had to be somewhere between the post office and the van, and there still was time. If I found them now, I'd just make it. Get rid of the mail, get out of there, go down to the statue and wait.

I loped along the sidewalk, playing the light like one of those guys who look for coins at the beach with metal detectors. An older man with a dog approached and I turned my head away, but still felt his stare.

"Lose something?" he said, ready to join the search.

"No," I said. "But thanks."

I crossed the wide walk in front of the entrance, trying to retrace the path I'd used, and I saw bottle caps, used lottery tickets, cigarette butts.

And then, as I approached the doors, I saw the guard turning his key in the lock. He closed the door behind him, gave it a jiggle and then turned. Through the window, I saw him hold something up and examine it. Then he twirled it and held it up again.

The key. The guard had it, and I had the mail.

I turned away quickly, and stood there for a moment, holding the mail, first against my chest, and then, as I strode away, under my arm. I thought of tossing it down a storm drain, or burning it in the woodstove. But there had to be some way to get it back into that box. Some way, I thought as I walked away from the building, back down the hill.

Sneak into the post office and just stuff it in myself? Mail it all again? Go back to Sandra Baker's house and leave it there, but that would be misleading. Or I could just give it to the cops and tell the truth.

I had never been much of a liar. I didn't need to start now. It was time to start telling the truth, the whole truth, nothing but.

And I'd told Crow Man and the ninja I'd meet them at Hannibal Hamlin at seven, and it was three minutes after, which probably didn't matter, though there was a chance that Crow Man would, for some hundred-dollar reason, manage to be punctual. So putting the mail on the passenger seat, I drove down the hill, up one red-brick block and over the steel-railed bridge that crossed Kenduskeag Stream. I parked the van in front of a shoe-repair place, which was closed, shut off the lights and motor, and sat.

The downtown had emptied like a tide pool, and the little park was dark and deserted. I couldn't make out Hannibal Hamlin from the van, but he had to be there, and maybe they were, too. Or maybe they'd walked a hundred yards, and, with the attention span of puppies, wandered off to sniff out some booze, huff down some fumes, forgotten all about me, and now here I was sitting in the dark in some frozen outpost of a city.

But then again, where else could they trade a skinny little boy for a hundred bucks?

I got out of the van and, reaching back in for the flashlight, crossed the street and walked back over the bridge. Below me, the stream was running fast and cold, a black gash in the center of the ice. The ground was icy and crackled like broken glass as I walked. The sound echoed off the buildings on the far side of the stream, but when I stopped beside the statue, everything was still.

In the distance I heard a siren, and thought of Sandra Baker. I'd wait fifteen minutes, then go make the call and come back. I started counting down. Waited some more. Stared up at Hannibal Hamlin, and his monument to the fleeting nature of fame. These kids wouldn't know him from Adam. But then, they probably didn't know much about Adam, either.

I stood some more, shuffling on my feet to stay warm, but the sound carried in the night air and I tried to hold still, me and Hannibal. But the cold seeped in like water, and my feet ached, my nose ran. I wiped it with a gloved hand, then turned as footsteps came from the direction of the van.

Someone was approaching, tapping along the icy sidewalk. I turned to watch, and the figure materialized. It was in a long coat, carrying a bag. As she passed under a light, I saw blond hair, but then a van came down the street, and slowed and I couldn't see her. The van stopped.

I saw the driver turn. Someone called something. The woman emerged from behind the van, walking faster with her head down. Someone laughed. The van motor idled loudly, and then there was a metallic scrape. The doors

opening. Feet crunching on the ice. Two guys came around
the back of the van, and then two more, and I thought of
Rusty's bunch and tensed. And then I saw him.

He was at the center of the huddle that crossed the street,
and I only saw glimpses of him as they approached. His
hair. His glasses. The gag tied over his mouth.

When they got close, Crow Man turned. He gave me a
gap-toothed, triumphant grin.

"Friggin' delivered to your door," he said. "Now hand
over the cash."

They separated, and there was Rocky, huddled like a
hostage. The gag was a blue bandanna. His hands were tied
in front of him, and his chin was on his chest. The rest of the
posse, bright-eyed and feral under their hoods, awaited their
reward expectantly.

"Wiry little scrapper," Crow Man said. "Had to practically hog-tie him to get him in the truck. You oughta throw
in another twenty bucks for wear and tear. And I gotta pay
the guy for the goddamn van."

"It's called overhead," I said. "Or didn't they teach you
that at Amos Tuck?"

He looked at me blankly.

"Take that thing off his mouth," I said. "And untie him."

"Why? You're just gonna tie him back up later, right?"

He grinned again and winked. On cue, the kids leered.
One tittered.

"So where's the money?" Crow Man said.

"Yeah," a kid seconded.

I dug in my jeans, pulled out the bills and counted.
When I reached one hundred, Crow Man snatched the cash
like a monkey taking peanuts, and the whole bunch of them
fell away from Rocky and tumbled back across the square
toward where the van waited.

Rocky stood there, like a broken dog. I walked to him and yanked the gag down from his mouth. Then I undid the knotted shoelace from his wrists. He didn't run. Didn't move. Didn't speak. Hannibal Hamlin looked on with disapproval of the whole sordid transaction.

"Sorry," I said. "I didn't think it would be like that."

Rocky said nothing.

"I'm parked across the street. Let's get out of here."

"Why should I?"

Again, good question, no answer. But I had to remain calm, matter of fact. Of course, he was going with me. Of course, he wouldn't run. Of course, he hadn't killed anyone. Of course. He was just a kid.

"Because you have to. For a whole lot of reasons. Where were you, anyway?"

"The mall," Rocky said.

I started to walk and after two steps, he started to follow.

"You hungry?" I said.

"Where we going?"

"We'll swing through Burger King."

"Where we going?"

"The one by the on-ramp."

"Where we going?"

We crossed the street, and I fished in my parka for the keys. I went around and opened the sliding door, and Rocky started to get in. He had one leg in when I remembered the mail and started to reach for it, but he was halfway in, and I reached under him and he reached down and the mail spilled onto the floor at his feet. Rocky leaned down, and in the soft light of the van, he froze.

I slammed the door shut. Ran around the front of the van and fiddled with the lock. When I climbed into the seat, Rocky still was bent over, staring at the floor. I watched him for a moment as he looked at each envelope, the address labels on the magazines. Sandra Baker.

"Somebody you know, isn't it," I said.

Rocky didn't answer.

"Kitty, too."

He eyed the mail, then slowly shook his head.

"I think this is Kitty's friend," I said. "How do you know her, Rocky?"

He didn't answer. He had come to the small envelope, the one I had held up to the light. He picked it up, held it in his thin, white hands.

"You know what it says inside? It says, 'No more.' That's all. That mean anything to you?"

Slowly he shook his head.

"Nothing at all? 'Kitty, kitty, kitty,' Rocky. 'How can you live?' You remember that, don't you?"

He stared straight ahead, lost in thought, then suddenly reached for the door latch. He yanked it twice but the door didn't open.

"Only opens from the outside," I said.

Rocky sat back. I leaned forward on the steering wheel so I could see him in the rearview mirror. He looked pensive, angry.

"My mom didn't do nothing," he murmured.

"I didn't say she did."

He stared, unseeing, the envelope still in his hands.

"You know whose handwriting that is, Rocky?"

Still he stared.

"Rusty's," he whispered.

I swallowed.

"Why would Rusty be writing to this lady?"

For a moment, Rocky didn't answer. I could see his face, pale in the streetlight, lost in thought.

"I don't know," he said.

"And do you know why he would say 'No more' to this lady?"

The pale face shook.

"He wouldn't be having an affair, would he? Not with a lady who might be his age. How old is Rusty?"

"He's forty, I think."

"No, if Rusty had a girlfriend, she'd be more like twenty. You think he was mad at this Sandra?"

Underneath the red plaid, the shoulder flinched.

"So he did know her, but he wasn't mad at her? Did he like her?"

This time he just stared.

"Were they friends or something, Rocky? Was Sandy a friend of your mom?"

"No," he snapped.

I paused, considered his clenched jaw, his angry scowl.

"So they didn't like each other?"

No answer. A car approached from behind, the lights painting us in glare. I squinted and adjusted the mirror so I could see Rocky full in the face. And then the car passed, leaving us in the icy cast of the streetlight.

"So how did you guys get to know this Sandra lady?"

No answer.

"She didn't live in Woodfield. You know where her house is?"

He looked at me carefully, then slowly shook his head.

"It's just outside of town here. Maybe a mile and a half from here. We could go there."

I watched for a reaction, but his face was a glowering mask. I put the key in the ignition and the dashboard glowed pale green like something from the space shuttle, and I started the motor.

"Why don't we? Just stop by for a minute. Maybe Sandra Baker will be home and we can ask—"

"No."

It was a bark. Almost a shout. When it had subsided, the van motor idled quietly.

"Why not?" I said.

"We just can't," Rocky said.

"Maybe she won't mind. Maybe she'll be glad to talk about—"

I put the van in gear.

"No," he barked again, and reached for the door handle, started to heave himself forward off the seat. I put my hand on his chest and shoved him back down. He bounced back up, and I shoved him again and this time he stayed down, tears running down his cheeks.

"Start talking," I said. "Or I'll park this thing in Sandra Baker's living room."

CHAPTER 55

At first he just sat there. I sat, too, arms across the steering wheel. Rocky cried, snuffling quietly and wiping his eyes with a dirty hand. I fought off pangs of sympathy by thinking of Sandra Baker on the couch, the smell in the room, Roxanne and the baby.

The child of a murder suspect.

I put the van in gear and pulled out. I'd driven fifty yards when Rocky said, "No."

I pulled over again, this time in front of a thrift store where mannequins wore hand-me-downs in the window. Rocky looked out at them and wiped his face.

"Next time, I don't stop until we're in her driveway," I said.

He bit his lip and then took a deep breath.

"She was dumping bad on my mom."

"And Rusty was telling her to stop saying this stuff?"

He shrugged.

"What kind of stuff?"

Rocky looked out the window. I waited. Slipped the gearshift down.

"Bad things." he said.

"Like what?"

No answer. I took my foot off the brake and the van rolled forward.

"Bad things," Rocky said, quickly. "About my mom and Rusty and Kitty, except she's dead."

"Sandra Baker said bad things about Rusty and Kitty, too?"

Rocky shook his head.

"No, not about Kitty. Kitty's dead."

"How do you know that?"

A pause. The van rolled. Rocky talked and it stopped.

"On account of what Sandra Baker said. About her being dead, I mean."

"What did she say about her being dead."

"I want my mom," Rocky said.

I turned and he was crying more, his eyes reddened and swollen as though they'd been punched, black dirty streaks like brush strokes across his face. I felt the sympathy start to well up inside me and I turned away and choked it back down.

"Rocky," I said. "What was it Sandra Baker said about Kitty being dead?"

Rocky sobbed. I waited, steeling myself to the sound. He sobbed again and again. I let the van roll.

"She said—"

I braked to a stop.

"She made it up. She was just making accusations and lying and—"

"About your mother?"

In the mirror, I saw him nod.

"What about your mother, Rocky?"

"Bad things, but they weren't true."

"Well, if they weren't true, then you shouldn't mind telling me, right? If they were just made up."

In the mirror, I saw him staring out the darkened window. When I looked ahead, I saw a car approaching the intersection. There was something stealthy about the way it moved, and I put the van in gear, and pulled out slowly.

"No," Rocky said.

"Just hang on," I said, and I drove up to the intersection and turned right, just as the patrol car passed through. The cop, a young man, glanced at me but drove on. A block up, I pulled into a convenience store lot and parked. I left the motor running and I asked him again.

"What was she saying about your mother?"

Rocky grimaced.

"We can be at Sandra's in five minutes. Is that what you want?"

He shook his head.

"I can't wait much longer, Rocky."

He swallowed.

"We can just pound on her door, Rocky. If she isn't home, we can just go in and wait. Sit right down—"

"She called my mom a lot of things."

"Where was this?"

"On the phone."

"She was talking to you?"

He shook his head.

"Talking to your mom?"

Another shake.

"Talking to Rusty?"

He hesitated, then nodded.

"And where were you?"

Rocky didn't answer.

"Come on, answer me. Where were you?"

"Listening," he whispered.

"Listening in?"

"In the family room. On the phone in the family room."

"Listening to Rusty talk to—"

"To Sandra Baker."

"And what were they saying?"

He started to cry again, to rock in place, rubbing the tops of his thighs.

"Rocky, just say it."

He closed his eyes, bit at his lips, rocked faster. I waited, and then the words came, choked out between racking sobs.

"She's a liar. A liar."

"What did she lie about?"

"She lied about everything."

"She lied about your mom?"

"She said my mom did it and Rusty did it, but my mom didn't. I know she didn't. The Baker lady just wanted money and Rusty said, 'Leave us alone.' And she said, 'Oh, yeah? There's no statute of limitations on murder. I'll go to

the cops and you know it.' And Rusty said, 'You blackmail-
ing bitch, you'll go to jail, too.' All this stuff about her being a cokehead and those days were over and she'll go down
for it, too. She says, 'No, I won't. I'll turn state evidence.
And I'll put—' "

Rocky paused.

"Put what, Rocky?"

He took a breath.

"She said, 'I'll put both of you away.' "

Rocky panted like he'd run up a flight of stairs. I waited
for him to recover, then asked as calmly as I could, "Put
both of them away for what?"

The tears ran, the finger brushed at them like mosqui-
toes.

"For—"

He started to break down again.

"For what, Rocky?"

I waited. Watched him in the mirror as his face became
almost distorted by a sneer, transformed by a scowl. When
he spoke, it was in the voice of a woman.

" 'That bitch ran her over and you left her there to die.
You left her there in the road, you bastards. You screwed
her, you bastard, and then you and your little wife ran her
over and you left her there to die and you've got to pay.' "

The last words came in a screech that ended in a sob. I
waited, my eyes closed, and I listened to him cry. And
when, after several minutes, his sobs had begun to wane, I
asked another question. I asked this one gently.

"What did she want, Rocky?"

"Money," he said, his breath coming in quick little
spasms. "More money."

CHAPTER 56

So we sat there, Rocky and me. I reassembled everything that had happened since he had pounded past the
restaurant window in Portland. He stared out the window,
breaking the silence with an occasional sniff.

"You okay?" I said, after minutes had passed.

Rocky nodded. Sniffed again. I turned in my seat to face
him and he looked at me and scowled. Was he angry with
himself for telling me? Angry that I knew?

"You know, just because this lady said this doesn't mean
it was true."

He turned away.

"And just because Rusty paid doesn't mean it was true. A
lot of people are paid off to keep things from coming out.
Just the accusation would be enough to ruin him, you know.
And once something like that is out, you can deny it all you
want. The damage is done."

"And all because I picked up the phone, and Rusty, he'd
said not to do that, it was for babies, and I was a baby and he
was going to grow me up."

I looked at him.

"So is that what he said this time?"

"He didn't say anything. He just came downstairs and
he started to say something, standing there, and I was just

sitting there watching TV and I was gonna act like nothing had happened, but then I looked at him and he looked at me and you didn't have to talk 'cause it was in our eyes, it was in both our eyes."

I waited.

"And then what?" I said.

"And then I stood up, like I was gonna just go get something to eat or something but I got, like, ten feet away from him and I just sorta bolted and I went up the stairs and he was chasing me, and my mom, she's saying, 'What? What's going on?' and she musta got in his way 'cause I grabbed my jacket and I'm out the back door and running and then he's out the door and he's running and I can hear my mom yelling, 'Leave him alone. Leave him alone,' like she thought he was just gonna smack me for doing something but he wasn't."

"What do you think he was going to do, Rocky?"

He considered it.

"I don't know. Something really bad. But he couldn't catch me."

"Big guy like that?"

"He's big but he's got something wrong with him. He's, like, wheezing and coughing a lot. He smokes. And sometimes he coughs up bloody stuff. It's gross."

"Did you go back home?"

"That night I did. He was asleep. I hid and he left in the morning and I went to school and I didn't come back. I'm not making trouble for my mom no more."

Rocky still stared through the window, which was opaque from his breath. He reached up and wiped it with his arm. I leaned toward him.

"Who have you told all this to?" I said.

He didn't answer.

"Rocky. Answer me. Who have you told this story to?"
He shrugged.

"Just Tammy," he said.

"You told her the whole thing?"

He waited, then gave a quick nod.

"So she knew," I said, half to myself. "And your mom. And your dad. And Sandra."

Rocky turned and looked at me with an odd expression. A half-smile. Almost smug, as though he'd managed some sort of ironic triumph. And then he looked back at the glass.

"And you," he said. "And you'll tell your girlfriend. And she'll tell somebody else and they'll tell somebody else. And everybody'll think my mom is a murderer or something, and she's not, she's great, and I can't let people think that, because they'll put her in jail and she can't go to jail 'cause she's sick."

So was Rocky the Grim Reaper? Or was the Grim Reaper trailing Rocky, sweeping up the dirt he'd scattered?

Flossie, Sandra, Tammy . . .

"You're going to have to tell your story one more time," I said, putting the van in gear.

"I don't want to."

"Well, Rocky," I said. "As you know, sometimes life is—"

"—a bitch," he said. "And then you die."

CHAPTER 57

He didn't fuss, didn't move, didn't say another word as I drove through the still streets to the Broadway intersection, made a U-turn and started back toward the downtown. But when I approached the Bangor police station, a long low brick building built into the side of one of the city's hills, Rocky sat bolt upright.

"These cops will just call my dad."

"No, they won't," I said. "There's a detective here who's working on Tammy. He'll know what to do."

We pulled up outside and parked behind a cruiser.

"What if he isn't here?" Rocky asked, panic rising up in him. "What if it's just some regular cop and they call my dad?"

"They won't. I'll tell them not to."

"So what. Who are you?" Rocky said.

Who am I? I considered it. I'm Jack McMorrow, I talked to Detective Bruno and this is Rocky and, no, he's not my son, he's just a . . . a friend and he's been on the streets and he's fourteen and I know Bruno would like to talk to us. Yeah, the name sounds familiar probably because there's an ATL out on the kid. Yeah, Woodfield. Yeah, parent will go for, but whatever you do, don't call his stepfather, because, well, it's a very long story, and what is my connection to all this? Just an interested bystander, and sure, I'll go and wait down the hall, but where's Rocky going? To see the juvenile officer? Oh. Well, just remember, you can't call his house. Will you tell the juvenile officer that? You're sure?

"What if we call first?" I said.

Rocky didn't agree, but he didn't try to kick the windows out, either, so I slowed as I drove along, looking for a pay phone, wishing I had my truck, my phone, and then remembering there was a pay phone in the *Clarion* foyer, up the block and around the corner.

I sped up, rounded the corner and pulled the van up in front of the door. Getting out, I looked back at Rocky, huddled in the backseat, considered him, then slid the door open.

"Come on," I said.

He looked at me, but then, without a word, got out of the van. Like a suspect being brought in for booking, he walked in front of me, waiting as I reached over him to open the door. I kept him within arm's reach as I dialed the operator and asked for the Bangor Police Department, and no, this was not an emergency. She gave me the number, and I put in a quarter and punched the number. Two guys from composing burst out of the door, headed for supper. They glanced at Rocky, then at me. I nodded briefly. They did, too, dubiously. A dispatcher answered and I asked for Bruno and she said he was off-duty, could someone else help me?

The composing-room guys gone, I said, no, could they beep him because it was important. How important was it? Well, it was related to a homicide he was investigating and, yeah, I could hold for the sergeant, and—

"Jesus Christ, you're here."

I turned, the phone at my ear, Rocky at my side, and Marna came over and grabbed me by the arm.

"I've been trying to call you," she stage-whispered. "I tried your car phone, I tried your house. This detective has been calling you. And Roxanne's called you, like, eight times."

I told the dispatcher I'd call back and hung up.

"Roxanne? Is she all right?" I said.

"I don't know. She says for you to call her in her car, but then she calls back, like, fifteen minutes later, and says it again."

She looked at Rocky.

"How are you?" Marna asked.

Rocky shrugged.

"Okay," Marna said. "Nice to meet you."

"This is Rocky. I've told you about him."

"Oh, yeah. Hi."

"Hey," Rocky said.

"So that's all she said?"

"Yeah. Over and over and over."

"Call her in the car?"

"Yup."

"And she was okay?"

"I don't know," Marna said. "I mean, don't tell her I said this. Never met the woman and I'm passing judgment, but she sounded kind of strange."

"Strange like what?"

"I don't know. Like she was, this is gonna sound funny, but kind of like she was on stage or something. She's not like that, is she?"

"No," I said. "Not at all."

"I wrote the number on—well, you don't need the number, you call it all the time."

I began to dial. Marna moved toward the doors, then turned back. She looked at Rocky. I put the phone down and walked to the door with her, and leaned close. She whispered.

"You know that woman you asked me about? The—"

She looked over her shoulder at Rocky, still by the phone.

"I talked to the funeral woman again, and she was saying something about the business, which I really may look into. I've got a strong stomach, and you know they make, like forty thousand a year? Anyway, she said—" Marna leaned close, and I could smell coffee on her breath, see the flakes of lipstick on her lips. "She said they ruled that case a suicide. You know one of the reasons?"

I shook my head.

"No."

"She was sick a lot. Some sort of kidney thing. And you know what else? The woman was despondent. Some problem with her kid."

I must have looked stunned.

"I know," Marna said, a tenderness creeping into her voice. "But you can get pretty wrapped up in kids. When things go wrong with them, it hurts pretty bad."

"Yeah," I said. "It must."

Marna shouldered her bag and pushed through the door.

"I gotta get a sandwich before I expire. Call Roxanne," she said, and the door hissed shut.

I turned to Rocky, who was standing by the phone watching me.

"You still gonna call the cops?"

"Yeah," I said, distracted. "In a minute. Just wait. Let me think for a second. You know, we've got to get you to somebody besides me. A social worker or something. There's a woman named Duguay who I met who I think would look out for you pretty well."

"I don't need no—"

"Yeah, right. You're doing just great. But we've got to talk to the cops, anyway."

"I'll talk to this detective but I'm not going into the police station. Can he come and meet us?"

"Yeah. I'm sure. Just sit tight."

" 'Cause I don't want them to try to take me into PC or something. I've heard of it happening. They say you're a danger to yourself or others and then they ship you to the hospital or the youth center or someplace. I don't want to . . ."

I was dialing. Rocky was talking. The phone was silent and then it was ringing.

Roxanne answered. Rocky turned away.

"You okay?" I said.

"Yeah," she said, her voice high-pitched and strange, like something that could spiral into hysteria. In the background was the murmur of traffic.

"What's the matter?"

"Nothing," Roxanne said.

"You sound like you're going to cry."

"Me? No. I'm fine. I'm just . . . just tired."

"You know you can't overdo it. It's not good for you, or the baby."

"I know."

She said it with an odd inflection, like I'd confided something.

"Where are you?"

"Well, I'm coming to see you. Where are you?"

"Where am I? I'm in Bangor, at the paper. But I'm not working. I thought I was supposed to come down there."

"I know, but I got out early. I thought I'd come up."

She paused. I listened but only heard the car-phone hiss, a surge and ebb that might have been a passing car. Rocky had walked across the foyer to the door to the circulation department, where a manager was pouring change into a sorting machine. The coins started to clatter and I turned away.

"You're sure you're okay? I can come to Portland."

"No, I just thought I'd sort of surprise you," Roxanne said. "And I was wondering, did you find our friend?"

"Rocky?"

"Yeah, Rocky. Did he turn up?"

She said it as though he were an amiable dog with a habit of wandering off.

"Turn up?"

"Uh-huh."

"Are you sure you're all right?"

"Uh-huh. I think maybe we should talk, the three of us. He's going to need services and I talked to somebody today who would . . . who would like to help him."

"Roxanne. Something's wrong, isn't it?"

"Yeah, that would be fine," she said, with a strange little-girl voice.

"Is somebody there? If it's yes, say 'Good.' If it's no, say, 'Great.' "

"Good, so I'll see you," Roxanne said, her voice bright and tinny.

Christ almighty. Somebody there. Somebody in the car.

"I'll call the police."

"No, that wouldn't be good."

"Somebody threatening you? Say 'better' if it's yes."

"That would be better."

"So who? How can you—"

"I thought maybe we could have a drink," Roxanne said. "I could use a Scotch and Drambuie. It's been a long day."

A what? Roxanne, who sipped Merlot. Roxanne who was pregnant. Scotch and Drambuie?

I tried to think, sorting back through the years to bars on the East Side, bars in the Village. Smoke and crowds and rows of bottles and bartenders pouring liquors, mixing drinks, saying, "You want that straight up?" and all the rest of the alcoholic ritual.

And then it came to me.

Scotch and Drambuie. A Rusty Nail.

Rusty.

"Is Rusty there? 'Great' is yes."

"Great."

"Is he armed? 'Okay' is yes."

"Okay. That sounds good."

"Knife or gun? 'Sure' is knife."

"Sure," Roxanne said.

"And he wants Rocky? 'Okay' is yes."

"Okay."

Oh, god, I thought. Oh, god almighty.

"So I thought we could meet, let's say, right there in Bangor," Roxanne said, blurting quickly, as though she'd been jabbed. "We could buy Rocky dinner."

"Where are you? Say 'Great' when I get close. Freeport. Yarmouth. Brunswick—"

"Great," Roxanne chirped, the hysteria pooling on the surface now. "How 'bout the Sea Dog pub? By the river. Rocky could wait in the truck."

"His idea? 'Sounds good' is yes."

"Sounds good," Roxanne said.

"What about cops? I could call the state police, they could stop your car. Would that be the right thing? 'Okay' is yes. 'Great' is no."

"That would be great," Roxanne said.

"He's close to the edge?"

"That would be okay, too."

"I need time." I said. "Can you just go along with him, can you make it up here, do you think?"

"Sure."

"Drive slowly."

"Uh-huh. Tell Rocky I said hello. Tell him I'm looking forward to seeing him."

"It's twenty of nine. You're two hours away."

I thought frantically.

"Is he nuts? What if the cops pull you over? Will he hurt you? 'Sure' is yes. No is—"

"Um, sure," Roxanne said.

"Where did he find you, your office?"

"Sure."

"Oh, god. I have a black van. A Windstar. It has black windows. Does he know I don't have my truck? No is 'I love you.'"

"I love you, too," Roxanne said, and this time her voice cracked. I thought I heard a sound in the background, a grunt, and then the receiver was covered, and she came back on and said, "Call me in an hour. Bye," and the phone went dead.

I hung up, my heart pounding, turned and looked at Rocky, still staring at the jingling change.

In a second, I was across the room and I had him by the shoulder and he said, "Hey, leave me alone."

"Just stay away from the door."

"What's the matter with you?"

"Nothing," I lied. "Just stay where I can see you."

"What's your problem? Who was that on the phone?"

"Nobody," I said.

"Didn't sound like nobody. I don't think I want to talk to that cop."

"What you want doesn't matter right now. Just stand there."

Rocky did, but sullenly, one eye on the door. I dialed

Clair's number, stood and waited with the steel phone cord stretched taut, as close to the door as I could get. Rocky watched me suspiciously from behind his glasses, and I watched him, too, but I saw him differently. I saw Roxanne's life, her ticket out of this nightmare. I saw our baby, its life in the hands of this bastard. I leaned against the cord even harder.

Clair's line was busy. I hung up.

"What now?" Rocky said.

"Just wait."

"I want to go."

"Just stand there."

"You can't hold me. You've got no legal right—"

"So report me," I said. "But right now, just shut up."

I dialed again. Still busy. It could be Mary talking to one of her daughters, and Clair said those conversations went on for an hour or more. I waited for what seemed like a minute, but might have been twenty seconds, and tried again.

Still busy.

I had to call the cops, I had to. They'd have the plate, the description of the car, they'd find it, they'd stop it, they'd take Rusty out at gunpoint, maybe shoot him. Call her in an hour, she'd said. Maybe he'd change rendezvous points. Maybe he'd change his mind and tell Roxanne to drive out to some deserted place and—

Or maybe he'd show up.

Rocky was scuffing at the carpet. I stood there with the phone in my hand, the cord stretched. The circulation guy came out and said, "Hey, how's it going?" and I said, "Good," and Rocky said nothing. The guy glanced at us curiously and swung through the door and stomped up the stairs. I dropped my quarter back in and dialed again.

It still was busy.

I thought. Forty minutes to Prosperity. Forty minutes back. That was eighty, and I had a hundred and twenty. I could call on the way. Or I could just go to the Sea Dog and wait, or I could go to the cops, explain, hope it was the right thing to do.

"Come on," I said, and I took Rocky by the upper arm and went through the doors and outside, with him in front of me. He tried to shrug me off, but I hung on tight as I walked him to the van, slid the door open, pushed him in.

"Hey," he said.

"Just sit there," I said.

I started the van and even as I started down the hill to Main Street, I knew. Main Street led out of the downtown, past the car lots and stores and vacant scrub. It had started to snow and I drove in the left lane, steadily and fast, eyes squinting against the pelting flakes. Then I swung onto the highway, blasted through the snowy backwash from tractor trailers, and swung off two exits down, at Route 202 south.

"Where the hell we going?" Rocky said.

"Home," I said.

"I don't want to go home."

"Not your home. Mine."

"Why you going so fast?"

"Because I'm in a hurry."

He quieted after that, buckling his seat belt and watching the road, wide-eyed. I drove the same way, silent and staring, eyes fixed to the pale splash of light that split the darkness that lurked on both sides of the road. In Maine, the city abruptly gave way to woods as though you'd passed through a walled gate into the blackness where the country people huddled around fires. You traveled the roads at your own risk, hurtling down long, steep grades, grazing oncoming trucks that reeled under their loads of logs.

There were a few oncoming, a few going our way. A loaded pulp truck, a ramshackle pickup, listing to the right, an old Chevette crammed with kids. I passed them and soon the city was miles behind and it was just me and Rocky, hurtling south, riding the fine line between killing ourselves because we were going too fast, and killing Roxanne because we'd gone too slow.

But I didn't think of it that way, not then, not consciously as I feathered the brakes, pressed the accelerator down, felt the van start to slide almost imperceptibly, not going quite straight, and then I'd let off as Rocky muttered, "Jesus."

And I said, "Jesus," too, oh, dear, Jesus, get us out of this one, don't let anything happen, not to her, not to them, as I hit eighty on a long downhill grade, the snow rushing at the lights like neutrons, and then the distant glow of a sign, red and white.

It was a store, in Newburgh Center, and the lights were on but there were no cars, except for a pickup, plowed in and snow-covered. I wheeled past the gas pumps, up to the door, saw the ice locker, the air hose, the phone.

I parked and said, "Don't move," to Rocky and got out. The quarter went in, but trickled out the change return. I tried it again, and again it jingled all the way through.

"Son of a bitch," I said, jamming the coin in. It took it and there was a dial tone and I punched the numbers with a cold finger. It clicked. Clicked again. The busy signal rasped.

"Damn," I said, hung up and grabbed the quarter and ran. Back in the van, Rocky looked at me coldly.

"Something's wrong, isn't it?" he said.

"Yes," I said, but that was all.

From Newburgh we climbed, still headed south, following a single set of black tracks on the now-whitened roadway. It was more slippery and the tracks swerved where the car had slid, losing traction on the long grade. I gripped the wheel tightly, narrowed my eyes against the snow glare, tried not to think of Roxanne, the baby, but tried to think of them, too.

Call the police? Hand over Rocky? What was the best way to get her back into my arms? Me and Rocky in the parking lot, and Clair in the van? Roxanne in view first, alone and unharmed? I pictured her running to me, falling into me, Rocky taken by the arm and led off to who knows what. Did that have to happen? Could I allow it?

The images turned, like the TV with Rocky at the remote, blipping and whirling as I drove. The snow was heavier now, more and bigger flakes, covering the tracks that had been my guide. I crested the hilltops in Dixmont, and then, starting to slide at sixty miles an hour, had to choose: Turn east and head for Brooks, or continue on toward Unity. The van waggled, the rear end swinging. There was a store in Troy, a store in Unity. I hit the gas and the van straightened and sped on through the blackness, past the shadows of dimly lighted trailers, the black shapes of houses, my passenger silent and grim.

In Troy, the store was closed, the parking lot white like the ice on a pond. I pulled in, saw footprints, a single set, leading toward the door, leading to the phone.

There was a young guy talking, tall, long-hair in a ponytail, college age. He turned as I pulled up, then turned back, huddling over his conversation. I told Rocky to stay put, and then got out and strode over.

"Emergency, I need the phone," I said.

"Yeah, right," the kid said. "You can get—"

I shoved him back hard, too hard, and he fell and said, "Hey," and got back up and came at me.

"Somebody's dying," I shouted at him, shocked by my own words even as I said them.

"Yeah, well, you don't have to knock somebody down, you asshole," he said, and he gave me a shove. But there was no force in it, just lost face. I jiggled the receiver and pumped in the quarter and dialed.

Waited, with him glowering.

Busy again.

"Shit," I said, and I slammed the receiver down, grabbed the coin and turned away.

That was it, the last call, and now it was a dash over the ridges, through the woods, twelve miles to home. I flung the van around the corners, crested the hills with the pedal down to the floor.

"You don't have to kill us," Rocky said suddenly, as we sped over Knox Ridge.

He was right, the little twerp, and I took a deep breath as I slowed. We'd be there in fifteen minutes, back on the road in twenty, explanations delivered en route. But how would I do that, with Rocky in the van? And what if Clair weren't home?

Well, he just had to be, if there was a God, if there was any justice, if there was . . . he just had to be. He just had to.

CHAPTER 58

But was he?

The barn was shut, the windows dark, the lights were on in the house.

I pulled in, wheeling the van close and crunching the front end into a snowbank so the headlights played on the door. The dooryard spotlight came on, the light spilling over the snow.

"Somebody sick?" Rocky said behind me.

"No," I said. "Nobody's sick."

Except Rusty, I thought, but then the door swung open, the storm door swung out, and Clair peered at us, then hurried down the steps. I shut the van off, taking the key, and got out. We met in front of the van, standing in the falling snow.

"What's wrong?"

I told him, speaking soft and low. Rocky. Sandra Baker. Roxanne.

Clair's face hardened.

"Where?"

"By now? Probably approaching Augusta."

"Police?"

"Not yet. She said he'd hurt her, that he was desperate. Desperate to get the boy back."

"Because the boy knows?"

"That's his version. The boy's, I mean."

"Whatever."

"We have to bring him."

"Bait," Clair said.

And without another word, he turned and went back into the house. I got back in the van and started the motor and sat silently at the wheel. Rocky watched me closely, and when Clair came back out with the Mauser, I glanced over and saw Rocky's owl eyes widen. Clair trotted with the rifle toward the barn.

"It's Rusty, isn't it?" Rocky blurted, and then he fell to a crouch, started to try to scramble between the front seats. I leaned over and strong-armed him back down.

"No, I'm not going," he said, and popped up again. Back down he went.

Back up. Back down.

"Rocky," I barked. "Sit there or I'll tie you down."

The words hurt both of us and I caught myself, but there was no choice. I couldn't allow myself to be nice or kind or compassionate. Not now, not yet.

Rocky resignedly sat back in the backseat, and when I told him to buckle his seat belt, he did. Clair came back out of the barn, hunched against the snow. I leaned over and opened the passenger door and he handed me the phone from Mary's car and a small canvas ammo bag. Then he got in, holding the gun in front of him, the muzzle pointing at the ceiling. Clair glanced at Rocky and gave an absent nod. He was distancing himself, too.

I followed my own tracks down the road, but the snow was falling steadily and the snaking lines were filling, turning a pale gray against the white undulating sheet of the road. Clair plugged the phone into the cigarette lighter, and as he leaned back in his seat, I took a crest too fast and the van started to skate. I let off the gas and the van snapped back straight and Clair steadied the gun.

"We aren't gonna be doing anybody any good sitting in a ditch," he said evenly. "You're letting your heart take over, Jack. Time to put it away and start using your head. Establish your objective. Devise a way of achieving it. Plan for old Mr. Murphy to show up and screw things up, and plan for that, too, as well as you can. And then execute."

I slowed but still skidded through the corner at the end of the road. The van went sideways, but we stayed between the snowbanks and straightened out and I hit the gas again.

"The objective is to get her back," I said.

"Then let's get to the drop zone in one piece."

"What drop zone?" Rocky said. "I want to get out."

CHAPTER 59

For ten miles, we didn't answer him, we didn't speak. I had to slow to fifty, as the snow piled up and drummed softly on the underside of the van. The defroster was blowing hard and hot and the wipers flicked every few seconds, clearing away the splattered flakes. Clair stared straight ahead, but approaching Dixmont, with the blackness on both sides, he suddenly spoke.

"Hour's up," he said.

"You dial," I said.

I gave him the number, digit by digit, and he punched it in. I took the receiver. After two rings, she answered.

"Hello."

Her voice was high-pitched, the gaiety bizarre and false. Static drifted in and out like clouds.

"Hi."

"Oh, Jack. How you doing? You getting this snow up there?"

"Can I talk?"

"Yeah, it's snowing to beat the band down here. I'm just coming out of Augusta, getting onto Route 3. Where are you?"

"Dixmont, coming up over the ridge."

"Well, I'll let you get back to work."

"And I've got Clair with me," I said.

"No, I don't mind. Really. I've got it in four-wheel drive and I'm just putt-putting along."

"And I haven't called the cops yet."

"Yeah, I'm starved, too. Can you take a break? Bring Rocky with you and I'll treat."

"What about police? Will he stay with this or should we have them looking for you?"

"No, you know I think maybe we should stay over. How 'bout the hotel at the airport? A night of romance at snow-bound Bangor International?"

"So no police?"

"Naah."

"No Sea Dog?"

"No, this'll be fun. I'll meet you at the front door, but why don't you call me in a half hour or so. And tell Rocky to put the old feedbag on."

"He's here, too."

"Good, I love you," Roxanne said, and even through the static, those words rang true.

"I love you, too," I said quickly, and then she was gone, once again.

I handed the receiver to Clair.

"Airport," I said. "At the hotel, but call in a half hour."

"He's moving us around, in case we know, in case we're trying to set something up. Next call, he'll move it again."

"Who?" Rocky said.

I paused, felt the truth rising in my gullet, on my lips, and then remembered the objective. I couldn't lie, so I said nothing. Instead, I turned the radio on, flipped the balance to the rear speakers, right behind Rocky's head. I turned up the music, a discordant flailing.

"Hey, turn it down," Rocky called out.

"Kind of a feeble attempt to be cagey, don't you think?" I said, leaning toward Clair.

"He's desperate, not thinking straight. They must've pushed him pretty hard. The cops, I mean."

"I'll bet it's Tammy. There had to be something on him."

I paused.

"Or he thinks he can beat that one, but if Rocky links him to this other thing, he can't beat two," I said. "I think we should call them. They could just follow her."

"I don't know. Pretty delicate thing to set up over the phone in a half hour. Could turn into a mess. What'd she say?"

"No."

"And she could have?"

"Yes."

"Another half hour?"

"Yup."

"Let's wait."

"I'd like to have them pull him over and blow his head off."

"Stay focused," Clair said, and as the music screeched and squawked behind us, he bent and picked up the ammo bag and unzipped it.

I drove at a steady fifty-five, eyes fixed on the vague outlines of the roadsides. Atop the ridge in Dixmont, the wind was blowing from the northeast and the snow turned and ran sideways across the road, drifting from the right side, and scouring the pavement bare on the opposite lane. It was harder and harder to see the where the road began and ended, and approaching Newburgh, I went off the road to the right.

There was a rumble and then the wheels caught the drifts and the van tipped to the right and Clair said, "Easy," and I fought the urge to turn hard to yank it back onto the pavement, and held on tight as the van bumped and lurched and finally slowed.

"We stopping here?" Rocky called, over the din.

I didn't answer, just shook my head, and pulled back on, pressing the pedal gently as the front wheels spun.

There was a pickup off the road, spun into a field on the left. Two guys in baseball hats were standing in the roadway and they tried to wave us down, but I looked them in the eyes and drove right past. They shouted something that was lost to the snow and wind.

And then there was just a white-flecked blackness, the snow slipping through the headlight glare like blips on a radar screen, the music thumping away, both Rocky and Clair staring straight ahead, thinking their disparate thoughts. I drove with hands and teeth clenched, eyes narrowed, feathering the accelerator as the van teetered on the edge of control. The driving kept me from thinking, kept me from screaming, but it didn't keep images of Roxanne from creeping into my mind. Roxanne and the way she drove with two fingers of one hand across the bottom of the steering wheel. Roxanne, how she held the baby in front of her, even now. Roxanne just before she went into court, how she sort of puffed herself up, steeled herself, and then let this disarming confidence come over her like a spell. Had she done that now? Was she talking to him? Reasoning with him? Disarming him with her empathy, her sympathy? Disarming him—

The headlights flashed through the trees, just a glimmer at first, to my right but moving toward us at a tangent. I looked ahead and there was a green sign that said NEWBURGH VILLAGE and an arrow pointing to the right, and then the headlights moving closer, snow showing in them, and the lights slowing but still coming and then they were there, and taillights, too, a car, sliding into the road and hitting the side of the van.

A tremendous booming bang. Then the van rocking and swerving, then rolling to a stop. All was quiet, but for the dinging of the door chime, like an odd sort of churchbell.

"Jesus," Rocky shouted.

"Damn," I said.

"Murphy," Clair said. "He rears his ugly head."

The van was in the middle of the road, fifty yards past the intersection. It had stalled, but the lights still were on. I turned and Rocky was turned, too, looking back at some old wreck, a Pontiac or Chevy, with the front end crunched in on the left side. The door opened and a man got out, followed by several little kids, exiting like clowns from a circus car. The guy glanced at the damage, then walked toward the van. I tried to buzz the window down on Clair's side, but it didn't work, so Clair opened the door and the cold and snow came in.

"Hey, I'm sorry," the man said, coming up to the door. "Jesus, that hill is slicker than shit. I put on the brakes and she just kept on coming. You people all—"

He stopped talking when he saw the rifle. Looked at Clair and looked at me, his eyes wide under unruly blond eyebrows. Clair smiled and I started the motor. The music blared.

"Don't worry about it," I said.

"Go," Clair said, and I pulled away as he closed the door, leaving the man and his children standing in the road like people looking up at a departing spaceship.

"Aren't you gonna get his license number?" Rocky said.

"Focus," Clair said.

And we did, turning off in Newburgh and cutting across to the interstate. I watched the temperature gauge, but it held steady and the van, slogging down the one tracked lane of the highway, handled same as ever.

"Good thing the air bag didn't go off," I said.

"Very good thing," Clair said. "But I'll bet that door doesn't slide anymore."

"You've factored that in?"

"Just removes one option."

"There are others?"

"We're going to have to talk about that," Clair said.

"In a minute," I said, and glanced toward Rocky.

His head was back against the seat, and his mouth was open. He snapped back to consciousness every few seconds, but as I watched, his mouth gaped one last time, and with his glasses perched crookedly on his nose, Rocky fell asleep. We waited a minute or two and he didn't stir.

"I'm going to head for the airport," I said.

"When's the half hour up?"

I checked my watch.

"Four minutes."

"We've got several things going for us," Clair said. "Several advantages."

"He doesn't know we know."

"We don't know that for sure," Clair said.

"But he probably doesn't know what I'm driving. And he doesn't know you're here."

"And we have the boy," Clair said.

"And he wants him, so that he can—"

I paused.

"We can't just hand him over," I said.

Clair didn't answer.

"Just to be hurt?" I said, "I can't do that."

The lights of Bangor's outskirts were showing through the snow. Clair started taking .30-.30 shells from the bag and slipping them into the magazine of the Mauser. In a pause in the music, I heard the metallic clack.

"This isn't about can or can't," he said. "It's about what you have to do, given the circumstances. And the circumstances have dealt him one card."

"Roxanne," I said. "And that's not one card. That's two."

CHAPTER 60

Clair started to punch the number as we approached the airport exit, but something made me reach out and touch his arm to stop him.

"Wait," I said.

I coasted to the end of the ramp, took a left and drove a hundred yards up the road to the entrance to some sort of industrial park. The park had grown up around a military base, long closed. The first building, called something systems, was dark, and I turned into its lot and parked. Shut off the motor and turned the key back on and the radio off. Rocky, who'd likely been up for thirty hours or more, slept through the chimes.

They rang, four, five, six times and then stopped.

I dialed the number and waited.

It rang. Once, twice, three times.

Then stopped.

"Hello," I said, cheerily.

There was no answer, just a faint hiss.

"You there, hon?"

Then away from the phone—

"Yeah, you've got the obits, but that story on the hospital, it doesn't pass the 'So what?' test. The information is there, it just needs to be interpreted, not regurgitated. No. Yeah, okay. Hang on one second, I'm on the phone."

"Okay," Clair said faintly.

Then back to the phone.

"Roxanne, is this thing working? Roxanne?"

The anxiety crept into my voice, and I tried to retract it.

"Roxanne?"

"Oh, hi," she said. "Sorry. I, um, I dropped the phone and I couldn't take my eyes off the road to pick it up. Sorry."

"No problem. I'd rather have you safe. Are you?"

"Oh, yeah. Getting a little slippery, but I'm just trucking right along."

"Safe?"

"Oh, yeah," she said.

"Did he answer?"

"Yeah, it's really not bad. Maybe a couple of inches on

the highway, but the sand truck came through here, and if everybody stays sane, we'll all be fine."

"How's he doing?"

"Okay. I mean, the judge didn't decide today, but I think we made a strong case."

"Police?"

"No, I don't think we'll be able to pull both of them. The older kid, he's sixteen, he can just go and live with the grandparents."

She paused, and the phone was silent for a moment, as though a hand had been placed over the receiver, and then Roxanne was back.

"Speaking of kids, Rocky still coming to dinner with us?"

"Yeah. He's asleep in the backseat."

"So—"

"How long?"

"How long?" Roxanne echoed. The silence again, and then the road hiss and she said. "Twenty minutes."

"At the hotel?"

"No, why don't we do the Sea Dog after all. They'll let underage people in, won't they? It is a restaurant."

"Okay."

The phone was covered for a moment.

"Listen, why don't you call me in fifteen minutes. Round up Rocky and we'll head over."

"I'm not going to meet you there?"

"Call me, Jack. Love you."

"I love you, too," I said, but the phone already was dead.

"Back to the Sea Dog. In fifteen minutes I'm supposed to call."

"Okay," Clair said. "That's what we expected. If we'd set something up at the airport, we'd have to move it all. He's just playing a game now."

I started the van and Clair looked over at me, saw the grimness, the fear. I hit the gas and the wheels spun in the snow as the van turned in a slow spin. Rocky stirred, rubbed his mouth.

"Calm down," Clair said, as though he were talking to a green private in his platoon. "I know it's Roxanne, it's the baby. But this isn't the time. You've got to keep it absolutely together."

I took a deep breath, and we pulled back out onto the highway and headed for the ramp, driving slowly in the two ruts in the snow.

"Okay," I lied. "I'm fine."

We drove into town, joining the long procession of cars that accompanies any Maine snowstorm. In Maine, when it says on TV that the road conditions are hazardous, you don't stay home. You go out to see for yourself.

So we threaded down the hill, past a fender-bender and a snow-covered cop directing traffic. Part of me wanted to roll the window down and scream, "He's got Roxanne," but I didn't, and the cop waved us through with his flashlight, while Clair pushed the Mauser under the dash.

"Loaded firearm in a motor vehicle," I said. "Five-hundred dollar fine."

"Just add it to the list."

"You're getting to be a regular outlaw. They'll be looking to write you up in the paper."

"It all started when I met this pansy reporter from away."

"That's 'Claire' with an 'E,' right?"

It was false bravado. We fell back into silence, driving slowly past the brooding Victorian houses, black shadows with lights showing high above us, glowing yellow through the snow. We coasted and braked, coasted some more, and

I checked my watch in the glow of the dash. It had been eleven minutes, and Roxanne had said fifteen.

At twelve minutes, we were sitting at a light. At thirteen, we were taking a right on Main Street. At fourteen we were squeezing through the back streets, heading for the waterfront pub. At fifteen, we were sitting in front of flashing red lights, waiting for a freight train to pass.

Rocky stirred and this time he woke up. He looked around.

"What're we doing in Bangor?"

I hesitated.

"Getting something to eat."

"I'm not hungry."

"I am," I said. "You can have water."

He reached for the door latch and jerked on it, but the door wouldn't open.

This wasn't going to be easy.

Finally, the last car passed, the barrier raised and the clanging stopped. I drove up and over the tracks and under an overpass and into the lot of the brew pub, a long low brick building right on the river. There were twenty cars in the lot, college kids headed in. I parked. Picked up the phone and, with a glance at Rocky staring at me from his seat, I called.

Again the silence.

"Roxanne," I said. "Pick up the phone."

I waited. Someone picked up.

"Yeah, that was better," I said. "No, I put it in city news. CLAR 1. It's slugged hosp. HOSP. Right."

There was a jiggling sound, like the phone being passed.

"Hi," Roxanne said, and this time she sounded weary, exhausted.

"Something happen?"

"Yeah, I'm fine," she said, close to tears. "Yeah, the driving isn't bad. Uh-huh, I'm in town now."

"Did he hurt you?"

"Yeah, well, nothing I can't handle. Four-wheel drive is a lifesaver. You were right."

"Cops now?"

"No, I'm fine. Just tired. When I see you I'll perk up."

There was a muffled rattle, like she'd covered the phone. "Rox?"

"Sorry. Had to drive. You know, you tend to forget when you're talking? Hey, I'm tired. How 'bout I swing by the paper and we can go to dinner together. Where's Rocky?"

"He's here."

"He's with you there? What are they doing, turning him into a copy boy?"

"Give me time to get over there. I'm at the Sea Dog. Give me five minutes."

"I'll meet you at the door. Wait, I'll call you right back. Gotta drive. Love you."

And she hung up.

"The paper," I said.

"What's going on?" Rocky asked. "What is it?"

"When?" Clair said.

"Now."

I wheeled the van out of the lot, just as the crossing lights started to flash. In the dark, I could see the same train backing up, thirty feet from the crossing. I floored it and the tires shimmied and then grabbed, and the bells were ringing and the red-and-white bar started to lower and it came down on the windshield and there was a bang and I blinked and the bar snapped off, and the windshield cracked in front of my face.

"Hey," Rocky said.

"Can you see?" Clair said.

"Not really. Tell me if we're headed for something big."

"I want to get out," Rocky said.

"Just sit there," I said. "I have to stop at the office."

I took a right on Main, pushing my way New York-taxi style into a line of cars, and drivers honked and one unrolled his window and gave me the finger. I drove two blocks up the hill, across the Kenduskeag and past the *Clarion* building.

"He'll expect her to call the paper," I said.

At the light, I dialed.

"Hello, Marna please. I have an obit."

The phone clicked. The light changed. I pulled ahead, but a car was timidly waiting to turn left and we sat.

"Hello, this is Marna, can I help you?"

"It's Jack."

"Jack," she whispered. "Those police still are calling. The last time, they wanted to talk to Randall."

"That's fine. But I need a favor."

"What? I'm not going to get in trouble, am I?"

"If my phone rings in the next five minutes, forward the call to this number."

I gave her the cell phone number. I pictured her taking it down.

"And Marna. Make it sound like I'm in the newsroom."

"Why? I mean, it's none of my business but—"

"Marna, please. It's very, very important."

She sounded doubtful but said she'd do it. I hung up the phone. The light turned red, but I bulled my way through. As we approached City Hall, I pointed to the spaces that faced the *Clarion.*

Clair nodded.

"I'll back it in, look right out at the door."

"But we've got to be in the lobby there."

"What if he calls?" Clair asked.

I thought.

"We'll wait two minutes. You drop us around the corner, and we'll go in the side door, cut through to the front. You can come back here and set up."

"What's going on?" Rocky said.

"Nothing. We're meeting Roxanne."

"No, you're not. I'm not going—"

The phone rang. I turned left into an alley and stopped. Picked it up.

"Newsroom. Jack McMorrow."

"Jack, Marna. When I hang up, you have a call and a call holding. I did it like you said."

"Who?"

"First call is Tippy. Second one is a man. Wouldn't say who he was."

"I'll take the second."

"I don't know how to do that," Marna said. "I think I'll have to connect you and then you hang up, and the next call will come through. It's a camp-on and a forward. You do pound three-eight, then star six, and pound and the number and—"

"Thanks," I said. There was a pause and a click.

"Newsroom, Jack McMorrow."

"Mr. McMorrow. Tippy Danforth. I've been trying to reach you since I had a rather distressing call from Mr. Randall. Before I reach any conclusion, I'd like to talk to you and—"

"Me too, Tippy. But not now."

I hung up. The phone rang. I answered.

"Mr. McMorrow."

Not Roxanne. Not Rusty.

"This is Detective Cobb. You're a hard guy to reach. We need to get together, sir."

"Yes," I said. "We do."

Clair looked. With the wipers off, the snow hit the windshield and ran down the glass, leaving watery trails over the cracks.

"So where can I meet you?"

"Well, I'm here at the *Clarion* and—"

"Good," Cobb said. "Be there in five."

And he hung up. I held the phone.

"Cobb's coming here, too."

"More the merrier," Clair said doubtfully.

"I don't like this," Rocky said.

"Me neither," I said. "Let's go."

I got out and Clair slid across, then tucked the rifle down by his right leg. I went around and tried to open the sliding door, but it was bent and stuck. I opened the passenger door.

"I don't want to get out now," Rocky said.

"Rocky, some things you just have to do," I said, leaning in.

Clair reached back and took one arm and I took the other. Rocky squirmed but I got him between the seats and out the door, half dragging him to the snow-covered ground. He went limp, then jerked away, but I held tight to his arm and kicked the door shut. Clair backed up and pulled out, and I led Rocky to the glass side door, marked EMPLOYEES ONLY. I unlocked it and pulled him in behind me.

"I could scream," he said.

"You could. And you'd be home in Woodfield with your dad within the hour."

"He's not my—"

"I know, I know. Come on."

Rocky followed as I made my way through a storage area and into the advertising department. There were lights on at two cubicles, and from one a woman showed her head.

"Hello," I said, as we passed, my hand still clamped on Rocky's upper arm.

"Newsroom intern," I said.

"Hi, there," the woman said, and then, as we reached the end of the room, "What, we have to drag them in here now?"

We left her standing there and passed into a corridor, up a half-flight of stairs, and then down. There was another glass door, but when I leaned against it, it was locked. I stopped. Tried my key. It opened, and we went out into the foyer, onto the brightly lighted stage.

I went to the door and looked out through the glass, Rocky standing behind me. As I was peering out at the dark, the door behind me opened.

"Jack," Marna said.

We both turned.

"Hi."

"I tried to call but somebody else answered. Your friend?"

"Yeah."

"Roxanne called. Your friend said to say you were down-stairs waiting for her. Was that okay?"

"Yeah. Thanks. But you might not want to be here."

"Well, why?"

Rocky tried to jerk away, but I hung on, and he cursed and swore and then gave up. Marna looked at me with doubt, then fear.

"It's okay."

"Jack, is it true what—"

"No. Tell Cobb, the detective, we're in a green Explorer." I recited the plate number.

"Tell him I'm with Rocky. Tell him—"

But she turned and half-walked, half-ran to the door, and it slammed behind her, and I could hear her pounding up the stairs. Rocky squirmed again, and said, "Let me go."

"I will. But you just have to stay calm for a few more—"

The Explorer rolled up, the driver's side away from the curb. I could see Roxanne at the wheel but no one else. She looked at me and her face was expressionless, like she was in a trance.

I said, "Let's go." Fingers clamped tight around Rocky's arm, I led him through the door and onto the sidewalk. The Explorer blocked the view of the van, but I knew it was there, knew I could trust Clair.

We walked to the car and I opened the door, Rocky behind me, and then I could see him.

Rusty was crouched on the floor, behind and to the right of the driver's seat. His eyes were wild, and his long arm was stretched across to Roxanne. Her sweater was hiked up and the blade was pressed against her bare belly.

"Get in, McMorrow," he said.

"No," Rocky screamed, and he flailed at the end of my arm like a trapped bird.

"Get in, or no baby," Rusty said. "Get the kid in."

I hesitated. Waited for a shot, for something. But Clair would see Roxanne at the wheel, nothing else, not through the dark glass. The knife pressed against Roxanne and she gave a little cry. I got into the passenger seat and pulled Rocky in behind me, cramming him onto my lap.

"Drive," Rusty said.

The Explorer pulled away with the door open, but the momentum swung it shut. Rocky was flailing at me, elbowing me in the sides, screaming, "No, let me go," over and over.

"I see a cop, the knife goes in," Rusty said. "I'll take her with me, McMorrow. Your little baby, too."

Rocky kept jerking his arms, but I held onto him tightly, smelled his odor, felt his hair in my face. Roxanne drove without looking at me. She was rigid and wooden, with only her hands and feet moving.

"Let me go," Rocky hollered, kicking at the dash, but I hung on to him and said, "Calm down. It's okay," between clenched teeth, praying that Clair was behind us.

"Turn right, honey," Rusty said, his voice a weary wheeze.

Roxanne turned, cutting through a side street, passing a young woman carrying a grocery bag. Rocky hollered, "Help," but the woman frowned and looked straight ahead, ignoring a carload of heckling kids.

"Straight," Rusty said, and Roxanne winced and doubled over on the wheel and I tensed and Rusty said, "Sit right there," and "Keep your panties on, honey" to Roxanne. "I just slipped, is all."

We drove through the streets, past the houses where life went on, normal and safe and secure, and Rocky tired of kicking and lapsed into giving an occasional sudden jerk. I eased forward to try to see in the rearview mirror, and there were headlights far behind us, but then Rocky bucked and our heads clacked together and I felt my lip start to bleed.

At the wheel, Roxanne turned her head and I could see that she was crying silently, tears running from her eyes almost to her mouth.

"It's okay," I said. "It'll be okay."

She didn't react, just bit her lip as the tears slipped down her cheeks, and she didn't reach to wipe them, just kept her hands on the wheel. I turned my head toward her, and saw Rusty, craning his head to see out the windshield.

"Straight again," he said.

"You know I can't remember anybody ever getting away with this," I said.

"Always a first time," he said, "and why don't you just—"

"What do you have, Rusty? A ten-year-old manslaughter? Hit-and-run? You could say it was an accident—"

"Yeah, it was an accident. I said, 'Drive,' I didn't say, 'Drive right over the bitch.' Jesus H. Christ."

Rocky was still in my arms, wide-eyed, listening.

"So you could plead for eight to ten, do five or six. No serious priors, right?"

I ignored Tammy, for the sake of argument. Sandra Baker, too. What he didn't know I knew . . .

"Who are you, my friggin' lawyer, McMorrow? Just shut up."

"You're just hurting yourself. Just pull over, take the car. You could be in Canada in three hours. Have a better chance that way than—"

"Shut up," he screamed, and Roxanne said, "Ohhh," and Rusty said, "Barely touched you, now keep driving."

We came to the end of the side street, and Rusty said, "Right." Roxanne turned gingerly, like she was driving on the edge of a cliff, and we started down another street full of warmly lit houses. There were kids in the road, Rocky's age, shuffling along defiantly in the headlights.

"Get 'em the hell out of the way," Rusty snarled, and Roxanne looked in the mirror, as if to ask, "How?" and he said, "Flash the lights."

She did and the kids turned insolently, squinting into the lights, and one of them gave the car the finger with a ski-gloved hand.

"Drive right through 'em," Rusty said, still crouched on the floor, the knife silver like a belt buckle on Roxanne's belly. Roxanne tapped the gas, and the kids fell to the side and we passed, and Rocky shouted "Help," again, but they shouted obscenities back, and one of them pounded the side of the car.

And then we were at West Broadway, and Rusty said,

"Right," and Rocky elbowed the window, trying to break it out, but it held and I held him, feeling the blood from my lip smear into his hair. Roxanne waited for a truck to pass, and then pulled out and we went south on West Broadway, past the looming houses, past Tippy's house, where the lights were on but Tammy wasn't there for feeding time. Rocky's head turned as he looked at the house, and he said, "How did Tammy die?"

I didn't answer, which may have been an answer, and he suddenly thrashed and I held him and saw Roxanne close her eyes, as though to pray. But then she opened them, and slowed the car, letting it coast softly over the snow, and Rusty said, "Keep going."

"I feel sick," Roxanne said.

"So feel sick. Drive."

Rusty must have felt me tense again.

"Don't even think of it. I'll slice her wide open."

"And I'll rip your heart out," I said, and then I remembered Clair's advice: head, not heart. I didn't say any more.

Roxanne was pale, the veins showing blue in her neck, her earrings incongruous, her breath coming in short pants. We drove down Broadway, down, down, down, through the lights, and I thought Rusty would say to go left, to the bridge over the Penobscot, but he didn't. He ordered Roxanne right, and then left, where there was no road, just a mall with offices and an auto parts store, and Roxanne stopped in the lot.

"Straight," Rusty said. "Then around the back."

And then I knew. We were going to the river, down to the trestles, down where the muffling snow would mask a gunshot, never mind a scream or a cry. They found Tammy; they didn't hear her.

I looked for headlights behind us, saw none, but had to

believe that a guy who could trail the enemy in the night
jungle could trail a car in downtown Bangor.

But if the van stalled, if Clair got hung up at a light, I
needed a plan, a plan to get Roxanne out, a plan to—

"Turn in," Rusty said.

Roxanne eased the car between two trailers, inching forward until the bumper touched a guard rail that separated
the lot from railroad tracks. The snow fell in the headlights,
but then he said, "Shut it off," and Roxanne did, and there
was a moment in which we could hear the tick of snow on
the roof and the vague black shapes of train cars and bridges
materialized in front of us.

"Now we go slow," Rusty said. "Turn off the dome light."

I did, fighting off the urge to bring my arm down hard
on his.

Wait, I told myself.

Clair.

"Better if you just let us out and left," I said. "Lock us in
one of these trailers. You'll have at least all night to—"

"Shut up. Out. You two first, and remember what I said.
I'll gut her if you run, cut that baby to shreds. Rocky, too.
Hang on to him for her life, McMorrow."

I did. As we eased out of the car, my hand gripped his
arm to the bone, and he said, "Ow," but I held him even
tighter. We stood as Rusty eased himself out of his crouch
and popped his door open.

"You come my way," he said, and Roxanne scrambled
backward between the seats, the heels of her pumps scuffing
at the console, the shifter. The knife stayed on her belly, as
she kicked her way through, and then he half-dragged her
out into the snow.

"Let's go," Rusty said.

Roxanne didn't have a jacket on, and her sweater was white

in the blackness, like a light in fog. I led Rocky to the railing, and Rusty led Roxanne, the knife still on her belly, and he said, "Go over it," and we did, and he and Roxanne followed. I looked around for some sign of Clair, but saw nothing in the snow-brushed darkness. I told myself that was good.

"Move," Rusty said, and we did, stumbling over jagged metal and trash and then crossing the railroad tracks, first one, then another. I could see the lights of the bridges, headlights moving vaguely across the river. It was snowing hard, the flakes dense and heavy and everything was hushed, even our footsteps.

A scream wouldn't carry fifty feet. A gunshot would be a muffled pop.

I looked to my right, but saw only snow and distant lights and train cars, still and idle. It was cold and no one would be out here, not in this wasteland, not at this hour. I looked over at Roxanne, already grieving.

"It's okay, hon," I said. "It'll be okay."

She looked at me, and with her eyes she said good-bye.

We weren't at the trestle, but fifty yards south of it, where the tracks skirted the river and work boats had been lifted onto the bank for the winter.

Rusty said, "In there," and I led Rocky between the boats and turned, blinking against the snow. He had his arm around Roxanne's chest, the knife laid against the left side of her neck. They were silhouetted against the white hull behind them, and I could see that Roxanne was shivering.

"Down on the snow," Rusty said, and Rocky jerked his arm away from me, started to run toward the river, but slipped and fell backward and rolled over. I ran to him and squatted and put my hand on his shoulder and my knee on his back, and his legs flailed like a swimmer's against the snow.

"No!" he screamed, looking up at Rusty and Roxanne.

"Stop it," I said.

"Stay right there," Rusty said, moving Roxanne toward us. "On your belly beside him, hands behind you, at your waist."

I looked at him, couldn't see the knife, but could feel it against Roxanne's skin, the blade poised over her life. And suddenly the hope started to drain from me, and the plan, what there had been of one, petered out. He'd cut her, leap on both of us. Two stabs to the back, to the lungs or heart, and we'd be gone, he'd be gone. I had to fend that moment off, hold it back until I couldn't hold any more.

Crouching, I felt Rocky sobbing on the ground. I looked at them.

"This how you did Tammy? Slaughter her like a pig? You're a real man, you know that? What, were you raised by a coward just like you?"

"My old man woulda chewed you up, McMorrow."

"Would he be proud of you now?"

"Christ, don't try that with me."

The words poured out of me.

"You're right. You don't have a conscience. How do people end up like that? Some people say it's biological. A gene left off the chain. You gonna kill your own kid? Maybe you're missing a whole bunch of genes. You killed Sandra, right? That was the worst faked suicide I've ever seen. Hell, you could practically take your fingerprints off her throat."

"You're nuts. I haven't seen her in ten years. She checked out, don't blame it on me. So just shut the hell up. You just shut the hell up or I'll hurt her."

"No, you won't. You hurt her, you've got no hold on me. You don't think very far ahead, do you? Jeez, DNA will put you away for Tammy. You think you stab somebody and walk away without a drop? Blood must have been spraying like a sprinkler. Cops take your shoes? Your pants? Your truck? One little fleck and you're gone. No, you'd better run now. Might buy yourself a few months, anyway."

He moved toward me, Roxanne clutched in his arms in a strange swaying dance.

"Oh, Jack," she said softly.

"Rusty, no," Rocky said.

"And Sandra Baker. What'd she do, squeeze you too hard?"

"Too long," Rusty said. "Wouldn't go away. Well, she found out there was an end to the gravy train."

"I guess she did."

"Once she was told, she backed right off. I tell her to kiss off and then I send her an envelope and she thinks there's money in it, but what is there? Two words. 'No more.'"

"You didn't have to go see her?"

"Never heard another word from the bitch. Shoulda said it a long time ago. Called her bluff, that greedy pig."

In my arms, I felt Rocky go still. Felt the pulse in his wrist and it seemed to quicken. A poor man's polygraph.

"And now your stepson is spreading the word."

"Thought it was over, and instead it's spreading, you know what I'm saying? A man can only take so much."

"A man? You've got to be kidding."

His eyes narrowed and he jerked back on Roxanne's neck. The blade showed in the darkness, and snow covered her hair.

"On your belly, McMorrow. On your belly."

"Nah," I said. "I'd rather talk."

He took a swaying step forward. I lifted my hand an inch off Rocky's back, eased back on my knees so I wasn't touching him. I saw him dig his sneakers into the snow, like a sprawled sprinter awaiting the start.

"Down, or I gut her, McMorrow," Rusty said, just eight feet away. "Down, you wise-ass piece a shit."

"Okay, I'm going. But I want to ask you something first. Why couldn't you just stay home? Why did you have to go running around and causing all of this misery? Just give me an answer. I want to know how you think, Rusty. I really do."

They were closer. Roxanne's head was pulled back, her throat exposed. Rusty's teeth were bared.

"I'll cut her, McMorrow. I'll do it."

I leaned away from Rocky, saw his knees start to pull up, his butt start to lift. I swallowed.

"And Rusty," I said, slowly and deliberately. "Is that why you killed your wife?"

For a moment, it all was suspended. My words. Rusty's mad stare. Roxanne in his arms. Rocky on the ground.

And then there was a shriek, a low, building bellow that erupted from Rocky as he came off the ground, sneakers and hands scrabbling at the snow, launching himself at Rusty, still bellowing as he flew through the air. The knife slashed out, Roxanne fell away and I flung myself toward her. Rocky was bulling Rusty back, his legs pumping, his hands on Rusty's throat and the knife was in the air and then it was raised behind Rocky's back.

Rusty hit the hull of the boat, put both hands back to keep from falling, and then the knife came up again and I ran toward them, shouting "No! Don't!" and watching as the knife made a half-hearted scrape at Rocky's back, and then father and stepson fell backward and the knife fell, not so much dropped as flung.

Rusty dove for it, scrambling in the snow and then there was a boom and a puff of snow. Boom and another puff, like smoke from a magician's wand. Rusty froze on his hands and knees, wavered for a moment and then sagged back on his haunches, like a wounded deer ready to die.

CHAPTER 61

Clair came up from the riverbank, the rifle in his arms. He trotted to Roxanne, who was sitting in the snow twenty feet away from us, crying quietly.

Rusty was on the ground on his back, motionless and silent, his hands over his face. Clair had fired two warning shots, hadn't even put Rusty down. Rocky was on his belly, sobbing into his crossed arms, saying, "Mommy, no. Mommy, no." I stood over them, wondering whether to hold them at knifepoint or offer a handkerchief.

Clair put his hand on Roxanne's shoulder and then under her arm and gently drew her up. Neither Rocky nor Rusty moved. Clair walked to the car with Roxanne and helped her in and started the motor. Then I saw him talking on the phone, and then hanging up. He came over, the rifle held low at his side.

"Sorry," he said quietly.

"Cut yourself?"

"Fell in the road. Slipped on the goddamn ice."

"Murphy?"

"Van ran out of gas. Pinched a line when it got hit, I guess, and it dripped out. It's in the road."

"Didn't matter."

"It could have," Clair said quietly.

"But it didn't."

"I didn't," Rusty said, his hands still over his face. "I didn't kill her, I didn't kill her then."

I started to answer, but Clair held his hand out to stop me, and I realized Rusty was speaking, not to us, but to his stepson, whose sobs had quieted.

"I didn't do it then. I did it a long time ago, without even knowing it. She was nothing, just Kitty from the bar, Kitty with the big—I mean, she wasn't important, but your mother, she thought it was gonna be the end, but it wasn't the end, I mean, I was still married, I was still around. It was just one of those things, I tried to tell her. But she got all wound up, went off the deep end and she followed us and there was this thing in the road and them screaming and everybody drunk and she's saying, 'You can have her, I'm leaving,' and I'm saying, 'Go ahead, you . . . whatever,' and it's this big goddamn scene and Kitty takes off and she's in the road and I'm half in the truck and your mother's saying, 'You can have him' and I'm hanging on the door and I reach in and I get the wheel and she hits the gas and there's this sound, like this bumping, thumping noise, like you ran over a raccoon or something. And it's her."

We stood still. Rusty paused. Shook his head under his hands.

"But Rocky, I didn't kill her. I didn't kill your mother. Hey, I paid that cocaine whore, I paid her, like, thirty thousand bucks. And then she comes back after me, after three years when we was supposed to be paid up, it's all over, and she wants to start it up all over again."

Another long pause.

"Rocky, why the hell did you have to listen on the phone?

How many times have I told you? How many goddamn times have I told you?"

To pick up your dirty clothes. Bring out your dishes. Put your bike away. And never eavesdrop on the phone when your parents are dealing with a blackmailer.

CHAPTER 62

It took minutes, but not more than three or four. The police streamed in first, then the ambulances, the scanner freaks, and soon what had been the blackest of wastelands was illuminated like a carnival.

They hustled us off, one by one: Roxanne in an ambulance, because she was pregnant, and Rusty in an ambulance with a policeman, because he was a murderer and kidnapper. Juvenile cops, a woman and a man, took Rocky from the patrol officers and drove off with him. Clair sat with Bruno and another cop. A patrolman stood beside me while we waited for Cobb to arrive.

He'd been waiting at the *Clarion*. Lori Child and a photographer followed him down to the riverfront. Child tried to talk to me but I just shook my head. The photographer took my picture, with the patrolman looking grim beside me and another cop in the background holding Clair's Mauser. The patrolman told the photographer to get lost, but it was too late. I could hear how it would play out at the news meeting:

"*And we got strong art, with the gun and everything . . . .
McMorrow full face with the cop holding the gun.*"

"*And Tippy liked the S.O.B. for some goddamn reason,*" Randall would say. "*I know he was trouble. But let's run that two
columns on the left, so McMorrow's not looking off the page. What
else you got for one?*"

Roxanne went to the hospital for observation, because of the
baby. I went with Clair and the cops to the Bangor police station. They separated us and I was assigned to a small tile-
floored room with venetian blinds and pictures of historic
Bangor on the walls. I thought of Rocky at the history house
and then I recounted that part and the rest of it to the cops.

It was Cobb and an older Bangor detective, a guy from
the old school who hammered me pretty good. They didn't
like the story about finding Baker dead and the post office
box and the mail, and they turned it every which way to see
if it would twist and break. The tape recorders whirred, the
lights hummed, empty paper coffee cups piled up like poker
chips and my story stretched like taffy. But it held because
it was all true.

After three hours the cops left the room. When they
came back the tension was gone, like we'd just finished a
chess match. They said they needed a favor.

"What?" I said.

"The kid isn't talking," Cobb said.

"Not at all?"

"Not one word," Cobb said.

"Like he's a goddamn mute," the other cop said.

"We know you two got along good," Cobb said. "We'd
like you to talk to him, tell him it's only gonna hurt him in
the long run if he doesn't cooperate. If he didn't do anything
wrong, if it was Clement who was responsible for most of

this mess, then the kid should tell us what happened. Let the asshole hang for it. Kid can maybe get on with his life."

Lots of ifs and maybes . . .

"I'd want Roxanne with me," I said. "She's better with kids like him."

"Fine."

"When?"

"Morning."

"Where?"

"Here."

"I'm not wearing a wire or anything," I said.

"That's not what we're after," Cobb said. "We just want somebody to get him started."

"It'll be like floodgates," I said. "Or it won't happen at all."

CHAPTER 63

They put us in an interview room in the police station. It had a window that looked out on a dirty snowbank and a brick wall. Three chairs loitered around a blond-wood table that had been inscribed like a high school yearbook. The walls were painted pea green, broken only by a bulletin board with nothing on it. The juvenile caseworker, a squarish woman with a mane of dyed-red hair, was sitting at the table with her hands folded and a grave expression. She looked at us and gave her head a brief shake. Rocky was standing at the window, staring out. There was a circle of fogged glass in front of his face, like steam on a bathroom mirror. His hands were crammed in his pockets. I was about to say hello when I heard him. He was talking softly, but not to us.

". . . Corinthian columns, as opposed to the Ionic out on the porch," Rocky was saying, in an odd sing-song voice. "This is all hand-carved wood, all the leaves and the scroll-work . . . . Note the detail."

He reached out with one hand toward the window and made a slow sweeping motion.

"Now, the black Italian marble fireplaces, who would like to guess when they were put in? Eighteen-sixty? Good guess, but the answer is we don't really know. Most experts think Sidney removed the white marble because there were four white marble fireplaces upstairs. As we said, Sidney wanted to have the grande salon of Paris . . ."

Rocky grinned to himself, and then laughed, a high-pitched laugh somewhere between a chuckle and a giggle.

It was like he was possessed.

"To understand this you must know the world of the wealthy American of the early nineteenth century. They felt—"

Roxanne moved past me and walked over to him. She took him by his upper arm and gave him a little shake, like he was sleepwalking and he needed to wake up.

"Rocky," Roxanne said. It was a command. "Rocky."

He turned to her and then to me, but he seemed to look through us. He smiled and turned back to the window.

"—a tremendous inferiority when compared to the gentry of their home country, namely England."

"Rocky," I said, moving to them. "You need to put all that aside now. We need to talk, buddy. Come on."

He continued.

"All these years after the Revolution, Americans were still the rabble in the eyes of the English. This led to—"

Roxanne turned him toward her and looked into his eyes.

"Rocky. You can talk about that later. We need to talk about other things right now."

He peered at her like she'd dropped into his dream.

"You're pretty like my mom," he said.

"We need to talk about your mom," I said.

Rocky didn't answer. I said it again. He didn't answer but after a minute he shook his head.

"Rocky," Roxanne said. "Your mom would want you to talk about her."

His expression shifted from passive to puzzled and he stared at the fogged-over window like it was a smoky crystal ball. We waited. Waited some more.

"Rocky," Roxanne said, leaning close to him now, speaking very softly.

"She was pretty," Rocky said, half to himself. "She said it didn't do her any good to be pretty. It just made bad things happen to her. She said she'd rather be ugly and have people leave her alone."

I thought of the M.E. saying women didn't usually shoot themselves. Maybe this was the exception—a woman who wanted to destroy her pretty face.

"Who didn't leave her alone, Rocky?" Roxanne said.

"Guys," he said. "Bad guys. Because she was pretty."

His expression sharpened and he looked at me.

"The old days were better. In the eighteen-hundreds—"

"Rocky. We need to talk about this now."

"Rocky, honey," Roxanne said. She put a hand on each of his shoulders and fixed her gaze on his. "Did you try to get people to leave your mom alone?"

He turned his face away and Roxanne moved with him.

"Rocky, you can't turn away. Your mom wouldn't want you to turn away. She'd want you to be strong and brave."

"No, Rusty would want me to be strong. And tough, like him. But I could never do that. I just couldn't."

"That's okay," I said. "You're fine. You're a good guy. You cared about your mom. That's the most important thing."

"I tried to look out for her," Rocky said, shaking his head. "But I sucked at that, too."

"What makes you say that?" Roxanne said softly.

Rocky looked at her and then the gauze moved over his eyes and he smiled. "To have gas lights in this era—that alone was—"

"Rocky," I said. "No. Don't leave your mom now. She needs you to talk about this."

"She would want you to," Roxanne said.

"It won't help her," Rocky said.

"It will help you," I said. "And that's what she'd want. She'd want you to get through all this and have a good life. You can't do that if you keep leaving. You tried to help her before. Try to help her now by helping yourself."

"Nobody helped her," Rocky said. "She was all alone. After I left—me leaving, that left her alone. That's what it did."

"And you think if you'd stayed she would be okay?" Roxanne said. So that was it, I thought. Guilt at not being there to prevent his mother's suicide.

Rocky shook his head and smiled but it was a sad, bemused expression, like we just didn't understand.

"No," he said, his voice barely audible. "She would have been okay if I never came back."

"When did you go back, Rocky," Roxanne said.

"It was at night. I don't know. I went back and I walked in and she was just sitting there, being sad. All by herself."

"But she must have been glad to see you," I said.

"I guess. At first. And then she was sad again. Really, really sad."

"Because you were leaving again?" Roxanne said.

Rocky didn't answer. He tried to smile but it was like his face was holding a massive weight and his mouth began to tremble. Roxanne took his hand in both of hers and said, "It's okay, Rocky, it's okay to cry."

Tears welled in his eyes and then spilled onto his cheeks and he wiped with his free hand while Roxanne held the other tightly. Rocky tensed and then let out a wail and started to sob.

"It's okay, Rocky," I said. "It's okay there, buddy."

He jerked his head around and bellowed into my face. "It's not okay. I screwed up. I screwed it all up and I can't fix it. I wanted to fix it and I wrecked it. It's what I always do. I wreck everything. I wanted to help her and I—"

Saliva sprayed from his mouth and he wiped at his face, his eyes and mouth. The caseworker rose from her chair. Rocky turned back to the window and banged his forehead on the glass. Once. Twice. Three times.

"I killed her."

It was a strangled whisper.

"What do you mean—" Roxanne began.

"I killed her," Rocky screamed, turning to us, his forehead red and splotchy. "I killed her. I did it to help her but I screwed up. Don't you see? Don't you fucking people see?"

"Rocky," I said. "The police say your mother wasn't killed by somebody else."

"No," he shouted. "I killed her by going to see the other lady. And when she said my mom and Rusty were murderers and they killed her friend Kitty and they would pay for it and if Rusty, if he didn't pay the money, she'd call the cops and she'd call the TV and everybody would know what my mom really was and I said, 'No, stop it,' and she laughed and I was crying and she said I was a crybaby and I should go home to my mommy and tell her."

"Kitty, Kitty, Kitty," I said. "How can you live—"

"—with yourself?" Rocky said. "It's what she said. It's what the lady said."

"On the phone when you were listening?"

"Uh-huh. And I wrote it down. I'd look at it and try to figure it out. What else could it mean? But I knew what it meant. She was asking my mom. How can you live with yourself after—"

Rocky paused. We waited and the room was still and silent for just a moment and then he sniffed.

"So I grabbed her to stop her from talking and she wouldn't stop and so I—" He paused. Swallowed. Wiped his eyes and sniffed. "I held onto her, onto her throat. And then she stopped. She just stopped everything."

I heard the caseworker breathe slowly in and out. Rocky had stopped crying, like the admission had calmed him.

"But your mom, Rocky," I said.

"I did the alcohol and the pills, put them all around," he said, in a voice that was sad and lost and broken. "I probably got that wrong 'cause I didn't even look at the bottles. Maybe they were, like, vitamins. That would be funny, huh. And then I went home. I took a taxi and I used the cat lady's money. Sorry. I'll pay her back."

"That's okay, Rocky," I said. "Just tell us what happened."

He leaned his head against the glass, let it rest there. He closed his eyes.

"I did another thing that was all wrong, even though everybody keeps saying it's what you should do."

No one spoke. I swallowed and took a deep breath.

Roxanne still was holding Rocky's hand. The caseworker took a step toward us and then stopped as Rocky began to speak.

"I did what she always told me to do," he whispered, more to himself than to us. "I told my mom the truth."

CHAPTER 64

Big, tough Rusty Clement tried to pin Tammy's murder on his stepson. Then he tried to pin it on me. Then Cobb lied and told him they'd matched Tammy's blood with the stains on Rusty's jeans, even though the lab results weren't in, and Rusty said Tammy had attacked him when he'd tried to question her about Rocky. In the struggle she'd stabbed herself in the throat.

I figured she'd told him to kiss off, said Rocky had told her about Kitty and she was going to the cops. Cobb said Rusty probably would get life. And Rocky? It depended on which judge heard the case, but Cobb said Rocky most likely would be in the youth center until he was twenty-one.

"He's going to need support," Roxanne said.

"We'll visit him," I said. "Bring him books."

"Yeah, and when he gets furloughs, he can come out to the farm and stay," Clair said.

"Don't try to teach him to cut wood," I said.

"I was thinking we could talk history," Clair said.

"The gasoliers," I said, and I shook my head.

We were in the Hilltop Restaurant atop Knox Ridge, eating a late lunch on the way home from Bangor. We sat by the window and looked out at the hills, the dark swatches of spruce against blocks of white, snow-covered pasture. The sky was a pale blue with streaks of clouds riding above the horizon and I thought of Rocky, locked up inside for months and months, seeing the sky only through Plexiglas and chain-link. Maybe it was best that he was an indoor kid.

"You know, that's what started all of this," I said.

They looked at me over their coffee.

"Rusty getting hooked up with Kitty. He had to have his way then. And then he couldn't stand Rocky not fitting his idea of a boy."

"And that idea was shaped by his own father, silent and controlling, beating the heck out of him when he did something wrong," Roxanne said.

"What he should have done is taught him that you can't control everything," I said.

"And you don't throw a tantrum when you don't get your own way," Clair said.

"The big, strong macho guy was really just a spoiled baby," I said.

"A weak man," Roxanne said. "And weakness leads to all these evil things. That poor little girl, preyed on once, and then having to be so tough and then this guy comes along."

"She didn't deserve any of it," I said. "Not one bit."

"And what he did to his wife," Roxanne said. "Even if he didn't shoot her, he killed her, little by little, day by day. And what he did to his stepson."

"Who's such a good kid in most ways," I said, "if only he'd believe it now."

"Good people do a bad thing and that defines them," Clair said. "A whole life defined by a single moment."

"And they won't be able to put Rocky back together again," I said.

"Kids never go back together," Roxanne said. "Not completely. Not even close."

"But we patch them up, maybe even save a few. Like Tippy and her animals."

"Then we send them back into the fray," Clair said.

We were quiet. I sipped my tea. Clair took a last swallow of coffee and pushed the cup away from him. Roxanne reached out and took my hand in hers.

"I hope life isn't a fight for our child," she said.

"We'll take good care of him, her," I said.

"Right," Roxanne said, and she forced a smile but she looked like she might cry. "We'll keep this baby safe and happy and healthy and—"

"All those things," I said.

"Because there are so many terrible things in the world," she said. "All of this tragedy. All of this awful sadness."

Roxanne looked away and took a deep breath and then I could see her gather herself up, her back straight, her belly and baby in front of her like some smuggled treasure. When she looked back at me and Clair her expression had hardened and she looked older, more resolute.

"We'll do what we have to do," she said.

"That's right," I said.

"Damned straight," Clair said.